# Murder
*in a*
# Scottish
# Garden

Books by Traci Hall

MURDER IN A SCOTTISH SHIRE
MURDER IN A SCOTTISH GARDEN
MURDER AT A SCOTTISH SOCIAL

And writing as Traci Wilton

MRS. MORRIS AND THE GHOST
MRS. MORRIS AND THE WITCH
MRS. MORRIS AND THE GHOST OF CHRISTMAS PAST
MRS. MORRIS AND THE SORCERESS
MRS. MORRIS AND THE VAMPIRE
MRS. MORRIS AND THE POT OF GOLD

Published by Kensington Publishing Corp.

# Murder
## *in a*
# Scottish
# Garden

# TRACI HALL

KENSINGTON
PUBLISHING CORP.

www.kensingtonbooks.com

KENSINGTON BOOKS are published by

Kensington Publishing Corp.
119 West 40th Street
New York, NY 10018

All Kensington titles, imprints, and distributed lines are available at special quantity discounts for bulk purchases for sales promotion, premiums, fundraising, educational, or institutional use.

Special book excerpts or customized printings can also be created to fit specific needs. For details, write or phone the office of the Kensington Sales Manager: Kensington Publishing Corp., 119 West 40th Street, New York, NY 10018. Attn. Sales Department. Phone: 1-800-221-2647.

The K logo is a trademark of Kensington Publishing Corp.

ISBN-13: 978-1-4967-2602-5 (ebook)
ISBN-10: 1-4967-2602-2 (ebook)

ISBN-13: 978-1-4967-2601-8
ISBN-10: 1-4967-2601-4

First Kensington Trade Paperback Printing: June 2021

10 9 8 7 6 5 4 3 2

Printed in the United States of America

To my family and friends, for encouraging my love of stories.
To my readers, for going along for the ride!

# Acknowledgments

I thank John Scognamiglio and the Kensington team for making each story a novel to be proud of—it takes a village, and I know it.

Evan Marshall, thanks for being the best agent in the industry.

Immense gratitude goes to Allan Thornton, my Scottish guru in Inverness, who gave me sheets of notes on Scotland—all mistakes are my own. Couldn't do this without Christopher Hawke, Sheryl McGavin, or Judi Potter. ♥

# Chapter 1

Paislee Shaw gritted her teeth as the school bus jounced over a crack in the paved road, and wished for a wee bit more padding to protect her bum from the hard plastic seat.

Mrs. Martin, Brody's P6 teacher, peered over her tortoiseshell glasses in reproof at the oblivious driver. "Almost there, dear," the older woman murmured to Paislee before turning to check on the sixty students aboard for the Fordythe Primary class field trip.

Paislee scanned the gray sky from her window and prayed it wouldn't rain. The dreich spring day was multiple shades of drab without even a hint of blue. She had rain gear for her and Brody, no matter. If folks cancelled activities due to the Scottish weather, they'd never leave the house.

"Did ye read the article in last weekend's paper?" Paislee asked Mrs. Martin once the teacher swung back around. "There was a full page about the life-size stag sculpture in the center of the maze."

"Aye. I clipped it oot for the class scrapbook. I'm keen tae see the wildflower garden," Mrs. Martin said. "I've a plot at home with spring bulbs, and this always inspires me. Do you grow flowers?"

"My gran had a container garden that I've let nature have its way with"—Paislee shrugged to show her acceptance that she couldn't do it all—"and it's still better than my brown thumb."

Mrs. Martin chuckled and patted Paislee's hand. The woman had dyed golden-blond hair and a square body in her brown and cream blazer and chestnut slacks. "My granddaughter is eight this year and ready tae help."

"You're sure tae get ideas here," Paislee said. The driver slowed as they rounded a traffic circle, then stomped on the gas pedal, lurching them forward. She gripped the seatback in front of her.

Her gaze traveled to Headmaster McCall in the row across from them, Hamish when they weren't at school. His dark brown hair was styled short and neat, his face was clean-shaven, his dark blue suit jacket unbuttoned to reveal khaki slacks.

They exchanged quick smiles. He'd become a friend over the last month or so, and the relationship, the *friendship*, was very new.

Bennett Maclean, Edwyn's dad, sprawled in the bench seat behind him. Bennett, single, owned a comic book store/arcade, which made Edwyn very popular. Father and son shared shaggy blond hair and jade-green eyes.

"Is this yer first time at the estate?" Mrs. Martin asked.

"Third as a chaperone," Paislee said. "I hope someday they'll open the manor house tae tours, and not just the gardens, but I understand. Can you imagine always having tae keep things tidy? I've a hard enough time picking up after Brody and Wallace."

"Wallace? Is that yer grandfather?"

"Our Scottish terrier—he's better behaved." *And* Wallace didn't always have an opinion, like Grandpa.

The noise on the bus from sixty excited children grew in volume as they left the business section of Nairn for homes with larger plots of land and more trees. Mrs. Martin shifted so that she faced the back, her knee on the seat.

The kids quieted with just a look.

Paislee's anticipation to visit the Leery Estate was twofold this morning. Aye, she wanted to wander the formal gardens and admire the stag sculpture, but she also hoped to get a message to Shawn Marcus, landlord of her knitting shop and son to Lady Leery.

He'd rescinded the leases on hers and five other businesses a month prior, giving them thirty days' notice of eviction, and then had the gall to disappear, ignoring all phone calls, emails, and attempts to find him. What better way to track Mr. Marcus down than through his own mum?

Her shop, Cashmere Crush, was Paislee's sole source of income to keep food in the Shaw family's mouths. She had *five days* to appeal to his compassion and stop him from going through with the sale. Paislee was tempted to petition Lady Shannon Leery herself, if Shawn kept playing games.

"Here we are," Mrs. Martin said. They turned off the main street at a wooden sign that read Leery Estate, rumbling down a narrower road barely wide enough for the bus.

The tires skidded on the packed dirt until the long vehicle slid into the strip of brownish-green grass to Paislee's right and a drop-off of about five feet to a rocky stream. She swallowed her alarm as the driver righted the bus.

The kids cheered like they were on a roller coaster.

She peered back at her son to give him a warning to behave. Brody's auburn hair made him easy to spot in the back of the bus—though he and Edwyn appeared to be arguing. Brody's cheeks were flushed, his head bent toward Edwyn's.

"That fence seems ready to drop at the next brisk wind," Hamish observed.

To her left was an emerald expanse of lawn, corralled with faded wood slats, running horizontally between slightly listing posts. With a minimum of effort both horse and deer could jump it, or knock it over.

By contrast the two ten-foot-tall stone columns on either side of the narrow road meant business although the wrought-iron gate was open. "Was the property surrounded once with stone walls?"

"Guid question," Mrs. Martin said. "We'll ask the guide."

They drove slowly down the dirt road, the stream to the right now blocked by a thick hedge of dark green yew bushes that separated the land from the water, all around to the back before trailing out of sight. The car park was empty, but it was early still, not even nine, and the estate had just opened today for seasonal tours of the gardens.

Paislee pressed her forehead to the glass. The slate roof matched the charcoal skies—the solid home a tribute to Scots durability. A wide stone porch with a four-foot railing was central to the three-story mansion, and had a staircase on either side. The old beige sandstone held a greenish tint from moss grouted between the rocks. A nymph statue spewed water into a pond centered directly below the porch.

She knew from past tours that the building had been erected in the eighteen hundreds with stone quarried from the nearby stream. The rock had turned light gray with age. They hadn't needed a garage in the old days, but a covered carport to the right protected four fancy cars. Two Mercedes, an Audi, and a Ferrari.

Paislee searched for signs of activity in the manor, but the lace curtains on the second floor didn't even twitch.

The driver reversed into a parking spot so they faced the sculpted green bushes and the horse stable. An arch of lavender bougainvillea marked the tour's entrance.

The volume from the kids' clapping and whistling grew louder now that the bus had stopped. Paislee returned her attention to Brody—he and Edwyn were all smiles again.

Headmaster McCall stood up and faced the kids, meeting each child's eye. "We've gone over the rules for the day. I expect guid behavior. Mind your manners, listen tae the chaperones, and stay together."

A little girl with braces asked, "Can we bring our backpacks?"

"No, Keira. Backpacks and lunches will stay on the bus." The headmaster spoke patiently even though this was the tenth time he'd addressed the lunch issue. "Yes, Brad?"

"Can we go straight tae the maze?"

"We're going tae follow the tour guide." The headmaster paused to let that sink in. "We'll have a quiz afterward, with prizes, on what flowers we've seen."

The driver opened the bus door with a *whoosh*, and Paislee filed out after Mrs. Martin, tugging her thick cardigan sweater around her waist at the chill in the air. The scent of roses drifted from the gardens.

"Ms. Shaw, please stand by the bench," Mrs. Martin instructed. "I'll send yer group of lasses tae you as they exit."

"All right." Paislee walked ten steps to the nymph fountain and the pond where orange and white koi swam.

A man strode from the gardens beneath the bougainvillea arch to meet them, a mobile phone in one hand as he called, "Fordythe Primary?"

Ten girls gathered before her. Paislee had met them at the school this morning and remembered Holly because of her happy smile with a wide gap between her teeth, and Britta, a blond cherub with pink cheeks. Kylie, a brunette with a constant sniffle, giggled with Moira, a freckled redhead. All the kids wore the school uniform of navy-blue pants and a white polo shirt. It was cool enough for them to have jackets on. Brody and Edwyn waited near Bennett.

"Yes," Hamish answered the man. "We're here for the tour. I'm Headmaster McCall."

"Welcome! I'll be yer guide today. Graham Reid." He stopped in the center of the lot, between the bus and the pond. They all gathered round him. The guide was tall, in his thirties, and wore a white pirate shirt tucked into jeans. His long wavy hair was the color of dark honey and had a black knit cap anchored loosely to the back. He swiveled on a bootheel to smile at them all with sparkling blue eyes, scruff at his jaw.

"I can't wait tae see the maze!" one of the boys said. "Will we get lost?"

"It's a *circular* maze, aboot this high"—Graham patted his broad chest, the silver from his thumb ring shining—"with a stag bigger

than me a beacon in the center. I'm the sculptor." Graham's cap
tilted. Paislee wanted to warn him that he was going to lose it but
realized it was part of his style.

Hamish buttoned his suit coat and braced his shoulders as if the
artist's laid-back demeanor might be as catchy as a cold.

Mrs. Martin sighed, smitten. "This means Mr. Reid created the
stag from metal, himself. How lucky for us tae meet the artist."

"It's me first year givin' the tours." Graham bowed dramatically, his hat sweeping the gravel before he straightened. "Lady
Leery thought it a fine opportunity tae speak about me work."

Mrs. Martin smiled reassuringly. "We'll have plenty of questions, tae be sure."

Graham stuffed his mobile into his back pocket, and exchanged
it for a bundle of brochures. "Anybody want one? There's a map of
the gardens, and the new hours. We hope tae expand even more by
next year."

The majority of the kids shuffled uncertainly. Paislee reached
for one, as did Mrs. Martin.

"Why don't I take them?" Hamish suggested. "We can pass
them oot later."

Graham released the stack, and Hamish tucked them in his
inner suit pocket.

"Ye might want them for the maze. Ta." The guide spread his
arms out to the sides, his white shirt billowing like a pillowcase on
a clothesline. "Who's been here before?"

About forty arms shot straight into the air, followed by a chorus
of children all speaking at once.

Mrs. Martin clapped twice, and the kids quieted.

"We've made some improvements. I'll point them oot along
the way." Graham raised his hand and led them across the lot beneath the bougainvillea arch. The light purple blossoms were paper
thin but abundant. "Let's start with the first garden tae the left of the
path."

Paislee gathered her blue-jacketed chicks and followed behind

Bennett's group, so she could keep an eye on Brody. He and Edwyn were elbow to elbow, whatever they'd been arguing about forgotten in the excitement of a day away from the classroom. She warily scanned the darkening gray sky as it threatened to drizzle.

Graham opened a wooden gate to a rectangular lawn surrounded by weeping willow trees with long rope-like branches. Yellow and white daffodils created a border before a three-foot hedge, and a variety of tulips and other flowers she didn't know beckoned them closer. "Go on and explore!"

"This is lovely," Paislee said. The layout of the grounds was part of the artistry with varying levels of flowers and greenery. The kids raced around the grass, swinging the branches of the willow trees around.

"Can ye tell me what's new?" Graham's eyes flashed.

In the two years since Paislee's last visit, scrolled metal benches had been added, inviting the guests to sit while they contemplated the birdbaths. "You created the benches?"

"Aye," Graham said, his scruffy cheeks pink with genuine pleasure.

Holly squealed from the willow tree, then giggled. Paislee excused herself from the adults to share in whatever the lass had discovered—a butterfly. They spent half an hour in the garden and could've stayed longer, but Graham was eager to continue.

Almost every time Paislee looked his way, he was on his mobile. She wondered, since he worked for Lady Leery, if he might know Shawn.

On the way out, Mrs. Martin said, "I remember when Lady Leery used tae do the tours herself."

Graham's expression turned wistful. "She's too busy for that, but mibbe I can convince her tae make an appearance after the tour. Nobody tells the history of this estate better—she knows it all in that beautiful head."

Paislee followed him and his drooping hat out to the path. "That would be really great." She had to find Shawn.

The coward had delivered the certified letters, his spray tan an off shade of orange, and then slunk away. Not even her best friend Lydia, who was a brilliant estate agent and had a right talent for uncovering gossip, had been able to discover the truth.

"I'll try." Graham clapped, silver rings clanging. "She is her own mistress," he said cheery voiced, though Paislee detected a strain. Why would a sculptor conduct garden tours for Lady Leery? She'd never heard of Graham Reid before Lady Leery's support. Maybe he suffered from poor starving-artist syndrome and needed the cash. Nothing wrong with earning your way, but he was a flirt—even winking at Mrs. Martin.

Holly attached herself to Graham's side, not subtle in her crush. "Can I hold yer hand, Graham?"

Paislee clasped the little girl's hand with a smile. "Hold mine instead."

Graham darted ahead of them on the dirt path. "The second garden is here tae the left." He opened a metal scrollwork gate.

"Why do they all have gates?" Britta asked, her blond hair in a crown of braids.

"Tae keep oot the rabbits." He ushered her in. Holly passed on Britta's heels, giggling up at Graham with her gap-toothed smile.

"I like rabbits," Kylie said, arm in arm with Moira. "Don't you, Moira?"

"I do, too," Graham assured them. "But they eat the leaves of the garden. Then it wouldnae be quite this bonny, eh?"

Paislee drew in an awed breath as she absorbed the bright colors. This garden had been framed with eight-foot box hedges. Blue impatiens, red hydrangea, white and yellow daffodils—spring flowers exploded from clay planters and wooden crates. It was triple the size of her narrow back garden.

"We have an ant colony, a worm farm, and a glass box with a spider making a web." Graham pulled his phone from his back pocket when it dinged a text. "See if ye can find where they are." The kids scattered.

Hamish and a quartet of braver boys tapped the box with the spider. The girls mostly stood back and watched, wide-eyed. Mrs. Martin waved. "We've got the worms here—who wants tae see?"

To her surprise, Britta, Kylie, and Moira all knelt in the dirt.

Graham was busy texting. Would now be a good time to ask about Shawn?

"Mum!" Brody called. "Come see the ants."

Paislee was not a fan of anything creepy-crawly, but as a single mum she knew she had to hide her fears.

Graham lifted his head at Brody's call and quickly strode toward the farm. "Who here has eaten chocolate-covered ants?"

He won the children's affections by offering to send them all a recipe that he swore was delicious. Graham held his ringed hand to his heart.

Holly touched the hem of his shirt and Britta tugged her back with a headshake.

*Chocolate ants? Yuck.*

After about thirty more minutes, Graham whistled for the kids to join him at the gate. "Next stop—the maze."

One of the boys raised his hand. "Is there a bathroom?"

"Aye." Graham looked to Mrs. Martin and the headmaster.

"A break before the maze is a guid idea," Hamish said. "From what I remember, ye had portable toilets?"

Graham waited for them all to leave the garden. "See the blue roof? Used tae be a toolshed but is now a restroom."

Paislee took a moment to get her bearings. If she faced the dense hedge from the garden, going left would be the toilets and the maze, and right would be the manor house.

"That's an improvement," Mrs. Martin said with approval.

"Aye, right?" Graham herded them all down the path. Hamish was already at the bathroom facility, directing the boys and girls to either side. "Lady Leery plans on expanding."

"What a delight!" Mrs. Martin said. "Janet, dinnae eat that grass."

Paislee's group of lasses had picked buttercups to see if a yellow reflection could be seen under the other girl's chin. "Let's all stop at the restroom."

"I don't have tae go," Holly proclaimed. Her brown hair had fallen out of its single long braid.

"I do," Britta said.

"How about everybody just try?" Paislee said.

Graham had walked ahead and now waited with Hamish and Bennett. Hamish passed out maps to the kids who wanted one— Brody and Edwyn each had their hands raised.

Paislee joined Hamish and Graham. "Stand in queue, girls."

Holly and Britta whispered back and forth. "Bossy" she heard Holly say, with a jerk of her chin toward Paislee.

She didn't take it personally. "Brody, what's your favorite thing so far?"

"The ants! Can I really make some at home?"

Bennett chuckled. "If ye do, Paislee, mind if I send Edwyn over? I dinnae want ants in my kitchen."

Graham's blue eyes shimmered. "Would ye like the recipe with nuts?" His tone teased Paislee, his manner charming. "It hides the crunch."

She pressed her hand to her stomach. "Thanks."

Moira and Kylie came out of the restroom, and Britta and Holly went in. The girls had gathered around Mrs. Martin as she talked about butterflies.

Faster than Paislee could blink, Holly exited the bathroom to join Mrs. Martin.

She shook her head. No way Holly was that fast. Oh well.

". . . but can't ye imagine a fall festival here? Or a Christmas-themed event?" Graham was saying. "Shannon has a host of ideas tae bring Leery Estate into the twenty-first century."

"I hope the manor doesn't lose its charm," Paislee said. "When I think of old Nairn, as a shire, I think of here." Beech trees and Scots pine had been cultivated behind the maze, and she could see the tall trees from where she stood. "The forest is so green."

"And full of deer." Graham scowled. "Shannon's thinking of culling the trees. We have tae balance the old with the new. Now, who's ready for the maze?"

Graham's casual use of Shannon's name, rather than Lady Leery, made her wonder if they were on friendly terms. She cleared her throat to ask about Shawn, when Brody raced by, followed by Edwyn.

Graham strode ahead to speak with Hamish, and she lost her chance.

The path followed a curve, the hedge of seven-foot-tall bushes at her right like a retaining wall that provided privacy from the stream on the other side. A three-sided gardening shed held a wheelbarrow and other garden tools.

After the shed, the bushes on the right had been cut back to reveal the water. There was a pavilion with ten wooden tables, where they'd eat their packed lunches after completing the maze. The beech trees shaded a trail into the woods.

Graham clasped his hands together with an infectious grin as he stopped before the chest-high hedge of the circular maze. "Get out yer maps, everyone. There are smaller sculptures, such as the stag and nymph, throughout. You'll get a point if ye find all ten, before reaching the center." His cap dangled down his hair like a loose thread.

"Pair up," Mrs. Martin instructed. "We'll go into the maze twenty kids at once. Mr. Maclean, will ye manage the first group?" She lifted her wrist to show her gold watch. "We'll see who has the best time."

Paislee counted her ten girls, from Holly to Britta. Brody and Edwyn were studying their unfolded maps like wildlife explorers as they lined up behind Bennett.

"Is there a prize?" Brody asked.

Graham scratched his scruffy chin. "Aye. Two free admissions back tae the gardens. You can bring your family." A beep sounded from his back pocket, and he answered his phone with a pink flush to his cheeks. "Excuse me a moment."

Holly suddenly held her stomach and pranced in place. Paislee recognized the potty dance. She'd thought the lass had been too quick.

Mrs. Martin slid her brochure into her blazer pocket. "Ms. Shaw, why don't ye escort Holly to the restroom? I can watch yer group. Girls, gather around."

"I don't have tae go," Holly whinged.

"It won't take long," Paislee assured her.

"I dinnae want tae miss the race."

It was her own fault she might miss the fun, but Paislee didn't say so. "We'll catch up with the others." She urged the reluctant Holly back the way they'd come.

Holly raced ahead, but Paislee could see her so she didn't say anything. A few minutes later, the girl barged into the restroom, the door slamming. Paislee waited outside, taking her phone from the pocket of her cardigan sweater. No calls—a good thing, since Grandpa was manning Cashmere Crush.

Graham's news that Shannon Leery might speak with them after the tour could be the golden opportunity for Paislee to ask about Shawn. Birds chirped from their hiding spots in the trees and bushes, the faint rush of the stream behind the tall thicket was as soothing as a fountain.

What a peaceful day.

A butterfly flitted from one daffodil to the next. Paislee relaxed her shoulders for the first time all morning.

What size was this girl's bladder, for heaven's sake?

A muffled *pop* sounded to Paislee's right, and the chirping birds scattered into the sky with angry caws.

Six feet down the path something rustled in the thick bushes. A branch snapped. The tall hedge bowed outward as if supporting a great weight.

Goose bumps dotted her skin. Her pulse raced. She instinctively stepped in front of the bathroom door, searching the path. Even the butterflies had gone. Things went eerily quiet.

"Ms. Shaw?"

"I'm here, Holly." Apprehension tickled her nape.

The strain of weight against the interwoven hedges gave way, and a man with dark brown hair crashed backward onto the dirt, eyes closed, pale face in a grimace. He wore a dark blue Oxford, denims, and loafers. His profile seemed familiar—oh no!

Shawn Marcus?

# Chapter 2

Paislee sucked in a shocked breath, taking a step toward the man in panic. From six feet away she could see that he didn't have Shawn's spray tan. His skin was pale, and getting paler.

"Ms. Shaw? What was that?"

"Uh, I'm not sure." She couldn't leave the restroom and allow Holly to walk into an uncertain situation. "Take your time, lass."

The toilet flushed. Not what she was hoping for.

She squinted to bring the man into focus—he lay on his back, arm outstretched on the dirt path, the skin on his hands scraped. Broken branches from the hedge bent down. Relief filled her that the man wasn't Shawn—but who was he? Was he injured?

Paislee couldn't see a wound, or his chest rising. She searched frantically for someone to explain what was happening. She picked up her phone. Two minutes had passed. Should she call emergency services? What if he'd had a stroke? She'd been trained in CPR as part of the process to be a chaperone at Fordythe.

"Stay here, Holly." Paislee stepped toward the supine man. If possible, he was getting paler.

Holly spoke from the threshold of the bathroom. "What was that?" The lass twisted the knob, not listening to Paislee's instruction to remain inside. "Fireworks?"

"Maybe." Paislee moved back and gripped the doorknob to keep Holly there. No way could she let the girl out! Paislee heard another rustling of the hedge—someone was on the other side. Hand on the knob, she peered into the brush to see who it was. A man, she'd guess. Someone about six feet. Was that brown hair? "Hey! What's going on?" The shadowy figure fled.

Hamish ran from the direction of the maze, followed by a man wearing a black canvas apron, rubber Wellington boots, and a broad-brimmed hat that shielded his face. She assumed he was the gardener, coming from the shed they'd passed. Graham arrived out of breath from a different direction, his knit cap gone.

The headmaster regarded the immobile figure and herded the curious kids who'd followed him back to the circle maze, leaving Paislee with Holly, the gardener, Graham, and the man.

"Ms. Shaw!" Holly rattled the doorknob, but Paislee wouldn't let go. The pale body was limp as a wet sock and the eyes partially open. Was the man all right?

The gardener yanked off a thick glove, pressing a finger to the still man's wrist, and then jugular.

"Is he . . . ?" Graham stood between Paislee and the man. His voice trailed off.

"Ach, I dinnae ken." The gardener rested back on his boots, the hat slipping to reveal a thoughtful expression. Was that a gun handle visible in his apron pocket?

Paislee gulped down her trepidation. Why would a gardener have a gun? She had to be mistaken.

"I thought it was Shawn." Graham stepped closer to the man and sank to his knees, his gaze intent on the pale face. "But naw, it's Charles."

"We should be so lucky," the gardener, on the other side of the man, murmured to Graham.

Paislee gasped, drawing both men's attention. The knob beneath her grip twisted and jerked as Holly said, "Let me oot, Ms. Shaw."

"Just a sec, Holly."

Holly shook the door. "Yer scaring me."

"I'm sairy, sweetie." She kept the knob tight and gestured at the shaken guide to do something. "Shouldn't you call an ambulance? Where's yer phone?" She knew he had one; he'd been on it the whole time.

The gardener grimaced. "Aye—Graham, go ahead. But I think it's too late."

Graham brought his phone from his jeans pocket. "How? I dinnae see anything."

The gardener rolled the body to show Graham the back.

*What did he see?* Paislee's stomach tumbled.

Graham scowled and dialed for emergency services, explaining only that someone was injured at the Leery Estate before ending the call. The entire time, Paislee kept Holly distracted by talking about her favorite flavor of ice cream.

Paislee was running out of possible flavors and feeling mounting panic herself—who was that man, alive or dead? Hamish appeared at the far end of the path. "Graham, is there an alternate way tae the car park? I'd like tae get the children on the bus."

Graham slowly rose to his feet. "Aye. By the stables—I'll show ye."

The headmaster made eye contact with Paislee and gave a single nod. "Can you get Holly tae the bus?" Protect the student was the subtext.

She nodded back, her skin chilled. Hamish and Graham raced toward the maze, leaving her with Holly. Her route to the car park would have to be beneath the bougainvillea arch without letting Holly see the man on the path behind them.

Holly had wanted to race. "Holly, I think I've got the door handle unstuck. Are you a fast runner?"

"Yes." Holly sounded suspicious.

"I bet you an extra dessert that ye can't beat me back tae the bus."

"What aboot the maze?" Her voice lifted in a whine. "I wanted tae see it!"

"Well," Paislee hedged, "there's been an accident, so all the kids are going tae the bus. Let's see if we can beat them there." Paislee opened the door, keeping her body between the little girl's and the man. "Can you do it?"

Holly grinned, showing her adorable gap. "Aye. I'm fast."

Paislee positioned the girl toward the car park. "Ready, set, go!"

Holly accepted the challenge and took off, not so much as peeking over her shoulder just as Paislee had hoped. After three strides Paislee stopped and spun around. The gardener was patting down the man's clothes.

"Can I help you? Should I get Lady Leery?"

He blinked as if startled by her presence. He stood, and she realized how tall he was. His eyes darkened in warning above chiseled cheekbones. "*I* will take care of Lady Leery. Go, now."

Paislee shivered as she hurried away from the ominous gardener. What had he meant, that he would take care of Lady Leery? Creepy! He seemed very in charge for a gardener, come to think of it. Graham had treated him almost deferentially.

Sirens sounded as she passed beneath the lavender bougainvillea arch to the car park and the bus, where a police vehicle preceded an ambulance. Graham waved at the ambulance, and it parked by the entrance. The path was too thin for the vehicle to drive down.

The EMTs jumped out.

"You'll have tae walk this way," Graham said. "Not far."

Paislee scooted between the vehicle and the house, by the pond. She trembled at the gardener's words "I think it's too late." She scanned the lot for the yellow bus and Brody's auburn hair in the chaos around the open bus door. The driver was outside, speaking with Hamish. Mrs. Martin herded the kids on board, Holly at her side gesturing wildly.

Where was her son? Was he still in the maze? Or lost?

She released an anxious breath when Brody and Edwyn stepped into view from the other side of the bus, where they'd been waiting their turn. Bennett had a large palm on each boy's shoulder. They were last in queue.

Brody broke away when he saw her, calling, "Mum! What happened?"

She fast-walked across the lot and put her arm around her son's skinny shoulders. He hugged her even though there were other kids around. "I don't know yet, love."

Holly cried against Mrs. Martin's side, Paislee hoped from only the excitement. She searched the bus windows for the students already on board for her group—there! Britta's blond crown of braids, Kylie with a tissue to her nose, and red-haired Moira, along with the others.

"We heard a shot!" Edwyn said. "Pow, pow." He blew on the tip of his finger as if it were a smoking gun.

The only gun she'd seen had belonged to the gardener. She contemplated the path and noticed that the ambulance doors were open.

"We were just startin' the maze when we saw the birds fly." Bennett's mouth was grim as he dropped his jade gaze to the kids. "We don't know what happened, Edwyn. It's best tae get back tae the school." He squeezed her upper arm. "We can talk later?"

"Aye." She turned toward the sound of metal clanging against the gravel as the EMTs unloaded a stretcher from the back of the ambulance and wheeled it beneath the bougainvillea down the path as Graham directed them. A second police car arrived, lights flashing, but no siren. Hamish and Mrs. Martin were both talking to Holly by the bus door. Hamish patted the girl's shoulder.

A police officer ambled toward them, his shiny black boots crunching the fine rock. His pants and shirt were black, his jacket and utility vest a bright yellow, and on it he wore a baton and spray. Their officers didn't carry guns. "Pardon me—I'm told there was a witness here? A woman?" He pointed to the yellow bus. "Ye cannae leave just yet."

Brody stuck to her side.

"That'd be me," Paislee said. "Paislee Shaw."

The officer tipped his black and white hat to Brody. "I'm Constable Vega."

Brody mumbled, "Hi."

"Can I ask a few questions?" The constable tilted his head away from the kids.

She appreciated his thoughtfulness. "Why don't ye get on the bus, Brody? This willnae take a second." Paislee shuffled a reluctant Brody toward Bennett, who loaded the boys behind Mrs. Martin and Holly. A female police officer—she could tell by the bun—knocked at the front door of the estate. The poor family.

Hamish saw that Paislee was with the constable and straightened his posture, his hand to the button on his suit coat as he crossed the lot. She smiled when he reached her side.

"I'm Headmaster McCall," he said to the officer.

"Constable Vega. I was going tae ask this witness what she'd seen." His tone suggested that the headmaster was intruding.

Paislee put her hand on Hamish's elbow to keep him there. "The headmaster arrived right afterward." She recounted the muffled *pop*, how the birds flew. Holly, the man crashing through the hedge, how she'd thought she'd seen someone, but they'd run away. "The man's name is Charles. Graham knows him. So does the gardener."

"Graham?" Constable Vega asked.

Paislee shifted to where she'd last seen the sculptor, by the ambulance. No longer wearing his hat or apron, the gardener's proper posture made him appear regal next to slouchy Graham. "There he is. He was our tour guide this morning."

"I've already gotten his statement. He was the one who phoned in the emergency. Awright, now, who is the girl, Holly…"

"Fisher. But she's only ten," Hamish said.

"I'll need tae get her statement," the constable said.

Hamish drew himself up tall. "I'll go with ye then. Don't you need her parents' permission?"

"No." The constable scowled and made a note in his tablet. "She's a witness. What school are ye from?"

"Fordythe Primary." Hamish reached into his wallet and handed the officer a business card.

Vega pocketed the card. "Nobody else saw anything?"

Paislee and Hamish shook their heads. "Holly didn't, either," Paislee said. "She was in the bathroom."

Just then, the emergency personnel brought the stretcher back out from under the flowered arch to the ambulance, followed by one of the first police officers, a short, rounder constable. The other, of medium height and build, went to the boot of his vehicle for a crime kit, including yellow tape to cordon off the path by the bougainvillea.

The gardener, his cheekbones sharp, his mouth grim, asked the EMT, "Is he alive?"

The man holding the foot of the stretcher gave a slight shake of his head while the other answered, "We cannae say."

"Stay here." Constable Vega strode purposely toward the others.

Sick at heart, Paislee was saddened to get confirmation the man was dead. Dead, and she might have been the last person to see him. She murmured a quick prayer for the stranger.

She heard voices from the porch and saw the female officer talking with a young blond woman in a short-sleeve dress, the lady nodding as she listened, clutching her arms as if cold. The officer said something else, and the young woman darted inside, closing the door behind her. The female officer descended the stairs and joined the three policemen.

"Holly thinks she heard fireworks." Hamish searched her face, a hint of their friendship visible in his concerned gaze. "What happened?"

Paislee tightened her sweater around her as a breeze kicked up. "Just what I shared with the officer—I told Holly the door handle was stuck, which is why she couldnae get out."

The headmaster unbuttoned his suit coat, then buttoned it again, a rare sign that he might be uncomfortable. "I'll have tae call her parents."

She didn't envy him the task. The front door of the manor banged. Would it be the young woman, returning to speak with the officer?

Her heart raced as Shawn Marcus himself traipsed to the edge of the porch, observing the ambulance and police cars. Even from across the lot she could see he wasn't well. His dark brown comb-over was unkempt, his black Henley partially tucked into his beige slacks. She took a step toward him, but he scuttled back inside.

"Blast it!"

"What's wrong?" Hamish asked.

"Did ye see that man? He is my landlord."

Hamish knew her personal situation. His groomed brow lifted. "Shawn Marcus? Paislee, ye cannae talk tae him right now. It's not the proper time."

"I realize that, thank you." A raindrop landed on her nose. "Can we go?"

"Constable Vega wanted tae speak with Holly." Hamish stuck his hands in his pockets as he eyed the overcast sky. "But I hope he'll wait for her parents."

A honk sounded and a dark blue SUV passed in front of the parked bus, blocking the second patrol car. Constable Vega rocked back on his heels. "The DI's here."

Paislee's shoulders dropped. She and Detective Inspector Zeffer had a very uneasy relationship since her helping with a murder investigation last month.

The detective exited his SUV, russet head bare, his custom-fit blue suit stretched across his broad shoulders impeccably. He studied the car park, the ambulance, and the stone house, before his cool gaze settled on Paislee.

The kids could be heard on the bus behind her—not shouts, just a raised volume of excited voices.

"May we leave now?" Hamish asked the constable. "The children are all wound up by what's happened. It'll be better tae get them into their routine at school."

"I have your information, Headmaster McCall," the constable said. "We'll need tae speak with Holly Fisher later, but, aye, ye can go."

"Thank you." Hamish's heel dug in the gravel as he shifted toward the bus, and Paislee started to follow.

"Not you, Ms. Shaw," the detective called from his SUV. He slammed the door closed. His long legs had him across the lot in eight paces. "I'd like ye tae stay."

"My car isn't here." Grandpa had it at Cashmere Crush.

The detective shrugged. "I'll have a patrol car drop ye off once we're done."

Paislee bristled at his high-handedness but didn't argue.

Hamish half-reached for her, then lowered his hand, uncertain as Brody had been when climbing on the bus with Bennett. "You'll be all right?"

"Fine," she said. "See that Brody and the others are, too?"

"Of course." Hamish's self-assured demeanor returned before he left them and climbed the steps to the bus. The driver closed the door and revved the engine.

Paislee tried not to feel abandoned as she faced the detective inspector and Constable Vega. "I already told the constable what happened."

"Show me where ye were, if ye don't mind?" Zeffer gestured toward the yellow tape by the entrance, his styled hair impervious to movement or the occasional raindrop.

"All right." The three of them crossed the lot, keeping toward the house. Paislee was careful of the reversing ambulance, before it drove down the narrow road, away from the estate.

DI Zeffer took point, Paislee in the center, and the constable behind her. She rubbed her arms against the chill of returning to the scene of the crime as they passed under the floral arch. "I thought at first it was Shawn Marcus. They look so much alike—who is he?"

"Charles Thomson," Constable Vega told her. "Lady Leery's nephew."

"That explains the similar build, and profile." Shawn Marcus's cousin. Paislee swallowed nervously when they reached the bathrooms a few moments later. Small orange cones marked the place where Charles had fallen, and yellow tape roped off the broken hedge.

A gust of wind lifted her hair, and she buried her hands in her cardigan pockets. She hoped it didn't pour before the officers got the information necessary to catch who was behind this.

"Did Charles reside here?" the detective asked his officer while he scanned the path. He kneeled down to observe some scuff marks in the dirt.

Constable Vega checked his notes. "I think he was here for a visit."

"We need tae *know*. Police work is not guesswork."

The constable flushed red. "I will find oot."

The DI straightened and focused on Paislee, who felt sorry for the other man—she'd been on the wrong side of the detective herself. "Where were you when it happened?"

She counted seven steps under her breath as she walked from the detective inspector to the bathroom door. "Here."

His mouth firmed. "What did ye hear before the shot?"

"Birds—it was a peaceful morning. The rush of the stream." *The man had been shot.* Her stomach knotted. "I wasn't clear that it was a gunshot."

Zeffer scowled. "Then?"

"Hamish showed up, then the gardener." She pointed to the smudged dirt he'd been interested in. "The gardener knelt there, after running from the shed," Paislee explained. "Graham was there, at his other side."

"And why were you here?" Detective Inspector Zeffer asked.

Paislee spoke calmly, though her insides were a trembling mess. "Chaperoning for the school field trip. Escorting Holly, one of the girls in my group, tae the restroom." She held the knob. "Holly was inside when I heard the commotion and then saw the body fall."

"Fall?" His brow hiked, challenging her word choice.

"Not 'fall' exactly," she said, doing her best to describe what happened. "There was more force than just a backward tumble."

"Did he seem pushed?" He shoved his hands against the air to demonstrate.

Paislee thought of the shadow she'd seen through the shrubs. "I'm not sure. I thought I saw someone, but they ran when I called for them."

His nose flared as if he'd gotten the scent of his prey. "Can ye describe this person?"

"I'm not *positive* I saw someone, but the hedge rustled up tae about here." She left her post by the bathroom door and put her hand at six feet next to the seven-foot hedge. Its branches were interwoven, but the spring leaves hadn't filled in all the way.

The DI sighed with exasperation. "What's behind here?" He peered through the hedge but jerked back, a thorn stuck to the sleeve of his blue suit. Not a friendly type of shrubbery. "Vega, have someone check it oot."

The constable observed the shrub and the brim of his hat caught a branch. "Aye."

"There's a stream, though I don't know how tae get behind this hedge." Paislee hugged her cardigan around her alert body. "It goes all the way down tae the circular maze and a picnic pavilion."

Zeffer stared at her. Waiting. Demanding.

She recalled Charles's navy-blue Oxford as he lay on the path. "I didn't see any wounds, but the gardener showed Graham Charles's back." Should she mention that they didn't like Shawn? Probably not—it would sound like gossip, and she knew the DI hated that.

Zeffer massaged his square jaw. "Constable, who is the gardener?"

Constable Vega read his notes. "Malcolm Gunn. Head butler— he runs both house and gardens."

"I want this area searched until a weapon is found." The detective inspector paced back and forth along the path like a caged tiger, russet hair electric and green eyes blazing.

"They're on it," the constable said with a gulp.

And what about the possible gun? If she kept mum and it turned out to be important, the DI would be furious. She cleared her throat. "Detective, I think the gardener-butler had a weapon in his apron pocket."

Zeffer whirled on his boot heel. "*What?* Why didn't ye say something right away—Vega, nab the butler!"

The constable clapped his hand on his hat and raced off.

# Chapter 3

Zeffer stopped pacing on the path and crossed his arms as he glared at Paislee. "What did ye see exactly?"

Paislee shuffled her feet with a nervous swallow. "Malcolm ran from the shed in wellies and an apron, the kind ye garden in, and I think I saw a black gun handle in his front pocket."

"Handguns have been banned for over thirty years," the detective informed her.

Paislee wasn't familiar with anything deadlier than her sharpest scissors. "I only saw the handle. Maybe I'm wrong." Her shoulders hiked defensively.

"You didnae think it was important tae tell us right away?" Zeffer stared down the path where the constable had gone as if willing his officer to return. She heard voices headed in their direction—male voices.

"I didn't know that Charles had been shot until you said so, and I *am* telling you." Paislee wished she was snug at home with a cup of tea, and this all a bad dream.

The pair arrived side by side. Constable Vega's crisp uniform was a sharp contrast to Malcolm Gunn's thick brown pants and bulky wool sweater. The man's dark brown hair was almost black, his brows heavy, his brown eyes piercing when they landed on

Paislee with disdain. He'd lost the apron but still wore the rubber boots.

"You have a handgun?" The detective had no problem going stink eye to stink eye with the butler.

Malcolm's demeanor became somewhat aloof as he answered the detective inspector. "Aye. With a permit, sir."

"Why?" Zeffer demanded. "I dinnae have a gun, and I track criminals for a living. What would *you* need one for? Trimmin' the rosebushes?"

Malcolm stiffened. "It's fer keeping pests under control, so they dinnae ruin our gardens." He finished with a slight lift of his upper lip. Borderline rude, but not quite. Blisteringly polite.

Paislee was oddly not comforted by this. Pests . . . like cute floppy-eared rabbits?

"I'll need tae see that permit, and the weapon will be entered into evidence, being that it was associated with the crime." The DI nodded at Constable Vega.

She glanced at the ground where Charles's body had lain. No bloodstains.

"I assure you, sir, that weapon had nothing tae do with any crime." Malcolm's chin raised a hair.

"Then it will be returned, but not until it's ruled oot."

"Fine, fine." Malcolm set his strong jaw. "I keep everythin' in the gun cabinet."

"Gun cabinet?" Zeffer repeated. "I'll need all the guns after we're through here. How many are there?"

"It's a hunting estate, sir. There are at least two dozen."

Constable Vega visibly quaked at that news like a bloodhound on the scent.

"Tell me what happened?" Zeffer lowered his arms, his voice deceptively inviting.

Malcolm scratched the hair at his temple. "I was in the potting shed with the hyacinth bulbs when I heard a noise."

"Could it have been an accident? Someone hunting?" Paislee

asked, trying to rationalize how Charles could have gotten hit by a bullet.

Malcolm gave a haughty laugh. "We had our first school event today fer the season's garden tours. No one from the family would be oot hunting. And no one else is allowed on these lands."

Thunder rumbled in the distance, and the friendly shire estate began to take on a sinister feel. Paislee eyed the dark sky with apprehension.

"Ye heard the shot," the DI prodded.

"I heard *something*, and I immediately ran toward the restroom, where I'd seen this young woman"—he jerked a thumb at Paislee—"and a lass pass by."

Paislee hadn't been aware of him at all. The butler exuded hard strength. Could it have been he somehow behind the hedge? She studied his hands and face for scratches but remembered he'd worn gloves and a hat. "Were you behind the hedge?"

Malcolm flexed his shoulders, puffing out his chest. "I was at the shed, I told ye."

She snuggled into her sweater against a brisk wind. "Graham arrived after you."

"Aye," Malcolm reluctantly confirmed.

Paislee waited for him to share the rest, and when he didn't, she said, "Graham thought that it was Shawn at first, just like I had."

"We'll need pictures of both men," the DI told the constable, who made a note on his tablet. "What next?"

"Graham called emergency services, and this young woman let the lass oot of the bathroom tae scamper tae the bus." Malcolm's tone faltered for the first time. "I knew Charles was dead."

Paislee bowed her head, her hair sweeping around her face. *Dead.* Leery Estate was one of her most favorite places. It would never be the same for her, or any of the kids, or that poor man and the Leery family.

"What's behind here?" the detective asked, not touching the thorny hedge as he gestured at it.

"The stream," Malcolm said. "Beyond that, Sharp's Park. Public land."

"Constable Vega, come with me and Mr. Gunn to get the weapons. I'll want every permit. If there is a single infraction, you will be fined the maximum penalty."

Malcolm clenched his jaw. "Everything's in order. I take care of it meself."

"Prove it," the detective told the butler. Zeffer cocked his head at her. "Why don't ye go wait by the pond? I saw a bench. Dinnae mention any of this tae anyone."

"Detective?" An officer hurried toward them, a black knit cap in his gloved fingers. "We found this caught in the arch," he said.

Malcolm drew in a sharp breath.

"What?" Zeffer asked. "You know who this belongs tae?"

She and the butler exchanged furtive glances. Malcolm said, "Graham Reid. The sculptor."

"Our tour guide this morning," she added.

The DI exhaled and waved for Malcolm to join him. "The house can wait. Show me your potting shed and where you stashed the gun. I highly doubt you locked it away in the last thirty minutes. Did you shoot Charles?"

"I didnae shoot Charles." Malcolm grimaced but followed the detective. Constable Vega sent Paislee a confused look and trailed after them.

Right—she was to sit on the bench and wait for the detective inspector. Her first instinct was to call Lydia, but the detective had told her not to say anything. She quickly hurried down the path, beneath the lavender bougainvillea, to the car park and pond below the large stone front porch. The bus was gone, and she breathed a sigh of relief.

Brody would be safe at Fordythe, with Hamish. The ambulance was gone, too, but two patrol cars and the DI's SUV remained.

The mansion's majestic door opened before she reached the bench, and Lady Leery—gorgeous at any age, but Paislee knew she was seventy-three—walked stiffly out, her chin high, her eyes red rimmed, escorted by Graham. The sculptor had changed from his white pirate shirt to a navy-blue turtleneck. His long hair had been brushed smooth. On the lady's other side stood a much younger blond woman in a blue sheath with a striped blue-and-white blazer—the woman who'd talked with the police officer earlier.

The star of the trio was no doubt Lady Leery. She was every inch an aristocrat in navy-blue slacks, white blouse, and soft blue sweater. Gold glinted at her ear lobes, her blond hair perfectly sculpted into a bob at her chin.

Paislee ducked behind the arch of the bougainvillea, feeling as if she didn't belong there to witness their grief.

Shawn was notably absent, yet Paislee knew he was around. As if thinking of him had forced him to show up, he stumbled onto the porch. Paislee gasped. Bags shadowed his brown eyes, and he'd hastily thrown on a suit jacket over his black shirt and beige slacks. His cheeks drooped loosely.

"Where did they take him?" Shawn demanded, keys jingling in his palm. "Where's Charles?"

"Tae the hospital," Graham said. "He's dead, Shawn. I'm sairy."

Lady Leery patted Shawn's hand as if to offer comfort. "I'll phone the hospital," she said. "It might not be too late. Miracles happen in medicine. I know a member of the hospital board—we'll do everything possible, son."

Had Charles and Shawn been close? Cousins . . . they'd probably been friends.

Paislee's skin pebbled from the cool wind as a few raindrops fell from the gray sky.

Shawn broke away from the group of people on the porch toward the carport and the assorted fancy cars. "I can drive faster than you can call," he announced over his shoulder. "He cannae be dead!"

"You're not well." Lady Leery snagged his elbow, and he

crashed against the stone railing. She urged him back toward the house, but he continued to struggle, so Graham and the young woman helped her get him inside, the two a team.

What was wrong with Shawn? What had they meant about doing all they could when Charles was already dead?

Malcolm and Constable Vega joined her beneath the arch and peered toward the mansion. The detective was two steps behind with another officer, who held clear bags containing items of interest, including Graham's cap and Malcolm's handgun. "I told ye tae stay on the bench."

She blew her bangs back. "The family was outside on the porch. It didn't seem polite."

"Who?" Malcolm asked. He brushed a raindrop off his forehead. The weather threatened to storm.

"Lady Leery and her son, Shawn. Graham, and a pretty younger woman. Graham's girlfriend?"

Malcolm snorted—very undignified, Paislee thought.

The detective walked with Malcolm to the bottom of the dozen stone steps leading to the porch. "I'd like tae speak with the family, and get those guns."

"I will see if Lady Leery has time for a meeting," Malcolm said imperiously. He was too snobby for those rubber boots.

Constable Vega bristled while Paislee bit back a shocked laugh.

Detective Inspector Zeffer brushed down the lapels of his blue suit against the rain. "Let her know that she should find time or answer questions at the station. I can have a warrant here in thirty minutes. My team needs me inside."

Malcolm straightened. "I'll relay the message." With that, the butler jogged up to the stone landing and dashed into the manor, leaving the others to cool their heels by the pond. Or, in Zeffer's case, fume. Paislee wouldn't have been surprised if steam rose from his ears.

"Should I call a cab tae take me home?" Paislee asked. Though she'd left her purse on the bus, she had her mobile.

The officer with the bags of possible evidence headed to one of the police cars. Detective Zeffer motioned for her to follow the man. "Constable Payne can give ye a ride back. Thanks for staying." Constable Payne had been the rounder of the two officers first on the scene.

"I didn't help much."

"Yer observant, Ms. Shaw. The sound of the shot, no blood on the trail. The gun handle." He speared her with his sea-green eyes.

She found it hard to swallow. "Do you think it was a hunting accident?"

"Too early tae tell." He hefted his chin toward the house impatiently.

Paislee palmed her phone, tucked in her cardigan pocket. "I just want tae feel safe, Detective. An accident is better than the alternative."

On purpose would mean somebody had killed Charles with intent. Murder.

"I suppose," he agreed dryly. "I dinnae want a killer on the loose, either—but somebody shot Charles Thomson. I will find them." He climbed the stone steps with a determined expression. "Starting with the guns in this house."

"Hop on in, Ms. Shaw," Constable Payne called. "Before it pours."

Paislee peered one last time at the front entrance of the estate. Malcolm opened the door to let the DI in, followed by Constable Vega. She searched for a glimpse of Shawn but didn't see him. Who had shot Charles and why? What was that shadow behind the hedge?

Unsettled, Paislee slid into the front passenger seat of the police car.

"You don't want tae ride in the back?" Constable Payne had dark skin and eyes, and the perfect deadpan delivery. His face was as round as his barrel-shaped body and laugh lines bracketed his mouth.

"For a second, I actually considered it." She couldn't laugh, too distressed by what had happened. "How can you keep your sense of humor? Don't ye think you should carry a weapon?"

"Well, lass, we're trained how tae defuse a situation. And it's better tae laugh than cry, I say."

"I agree . . . in theory." Right now, she felt too sad. Too scared.

The officer drove slowly down the dirt road until they reached the sign on the main street. "Where tae?"

"Cashmere Crush. Take A96 tae Market Street."

It was only eleven and traffic was quiet. Constable Payne kept up small talk without divulging much. The officers in the station had been reprimanded for talking out of turn during the last investigation under the detective inspector.

"What's Cashmere Crush?"

"A knitting shop. I sell custom sweaters as well as local yarn." She tried to imagine her friend Amelia, who was considering officer training, behind the wheel instead of Constable Payne. It was difficult; the woman's petite features reminded her of a pixie. Right now Amelia worked as a receptionist at the police station. Would she be able to defuse a situation without getting hurt? "Do you ever wish you had a gun?"

"Around Nairn? No. If I was in Edinburgh, mibbe." Constable Payne winked. "Glasgow, definitely."

"What would ye tell someone interested in joining?"

Constable Payne looked over his nose at her, and Paislee raised her palms. "Not me."

The officer grinned. "I heard ye talking tae the DI—observation is a great skill tae have for an inspector."

"I'm a mum, thank you. A knitter. A business owner." A reluctant witness to a murder.

"Have the person call me if they want. Inspector Shinner had a knack for gathering new recruits. Made sure we were seen as allies in the community, not the 'cops' ye ken?" The constable slowed around a traffic circle. "I sure miss him."

"I've heard that he was amazing." Nobody heaped praise on the new DI, according to Amelia.

"Not that Zeffer doesnae have his own strengths," the officer said quickly. "He has some big, shiny Shinner shoes tae fill, that's all." Constable Payne parked in front of Cashmere Crush. "Here ye are. I cannae believe how many times I've driven by this place but never knew what it was. Yarn, huh?"

"If you ever want tae take up knitting, let me know. Thanks for the ride!"

"If you change *your* mind," he teased and pointed to the station. "Come on down. Ye can help catch who shot Charles."

"Very funny." Paislee got out and watched the officer drive down Market Street, past the five other businesses that Shawn Marcus had sold from under them, ending at the turquoise blue awning of Theadora's Tea Shoppe, to the police station on the right.

Detective Zeffer had a lot to prove—and not just to her but to his own team. Paislee, an officer of the law? As if she had time for one more thing.

# Chapter 4

From the slightly crooked sidewalk on Market Street, Paislee studied the outside of her shop, wanting to memorize each detail in case she was evicted. This had been her life for the last eight years. The block-long building was made of brick, and each individual business had a flower box before a frosted window. Hers was filled with vibrant red geraniums, mustard marigolds, and lush green ferns from all the rain.

Her sign read Cashmere Crush, with interlocking *C*'s for her logo. She'd burned the midnight oil to make her business successful enough to support her and Brody, and to be part of the community, as Gran had urged. Inspector Shinner had known the value of a tight-knit town, and had taught community mindedness to Constable Payne.

The citizens of Nairn stood together.

Shawn Marcus *couldn't* take this away. She peered down the block—James the leather shop repairman, Ned the dry cleaner, Margot at the medical lab, Lourdes and Jimmy had the office supply, and of course Theadora and Dan's bakery jewel, on the opposite corner. Oblivious to her, Dan swept beneath white tables, shaded by turquoise umbrellas.

Across the street at the florist, Ritchie waved from his front door. He'd probably watched her being dropped off by the police car like a criminal and wondered what was up—she could just imagine the gossip! And to top it off, she was standing outside staring at nothing like a numpty idiot. Paislee yanked open the door as a customer exited, carrying a large white shopping bag with the *CC* logo on it.

"Cheers," Paislee said as the woman passed. She entered her shop on a lighter note. Wall-to-wall shelves of yarn, sorted by color, created a rainbow of wool to rival any formal garden. A chest-high table was to her right, and she'd designed a special nook for her hand-knitted goods. What had been sold?

"Ye're back early," Grandpa Angus said. He was a handsome seventy-five, with silver hair, a square-edged silver beard, black glasses, and the same brown eyes her father'd had, and Brody, too. He'd arrived in her life on a blustery wind, but they'd settled into a routine as they waited for word of his son Craigh, supposedly out on an oil rig called the *Mona*, though there was no record of the company's existence.

"I saw a happy customer," she sang. Paislee'd get each new customer's information to inform them of her move, once she found a suitable space. She felt sorry for Shawn, him sickly, and his cousin dead . . . but she had to take care of her family, too.

Grandpa leaned conspiratorially forward. "She bought the yellow cable-knit sweater and took a card. Talked her into special ordering a matching one for her husband for Christmas."

"That's great, Grandpa." Paislee tucked a stool beneath the high-top table. There was a lot to do if she had to move! Lydia told her to be patient, but there was so much yarn to crate that the mere idea made her bones ache. She couldn't have, in good conscience, asked Shawn about the sale of the building this morning.

"How was the maze?"

"Well." She brushed her bangs from her eyes. "Somebody was shot and killed."

His wrinkled hand went to his heart. "Eh?"

"Aye. Shot." Paislee started to tremble at the memory of the man's limp body crashing backward through the tall brush. "His name was Charles—Shawn Marcus's cousin."

Grandpa's forehead bunched in confusion. "Yer landlord?"

"One and the same."

"Ye've got the worst luck, lass."

"I feel like it some days." She tossed her keys on the shelf below the register. "My heart goes out tae the family. Lady Leery, especially." She frowned—the lady had only one son. "I wonder if Shawn ever married? Or has kids?"

"Dunno." Grandpa shrugged, his thin shoulders filling out his flannel shirt better than it had when he'd first arrived on her doorstep.

Paislee slipped off her cardigan and pulled the folded-up map from inside her pocket, then draped the sweater over a hard-backed chair.

"What's that?"

Paislee smoothed the brochure flat on the counter. There was a gorgeous picture of the maze and the stag sculpture in the center. "What a field trip tae remember P6 by!" She sent Hamish a personal text to ask how everyone was doing.

Grandpa propped his elbow next to the register and scanned the images. "I remember when you had tae have an invitation tae be at the manor."

"Did ye ever go?"

He waggled a crooked finger. "Officially? No. I was a fisherman, not a peer, and Shannon Leery was a goddess. That said, she didnae mind us using the land."

"You knew her?" Paislee couldn't help but smile at his enthusiastic pronouncement.

"My sights were not aimed that high, but all of us local boys had crushes."

"So you've never been tae the estate?" It was on the tip of her tongue to suggest a trip to the gardens, but she couldn't. Not until the killer was found. Maybe not ever again.

He pinched the bridge of his nose. "I didnae quite say that. The property isnae fenced all around and has plenty of acreage. Good fishing on the stream. Hunting too. Fox, deer. We used tae eat squirrel, you ken."

"Grandpa!"

He tapped the glossy brochure. "The only time I was there as a sort of guest was when Shannon married George Marcus. It was for his money y'know—that was no secret tae anyone in the shire. They opened the house tae the public with a dram of cheer for everyone."

Paislee tried to imagine the lady she'd seen on the steps today involved in such a scandal. Lady Leery seemed the epitome of class right down to her gold earrings. "She married for the cash?"

"Aye, and George knew it, too, but Shannon was beyond lovely. The money revitalized the estate. There were no male heirs, so Shannon had inherited as oldest."

"Poor George!"

"My foot," Grandpa bellowed. "He was married tae the most beautiful lass in three shires."

"She still is beautiful."

His silver brow lifted twice in consideration. "Maybe I should give her a call. Show her a night on the town."

Paislee was tempted to plug her ears. He and Gran's long marriage had ended when her grandmother had discovered (decades later) that Angus had an adult son with another woman. The story went that the night before his wedding to Agnes, at his stag party, Angus had gotten very intoxicated and strayed. Gran couldn't forgive the proof of his infidelity—Craigh.

Paislee was in no position to judge that particular situation.

"It's a shame that happened today of all days, lass. Did they catch who did it?"

"No. Tae be sure, Detective Inspector Zeffer will be under the microscope at having another murder in his district so soon."

He removed his glasses and stared at her. "What happened exactly?"

Paislee explained about the *pop*, the birds flying into the air, and holding Holly in the bathroom.

Grandpa bowed his head and groaned. "Sounds like ye were in danger, lass."

She forced herself to recall the pale figure. "The thing is, Grandpa, that I didn't notice an injury. There was no blood on the path later, either, when I showed the detective what happened."

"Did ye see anything?"

She tucked a lock of hair behind her ear. "On the other side of the hedge, aye, but it was shadowy. Nobody answered when I called out. It could've been a deer." Paislee nodded to convince herself. "Yeah, someone might've been shooting at the deer, and gotten Charles instead."

"A man doesnae resemble a deer, me girl."

"You're probably right." Paislee filled him in on the rest of what she'd seen, including Malcolm and the gun.

"*Gun?*"

"The butler had a permit—the DI was all over that, believe me." She lifted her hands, the sleeves of her white peasant blouse fluttering.

The store phone rang. Grandpa answered and gave the business hours, then hung up. He glared at her. "You were worried the girl in the toilet might be in danger, but what aboot yerself?"

Paislee shook her head, the trepidation she'd felt out in the open eased by being safe in the shop with Grandpa. "I'd rather think it was an awful accident than on purpose. Said the same tae Zeffer."

"I guess I cannae blame ye." Grandpa read the brochure and slapped his forehead. "Now that's a pricey tour! Was it all ye could drink?"

Paislee chuckled. "Just what all the primary kids need, *not*. The teachers perhaps. But the price is on par with Cawdor."

"Cawdor has a golf course and restaurant." Grandpa tugged his beard. "And ye can go inside the house tae see the rooms and antique furniture."

It was hard to argue. Her mobile phone rang from the pocket of her khakis, and she noticed that Hamish hadn't returned her message. "Lydia!" She held a finger up to her grandfather and stepped into the back storage area. "How's it going?"

"I have another two shop locations tae show you—still no sale pending on yer building, though. It's beyond strange at this point."

Paislee quickly caught her bestie up on what had happened earlier and ended with "So as ye can imagine, it wasn't the time tae ask Shawn or Lady Leery about the eviction. I think Shawn is sick again, and with the death of his cousin, I just couldn't." And to think she'd started off the morning so determined to demand answers.

"Paislee Ann, what are ye goin' on aboot?"

Paislee repeated the events, speaking slower and answering questions until at last Lydia heaved a sigh and spluttered, "Even if it was an accident, like ye hope, you might have been winged by a stray bullet."

The severity of the situation was starting to sink in. "Brody was there, too!" Her stomach rolled at the idea of anything happening to her son.

"I cannae believe it." Static sounded then cleared. "I'm glad you and Brody are all right. We're supposed tae have the quarterly party for Silverstein's there on Friday. I wonder if it will still happen?"

"Oh, I wouldn't think so. Opening up the home for a party after the death of a family member?"

"Our accountant, Gavin Thornton, set it up for us since he has an in with Lady Leery. The plan was a formal dinner with drinks and dessert."

"I don't know, Lyd. Could ye reschedule? Or have it some-where else?"

"Ye dinnae understand—this party is a pretty big deal. Having it at the estate makes it extra special for our owner, Mr. Silverstein. And"—she waited, almost shy—"I might be up for an award."

Lydia's successful career had landed her a position at the best agency in all of Scotland, making a high-end salary. Paislee knew she earned every pound by listening to what her clients really wanted.

"Congratulations, Lydia!"

"Don't jinx me. I called for three reasons. One, tae view the properties, and two—tae see if you'd be my date. You always say no, but now that ye have your grandfather, mibbe ye can? I'd love to have ye there."

Paislee hadn't gone on a real date since her fateful graduation night. Her energies were all poured into raising her son as a single mum in old-fashioned Nairn.

"Don't say no," Lydia begged sweetly. "Think aboot it."

Paislee considered her options. Asking Grandpa was uncom-fortable, but he would probably do it if she tossed in a bottle of Scotch as payment. Perhaps the DI would have caught the killer by then. In which case, going to the estate might give her a chance to speak with Shawn and allow her to plead her case.

In her heart, she imagined that Lady Leery would cancel the event, after the death of her nephew. "It'll probably be rescheduled, but if it's not, I'll ask Grandpa." Bribe, more like.

"I'm really gonna like ye having a babysitter, Paislee."

"Don't get used tae it." Grandpa Angus was very vocal about moving on as soon as Craigh returned from his job on the oil rig.

"It's time ye had some fun. I know why you dinnae date, but ye cannae be a nun, for heaven's sake. I know of a certain head-master who'd like tae change yer mind."

"Hamish was brilliant today—he handled the emergency like he faces down crazed shooters all the time."

"Do ye like him?"

"As a friend, aye." She refused to think of him as anything more.

Lydia hooted but didn't rest on her victory laurels. "Third thing—I want tae show that notice Shawn Marcus gave you tae the guy in legal I've been conferring with."

"Sure. Why?" Paislee paced before the boxes of yarn. There hadn't been any number to call on the letter—she'd searched the document for somewhere to protest. She and Lydia had studied it carefully.

"I have a hunch, that's all. You still have the envelope?"

"Aye."

"Great. When's a good time tae view those properties?"

"After I drop Brody and Grandpa at home, before dinner? I hope you can pull a rabbit from the hat, Lydia. I'd rather not move at all, and I know that every business in this row feels the same way. Theadora tears up every time I see her. It's all she can talk about. She and Dan have sunk everything into their business—we all have."

"Bring the certified letter this afternoon? It would save me a trip."

"No problem." Thinking of Theadora and Dan made her think of happy couples, which made her think of how crazy it was that Lydia was single. "Hey, did you ever get in touch with Bennett Maclean?"

"The gorgeous comic book god? Oh yeah, I sure did."

"And?"

"He never called me back. I am *not* going tae chase him down."

Paislee thought of how well Bennett had dealt with the chaos at the Leery Estate. Not rattled, but calm with Brody and Edwyn. "Maybe try again? He's probably busy."

"What, raising a kid and running a business, like some other single parent I know?" Lydia laughed. "I dinnae ken how ye do it. I like tae go home and relax with a cocktail and some quiet music . . . put me feet up."

"I don't think I've ever done that in my life—you're being a tease." God, she dreamed of quiet moments that didn't require her doing laundry or catching up on sweater orders, which is what she did after Brody, and now Grandpa, went to bed.

Lydia's office phone rang. "I have tae go. See you later?"

"Cheers!"

After the call Paislee hurried to get the certified letter from her safe and put it in her pocket before she forgot. Some days it was her lists that kept her from forgetting to buy groceries or detergent. Hard to hang on to "good mom" status if there was no orange marmalade for toast in the house, or there were dirty school uniforms.

In the front of the shop, Grandpa played solitaire with a deck of cards at the high-top table and watched folks pass by through the frosted glass window. A spot of sun had broken through the gray sky to shine on his silver hair and fill the room with light. Paislee's heart warmed.

Grandpa's payday was every other Friday, so along with new clothes and a haircut, he paid for a storage unit in Dairlee in full belief that Craigh would return. They'd cleared through Gran's things so that Grandpa could have more space, and piled the other boxes in Gran's remaining room. There were pictures and heirlooms— things she wasn't ready to part with, or sort through. There was even a box of her dad's in there.

Death happened quickly and changed things so fast your head spun like a top, and all you could do was hang on. Like with Charles, for the Leery family. She jotted a note to send a sympathy card.

"You awright, lass?" Grandpa shuffled his cards and tapped them on the table. "That was one heavy sigh."

Had she sighed? Paislee blinked at her grandfather, who'd known Shannon Leery in her youth. "Yes. Thanks. Grandpa?"

"Aye?"

"You said that Shannon was the heir for the Leery estate. Were there other siblings?"

"Just the younger sister, Shayla. Never could measure up tae Shannon."

"Do you know if Shayla got married? Well, she must've, tae have Charles." Paislee fired up her laptop and typed "Shannon Leery Marcus" into the search bar. Lady Leery had her own page on Wikipedia, with a list of her kin. Just another wee difference between the peerage and the common folk, she thought, tongue in cheek.

Shayla, two years younger than Shannon, deceased, had married John Thomson, and they'd had Charles Thomson. John was also deceased. The family wasn't winning any ribbons in the longevity department.

Shannon had only one son, Shawn Philip Marcus. He'd never married. No children. Shannon's husband, George, had died two years after their marriage, from being—*shot*. Chills raced up her spine as she pictured Charles on the path before her, eyes half-open.

Paislee did another internet search and gasped at the headlines. "Grandpa, did you know that Lady Leery was under suspicion of killing her husband, who'd been shot?"

He laid a card down. "That was nothing but rumors and gossip, lass. The shire was in a frenzy, but Shannon was cleared of all wrongdoing." Grandpa looked up at her, his glasses glinting beneath the overhead lights. "Everybody used tae shoot, back in the day. It was a genteel sport."

Paislee closed her laptop and resumed knitting on a cinnamon-colored cashmere vest. Should she feel sorry for the lady, or was there more to the story?

What reason would Lady Leery have to shoot her nephew?

"Genteel," she said in a dry tone. "Until you're on the wrong end of the gun."

# Chapter 5

Paislee left that afternoon at three to pick up Brody from Fordythe, deciding to prep a casserole for dinner before she met with Lydia to examine properties.

With Grandpa supervising the meal at home she had a better than fair chance the cheese topping over the tattie-and-neeps wouldn't burn. Brody, distracted by video games, didn't always hear the timer go off.

Hamish still hadn't answered her text, so Paislee parked rather than wait in queue to check in with Mrs. Martin and make sure the bairns were all right. In P6, they were toward the top of the food chain, with only one year left before secondary. To Paislee, they were still babes.

She nabbed the space nearest to Hamish's office and noticed the window blinds were drawn. Paislee followed the paved path in front of the building, eyeing the grassy field to her left. In fifteen minutes, once the bell rang, the lawn would be brimming with rowdy kids, excited to finish another day in class.

Opening the blue door of Fordythe, Paislee inhaled the scents of busy children: popcorn, project glue, hand sanitizer.

Paislee signed in at the reception desk and greeted Mrs. Jimenez. The woman's thick dark hair was cut in a shag at her round shoulders, and she held a phone receiver to her ear as she waved for Paislee to go on ahead. Mrs. Martin's class was at the farthest end of a beige, linoleum-tiled hall.

Paislee peeked through the sliver of glass in the door. To her surprise, Mrs. Martin's classroom was crowded with all the kids from P6. Headmaster McCall and the school counselor, Ms. Peterson, stood before the children clustered in seats, on the desks, or on the floor. This was not the usual tight ship.

Brody hunched over his desk, situated farthest from the doorway, but she picked out his auburn mop. She couldn't put off a haircut for him much longer. Mrs. Martin saw her through the glass and gestured for Paislee to join them.

She didn't want to intrude but was curious as to what was going on. A free-for-all, as it turned out. Holly was center stage, crying crocodile tears, overdramatizing the horror of being *locked* in the bathroom while a crazy shooter rattled the door, threatening to kill her.

Paislee wanted to explain herself but realized it was best to shut her gob, so she leaned against the wall closest to the door and kept out of the way. Hard to believe that just hours had passed since the disastrous field trip at Leery Estate.

Mrs. Martin shuffled across the room to Paislee with a slight negating shake of her head, as if to assure her not to worry.

Paislee nodded and observed the throng of children. There was Britta, her crown of braids not as tight as it had been this morning. Sweet girl. Holly continued to cry.

It was a shock to be so close to a crime, and Paislee, very much an adult, still felt off-center about it—she planned on numbing the tragedy with a raspberry scone after dinner. "Any word from the DI?" she whispered to Mrs. Martin. She hadn't heard a peep.

"None," the teacher murmured. "We tried tae carry on like a normal day, but it's not fair tae the children tae keep things bottled up. Ms. Peterson and the headmaster decided tae call a class meeting."

"What did Holly's parents say?"

"The Fishers are driving home from Edinburgh. Dad had a job interview there. They requested that Holly not talk with the police until they get back."

"She was in the bathroom the whole time. What's there tae say?"

Headmaster McCall glared their way, and Paislee shrank back. Mrs. Martin straightened her brown-and-cream blazer and returned her attention to the students.

Ms. Peterson listened with strained compassion as Holly finally calmed down enough for her to get a word in. "Thank ye for sharing, Holly. Now, does anyone *else* have anything they'd like tae say aboot what happened today?"

The red-haired girl from Paislee's group raised her hand.

"Moira?" Ms. Peterson encouraged.

"I heard a bang and thought it was a truck. I didnae know there was a person *dead* by the bathroom." Moira's lips quivered. "Is he goin' tae turn into a scary ghostie now? Forever?"

Her friend Kylie shrieked. "The garden is haunted!"

The class erupted at the idea of a haunted estate, and Hamish winced. Ms. Peterson did her best to calm the situation, but the kids had gotten their teeth into the idea of ghosts, spirits, and mad killers like her Scottish terrier, Wallace, to a beef bone.

With patience earned from years of teaching primary school, Mrs. Martin regained control of her class by flicking the light switch off, on, and off before taking her place before her desk, hands folded. "Be. Seated."

Hamish and Ms. Peterson faded to the right, toward the door, but didn't leave as they gave way to the person in charge. The kids sat where they were and faced front.

Mrs. Martin centered her glasses on her nose. "Today there was a tragedy at Leery Estate. There are no ghosts. No mad killer, and I will thank ye tae keep yourselves under control. Spreading stories about *ghosts* is not how you set an example for the younger kids at

Fordythe. Show me that you're ready to be in P7." She eyed Moira and Kylie, then scanned each child in the room. "We should be thinking of the Leery family today, and their sorrow. As a class." She looked to Hamish, who nodded. "We will send a sympathy card conveying our condolences. That is what one does after a loss. How many of you have lost someone in your family? Raise your hands, please, no shouting."

A surprising number of little hands shot up.

"Did it make you feel sad?"

A round of nods, and the teacher called on a few kids to share what they might do, which ran the gamut of prayers to planting a tree.

"It's important when we lose someone tae remember them in a loving way." Again Mrs. Martin let her glance land on each child, as if to banish the thought of ghosts permanently. "We didnae know Charles Thomson personally, but the Leerys are part of our community, and *that* is why we will act with compassion."

Mrs. Martin switched the lights back on, with five minutes left of class. "You may talk among yourselves *quietly*."

"See me in my office before you leave?" Hamish murmured into Paislee's ear.

He must have her purse, she thought. "Sure."

Ms. Peterson left, and Hamish joined Mrs. Martin in front of her desk. The two spoke in hushed voices, so Paislee walked over to Brody and Edwyn. "How are you guys?" Was Brody worried about ghosts or killers?

"Mum, can I play football after school?" He pushed his auburn hair from his eyes. "Edwyn's gonna stay, too."

"For a few minutes while I meet with the headmaster." She had two orders for sweaters to complete at the shop, but it might be healthy for Brody to hang with his mates and burn off some steam.

"Class," Mrs. Martin called. Hamish had gone. Two minutes until the bell rang and the antsy kids perched on the edges of their seats, ready to bolt from the room like hounds at a whistle.

"Yes, Mrs. Martin," they said in unison.

"Thank ye for listening. I'll see you tomorrow—with an extra ten minutes of morning recess as a reward for guid behavior."

They cheered, and the bell clamored. Brody was about to dart after Edwyn when he remembered Paislee and turned back with a squeak of his sneaker sole on the linoleum floor.

"Go," she said. "But I don't think yer supposed tae run in the halls."

He fast-walked out of the classroom.

Paislee straightened some of the desks on her way to Mrs. Martin. "You were amazing. Tae give the kids an outlet for their grief."

"Unfortunately, it's not my first bout with death and the kiddos. We all feel helpless and dinnae ken what tae do, so we'll send a signed card from P6, along with flowers. Poor bloke."

"Charles Thomson. He was Lady Leery's nephew."

"Nephew?" Mrs. Martin's mouth pursed, fanning wrinkles between her nose and upper lip.

"Aye, did ye know Shannon Leery had a younger sister? Now that branch of the family is all deceased."

"Tragic." Mrs. Martin pointed to a family photo on her desk. She and her rotund husband sat in the center of four kids and six grandkids. "Family is tae be cherished."

On that Paislee agreed.

"Did ye see what happened?" The teacher's eyes rounded behind her tortoiseshell frames. "How are *you*, dear?"

"I'm fine." Paislee didn't want to go into detail of how scared she'd been that the dead person might have been Shawn. "It was shocking, tae be sure"—her throat caught as she recalled the pale body on the path—"but I'll manage."

Mrs. Martin peered closer at Paislee as if to see for herself. "We'll have closure once the police discover whoever is responsible."

"I'd like for Nairn tae feel safe again." She'd given this a lot of thought, to be fair to Lydia and the others who wanted Nairn to be more prosperous. "It's the downside of growing the town—more people, more crime."

"Which should mean a bigger show of force." Mrs. Martin tucked a strand of hair behind her ear, showing a little pearl. "Paislee, I meant tae ask how things are at home? You'd mentioned your grandfather this morning."

"He's settling in, thanks."

"It will be good for Brody tae have him around, since ye've no da in the picture."

Paislee bristled at her observation—it was a sensitive subject. "The right *people* make a difference." Male or not.

"Calm yourself, lass. Brody's smart, and has a guid heart. I've a son aboot yer age, single." Mrs. Martin leaned her hip against her desk as she studied Paislee. "A teacher, like me."

Surprised by the direction of the conversation, Paislee folded her hands behind her back to distance herself. "Uh. I'm sure he's very nice." To be clear she wasn't interested, she added, "I don't date."

"Ye should. Life is for the young. It passes by in a trice. Who'll be at yer side in your golden years?" Mrs. Martin gestured to the photo on her desk as if offering a prize membership into a special club.

"Lydia, probably," she joked, taking a half step back.

"Who?"

"My best friend," she said. "Thank you for thinking of me. Have a nice day." Paislee squeezed Mrs. Martin's wrist and escaped from the classroom, leaving Mrs. Martin humming softly at her desk as she sat down to tidy papers.

Paislee reached the end of the hall out of breath from rushing. Mrs. Jimenez hung up the phone. "Can I help you, Paislee?"

She glimpsed behind her, her mind in a whirl over Mrs. Martin suggesting Paislee should date her son. "Is Headmaster McCall in? He wanted tae see me."

"Aye." The receptionist leaned her ample bosom forward. "I heard ye were with Holly when the shooting happened."

"True." She buried the immediate memory of Charles breaking through the hedge to the path. It wouldn't serve her in her quest for calm.

"We sent an email home tae the parents of P6-ers and the phones are ringin' off the hook. Demanding tae know what our safety measures are for field trips." Her high tone was laden with drama. "Who can predict where a killer will hide?"

"All of the kids are okay—focus on that?" Paislee suggested.

The headmaster cleared his throat from his open office door. His suit coat was properly buttoned, though his tie was askew. "Ms. Shaw?"

"Good luck," she told the receptionist, gladly crossing the hall to Hamish.

Their eyes met; then he averted his gaze.

Apprehension tickled between her shoulder blades. Maybe this wasn't about her purse?

Paislee entered Hamish's office. A month ago she'd sat across from his desk when he'd reprimanded her for being tardy and making Brody late.

Since then, they'd met casually outside the school at community events or when he had a question regarding a knitting project for his sister. Hamish made her laugh, and she liked to poke him when he acted too superior. He had the cutest dimple on his cheek when he forgot himself and smiled.

She took the same wooden seat and faced him as he sank into his dark brown leather chair. His diploma and certificates were centered on the wall behind him.

Hamish laid his arms on his desk and interlaced his fingers. There was no hint of a dimple. "I'll need tae get a statement from you, aboot what happened today. Thankfully, nobody was hurt, but the parents are already up in arms."

"Mrs. Jimenez mentioned that." Paislee reached into her cardigan pocket for her phone and held it for comfort. "I thought you were going tae give me my purse."

Hamish flinched. "Och, hang on." He unlocked a bottom drawer and brought out her brown leather slouch bag. "Here."

"Thanks." She placed it on the ground by her feet.

"The statement?"

"Of course, though we've already talked about what happened, with Constable Vega." The air was thick between them, and she tried to lighten the tension she didn't understand. "I'll write it tonight. Ye ken Holly's destined for the stage, right?"

"A bit of a drama queen, aye." His mouth twitched, but he didn't smile. "She claims you *locked* her in the bathroom?"

Heat filled her cheeks at the implication she'd done something wrong to the girl. "I held the bathroom door shut, so Holly wouldn't see the body on the path, or run into danger. We had no idea what was going on." It was a good thing she'd come early today to hear the lass herself. "Holly also claimed the shooter threatened tae kill her."

"I ken, I ken." Hamish leaned back, his elbows on his armrests, his expression disgruntled.

"Nobody said such a thing."

His features grew pinched around the eyes and mouth. "Mr. and Mrs. Fisher are driving in from Edinburgh and should be here within an hour. It would be best if I knew exactly what happened from your perspective."

Paislee's mouth dried. Didn't he believe her?

"I know what ye told the constable, but please go over it again." His pointer finger tapped the armrest.

"Mrs. Martin asked me tae take Holly tae the restroom before we entered the circle maze. She didn't want tae, but she was doing the dance, you know?" Paislee bopped her feet against the floor to mimic dancing.

"Holly said she didnae want tae go, but ye forced her anyway?" His confusion revealed that he had no kids of his own.

Paislee scowled. "Would ye rather she had an accident in front of her mates?"

Hamish leaned forward, blackish brown hair falling over one brow. "Then what?" His tone was clipped and he ignored her question.

Stung, she straightened and tightened her grip on the mobile in her cardigan pocket. Paislee didn't care much for this version of Hamish McCall, arrogant headmaster.

How had she imagined they might be friends? She should never have lowered her guard. But his smile . . . she shook her head.

"Then we retraced our steps back tae the bathroom," she said as calmly as she could, given the circumstances.

"And?"

She focused on the scene. "Holly dashed in tae use the facilities. I waited outside for her."

"Were you holding the knob at that time?"

"What?" She'd been enjoying the birdsong. The butterflies. "Why would I?"

"At what point did you grab the knob?"

Flustered, she frowned, her brow tight. "After Charles fell back through the hedge."

"And when did you release it?"

Tears stung her eyes at his cold questions.

"Not until after you gave me the nod—Graham was going tae show you and the others a way back tae the bus by the stables so that you didn't have tae be on the path, but I had tae get Holly there without her looking back." Nausea flipped in her belly.

The headmaster nodded his encouragement for her to continue. "And how did you do that?"

"I bet Holly an extra dessert"—which she still owed the lass— "that she couldn't beat me back tae the bus." Paislee's stomach gurgled with nervous guilt, though she hadn't done anything wrong.

He leaned forward inquisitively. "Why didn't ye just ask her tae stay inside the restroom?"

"I did." *Calm. Calm. Calm.* "She tried to leave anyway, so I held the knob."

"And locked her in." He blew out a noisy breath.

"What would you have done?" Paislee released her phone before she might break the plastic from clutching it too hard.

"Unfortunately, it doesnae matter what *I* would have done." He raised a palm. "You were there."

"I assessed the situation the best I could." She drew herself up. "Why do I feel like you don't believe me?"

"I *do* believe you. But there's no denying that Holly was scared. She wanted oot of the restroom. You didnae let her." His brow furrowed. "'Locked her in' sounds bad, ye ken?"

"There was a shooter. With a gun. Holly could have been shot. Any of the kids could have been shot." She thought of Brody and bile rose up her throat—she swallowed the sour taste.

He scrubbed his clean-shaven jaw. "Aye. On my watch."

Paislee shielded herself from feeling empathy for him—his disregard for her feelings really hurt. She'd done her best. She focused on his diploma, her back rigid.

"I've already cancelled the other field trips scheduled for Leery Estate this year." His eyebrows lifted with mock cheer. "We're golfing instead." He drummed his fingers on his desk. "Nice open range where you're sure tae see someone coming."

"Golf?" It was a popular sport here in Nairn, but not one she'd learned. "I don't play."

"It willnae matter for you this year."

The hair on the back of her neck rose. What could that mean?

Hamish's professional mask didn't budge. "I know yer busy, but if ye could write oot what happened before ye leave? Just so that I have a record when talking with the parents."

Holly's parents, he meant.

"Sure." She could tell her side of the story and let them know that there was no shooter threatening their daughter, by name, for heaven's sake. "If you'll give me some paper?"

Hamish didn't meet her gaze as he opened his drawer and pulled out a manila folder. "There's an incident report. . . ."

Hamish and his reports. Paislee said nothing but bent down to retrieve a pen from her purse.

He slid a black ballpoint across his desk. "Black ink, please."

She gnashed her back teeth together, anger replacing the sick feeling in her body.

"Take yer time," he said, "and be thorough." He hustled out of his office, leaving the door open a crack.

Hamish's pointed questions were directed at finding out what had happened to Holly during the shooting, while Detective Inspector Zeffer's inquiries were meant to find the shooter.

A half hour later, she left the report on the headmaster's desk without bothering to wish him a good night. She grabbed a jubilant Brody from the field, inwardly fuming over which man's line of questioning bothered her most. She didn't dare ask herself why.

# Chapter 6

That evening, after dinner and dishes were done, Paislee, Brody, and Grandpa hunched around the kitchen table with a puzzle of London's Big Ben.

When her granny wasn't knitting she'd adored intricate puzzles. Grandpa Angus had continued the hobby after he'd discovered a stash of brand-new boxes in Gran's room.

Paislee picked up Wallace and set the pup in her lap, stroking his black fur. He relaxed against her body, baring his tummy for a scratch. Her finger snagged on a tangle in his fringe, and she gently separated the knotted strands. "Wallace has an appointment with the groomer next Friday."

"Speaking of—you never said how the appointments with Lydia went." Grandpa fit a square edge against a round space, then pulled it back with a grunt.

"You distracted me with dinner on the table." The golden-crusted mashed potato and turnip casserole and a green salad had been ready to eat. "Both locations were a nightmare."

"Why?" Brody's lower lip pouted as he concentrated on a piece of the clock, his body half-sitting on his chair.

"They're on the outskirts of Nairn. Lydia tried tae sell me on being ahead of the curve, as our town is spreading." She rubbed

Wallace's ears, and the dog exuded love from his shiny, nearly black eyes.

"I read in the paper that we're getting a new traffic light off of Foss Street." Grandpa sat back and crossed his ankles once he'd finagled the piece, his expression victorious.

Foss and Hawthorn was a busy intersection that was only getting busier. "It's a good thing. I hate the traffic circles—they make you go *so* slow."

"That's the point, lass, that's the point." Grandpa smacked his lips. "I could use another cup of tea."

Brody pressed down on the clock piece, and it snapped in to complete the corner nearest him. "Yes!"

Grandpa tousled Brody's hair as he got up to refill his tea mug from the electric kettle. "Anybody else?"

"Naw," Brody said, his decaffeinated tea halfway gone. He added enough honey and lemon to make it pass for a dessert, but Paislee allowed him one cup before bed. To her mind it was still better than soda.

"No, what?" she prodded.

"No, thanks," Brody grumbled.

"No, thank you," she said to her grandfather. "I'm full. What a delicious meal."

Brody'd wolfed down two helpings of dinner and a scone. He didn't seem to be fazed by what had happened this morning. Charles falling backward through the brush popped up randomly in her thoughts, bringing with it physical trembling and cold sweat. Ten minutes of doggy snuggles had helped lessen her anxiety, but it wasn't gone.

Grandpa slid his glasses to the bridge of his nose. "Mind if I borrow the Juke on Saturday? I'll bring it back with a full tank."

"What for?" He hadn't asked to borrow the car before.

Wallace stretched, and she placed the pup on the braided rag rug at their feet. He sniffed Brody's socks, and Brody giggled, wiggling his toes.

Grandpa Angus brought his full mug to the table. "There's somethin' in Dairlee I need."

"From where?"

His cheeks tinted pink. "Storage unit."

"Oh." The storage unit? She couldn't think of any reason to deny his request. "Do you even have a driver's license?"

Grandpa tugged his beard and snapped, "Ye need tae see it?"

"No, no." He'd driven just fine the few times he'd been behind the wheel. Grandpa was probably covered under her vehicle insurance, but she made a note to call the insurance agent to ask for sure.

She chose a straight-edged piece of the puzzle. "So long as you're at the shop by four."

"Can I go with you, Grandpa?"

Paislee searched for a matching black-and-brown stripe with an edge. Was this a sign of them getting along? She knew that Brody didn't like being cooped up at the shop with her, but she tried to make up for it with Sunday Fundays.

"Not this time, lad."

She waited to see if Grandpa would explain. Nothing. He simply slurped his tea. Brody didn't question his grandfather, but he left the table in a huff and turned the telly on in the living room extra loud.

Paislee didn't blame Brody for being upset. Grandpa continued with the puzzle. Why was he being so secretive? She didn't press. Between witnessing a man die, Hamish not supporting her, Lydia showing her two awful properties, and the threat of losing Cashmere Crush's location, she had a full plate.

She tossed the piece in the center of the table and joined Brody in the living room. He was curled on the corner of their cozy old sofa to watch his favorite sitcom. Two armchairs were snugged into the space beside the fireplace, but she sat beside Brody.

Her grandfather shuffled loudly to his room and closed the door. She realized with a pang that she no longer thought of it as Gran's room.

"Hey, Brody, are things okay between you and Edwyn?"

He scrunched his nose as he glanced at her. "Why?"

"It's just you two were arguing on the bus."

His brow furrowed, too, then relaxed. "He wanted tae know if I thought Britta was cute."

Britta? The sweet blonde with braids? Noooooooo—Paislee wasn't ready for this! "And do you?"

"No, Mum. Ew." Wallace jumped onto the couch between them, circled twice, and plopped down with a tail wag and a chuff. "He wants tae marry her."

"Oh . . . that sounds serious."

Brody pulled his gaze from the TV show to Paislee. "I think he's gone mental."

She concurred. "Why's that?"

"Everyone knows that if you want tae make it in sports, you cannae get married."

It was news to her. "Are ye serious about sports?"

Wallace rested his head on her son's lap, ears up.

Brody stroked the dog's muzzle. "Football, duh."

She hadn't known until this moment that her son wanted to play football professionally, let alone that he was thinking of his future, or had an opinion on marriage. "Well, I don't think ye should worry. Edwyn's too young tae get married."

He traced his finger down Wallace's nose, tapping the pink tip. "I told him that, Mum. He didnae listen. He's going tae ask her tomorrow at recess."

"Why Britta?"

"She's a verra guid drawer."

An important skill for a boy into comic books. At ten, Paislee vaguely recalled wanting to be an acrobat. Where and when did childhood dreams die?

Paislee hugged Brody to her side and kissed the top of his head—she would help him be whatever he wanted to be. "You're pretty smart, kiddo."

"Not math. Are ghosts real, Mum?" He looked her in the eye, demanding honesty.

She considered how to answer. "I've never seen nor heard one." There'd been times when she'd felt her grandmother's presence or smelled her perfume, but that was just memory . . . maybe.

"Seein' a ghost would be scary."

"Well, we're safe here. If ye want, we can do some research on them. Tomorrow." She had a feeling that even though Brody hadn't seen Charles's body, the group hysteria from class might unsettle his usually sweet dreams.

Brody yawned. They got ready for bed, singing silly songs. She tucked him in and made sure that Wallace was curled at his side. As usual, she said a prayer for Gran to watch over him during the night.

The next morning, Paislee bit back a squeal as she got a gander at the dark circles under her pale blue eyes. *Yikes.*

Neither she nor Brody had slept well—she'd had her door open to listen for him, so she hadn't allowed herself a deep sleep.

She expected him to be sleepy when she woke him for school, but he virtually sprang out of bed and finished his breakfast with his usual bounce.

"Grandpa, can I stay home with you instead of going tae Mum's Knit and Sip tonight?"

Theirs was a new relationship, and Grandpa had knocked it back by not allowing Brody to go on his mysterious errand on Saturday.

Grandpa nodded. "Aye. Let's rent that superhero comedy you wanted tae see last week, *Stupid Man,* or *Antmouse,* or whatever."

"*Ant-Man!* Thanks, Grandpa."

She crossed her fingers and hoped for a mended fence. "Don't forget your class earned extra recess today." Where Edwyn just might get engaged to Britta. It was sweet—so long as it wasn't her kid.

"Whoop!" Brody leapt toward the door and picked up his backpack by a single strap. Grandpa sat at the table, a steaming mug at his side, the paper open, his glasses hanging on by the tip of his nose.

She acknowledged being a wee bit jealous of him leisurely enjoying the newspaper. "See you later," she said, shutting the front door.

Paislee dropped Brody off at school, where Hamish waited in the blue doorway of Fordythe. She pretended not to see him. He owed her an apology, to her way of thinking. Still, she hoped his meeting with Holly's parents had gone well.

She arrived at Cashmere Crush at quarter past nine and parked in the alley next to the back stairs. To her surprise, Theadora Barr waited for her on the stoop.

Had she been locked out of her tea shop? Where was her husband, Dan?

"Hi, Theadora." The two ladies were friendly acquaintances through their businesses, a family of sorts. Theadora had dyed her platinum-and-teal locks to a golden brown and styled them in shoulder-length curls. She wore a collared dress with a subtle floral pattern.

"Paislee!" Theadora brushed her palms down the front of her dress as if nervous.

"Want to come in?" Paislee gestured to the shop.

"If ye don't mind?"

The hair on the back of her neck rose in caution. Paislee unlocked the door, scooting by Theadora, who smelled like perfume rather than sugar. This was the first time in five years that Theadora had wanted to speak with her so early in the morning.

Paislee flipped on the lights at the storage section and then the overhead lighting for the shop. "I ate the last raspberry scone last night, so I'd planned tae swing by your bakery later. Is everything all right?"

Theadora's eyes welled, but she swallowed and looked away. "Aye. Are *you* all right?"

"Sure, love, why wouldn't I be?" Paislee settled her arm around Theadora's shoulders.

Theadora raised her gaze and clasped Paislee's wrist. "Amelia told me this morning that you were at the Leery Estate when Charles was *shot*."

Alarmed, Paislee asked, "You know Charles Thomson?"

"No." Theadora folded her hands before her, and Paislee ushered the woman to the register counter. "He was part of the Leery family, right?"

Paislee recalled the DI's request for her not to share what she knew, but this was something Theadora could find on a Google search, as Paislee had the day before on Wikipedia. She hadn't had the chance to read the morning paper, but she'd be surprised if the shooting wasn't the headline. "Charles was Shawn Marcus's cousin. Son of Shayla Leery Thomson, Shannon Leery's sister."

"I didnae even know she had a sister, or family other than Shawn, er, Mr. Marcus." Theadora wandered into the front of the shop, her eyes taking in the shelves of vibrant yarn. "Was Shawn there? Were you able tae speak with him?"

Theadora and Dan were in a tight bind, just as Paislee was, if they needed to move right away. Their bakery on the corner of the street closest to the beach was a premium space for tourist traffic. They had to be going crazy waiting for the ax Shawn wielded to fall.

"My plan yesterday morning was tae find out from Lady Leery where Shawn was staying, tae track him down. Then I saw him on the front porch with his mother, but it was a bad time, with the shooting." Paislee paused. "You don't think he lives with his mother? At fiftysomething?"

Theadora paled. "That'd be strange, though the estate is large."

"True. Maybe he was there for business." She recalled the purple circles under Shawn's eyes. "He stumbled out of the manor, tucking in his clothes. He wanted tae drive tae the hospital for Charles. His mother wouldn't let him leave, saying he wasn't well."

"I dinnae ken, Paislee. That family has enough money for Shawn tae have ten houses." Moisture filmed her eyes and she tucked a curl behind her ear. "Stumbling could be grief from losin' his cousin, not just illness."

"If you'd seen him, you'd know what I mean." Last month, Theadora had been ready to hang their landlord up by his toenails, cover him in honey, and leave him for the ants.

Theadora wiped at her lashes. "I'm being dafty. Dan blames my amped-up hormones." She gave Paislee a half smile, her lips a signature brick red that hadn't changed with the new hairstyle. "Ye havenae gotten another notice about moving, have ye?"

"No, I would've told you, believe me." Paislee leaned her hip against the counter.

"Do ye think people can change?"

"Tae be sure. We grow all the time."

Theadora tugged the collar of her dress, her throat flushed. "I'm beyond impatient with all of this . . . waitin'. Not just the business, which is bad enough, but gettin' pregnant. We've tried a new fertility specialist, who isnae cheap."

Paislee patted Theadora's arm in commiseration. "That's rough."

"Things are verra tense between me and Dan." Theadora's voice cracked. "He wants tae find another location and tell Shawn tae take a hike, but you and I both know *this* is the best in Nairn."

It was. "Dan's changed his mind about keeping the tea shop here?"

Theadora placed her hand protectively over her stomach. "He's frustrated by this process, too. We're both healthy. Why cannae I get pregnant?" She sniffed and dabbed her nose with a tissue from her dress pocket.

Paislee hugged Theadora tight. "Gran used tae say, 'Everything in its own time,' but it's hard tae be patient when ye want something so much."

"We've gone through our savings. It's *my* fault." Theadora flicked her gaze up to Paislee, deep pain in her eyes. "But I cannae stop trying."

Her heart broke for Theadora. "If ye want a family, what about adoption?"

"That would feel like givin' up. Like I failed." Theadora forced a watery smile. "I'm sairy tae be such a downer, but I truly just wanted tae make sure that you're fine?"

"It was no bother, Theadora. You're welcome tae chat anytime."

They hugged again, and Theadora pulled away with a raised chin, no more tears. "Come tae the bakery for a business meeting Saturday morning at eight. I may have news of me own tae share." Theadora waved over her shoulder and hurried out the back door.

How could she help Theadora and Dan through this time? Paislee flipped the closed sign on the front window to Open. Did Theadora's cryptic words mean the bakery owner was pregnant at last?

Humming, Paislee scanned her shelves for just the right shade of pale pink, or baby blue. Or what about a mint green? No matter what gender, the Barr baby would be loved.

Paislee's morning was filled with walk-in customers, which only solidified her worry over losing this location. She couldn't wait ten years for Nairn's sprawl to reach her on the outskirts as Lydia had suggested. Much of her success was due to being visible.

At noon she ate a sandwich for lunch in the shop and scanned the local news online. There was nothing about the murder. Amelia would be at Knit and Sip tonight, so Paislee could ask about the investigation then.

Was Shawn Marcus living with his mother? Of all the places she'd searched for Shawn's address and contact information this past month, the Leery Estate hadn't been one. In hindsight, it seemed so obvious.

Lydia had access to a private site her company paid for that showed past known addresses, which had given locations for Shawn from Wales to South Africa.

The Leery Estate hadn't been listed—she would have remembered. Paislee searched the Nairn directory for Shannon Leery. It was the same number on the brochure by the register.

Without stopping to talk herself out of it, Paislee dialed from her mobile. A man answered. "Leery Estate."

Her stomach did loop-de-loops, and she bit her lip to keep from giggling nervously. She'd never make a good criminal. "Is Shawn Marcus in?"

"He's unavailable at the moment. May I take a message?"

Paislee pictured the tall butler who'd made the remark about them "being so lucky" if Shawn had been the one dead. Would he recognize her voice?

"Ma'am?" he prodded in a snooty tone.

"Sorry." She dropped an octave. "Is there a better time tae reach him?"

"I believe he will return within the hour."

Paislee hung up, her hands shaking. "Woot! Shawn Marcus officially lives at home." Now she just needed to get onto the estate to meet with him and convince him not to sell their building.

Before it was too late.

# Chapter 7

Over the next two hours, Paislee was thwarted from driving to the estate by constant foot traffic in Cashmere Crush. She sold a scarf, lemon-yellow yarn, and a pattern book for an afghan. She walked an older woman with a silver eyetooth to the door. "Thank you. Call or email if ye have questions!"

She locked up, tempted to break all speed limits to get to the estate. A niggling voice suggested that she check one more time to make sure Shawn was there. The way sales were flowing in today, she hated to leave.

Paislee called from her car. Her palms were damp, her breaths sharp, her nerves jumpy. She had to stop Shawn from selling the building. "Leery Estate, this is Midge, may I help you?"

She was relieved that it wasn't the butler, Malcolm—his intensity was a bit much. And she just couldn't trust a man who shot rabbits. "Is Shawn available?"

"I'm sairy, but no. The family is at the church. May I take a message?"

That was a brutal reminder that Shawn really was busy, and why. Paislee didn't want to leave her name and number because Shawn Marcus already knew that she wanted to speak with him, and had been avoiding her calls. Her only hope was to catch her landlord by surprise.

Tomorrow. She couldn't just drop it as there were only four days left of the thirty from his eviction notice.

"No, thank you." She hung up with a sigh and glanced at her watch—shoot—three fifteen. Time to pick up Brody! The last thing she needed was to be late, especially since she hadn't heard a single word from Hamish regarding the Holly situation.

She arrived in twelve minutes, after breezing around the traffic circles, to find Mrs. Martin on the curb with Brody. There was no sign of the headmaster. The bell rang, and kids trickled out the front doors of the school. Paislee rolled her window down and glanced to Mrs. Martin as Brody hopped in the passenger side and buckled up.

"Is everything okay?" She looked at Brody, who ignored her. "What's wrong?"

Her son's teacher stepped up to Paislee's window. "Brody and Edwyn had a wee disagreement over Britta. I'll let him tell you aboot it. Nobody's in trouble, but if it happens again, there will be consequences, ye ken?" She removed her tortoiseshell glasses to peer at Paislee, then Brody.

Brody ducked his head. "Yes, Mrs. Martin."

Consequences? Paislee thanked the teacher and carefully pulled into traffic, driving back to the house so that Brody could be with Grandpa for the evening. Brody rode home with his head down. She was glad to have an idea of what the problem might be.

"So, Britta?"

His lower lip jutted out. "I tried tae talk him oot of askin' Britta tae marry him, but Edwyn got really mad—like supermad. Bulgy eyes and everything."

What an image! "Did ye *fight* fight?"

"Naw." Brody kicked his backpack. "Just yelled."

"Well, tomorrow you'll both be cooled off and can talk about it."

He shrugged. "It's stupid, anyway, because he asked Britta, and she just ran inside all scared."

"Och. Ye think he felt bad about asking? Edwyn might not want tae do it again, until, you know, later." Like in his twenties or thirties. Paislee wondered if she was under any obligation to call Edwyn's dad? If it were Brody, she'd want to know but it wasn't like she and Bennett were friends. And Britta's mum?

On second thought, she'd speak with Mrs. Martin and let the capable teacher handle it.

"Why can't we just play football?" Brody grumbled.

Paislee dropped her son off at home, walking in to chat with her grandpa and get her dog hugs from Wallace before going back to the store for Knit and Sip night.

She'd created the event to bring together a community of ladies who wanted companionship as they crafted. It had been Gran's suggestion, and a good one, to move away from an online-only business and build a venue to gather.

It started at six, and went to eight or nine, depending on, in the past, when Brody was tired of watching movies in the television nook she'd created for him. Tonight, she was lucky enough to have Grandpa—she hesitated to think what kind of advice he might give Brody about the lasses.

Paislee placed cups, plates, and napkins on the high-top table and played pop music on low in the background, choosing to finish her bespoke cinnamon-colored cashmere vest for tonight's project.

Lydia was first to arrive, sailing in on a wind of expensive perfume. She'd changed her hairstyle to a dramatic cherry red—spiky on one side and bobbed on the other. Her gray eyes were the color of river rock and she emphasized them with dramatic liner and mascara. She was tall, thin, yet curved, and as nice as she was beautiful.

"How are ye, love? Any word on the murder? I havenae seen a thing on the news, not that I've had a free second tae do more than breathe." Lydia kissed Paislee's cheeks. "Rough night? You look knackered."

"Thanks. Nothing from the DI, but I'm hoping Amelia will

have news." Or better yet, the detective inspector would have the shooter behind bars. "What about your legal department? Anything tae save us?"

"I've given the certified letter tae Grant Cooke, the solicitor for our agency. The man's a wiz. Let him work his magic." Lydia's tone held admiration.

"Is he handsome?" Her bestie deserved someone in her life to treat her special. "Single?"

"Stop." Lydia lifted an insulated bag to the high-top table. "I brought a pear cobbler."

"All the businesses on this block are meeting Saturday morning. What can we do tae stop the eviction? Lyd, everybody's on edge with waiting." She used her most cajoling gaze on her best friend. "I'd love tae offer hope."

"Ye cannae say anythin' aboot Grant just yet." Lydia slid off her lightweight sweater to show a cherry-red silk blouse loose over jeans. "He's makin' it a priority, but it could be awkward. The Leerys are a prominent family."

Her shoulders hiked—Lydia suspected something specific but wasn't spilling the beans. "A hint?"

"I *can't*. Grant wants tae get tae the bottom of it. Stop with those eyes!" Lydia sighed. "You have tae understand that Shawn Marcus will one day inherit the Leery Estate. Our firm cannae make false accusations. Grant needs proof if something is amiss with the sale."

"There are times I hate that P word." Paislee folded her arms at her waist. "Hey, I found out that Shawn lives at the manor house."

"He does? But that didnae come up when I searched." Lydia's gaze narrowed. "Unless it was because it was his original address, like from birth? I cannae believe I missed that. I'm not on me game these days. I've been so busy at work—"

"Nice tae know you're human," Paislee joked. "I'm going tae

see Shawn tomorrow. I'll march up those stone stairs, pound on the front door, and make him listen. I'll appeal tae his sense of right and wrong." Paislee thought of the customers she'd had all month. "Business has been so good. How can I lose Cashmere Crush?"

Lydia squealed, "No! You have tae wait. Let me talk tae Grant first." She lowered her voice even though it was just the two of them. "He knows something's off. Why give ye a thirty-day eviction notice and then never follow through?"

"I'm not going tae show up at work on Monday and find my door padlocked, will I?" Paislee was tempted to sleep in the shop.

"Highly doubtful." Lydia put her hand on her hip. "According tae that letter, you have thirty days from the point of sale—which didnae happen."

Paislee plunked down in the high-backed chair and pulled her wooden knitting needles from the ball of soft cashmere; the familiar action soothed her frazzled nerves. Another thirty days. How long would Shawn keep them dangling on the line?

"Och!" Lydia smacked her palm to her forehead. "I talked with Gavin today—Lady Leery's still hosting our party. He says she doesnae want tae let us down."

*Oh no.* Paislee looped yarn over her trembling finger. "That's taking good manners too far, don't ye think?" Her voice sounded funny to her own ears. Going to the estate to confront Shawn was different somehow than sitting down to a meal where someone had been killed.

Lydia shrugged. "Mibbe she didnae like Charles. My mum threw a party when her stepdad passed."

"They haven't caught the killer yet, Lydia. This is different." But even as Paislee's imagination conjured a madman stalking the halls with a gun, another part of her wanted to confront Shawn in a dark corner and demand that he leave Cashmere Crush and the other businesses alone.

"It's a verra big deal tae Mr. Silverstein tae celebrate at the estate. The antiques are genuine tae the house. It's like being back in time, Paislee. I hope you'll ask Grandpa if he can watch Brody?"

"I don't know. . . ."

"You said you would! Besides, Gavin promised Natalya Silverstein that there would be loads of extra security, so dinnae fash, all right? What if this turns out tae be a tragic, yet accidental, shooting? Then you'd miss an amazin' night for nothing."

"I'll ask Grandpa," she said. She envisioned a dozen men with hulking arms in bad-fitting tuxedoes. She and the dead man had a connection, since she'd been there to witness his passing. How could Lydia understand that? She gulped over the lump in her throat.

"I'll bring a dress tae your house. This is a high-end party, and you deserve tae shine and have fun."

Paislee told herself to shake off the blues and celebrate another thirty days in this locale. "Nothing that makes me uncomfortable. Like those heels you tried tae make me wear last Christmas," Paislee said. "I looked like a hooker."

Lydia snickered. "No hooker heels. Got it."

The door banged open, and Mary Beth Mulholland entered, her fleshy arms laden with a platter of fruit, her knitting bag looped over one wrist. Forty years old with twin daughters, and married to a successful solicitor, Mary Beth claimed knitting kept her sane. "Paislee, how are you and Brody? Mrs. Jimenez told me aboot the scare at Leery Estate during the field trip. How terrifying!"

"We're fine" was all she had a chance to say before Amelia Henry, her good friend who was also a receptionist at the police station, arrived. The thirty-year-old rocked a short, spiky haircut. Her eyes were sapphire blue, compared to Mary Beth's cornflower.

"Amelia will know what's going on," Mary Beth declared.

"I will?" Amelia carried chocolates, her knitting in a leather backpack over her shoulder.

"Have they caught the killer, from the shooting at Leery Estate?" Mary Beth gave Amelia a hug, just about dwarfing the petite woman.

"Not yet." Amelia blew a kiss to Paislee and put the candy on the table next to Lydia. "The DI is in a mood."

That was nothing new, Paislee thought. "Do you know Constable Payne?"

"Tae be sure—he's always crackin' jokes." Amelia stepped over Paislee's knitting basket to a vacant chair across the circle. "Why?"

"He drove me here after the shooting yesterday. He seemed really nice, so I asked him if he liked being a constable." He *had* been funny.

Amelia dropped her backpack with a *thunk* and sank down. "Why did ye do that?"

Paislee blushed at being caught butting her nose into Amelia's business. "I didn't mention your name, but he offered tae talk tae you about being a police officer."

"I'm sairy I ever told you aboot that." Amelia unzipped her backpack with jerky movements.

Lydia raised her brow in question at Paislee.

"Oh, don't be," Paislee said in a rush. "I swear I didn't even hint at who you might be—he thought I was asking for myself, at first, but—"

"You, a constable?" Mary Beth asked in horror. "You are a knitter, Paislee. That's what you do."

"I know that!" She felt bad for upsetting her friends. "That's what I told him, too."

"You've changed yer mind, Amelia?" Lydia sipped her wine.

Elspeth thankfully stopped the conversation when she arrived, balancing a tray of crackers and a cheese ball. She was tall and slender, with an iron-gray mane—it was hard to believe she was seventy. Each Thursday, she left her blind sister at home to have an evening with her fellow crafters.

"The hot topic of the night is the shooting at Leery Estate,"

Paislee said once they were all seated. She carefully didn't return to the subject of Amelia being a police officer. Lydia leaned against the high-top, ready to serve drinks, snacks, and gossip. Paislee's mouth watered at the scent of sugary pear from the cobbler.

"I only know aboot it because I volunteer at the church with Father Dixon. Shannon Leery and Shawn Marcus were both in his office today." Elspeth removed her needlepoint from her craft bag. "There's been nothing in the paper."

"Which I find odd," Mary Beth said. She chose a sturdy wooden chair and dug around in her knitting bag until she found her yarn and pulled it to her lap. Dark purple.

"Your usual whisky, Amelia?" Lydia lifted the bottle, poured, and delivered.

"Aye." Amelia crossed one booted foot over her knee, knitting needles to the side, glass in hand. "Thanks. It's been a rough week."

Paislee completed another row of her vest, her hands moving independently of her thoughts, which zeroed in on the shooting. Amelia had to know something.

Lydia returned to her customary spot. "Our firm is havin' a quarterly celebration at the Leery Estate tomorrow night and Paislee is going tae be my date."

Amelia sputtered her whisky. "Beg pardon?"

"*Maybe*. I'm going tae ask Grandpa tae watch Brody for me."

Mary Beth's brow winged upward. "Arran's firm had a holiday party there once and it was spectacular. I was able tae actually use me finishin' school manners and choose the correct forks during the formal dinner."

The ladies laughed, but Paislee would have to do a Google search on etiquette.

"We had an excellent quarter," Lydia said. "The company can easily afford it. Elspeth, white wine?"

Elspeth lowered her needlepoint. "Aye, that'd be lovely."

Lydia brought it over. "Mary Beth? Anything tae drink? I made a pear cobbler with nutmeg whipped cream for later."

"I'll stick with iced tea. I've lost a pant size since giving up alcohol. Doesnae mean I won't enjoy yer dessert, Lydia. I brought fresh fruit and an apricot tart."

"Delicious." Lydia admired the colorful platter of perfectly cut melon. "Paislee?"

"White wine, please, and some cheese and crackers." Paislee set the expensive cashmere and needles aside until she was finished eating. "Lydia, you're sure it's all right to bring me?" She didn't do fancy.

"Stop stressing aboot it." Lydia plucked a strawberry from the fruit platter and put it next to a plate of cheese and crackers. She brought that with the wine to Paislee.

"I cannae believe they're holding the party there." Amelia cupped her glass and stared at Paislee, then Lydia. "The Thomson *murder* is an open case."

Paislee couldn't miss the emphasis Amelia put on the word, and shivered.

"Aren't ye worried that the killer is still oot there somewhere? What if he's got a grudge against the Leerys, and yer in the wrong place?" Elspeth swigged her wine, clearly agitated.

Lydia held up her hand, her nails giving off a cherry-red glimmer. "Calm down, ladies, calm down. There will be extra security, so no danger. Besides, it may turn oot tae be a hunting accident. Tragic, but not deliberate. Right, Amelia?"

Amelia drummed her fingers against the whisky tumbler. "Not exactly."

"What do you know?" Paislee leaned toward Amelia.

"You *have* tae tell us," Lydia said in her sweet pout. "We're supposed tae be there tomorrow for dinner and dancing."

Amelia studied the ground for a moment, her forearms on her knees; then she looked up at Paislee, not Lydia. "The DI doesnae believe it was a hunting accident. I cannae say more than that. It's pure numpty tae still host the event." She shifted toward Lydia. "Sairy."

"Does he have a suspect?" Paislee asked.

"Och, no." Amelia tapped the toe of her boot and drank her whisky.

"How aboot a murder weapon?" Elspeth held her empty glass out to Lydia to top off. "I dinnae ken how I'll sleep at night until this killer is caught."

Lydia poured Elspeth's wine. "Come on, Amelia, I need more than that if I'm tae call off the event of the year. It's a big deal."

Amelia hesitated, torn between her job security and her friends. "I saw the ballistics report." She glanced to their reflection in the darkened window and lowered her voice. "The murder weapon was a rifle."

Paislee was no longer hungry. For some reason when the detective inspector had been talking about gunshots, she'd imagined the black handle in Malcolm's apron. That was not the same thing. "A rifle? But the sound I heard wasn't loud at all. It was kind of, well, muffled?"

"If it had a silencer, it might sound like that," Amelia said thoughtfully.

Lydia passed around the fruit platter. "A silencer?"

Amelia waved the offer of food away. "I've been huntin' with me dad and brothers since I could toddle. I know my way around a rifle. A silencer doesnae completely stop the sound but dilutes it. Another name is suppressor, which is more like it."

"So, if this diluter thing was used, doesn't that make it more likely tae have been an accident?" Paislee sipped her wine to relax her jumpy stomach.

"Not necessarily," Mary Beth chimed in. Her metal needles clacked rhythmically. "The DI might be onto somethin'. A silencer *could* mean the murder was premeditated. What do we know aboot the nephew?"

"Charles Thomson." Elspeth's mouth thinned. "I dinnae recall him ever being in Nairn. Grew up in London with his mum, according tae Father Dixon."

No way could Paislee or Lydia go to the party if there was a killer hunting the Leery family, on the loose. "What kind of crazy person would want tae shoot somebody on purpose?"

Amelia closed her eyes and groaned. "I'm not supposed tae talk aboot the case. Can we *please* talk aboot somethin' else?"

Lydia traded the fruit platter for her glass and swirled the wine, her smoky eyes mischievous. "Fine. I have a bit of gossip that cannae leave this room."

What a pronouncement! They all swiveled to keep their eyes on Lydia, who flipped her red hair. Paislee nibbled on a cheese cube.

After a dramatic swallow of her wine, Lydia said, "As we all probably know, Lady Leery is infamous for her lovers."

Paislee choked on the cheese. "What?"

Mary Beth burst out laughing and smacked Paislee on the back while Amelia shot her a concerned look.

Elspeth nodded, in the know. "I was the same age as her younger sister, Shayla, and in the same classes. Shannon was the kind of beautiful that made men stupid."

Lydia sighed dreamily. "Well, her current love is a sculptor. Graham Reid. Gavin told me. Thirty-five tae her seventy-three." She dipped a strawberry in her wine and bit the end.

"You've got tae be kidding—Graham Reid? Her lover?" Paislee pictured his long, dark honey hair, his flirtatious manner and blue eyes. "I met him yesterday," she told the ladies. Her mind raced as she recalled Graham, Shawn, Lady Leery, and another young lady on the porch. "He was our tour guide." His black knit cap had been collected as evidence. Her smile faded. Graham didn't like Shawn, yet the three of them had helped Shawn inside the mansion when he'd wanted to leave.

"Her lovers were legendary." Lydia spoke in a wistful tone as she named top celebrities from the past fifty years. "Back in the day, such things were teatime conversation, not like now, with the internet and zoom lenses on cameras or drones."

Elspeth clucked her tongue. "Her overt femininity made her younger sister, Shayla, sick with jealousy. Drove her off tae London, once she turned eighteen. I dinnae think Shannon meant tae be cruel. She was just thoughtless of Shayla's feelings."

"Grandpa told me that Shannon married for money," Paislee said. This was the kind of gossip that she liked best—slightly scandalous, but harmless. "Everybody knew it, even her husband."

"Aye." Lydia paused dramatically. "And then George Marcus, her husband, died in a hunting 'accident' on their property two years later."

The pinot grigio suddenly tasted bitter against Paislee's tongue. "I read that on Wikipedia—but Grandpa said the rumors of murder were just gossip."

"I remember that. What a scandal," Elspeth recalled, her eyes narrowed. "Shannon and George had a stormy relationship, tae say the least. When he died, everyone wondered if she'd done it— including Shayla, but that might be sour grapes, because her sister was left the estate." Elspeth lifted a shoulder. "The courts ruled her innocent."

Mary Beth uncapped her bottle of tea. "Well, I hate tae speak poorly of her. Lady Leery has certainly been guid tae our community. She donates tae everything."

"I agree, Mary Beth. The woman is gorgeous tae this day. Have all the lovers you want, I say." Lydia raised her wineglass in tribute. "It isnae such a scandal these days."

"It's no different than Widower Mann and his flock of elderly women," Mary Beth said.

Elspeth disagreed. "There should be different standards for a lady."

This broke off into a heated argument that only cooled when Lydia brought out her pear cobbler.

Paislee dug in. "So let me get this straight. Graham, Lady Leery's current lover, lives at the estate. Shawn Marcus, her son, also lives at the estate. I wonder who the pretty blond woman was on the porch with them? I thought it was Graham's girlfriend but that can't be true if he's with Lady Leery."

Amelia set the delicious, uneaten cobbler to the floor. "You ladies are relentless."

"You know who she is?" Paislee asked.

Amelia stood and eyed the ceiling. "Aye. There's going tae be a full spread in the paper tomorrow morning aboot it."

"Why hasnae it been in before now?" Mary Beth faced Amelia.

"Lady Leery knows the man who runs the paper. He's an old"—she glanced at Lydia with a twitch of her mouth—"friend. But she could only hold the local news back so long, ye ken?"

"That's a lot of nerve," Mary Beth said indignantly.

"The peerage has different rules." Elspeth sipped at her second glass. "You were saying, Amelia?"

Amelia's cheeks turned pink at being prodded to speak about the case again. Lydia added another inch of whisky to Amelia's empty tumbler. "Well. Lady Leery's legion of lovers certainly explains Aila Webster."

"Who?" Lydia asked.

"You promise not tae say anything? I mean, I'm just tellin' ye early, is all." Amelia crossed and then uncrossed her arms.

The ladies promised immediately. Paislee felt no guilt in hearing what was happening since the DI hadn't been in touch. He didn't owe her, but it wouldn't hurt him to be polite. She'd done her duty as a witness by sharing what she'd seen on the path, and pointing out Malcolm's gun.

Amelia took a deep breath. "Let me back up—it seems that when the DI and Constable Vega interviewed the residents of the house after the shooting, the keys tae the gun cabinet were missing. The DI couldn't immediately collect the guns locked inside the case."

"Is that legal?" Mary Beth asked. As a solicitor's wife, she'd probably listened to a lot of her husband's cases.

"Aye," Amelia said. "They're investigating a murder on the Leery property. They have tae account for the guns. I cannae be more detailed than that—I'm just sharing what will be in the paper tomorrow mornin'. Eh?"

They all nodded.

"The butler claimed the guns were all in order." Paislee wiped her hands on a napkin and brought her knitting needles out. She had a feeling the DI wouldn't like her sharing that the butler'd had his own gun. Although if Amelia was right and the bullet had been fired from a rifle, well, did that clear him?

"The butler, Malcolm Gunn, is also the one who swore the keys were missin' all morning." Amelia's expression showed what she thought of that.

Mary Beth scoffed. "Uh-huh."

Paislee shifted to get more comfortable on the wooden chair. "He was the first tae realize that Charles was dead."

Elspeth sucked in a breath. "It's like something from a true-crime show—my sister loves listening tae those." She tugged out her stitch and did it again.

"Who's the blonde?" Mary Beth asked, keeping them on task.

Amelia lifted her glass of whisky to her lips as if she hadn't heard Mary Beth. "Wednesday night the station received an anonymous call accusing Aila Webster of killing Charles."

Paislee looped yarn over the needle. The blond woman must be this Aila, but who was she to the family?

"The thing is," Amelia continued, "we traced the call back tae the estate. So the DI sent a team, and they found the keys under the mattress in Aila Webster's bedroom."

*Family.*

Paislee scooted to the edge of her chair as an idea blasted into her head. She'd thought them a united front on the porch when she'd seen them together after the tragedy.

"Aila Webster is Lady Leery's daughter," Amelia announced, confirming Paislee's suspicion.

# Chapter 8

The brick walls and shelves of yarn in Cashmere Crush absorbed the shouts as the ladies all questioned Shannon Leery's having a secret daughter. Where had she been keeping the lass, Elspeth wanted to know. Shannon lived in the public eye!

Paislee shook her head and knitted another row on her cinnamon vest. "I don't understand, Amelia. Did Aila steal the keys?"

Amelia drained her glass and grabbed the socks she was knitting from her backpack. "Aila Webster manages Lady Leery's Feed the Poor Foundation. Because the keys were found under her mattress, she's a person of interest."

"That would make Charles her cousin, too." Mary Beth finished a purple square the size of a coaster, then started a new one. She was so fast she'd already completed a dozen.

Paislee balanced the vest on her lap and lifted a brow. "I'm sairy. I just don't think it makes sense that she'd steal a gun from a cabinet, shoot her cousin, and then hide the keys under her own mattress."

"Unless she's an eejit," Mary Beth said.

Elspeth lowered her needlepoint. "I suppose she was the one tae call in the accusation, too?"

Paislee raised her gaze to Elspeth at the blatant sarcasm and smiled.

Amelia's mouth twitched. "Probably not. Though the person used a voice scrambler, the DI thinks it was a male. But they cannae be one hundred percent sure."

"Aila is very petite." Paislee tried to imagine the polished young woman she'd seen with a long rifle. A killer.

"Doesnae matter." Elspeth shrugged. "Like Amelia, I used tae hunt deer with my dad and could handle me own gun."

"There are ways tae make it work—you might've noticed I'm on the wee side meself." Amelia wrinkled her nose. "Anyway, Aila is too obvious, and being set up, in my humble opinion."

The ladies all chorused their agreement.

Lydia smoothed a cherry-red spike. "Since Aila is family, I wonder if she'll be at the dinner tomorrow night?"

Paislee was torn between fascination and fear. "The police *have* tae find the killer before tomorrow's dinner. Do you really want tae still go if they don't?"

"It's important tae me, Paislee," Lydia said, her palm to her heart. "We'll have paid security."

How could she argue with that?

Amelia's shoulders drooped as she turned to Paislee. "I overheard the DI saying he wished he knew who had access tae the keys, besides the butler. Someone from inside that house made the anonymous call, but no one's fessin' up—they're all playing possum. What if there's a *real* problem?"

Paislee stopped midstitch, mulling things over. By going with Lydia, she could locate the gun cabinet and see the inner workings of the mansion. That might help the DI find the killer before someone else was hurt, or worse.

And she might see Shawn. Her landlord couldn't ignore her in his own house.

Lydia's firm had hired extra security. Paislee lowered her knitting needles, scared that a million things could go wrong, but she couldn't let Lydia down. "If the event still goes on at the estate, then I'll see what I can find tae help."

"Hey now," Lydia said in alarm. "I don't want ye shaking the bushes, Paislee. This is a swanky affair. We're there tae dine on caviar, drink Dom Pérignon, and celebrate a successful quarter, not ask aboot keys."

Paislee squashed her trepidation and forced a smile. "Much different than my usual Friday night of sorting socks."

"Please be careful," Mary Beth said, and Elspeth nodded.

Lydia spread her arms to her sides in a sulk. "The only danger we'll have tae watch out for is old Mr. Silverstein's hands. He owns the company." She shook her palms like she was in a musical and they all laughed, but the sound was forced.

Paislee glanced at the time on her mobile and jumped—how had it gotten so late, so fast? "Nine on the nose."

"Remember—secrets said here need tae stay here." Amelia stuffed her sock project into her backpack. "Let's talk Saturday? After the party."

Mary Beth, Amelia, Elspeth, and Lydia were cleaned up and out the door by quarter past nine. Paislee had to power down the laptop and close the till.

Five minutes later she was locking up in the back alley and dreaming of hot tea before the fireplace.

Angry voices echoed in the cool night. She recognized Dan's deeper tones as he murmured something, and then Theadora yelled, "Ye've changed yer mind? After all this!"

"Every sacrifice was for us," he shouted.

Paislee's heart skipped as she waited in the silence, then: "And I've failed. Is that what yer saying?" Theadora's hurt words warbled on the wind.

"We both have. No more, Thea. I cannae take it." Dan's voice broke.

Tears welled in Paislee's eyes at the pain between them, and she looked down the alley from her top stoop, hoping she wasn't visible. They didn't need to know their argument had a witness.

Theadora, crying, got in the passenger side of their SUV and slammed the door. Dan wrenched open the driver's side, climbed behind the wheel, and peeled out of the alley and onto the main street.

Paislee said a little prayer for the couple. Just that morning, Theadora had mentioned a possible surprise. She'd talked about people changing. Was she pregnant, and Dan not on board? Or had it been another false hope?

Paislee arrived home and sat in the driveway, considering her next move. Tomorrow night, she'd find Shawn and plead her case, make him listen. He had to know how his actions affected others. What if Grant Cooke could actually stop the sale, or prove that Shawn was up to something? If she could share that news with the other businesses, it might alleviate some of the pressure on Theadora and Dan.

One thing was for certain: she couldn't wait to read the morning news to find out about Aila Webster.

Friday morning, just as Amelia had told them, Aila Webster was in the paper as a person of interest regarding the death of Charles Thomson. There was a blurred photo of the pretty blonde and a caption that read "Killer Cousin?"

"Did they discover the shooter?" Grandpa had nabbed the newspaper while Paislee fixed breakfast. Her dreams last night had been of confronting a giant talking hedge with brown eyes and an orange tint to its branches.

Brody crunched toast that he'd piled high with marmalade. Wallace, on his haunches, black tail sweeping the braided rug, watched his boy carefully for any dropped crumbs.

"Listen tae this!" Grandpa shook the paper and clucked his tongue behind his teeth. "Aila Webster is Shannon Leery Marcus's *daughter*. She was educated abroad."

True to her word, Paislee didn't mention that she already knew. "Does it give the age of the young woman on the porch?"

Grandpa scanned the print. "Thirty. Lady Leery brought Aila Webster into the family business two years ago tae manage the Feed the Poor Foundation."

Paislee did the math. "Shannon Leery was *forty-three* when she had Aila." She was unable to fathom raising a child at that age. "I'm dog-tired all the time and only twenty-eight."

"And no husband. Back then, it woulda been a huge scandal for a peer. Mibbe that's why Shannon sent the lass tae Switzerland?"

It had been a scandal as well for Paislee, but she and Gran had overcome the snide gossip. In retrospect, she acknowledged that it helped not being a pillar of the community. Lady Leery would have been judged very harshly, with a lot to lose. Paislee had started with nothing and had worked hard, every day, to prove the naysayers wrong.

Grandpa lowered the paper and told Brody, "Mind the time."

Brody scowled. "I know. Yer not me mum."

"Manners," Paislee said, and tugged the paper, wanting to avoid an argument. "What else does it say?"

"There's a photo of Charles Jonathon Thomson. Born tae Shayla Leery Thomson and Jonathon "John" Thomson in London, died at age forty-seven, on the Leery family estate."

Paislee studied the grainy image sideways. "Looks like Shawn only a few years younger."

"Says Charles was shot, but there are no other details of the crime. There's a number tae call if you have information regarding the murder. Ah, says Ms. Webster was brought in tae answer questions aboot her relationship with the family due tae an anonymous phone call. The reporter asked Detective Inspector Zeffer if he thought she'd killed her cousin."

Paislee wanted to read the article later for herself to gather any nuance. "How did that go over?"

"The DI declined tae comment," Grandpa drawled. They exchanged amused glances since they'd each had run-ins with the detective, and their relationship was just short of antagonistic.

"No surprise there," she said. "Grandpa?"

"Aye?"

"Would ye mind staying home with Brody tonight, while I go with Lydia tae her quarterly company party?"

Brody kicked his heel back against the leg of his chair. "Mum! You were gone last night."

Grandpa gave Brody a doubtful expression.

"Why can't I come with ye?" Brody asked.

"You weren't invited, for one," Paislee said, "and for two, it might be nice if I had dinner with a friend. When was the last time I went out?"

Not since Gran had passed, and even then only on a rare occasion.

"Fine, fine," Grandpa said, primly crossing one leg over the other, dangling his slipper from his toe. "So long as ye dinnae plan on makin' a habit of it."

She wouldn't dream of it. "I think you guys can get along for one night." Paislee glared at Grandpa, then Brody.

"I already did," Brody said. "Yesterday."

"You're welcome tae be at the shop Thursday nights for Knit and Sip. The ladies always ask about you."

Brody glanced at Grandpa with a grimace.

"Your choice," Grandpa said as if it were nothing to him one way or the other. "Where is the party?"

"The Leery Estate."

"It's odd they're hosting an event there so soon." He took his glasses off and placed them next to his mug.

"Why would you go there, Mum?" The concern in Brody's brown eyes was a replica of his grandfather's, never mind the age difference between them. "What if something happens again?"

"It won't," she quickly assured them. "We'll all be very safe. Lydia's company has hired extra security. A lot can happen in a day, and maybe they'll find the shooter before then."

Her son didn't seem convinced.

"I'd like tae know that you and Grandpa are having fun while I'm out. Please, Brody?"

He exhaled loudly, the rush of breath ruffling his auburn bangs. "Awright." With a sly glance at her he asked, "But can we have pizza, and crisps?"

She pretended to think about it—but it was a small price to pay for a night out. "The small bag."

"Ice cream?"

"That you have tae ask your grandpa, since he'll be the one dealing with you bouncing off the walls."

Grandpa smoothed his beard. "I want sausage on half the pizza."

Brody's favorite was pepperoni, which is usually what she bought because she didn't really care that much.

Brody nodded as if the deal was struck. "Done."

"Mushrooms?" Grandpa suggested.

Brody fell back against his chair as if he'd just been poisoned by the mere suggestion of the fungus.

"And I *do* like sardines." Grandpa hid a grin behind his tea mug as he lifted it to his mouth.

Their night *could* be fun, if they didn't kill each other, and she hadn't even had to bribe her grandfather with Scotch.

A hint of excitement warmed her blood. "Lydia will be over after work today tae help me get ready for the party. It's a fancy affair."

"Girls," Grandpa said. "Getting all glammed up. I wonder if you'll meet this Aila tonight? A possible murderess."

Paislee's heart sank. She would be on her guard, even with added security at the estate. "Aila was brought in for questioning, which isn't the same. If the police thought she'd done it, then they would have arrested her." She couldn't mention anything about the gun cabinet, or the anonymous call being traced back to the estate, since it hadn't been in the article. Perhaps Lady Leery still had some clout with what was being printed in the news?

"Unless they just dinnae have the evidence tae hold her," Grandpa said with a waggle of his silver brows. "You know what's missing? A motive."

"A motive?" Paislee repeated like a parrot.

Grandpa was on a roll. "Why would Aila shoot Charles? Mibbe she's not the shooter . . . but what if she had an accomplice?"

Her mealtime agenda was more than just to taste the soup, but to see how everyone got along. To talk to Shawn. To discover if Aila had been set up. If it helped the detective catch the killer, Paislee wasn't opposed to engaging in pointed dinner conversation.

Brody finished his cereal and juice, and brought his empty dishes to the sink. "What's an accomplice?"

She centered her mug on the cloth napkin next to her toast plate. "It's a person who helps someone else commit a crime."

Understanding dawned on his face. "Oh. Like when Brian was nabbing crisps from the kitchen."

"Aye, like that."

Brody had told the kids that they needed to stop stealing or else he'd let the cook know what they were doing, and they'd stopped. He'd lost Brian as a friend, but he'd kept Edwyn.

Paislee couldn't have been prouder of her son for standing up for what he believed was right. She hoped that things with Edwyn went well today. She couldn't recall learning such tough life lessons in primary school.

Brody raced upstairs to brush his teeth and comb his hair, while Wallace snuffled like a furry vacuum around Brody's chair.

Paislee swallowed her last bite of toast with the dregs of her tea. "Grandpa, did Brody bring up an argument with Edwyn last night?"

"Naw. He did his homework and we watched *Ant-Man* till bed. Why?"

"They had a tiff is all," she hedged, not wanting to give details if Brody hadn't.

He waved it off. "Boys. We were always brawlin' at that age."

"I'll keep that in mind." She mentally rolled her eyes. Grandpa's confidence was that of a head psychologist for children's development. "I'd like tae bounce something off you, but it can't be discussed outside the house," she told him. He had a habit of blurting things out.

He crossed his arms over the paper. "I have no plans tae leave today."

"Lydia's got a guy in her legal department delving into Shawn's sale of the building." Paislee's mind couldn't leave the issue alone, like an uneven stitch in an otherwise perfect row—this particular idea had come to fruition right before her alarm clock had blared this morning. "If the businesses had already left Market Street—say Margot moved the lab, and Theadora and Dan opened a bakery across town, and then the sale fell through, would we be at fault for breaking our leases?"

Even while sleeping, Paislee tried to make sense of Shawn's disappearance after the eviction notice.

"Sounds underhanded." Grandpa tapped the side of his nose. "If you all moved and then the sale 'fell through,' would you have broken your lease? Shawn wouldnae be responsible then." He slurped his tea. "And he'd have a vacated building tae do what he wanted with. Get new tenants. Raise the rate. That's verra twisted, lass."

"It's devious all right." Paislee crossed her legs beneath the round table and leaned forward. "I must talk with Shawn tae see if it's true." She also hoped he'd offer insights into Charles's death. He might know if Graham or Malcolm resented Aila's position in the house enough to set her up with that stupid phone call.

Grandpa's brown eyes glimmered. "Ach, well, if I've learned one thing aboot you, lass, it's that you're good with people because you care—folks respond tae that. Find the right time tae ask yer questions. Not over the pot roast, in front of everyone. Be *subtle*."

Subtle. It would be difficult, but she'd be polite and not lock her landlord in the closet until he answered her. Her chest tightened at losing the business she'd struggled so long to build. "I have tae save our building if I can." And the people whose lives were being torn apart inside it.

"And just mibbe ask him aboot his cousin? I see the sheen of curiosity in yer eye." Grandpa smoothed his beard to hide his smile.

She smooshed a toast crumb with her finger. "Ye can't blame me! I was there when Charles died. It's only natural I have questions."

He watched her closely. "And would the detective approve?"

"Probably not." Paislee shook a corner of the newspaper. "The DI didn't see the room of scared students in Mrs. Martin's class. Poor Holly will need therapy from being kept in the bathroom. But what else was I tae do?" Paislee hurried to the counter and turned on the teakettle, her shoulders hunched under the weight of her confused emotions. "Zeffer has tae understand that this is personal tae me, and yet crickets! How difficult is it tae send a bloody text?"

Paislee straightened with determination. The same question could be asked of Hamish, another man she hadn't heard from.

She whirled toward Grandpa in full-on defense mode. "Detective Inspector Zeffer doesn't care about the people here in Nairn like we do. Even the officers at the station know it."

"You're a good ally tae have, but take care." Grandpa's body language exuded caution, from a wrinkled brow to clenched hands on his knees. "Especially after what happened last time ye poked around, when folks didnae like it."

Paislee rubbed her neck, where she'd worn a brace for a week after being run off the road. It'd been a close call. "This is different." She brought her dishes to the sink, recalling how she'd overheard two members of the household lament the body hadn't been Shawn's. Graham Reid, sculptor, tour guide, and Lady Leery's lover; and Malcolm Gunn, head butler.

"Leave those," Grandpa said. "I'll do them after you and Brody leave. Pick up a bit."

"Thanks." Having an extra pair of hands to help with chores freed up time on Sundays to spend with Brody and Grandpa Angus. "What's your plan for the day?"

His body tensed. "I'll be calling the Dairlee police station again for me weekly update on absolutely nothing."

She wished she could help, but Grandpa was determined that they wait to take action. To give Craigh a chance to come home when he said he would, from an oil rig that the authorities said didn't exist. "Just another month, Grandpa."

A part of her worried that Craigh had possibly deserted him, that Grandpa Angus had gone mental and was in denial. But he seemed mostly sane to her.

"Waiting is agony, wondering if ye should be doing more." Grandpa smacked the table with his palm, his voice warbling with age and emotion.

"What else can we do?" Her chest ached for him. She'd called the police station and gotten the same information. There was no oil rig named the *Mona*. She'd searched for it on Google and found nothing.

If Brody were missing, she'd turn over every grain of sand to find him, so she was one hundred percent on Grandpa's side. She knew in her gut that he was hiding something, probably in the storage unit he planned on visiting.

He stared forlornly into his mug. "Wait some more."

She squeezed his shoulder in commiseration and climbed the stairs to the second floor to see if Brody was ready for school.

Brody, auburn hair wild, crooned to a cereal commercial, using his brush as a microphone to sing by his bed. Wallace wagged his tail and barked like a furry backup singer.

A boy needed a dog, and they'd gotten Wallace to help with their grief when Gran had passed. Now she couldn't imagine life without their pup.

She applauded, and Brody was embarrassed for all of two seconds before taking a bow. "Thank ye, thank ye verra much."

Elvis had nothing to worry about. "Got your backpack and your homework?"

He tossed the brush—which had missed a few spots on Brody's head while subbing as a microphone—onto the counter and dashed to his closet.

She went to her room, smoothing her shoulder-length auburn strands. Her eyes were pale blue, while Brody had brown. Her skin was pale and didn't freckle, whereas Brody had a smattering of freckles. Yet they had the same hair, the same slope of nose.

Family.

And tonight, thanks to Lydia, she'd get a table-side view of the Leerys, to "subtly" question them about possible building scams and murder. Grandpa said people talked to her because she cared, but this was a different level.

Brody ran past her open bedroom door to the stairs, his hand sliding down the wooden rail as he reached the last step with a *thunk* of feet. "Brody! Slow down before ye crack your heid!" One of these days he was going to take a tumble.

Wallace barked excitedly. Paislee stepped into the hall and peered into Brody's room. His backpack sat forgotten on the unmade bed. "Thanks, pup." She patted the dog's head. "Let's go."

Brody was in the kitchen, holding his insulated Avengers lunch bag. Inside was a cheese sandwich with two slices of pickle, an apple, and a bag of crisps. For dessert there were two chocolate biscuits. He bought milk at school.

Grandpa was in the shower when they left, on time, again, and they arrived at Fordythe at quarter till nine. Hamish waved her over when Brody hopped out.

She rolled down the passenger side window, still a wee bit upset at him about Holly. "Morning."

"Morning." Handsome in a dark brown suit, he didn't quite smile. "Can you park? I need tae speak with you in my office."

Her pulse skipped with foreboding and her skin pebbled. Her mouth dried. "Sure. What's wrong?" She wondered if this had to do with Brody and Edwyn, and Britta.

"I'll explain inside." He unbuttoned his suit jacket.

She arched a brow, wanting at least a clue. "Am I going tae get a detention?"

Hamish leaned inside the car, his mouth stern. How she missed that dimple of his! "'Tis no joke, Paislee."

She held his gaze, not backing down. He could give her something.

He realized she wasn't going to move and pulled back, his fingers on the window sill of the Juke. Tension seethed between them. Her stomach knotted.

"You know I met with Holly's parents yesterday?"

The little girl had been quite dramatic over what had happened. Paislee didn't blame her for soaking up the spotlight, but Holly had not been shot at directly.

"Aye?" She kept her hands loosely on the steering wheel, her car in park.

He flinched at her stubborn response. "Wednesday evening, the Fishers claimed tae understand what had happened. I showed them your statement and explained the situation."

"And?" She hoped to hear words of thanks for keeping Holly safe, but that wasn't the vibe she was getting from the headmaster of Fordythe.

"Well . . . this morning I've been notified by their solicitor." Hamish buttoned his suit, fiddling with the brown button. "They've threatened tae sue the school."

Paislee sucked in a sharp breath—the school and the students meant so much to Hamish. No way could she let the Fishers do that. How could she help?

His jaw flexed. "They're filing a complaint against you for locking their daughter in the bathroom against her will."

Personally sued?

All she had was Cashmere Crush. No, she had Gran's house. Cold nausea rose up her throat, and she broke into a sweat. It was a good thing that Brody was already inside the school or she'd owe a million pounds to the swear jar.

# Chapter 9

Paislee opened Cashmere Crush at nine fifteen, so angry about the headmaster's news that she found no solace in the rainbow glow of her sweater shop. She counted out the till wrong *twice* before getting it right. She swept the front, straightened the yarn, and paced before the frosted window. What was she to do?

Mary Beth dropped in at ten for the platter she'd forgotten the night before, and Paislee was still in a mixed state of fury and guilt. She explained what had happened in shock. "Can ye believe it? They're claiming child endangerment. As if!"

"Let's call Arran," Mary Beth said immediately. "It's obvious they've talked with a lawyer, and so should you."

"I can't afford a solicitor."

"He'll do a free consultation. Then, if he decides that he can help, he'll work oot a friend's plan for payment. He does it all the time."

She recognized that for the well-meaning fib it was. "I cannae take advantage, Mary Beth."

"The consultation is free, Paislee, just tae hear what Arran thinks. But I dinnae like how they suddenly want tae sue. Someone's been talking tae them and convinced them tae go after 'easy' money."

"Well, they're targeting the wrong person. Just because I own a shop?" Now that the anger was fading, fear reared its ugly head. She swallowed her pride, but it hurt like a fish bone caught in her throat. "All right. I'll call him."

"I'll do it, love. How soon can ye meet?"

"Whenever he can fit me in—I really appreciate it, Mary Beth." She rubbed her arms to lessen the arctic chill on her skin.

"That's what friends are for, right? We care aboot each other. I bet that Holly and her parents aren't from Nairn."

She'd ask Hamish later. After her extreme reaction, he'd postponed their meeting till the afternoon, when she'd pick up Brody. He'd texted twice to make sure she was all right. She hadn't responded. Did he really think she'd let a child be hurt?

How could the Fishers sue her or the school?

"So." Mary Beth's eyes glittered as she pulled the morning's exposé on Aila Webster from her purse. "Guess what firm is being used tae represent Ms. Webster?"

"Arran's?"

Mary Beth proudly tucked a brown lock of hair behind her ear, her large diamond stud winking hello. "Uh-huh. Shannon Leery had representation for Aila the second the DI called her daughter tae the station. From all accounts, Shannon is furious with the new detective for requesting Aila go tae him for questioning, when Inspector Shinner would have discreetly driven tae the estate."

"He probably doesn't even realize his faux pas."

"You don't think?" Mary Beth sniffed. "I'd guess he's makin' a clear line that things are not goin' tae be run in the old way."

Paislee thought of the detective's cool green gaze, and his determination to speak with the family on Wednesday after the shooting. He must have decided that was all the special treatment they were going to get. "You could be right."

"It's always been that way, a little extra courtesy for the peerage, and what does it hurt? Castles and old estate homes are part of what make this country unique." Mary Beth unfolded the paper and frowned at the blurry picture of Aila, then Charles. "Did you notice that we were told a wee bit more than what made the paper?"

Mary Beth had changed her tune about the peerage since last night, now that Aila Webster and Shannon Leery were her husband's clients. "Aye. I wondered about that." Paislee's mind was on permanent spin mode, and she couldn't focus.

"Old McRiley has final say over what his nephew prints, and I imagine he did Lady Leery a favor. She must be something under the covers tae garner all this male devotion, eh?"

Lady Leery's sexual appetites were not something Paislee wanted to add to the mix in her head. "Ew."

Mary Beth picked up her platter and the paper. "I'll call ye later aboot the appointment with Arran. I don't want you tae be concerned, all right?" She strolled toward the front door, just as it opened.

Detective Inspector Zeffer held it for Mary Beth, who thanked the DI and sent a quick wave back at Paislee.

"Cheers," Paislee said, her stomach tight. Could he be here about Holly? Could he arrest her? Dizzy, she leaned against the counter.

"Hello, Ms. Shaw."

"Paislee."

Zeffer wore yet another stylish blue suit that looked tailored for him. Ned at the cleaners said the DI had seven on rotation. Snug but not tight to the shoulders and waist, slim trouser legs and black leather oxfords. He had the striking cheekbones and sea green eyes of a high-end fashion model—and the manner; heaven forbid the man crack a smile.

Which reminded her painfully of Hamish. Paislee cleared her throat. "What can I do for you today? Interested in some yarn, or a hand-knit sweater?"

"I'm here aboot Charles Thomson's murder."

Goose bumps raced along her spine, and she shivered. "Oh?"

"I'm sure you read the paper this morning?"

"Aye. Aila Webster was front-page news." She rather liked having insider information from Amelia. It made the detective's haughty attitude a wee bit easier to swallow.

He rested his clenched hands on the counter between them. "As was my lack of comment. The station's phones have been ringing nonstop."

She bit her lip to keep from saying anything.

"I don't feel the need tae explain myself, however my no-comment comment was in regard tae if we had the killer in custody. The reporter took what I said out of context, as they tend tae do."

"So, what can I do for you?"

"Amelia told me you're going tae the Leery Estate tonight for a party with your friend. Understandably, she was concerned with your safety." His eyes narrowed. "Who can tell what's in a killer's mind? I wanted tae speak with you before you went."

"About what?"

He leaned so they were nose to nose, his cool green gaze filled with concern. "I dinnae want you snooping around and messing with my investigation."

The concern was for himself, not her. He was afraid she'd ruin his case. The man grated on her last nerve.

Still, she'd been raised to be polite. "Detective Inspector Zeffer, the sooner you find the killer, the sooner I can be at ease knowing that me, my family, and my friends are safe. You said you wanted tae discuss Charles? Or is this visit about Aila, and the anonymous call mentioned in the paper?" She added a thin layer of doubt to her tone. "Do ye really think she'd shoot her cousin?"

Color mottled his smooth-shaven cheeks. "No, I *don't* think she shot him. No gunpowder residue was found on her fingers nor on the clothes she was wearing that day—it's all been tested and confirmed. But I dinnae ken who did yet, and that makes me nervous when you want tae tweak the devil's nose by showing up at the estate!"

Paislee drew in an offended breath. "I don't plan on tweaking anything." She pressed her fingers to her chest. "My 'plan' is tae have dinner conversation with my hosts, if that's all right with you."

Dismayed, he stared up at the light fixtures on the ceiling. "Remarks like that will have me putting you in a cell for your own safety."

"You can't do that." Could he?

"Try me."

"Lydia's company has hired extra security for tonight, so I feel safe, in the event you don't find the killer by then. She's been nominated for an award." Paislee didn't know why she'd thrown that in, as if she had to explain herself to the infuriating man.

It was the first time she'd been out in years, and that was no exaggeration.

Paislee was going to dress pretty, eat delicious food, drink champagne, and then curl up in her own bed—filled with ideas of what it must have been like two hundred years ago in a great manor house. If by chance she also got to speak with Shawn about possibly not selling the business from under her, by appealing to his humanity, all the better.

If the opportunity arose for her to observe the inhabitants of Leery Estate and determine for herself what motivation someone living in that house had to kill Charles, well that would be the cherry on top.

Zeffer studied her closely, then took a step back and crossed his arms. "Every member of the Leery household has the license to carry a gun, even the maid. They are superior marksmen from years of hunting fowl, deer, fox, and rabbit. None of them think twice about pulling a trigger."

"I know that." Paislee sent a silent thanks to Wikipedia and her grandpa.

"Any one of those people could have killed Charles. I've already caught them lying for one another."

"What are you saying?"

He winced. "I want you tae stay home."

"No."

Zeffer slammed his fist into his open palm, frustration evident in the wrinkles around his eyes. "Since you are ignoring my advice, please do be careful. You were on the path that day. What if the killer thinks you saw something more than you did?"

"I didn't!" She was connected to Charles because he'd died before her. That was all.

"Oh, I believe you, but what if the killer doesnae?" Zeffer paced in front her counter, his arms at his sides, his gaze on her. "What if they think that Charles told you something secret in his last breaths? If you go in there and start poking your nose around, you'll draw suspicion. Think of your son, if you willnae think of yourself."

The anticipation she'd felt in going to the party ebbed, and she really didn't like the detective for that. "Do you think it was a family member?"

"I don't know who it was, or they'd be in custody." Zeffer took another turn, his sole squeaking against her polished cement floor. "Now, what did you see exactly that morning? Tell me again from the beginning."

Paislee did, ending with Hamish and Malcolm arriving.

He pulled his notepad from his coat's inner pocket and opened it. "The day of the murder, you said that Hamish McCall and Malcolm Gunn had run from the maze tae the body."

Not just a body. She gritted her teeth. *Charles.* "Yes. Graham arrived from the opposite direction. He was missing his cap, which your men found later. Where was it?"

He waved away her question. "Graham Reid was your tour guide, for the students."

"Yes. And the sculptor of the art within the maze itself, as well as Lady Leery's lover."

His green eyes blinked. "What?"

"It's true, according tae Lydia, who heard it from Gavin—oops, that's supposed tae be a secret." Lydia had to forgive her—her exact words were *not to leave this room*. "Where did you find Graham's hat? I worried all morning that it was going tae fall."

"By the bougainvillea arch at the entrance."

She frowned. "How did it get there? He'd had it on by the maze, which was on the other side of the restroom."

The detective jotted this down in his notes. "Mr. Reid doesnae remember when he dropped it. You're sure of this?"

Paislee thought back. "Yes. I'm very certain he had it on." She'd wanted to fix the thing before he lost it.

"We have the time of the children and Mr. Reid reaching the maze at ten thirty. Does this sound right tae you?"

Everyone, even the adults, had been excited about seeing the maze. "Aye, the shooting happened at ten forty-three, I'd checked my phone tae see how much time had passed from Charles being on the path and when I'd put my phone away, only two minutes." She shrugged in disbelief that time could be so slow and yet so fast.

Zeffer tapped his pen to his notebook, urging her to continue.

"Graham answered a phone call, probably at ten thirty? I took Holly tae the restroom. We heard *that noise*, and then Graham ran *from* the bougainvillea arch. He must have come from the other side somehow, because he never passed by me." She curled her fingers on the counter. "I'm sure I saw someone behind the hedge."

He read his notes. "Yes, yes, a shadowy figure of unknown height and weight," the DI said flatly. "Unfortunately, this doesnae give me anything."

Paislee rolled her eyes. "Well, it tells you there was someone back there."

"It tells me *you think* you saw someone back there."

"There was. I assure you." She bit the inside of her cheek. "I think. Perhaps Graham? Also, and it's probably nothing, but Charles really did look like Shawn, and at first I thought it was him." She patted her fast-beating heart. "When Graham knelt by the body, Malcolm was on his knees on the other side, checking for a pulse, and Graham said that he thought it was Shawn, and Malcolm said"—she swallowed, her throat dry—"*we should be so lucky.*"

The detective's brow bunched. "Why didnae you mention this earlier?"

"Because I don't want tae cast suspicion on people who might be innocent." She blew her bangs back. "Is it possible someone from outside the family wanted Charles dead? Someone from his past? Who was he? What did he do for a living?"

"We're digging into that, but it's not so cut-and-dried. Charles was a scam artist from London, with an arrest sheet as long as my arm." He stretched said arm to his side.

The type to attract enemies. "Anybody with half a brain could have gotten onto that property." If it was someone from his past, the murder would be personal to only Charles, which meant that the rest of the family wouldn't be in danger. Feeling hopeful she said, "Maybe the killer's already gone back tae where they came from."

The detective rested his forearm on the high-top table. "I'm not trying tae scare you, but the facts are that Charles was killed, you were a witness, and I don't know who pulled the trigger. If you willnae listen tae reason, at least be on guard tonight."

The surprising burn of tears sprang to her eyes. "I will."

His phone beeped a text, and she could tell she'd lost his attention. She hoped the message was about whoever had killed Charles so Zeffer could arrest them and they'd all be safe.

Raising his palm as a goodbye, he left with an abrupt *swoosh* of the door behind him. The store phone rang.

She swallowed her unshed tears. "Cashmere Crush."

"Paislee?" Mary Beth called as if she'd been watching the shop. "What did the detective want? I didnae want tae leave ye alone, but I couldnae think of an excuse tae stay. Has he found who shot Charles?"

"No, though he did say he doesn't think Aila is responsible."

"Ha! I told you that Arran's firm is good. Speaking of which, my husband can see you on Monday morning, nine sharp. I asked if he could make it sooner, but he assured me that Holly's family will-nae be able tae take any action over the weekend."

"I'm going tae meet with Hamish today when I pick up Brody. I'll let you know if I hear anything at all, okay?"

"Sure. What a mess, love."

A customer walked into the yarn shop. "I have tae go, Mary Beth. Thank you and thank Arran for me, too."

She hung up the phone and got to work, doing what she had to do to support her and Brody, and possibly Grandpa. "Welcome tae Cashmere Crush."

At three twenty, Paislee closed shop for the day and drove to Fordythe.

She parked and made a promise to herself that she would stay in control of her emotions no matter what Hamish said, or what claims Holly's family made.

She knew the truth. She *couldn't* lose her business *and* her home.

Paislee walked into the school and waved to Mrs. Jimenez, who was chatting on the phone. The receptionist flashed an empathetic smile. Blast it. That must mean that everybody knew what was going on with the Fisher situation. No doubt in part to Mrs. Jimenez being the sharing type.

Paislee had been a chaperone at Fordythe since Brody first started school. She knew these halls, the grounds, and the teachers, probably better than Hamish did—though to his credit, the headmaster cared deeply for their educational community.

Hamish stood at his doorway and gestured for her to enter his office. He didn't smile, or allude to how she'd (over)reacted to his announcement of being sued this morning. She searched for a way to apologize but couldn't find the opening in his armored demeanor. His brown suit might as well have been made of steel.

Defensive, Paislee perched stiffly at the edge of the hard chair.

Hamish paced before the file cabinets, his hands behind his back. "Our legal department is now involved."

She swallowed, her mouth dry. "What does that mean?"

"Your chaperoning privileges have been revoked."

His decree was a punch to the gut. "Is that what you meant yesterday when you said that golfing wouldn't matter for me?" Paislee interlaced her fingers over her purse on her lap to stop them from trembling.

"I wasnae sure that would be the directive."

Paislee had to keep her cool especially since she'd lost her temper with Hamish earlier. She'd already signed up for the end-of-year party at the skating rink. Brody had only one more year of primary school. "That's not fair."

"I agree." He rested his hand over the button of jacket. "But this isnae my decision."

She placed her purse on the ground for something to do and immediately missed the weight of it on her lap. "Can you revoke it?"

Hamish sat at his desk, his usually neat hair mussed. "Perhaps if the Fishers drop the charges?" He shrugged. "This is verra serious."

She blinked back the sting of tears and cleared the lump in her throat. *Don't be weak.* "I'm seeing a solicitor on Monday."

His shoulders eased. "Thank God."

"What else aren't you telling me?"

"The Fishers are also going after the Leerys."

"Mary Beth was right—this is all about the money."

"I cannae discuss anything aboot this lawsuit with you." His skin had a gray tinge to it, and his gaze settled on her face. "I'm sairy."

Paislee felt him pull away from her emotionally and realized she would be on her own. His loyalty was to the school. Sick, she said, "I don't have the money that the Leerys do, or the school system. I only have me." And her list of responsibilities was long.

"I know, Paislee." He put his hand on his desk, his palm up. "It isnae right."

"What else could I have done?"

"Run scared in the opposite direction, but you didnae." His voice deepened. "I've told everyone who will listen that."

"I wouldn't leave a child in danger."

His eyes closed briefly, and when they opened again, he'd donned his professional mask. "Who is your solicitor?"

"Arran Mulholland."

"He's guid." Hamish nodded, and she could see him process how she could afford one of the best solicitors in Nairn. He didn't ask.

"Shannon Leery is using him, too." Paislee didn't tell him that she was getting the friend rate. Something fragile had broken between them in this room. "Now what?"

He brought out a stack of papers from his middle drawer and handed it to her. "Do ye mind reading and initialing that your chaperone rights have been rescinded?"

Her nostrils flared in anger. She breathed in once, twice, three times. Exhaled. Stayed in control outwardly, thank heaven. Her insides were a jumbled mess.

"I'm not signing your blasted forms." The rest of Brody's P6 school year stretched before her. Then next year, when his class would be top dog in P7. She raised her eyes, locking her gaze on Hamish's unsmiling face. She'd never see that dimple again.

"I have tae do my job, Paislee."

"You're right, *Headmaster* McCall. I guess I'll wait for my solicitor tae be in touch?" The bell rang, and she rose unsteadily.

She left, escaping the touch of his outstretched hand.

# Chapter 10

Paislee, needing to keep busy so as not to dwell on things like Hamish McCall, or Detective Zeffer, or Shawn Marcus, Charles's death, or being sued, or the imminent loss of her business location, unloaded the socks from the washer-dryer that was on its last whirl.

If she was ever to win the lottery, the first thing she'd buy (after starting Brody's college fund) would be brand-new stainless-steel appliances. A full-size washer, and dryer . . . it made her feel warm and fuzzy inside just to think about it. She didn't need a new house or car, but a refrigerator with an automatic ice machine? A matching cooker. And glory be—a dishwasher, something that cleaned each plate to a glossy, spot-free finish.

"What's finally bringing a smile to your face? You've been glum since ye got home," Grandpa Angus remarked as he lined up a piece of the Big Ben puzzle to an empty space. They'd completed all of the clock tower and half of the clockface.

"A new kitchen."

He pointed a puzzle piece at the cracked laminate counter, yellow with age. "What's wrong with this one?"

"Nothing, if ye don't mind old."

"Hey! We replaced things as needed when we moved in."

"That was fifty years ago." It always startled her to remember that he and Gran had once been young in this house, that her dad and aunt Mora, both dead, had been raised here. There had been a time when Gran and Grandpa had been happy, before Gran had discovered that Grandpa had an adult son a few months older than her dad. Love had turned to bitterness, whenever Grandpa's name arose.

She'd been fourteen when the scandal happened and hadn't understood. Gran never explained. A few times, Grandpa had let slip how he still loved his Agnes. It was a tragedy that Gran hadn't known.

Paislee patted the washer-dryer. "I pray that this old beast is good for another thousand spin cycles, but I have my doubts." She held up a mostly damp sock before hanging it on the drying rack against the back wall. Not wanting to add to Grandpa's worries, she'd kept the possible lawsuit to herself.

"I wish I could help ye, lass, but ye know my finances are strained, for now. But who knows what the next fair wind may bring?"

"Have you been in the Scotch?"

He smirked and fit another piece without answering.

The doorbell rang, and her gaze flicked to the round kitchen clock above the cooker. Half past five.

Lydia entered the two-story house without waiting for anybody to answer the door. "Hellllooo! I've arrived tae dress Cinderella for the ball—Brody, be a love and help me with the bags?"

Brody raced from the living room, yelling, "Aunt Lydia!" at the top of his lungs.

They exchanged quick hugs, and Paislee didn't miss the cash her bestie tucked in Brody's pocket. Her son grinned, extra eager now to be of assistance.

Black and silver garment bags, actual luggage, and a silver make-up case to rival that for a theater production were lugged upstairs. Grandpa watched from the hall, bewildered by all the trappings.

Paislee waited for Lydia and Brody in the foyer, arms crossed as they descended toward her. "You said you were bringing a dress."

"I wasnae lying." Lydia wore jeans and a black T-shirt, which meant she had a ways to go herself. Yet the charcoal liner and long lashes of her eye makeup were impossibly perfect.

Stopping her friend at the bottom step, she took a close look at the intricate palette of the gray-to-black eyeshadow. "How did you learn tae do that?"

"YouTube videos and lots of practice." Lydia slipped her hand through the crook of Paislee's arm. "Now, I brought a bottle of white wine to start the festivities and get you tae relax. Angus, do you mind being a dear and opening the bottle for us?" She pointed to the insulated bag by the foyer closet. "There's a little something for you in there as well. Single malt?"

Grandpa leapt into action and brought the bevvies to the kitchen, digging in the drawer where they kept the corkscrew.

"The company hired drivers for all of us tonight," Lydia said in high spirits, "so that we may get wrecked safely."

Paislee did relax at that. How could she preach "don't drink and drive" if she was not following the rules herself?

Brody opened the front door and peered out. "You have a limo? Cool!"

"Not yet," Lydia said. "The town car will be here tae take us at six thirty, so we must hurry!"

Grandpa returned with the open wine bottle and two glasses, which Lydia accepted.

"Thank you, sir. You didn't want a nip?"

"Naw. Brody and I have our own party supplies, right lad?"

Brody nodded and dashed back to the living room. "Ice-cream sundaes!"

"Go on," Grandpa said, ushering her up the stairs after Lydia. "Let her work her magic."

Paislee wasn't sure how to take that, but Grandpa was already scuffling in his slippers down the hall to the kitchen.

Lydia cleared Paislee's vanity table so that her notebooks, receipts, pens, and crochet hooks were in a pile in the floor beside it. Her friend took her by the arm. "Before makeup, let's choose a dress."

"We haven't done this since high school. That had conse-quences." Paislee patted her flat stomach. Having a child out of wedlock, without naming the father, had been very difficult in the old-fashioned town, but she'd never regretted her choice. She had Brody, and Brody had her.

And now they had Grandpa, for as long as he decided to stay.

"I promise not tae knock you up," Lydia teased. She laid two garment bags across Paislee's mattress.

Lydia unzipped the first bag and pulled out the dress. The black fabric shimmered like a living thing. "This is not your typical little black dress," she said reverently.

Paislee gulped and brought her hand to her cleavage. "It's defi-nitely little—how is that supposed tae keep me decent?"

"Magic underwear, and magic fabric. It clings without bunch-ing. I had two marriage proposals when I wore it tae last year's Christmas party."

"What?"

Lydia waved her hand. "The men were already married, so I hardly took them seriously. Felt sorry for their wives. Marriage is a cruel business, not that you would know. You were smart and skipped tae the best part. Brody."

Paislee laughed at that—trust Lydia to put a positive spin on single motherhood. "You think you'll ever change your mind about walking down the aisle again?" Her best friend had moved away for five long years for college, got married and divorced, then returned home.

"Why bother?" Lydia smoothed a cherry-red strand of hair across her cheek. "I have plenty of money, a career, a town house on the water. And I have Brody when I need a kid fix. Nope, I'm good." She unzipped the second garment bag and lifted high a blue dress. "Now, what would you like tae try on first?"

The black dress had danger written all over it. "The blue, please."

"I knew you'd choose that one. It does go with your eyes." Lydia's tone was smug.

"Oh!" Paislee accepted the dress by its velvet hanger, her fingers slick over the silky fringe that reached the floor. Silver beads glistened over the icy blue fabric. A beaded halter top, an open back, a thigh-high slit to reveal her leg when she walked. It was as petite as her five-foot-three frame. "It's beautiful, Lydia."

Lydia held up silver heels. "Wait until you try them on. They even fit my giant feet like a dream."

In a flash Paislee was dressed in the gown and heels. Eyeing herself in the mirror, she stepped back and brought her hand to her heart. "Is that me?" She touched the deep décolletage, not normally on display, then twirled, her bare leg peeping through fringe.

"Oh, aye. If only Hamish could see you now."

Her shoulders slumped at the reminder of the cruel turn her life had taken that afternoon. "It wouldn't matter."

"Why not?"

Paislee told her friend about how the family of the girl was going after the school, the Leerys, and her. She choked up when it came to possibly losing her home. "Hamish has tae abide by the school rules."

"We'll get a lawyer," Lydia said instantly.

"I have an appointment with Mary Beth's husband, Arran, on Monday morning." She couldn't even fathom where she'd find the money to cover the cost, even at the friend rate.

Lydia pressed on Paislee's shoulder to guide her down on the padded bench, then poured them each a glass of white wine. "Tell me everything while I do your makeup."

"I can't talk about it"—*Hamish*—"without tearing up, and I'd rather have fun tonight."

"All right, for now. But you arenae off the hook." Lydia shook her head. The cherry-red spikes at the right didn't move while the bob on the other side swayed at her jawline. "How crazy was the paper this morning? Most of what Amelia said aboot Aila—front page."

"DI Zeffer stopped by the shop. He's feeling the heat of public opinion." She met Lydia's gaze in the vanity mirror. "Folks don't like that he'd called Aila Webster into the station like a commoner tae answer questions."

"That was the topic of conversation at the office as well." Lydia combed out Paislee's hair. "One of my clients swears he's ready tae haul Inspector Shinner oot of retirement tae show the new lad how tae run Nairn."

Paislee groaned, caught by a pang of sympathy for Zeffer that she wouldn't admit to anybody. "I'd hoped he would've caught the killer by now." No phone calls, no texts. "But I did find out that Charles was a scam artist when he lived in London. Maybe he ripped off the wrong person? This was revenge?"

"Way more reasonable than havin' your cousin shoot ye while you're visiting the family estate." Lydia plugged in a curling iron that had multiple attachments, then opened the silver makeup case and pulled out one of its dozen drawers.

Paislee half-turned on the padded vanity bench. "From what I understand from Mary Beth, the article was heavily edited by an admirer of Lady Leery's, Mr. McRiley."

"Brilliant!" Her best friend sighed with admiration. "I've met Shannon Leery twice. She's remarkable." Lydia focused on the task at hand and dabbed powder across Paislee's face. "You're so pretty, Paislee. Why not give Hamish a chance? This lawsuit will blow over."

"No." She'd let her guard down with Hamish and gotten burned—not his fault that his career came first, as it should. "I have a son tae raise."

"So, what, you're just going tae be single until Brody graduates secondary school?"

"Perhaps forever. Like you, I don't require a man tae make my life easier. The only semi-happy couple I know are Theadora and Dan, and even they're having problems."

"From the tea shop? He's a cutie, and I loved her hair, white and teal."

"She dyed it golden brown and traded her jeans for floral dresses. I think as part of the 'new mom' territory. They're trying fertility treatments."

Lydia curled a strand of Paislee's hair. "Those arenae cheap. How long have they been at it now?"

"At least two years. I hope she'll announce a new baby on Saturday." Paislee crossed her fingers. "Last night they were arguing in the alley when I left Cashmere Crush."

Lydia sighed. "How long have they been married?"

"Twelve years."

"That's forever in today's world." Lydia reached into the silver case and withdrew a number of different tubes, before casting her critical eye on Paislee's face. She felt like a blank canvas and her bestie was van Gogh.

"Lourdes and Jimmy are acting strange, too. I hardly see Ned at all, or James. Margot hasn't changed, but she's the only one that will be fine if we have tae move. Did you ask Grant about the certification letter?"

"Nothing for certain."

Paislee got a peek at herself in the mirror and choked on her wine. Half her hair was straight, the other curled.

Lydia giggled. "Trust me, Paislee. I'm not done yet."

Somehow Lydia used her special skills and twisted Paislee's auburn hair up in a clip, coaxing side curls from her normally defiant thin strands. Crystal earrings dangled from her lobes. Her makeup was flawless: a hint of pink to her pale cheeks, ice-blue and gray around her eyes that sparkled like tiny stars.

She slung her silver cashmere wrap over her arm and borrowed a silver bag from Lydia's stash.

"Hurry, hurry." Lydia drained her second glass of wine. "I cannae wait tae see Brody's face when he sees how beautiful his mum is."

Paislee carefully made her way down the stairs—the creaking third and fifth giving her away. Brody and Grandpa lined up in the foyer, whistling and giving her two thumbs-up.

"You look so glittery, Mum."

"I do," she said, suddenly feeling self-conscious.

Wallace snuffled her sparkling toes, then tugged on a piece of fringe at the bottom of her dress as if he wasn't sure what to make of it.

Brody quickly grabbed the dog up before she unraveled.

When the driver knocked on the door, Grandpa cautioned her to be subtle over the roast.

"What does that mean?" Lydia asked.

"Nothing. You know Grandpa," she said. She waved goodbye, whisked away from her regular life into a limousine. The fact that that she and Lydia were driving to the scene of the crime was never far from her mind.

# Chapter 11

Arriving at the Leery Estate in the back of a limo was much different from the last time Paislee had been here, bumping along on a crowded school bus with hard seats. These were soft leather that her bum sank into.

It was nearing dark as the gate opened, and the lights from the estate shimmered in the dusky evening to give the stone building an ethereal quality. She wouldn't have been surprised to see nymphs emerging from the lawn and gardens.

"I can't believe it," Paislee said, leaning so close to the window her breath steamed the glass. "It *is* like traveling back in time."

"Didn't I tell ye so?" Lydia squeezed Paislee's hand. "This is my third event here, and it's worth every cent that old man Silverstein shells oot. I'm so glad tae finally be able tae bring you."

"Me too."

Paislee straightened when the vehicle stopped before the long stone porch. The nymph statue in the koi pond now spewed golden water. The daffodils and tulips were pale shadows of themselves as they swayed in a slight wind.

A very handsome lad in his teens, dressed in solid black, opened the rear door to escort them from the limo, which drove off once they'd stepped out.

Peering up at the stone mansion, the roof and porch covered in fairy lights, Paislee was swept away by the magic. But not so swept away that she didn't notice a man by the bougainvillea arch in a black jacket that read SECURITY.

The teen escorted Paislee and Lydia up the stone steps to the main entrance, where Malcolm Gunn waited with a silver tray and pen. Dressed in a black tuxedo; a blue, green, and white plaid vest, with a white bow tie; and black gloves, the tall man resonated power. These were quite different from his gardening togs—she couldn't help but wonder if he'd concealed a gun in his jacket pocket. Dark brown hair, sharply chiseled cheeks. Serious brown eyes. "Lydia Barron and Paislee Shaw," Lydia told him.

"Welcome tae Leery Estate." Malcolm didn't give away that he knew Paislee from Wednesday—unless he'd forgotten, or Lydia had truly transformed her. "Midge will escort you tae the drawing room for a cocktail. We ask that you refrain from taking pictures. This is the family's residence, and they are pleased tae share their private residence but ask that you respect their privacy."

Paislee remembered that Midge was the woman who'd answered the phone yesterday when she'd called for Shawn.

Midge was in her forties, wearing a black maid's dress and white apron, and a white-and-black cap over brown hair. She introduced herself with a pleasant nod. They followed her down a dim hall with gilded portraits on either side.

Paislee swallowed a squeal of excitement as she tried to look everywhere at once and just couldn't. Brick-red carpet runners were laid over plush dark green–and–beige carpets. The Leery family plaid—blue and dark green with stripes of black—had been framed as art upon a wall. Malcolm's vest had been fashioned of the same plaid. A blond server in black on black passed them in the hall, his silver tray empty.

Lydia tugged her hand as they glided behind Midge. "Lady Leery loves her male eye candy. And that butler? Yum."

"I met Malcolm on Wednesday, as well as Graham—when Charles . . ." Had been shot. Her joy faded.

"You said you wanted tae have fun tonight. No asking questions!" Lydia didn't wait for a response. "I love this place. No such thing as an ugly man in her home."

"That's one way tae decorate," Paislee said, attempting a joke.

Midge whistled low as she led the way down the hall.

"It has its merits," Lydia said with a gleam in her eyes. Her friend's red dress matched her hair, her bare legs long and tan in her high-low gown. Red chiffon trailed her tall form in an elegant wake.

Paislee had so many questions she feared she might mess up when Lydia just wanted to share her world. Who here would have set Aila up as a killer and why? Was someone who lived here guilty, or could it be someone from Charles's past?

When they entered the drawing room, it was like going back two hundred years. A grand stone fireplace with an intricate wooden mantel, carved with stags and nymphs, took up an entire wall to her left. A scattering of sage and dark green sofas created a sitting area large enough for thirty.

Clusters of men, and some women, all dressed in their finest, spoke in varying pitches, their voices bursting with merriment. The guests dripped with gold and diamonds, from watches to rings to jeweled hairpins. Two waiters in solid black carried trays of champagne about the room. Another offered appetizers.

Paislee's pulse sped as she tried to acclimatize to the glamour. "How many people are here?" Lydia belonged, but Paislee felt like an extra on a movie set.

"Twenty-four for dinner, because that's all the antique Victorian table can seat. Only the shining stars of the company have been invited."

A waiter brought them champagne.

"See the older gentleman with the white hair and mustache?"

Lydia discreetly tilted her head toward a man who had to be as old as Grandpa. He had on a diamond tiepin that flashed from across the room.

She nodded.

"That's the owner of our real estate firm, Mr. Silverstein. He's the one tae watch oot for, with the groping hands."

Paislee giggled, taking note to stay clear.

"Next tae him, the woman in the black sheath, is his wife, Natalya. Aye, twenty years younger and sharp as a tack. She plans on running the firm after he's gone, which is guid for us all. See the man with the bright copper hair?"

"Aye."

"He's Grant Cooke, from legal. I'll be sure tae introduce you." Lydia craned her neck to see around the broad shoulders of a gray-haired man with the profile of a gladiator. "And that's Gavin Thornton—he's the connection with Lady Leery, and why we get tae have our private events here, with the family. Silverstein loves what others cannae have."

"What does Gavin do?"

"He's the accountant for the firm and the Leery Estate. It's rumored that decades ago he was Shannon's lover. Tae be sure, he's far too old for her now," Lydia said with admiration.

"Where is Lady Leery?"

"Oh, we willnae meet the family until dinner. This is for cocktails with our agency." Lydia tipped her champagne flute to the left. "Our two best ad execs over there, with their spouses. Last year at the Christmas party their wives made out under the mistletoe."

"Are you kidding?"

"Nope."

Paislee sipped her bubbly, liquid courage flooding her veins.

"Ready?" Lydia asked.

"Aye. Let's do it." Paislee had never in her life been to an affair like this. The lad they'd passed in the hall had returned carrying a platter of caviar on toast points into the room. Over the next hour, there were a variety of canapes that she was mostly too busy smiling and making polite conversation to eat.

Twice Malcolm called Gavin from the party for a whispered conversation near the doorway to the hall. They both looked grand, Malcolm in his signature head-butler black, Gavin in a charcoal designer suit made of fine wool. She noticed both times Gavin had wiped the annoyance from his expression before joining his associates. It was clear that Malcolm conducted the evening's happenings, but he and Gavin knew each other well.

Wanting to regroup before dinner, where she might get a chance to see Shawn, Paislee stood next to the cinnamon-scented fireplace, crackling with low flames, and watched the crowd. Lydia had left her to talk to Grant, and Paislee was grateful to catch her breath. Her bestie came alive in these situations, bubbling over with effusive energy that was genuine and sincere.

"How is it we havenae met?" a low voice asked.

She turned to see Gavin at her elbow, offering his hand. Up close, he exuded warmth, his green eyes bright, his gray hair a well-styled mane around his rugged face. He could have passed for the lord of the manor.

"I'm Paislee Shaw, here with Lydia." His clasp was just right—confident but not lingering. Old-school charming.

"I'm Gavin Thornton. Boring bean counter for Silverstein's firm. Lydia is one of the highest-ranking estate agents in the company's history. How do you know her?"

The man emanated charisma from his pores. His white-toothed smile hinted at mischief just around the corner. "We've been best friends since primary school."

He tipped her chin and studied her. "I've never seen such eyes—you have a classic beauty."

Paislee's cheeks heated, no doubt ruining the makeup Lydia had piled on. Blushing was a redhead's curse.

"My apologies for speaking my mind," he rumbled. "Let's blame the champagne."

"I always blame the champagne. Hello—Paislee, is it? I'm Natalya Silverstein. Dinnae be bowled over by Gavin." She tucked a bejeweled hand into the crook of his arm, her manicured nails long and crimson. Her dress was black, fitted to her body like a second skin, and her hair had been dyed a soft caramel. Her imperceptibly lined face beneath the layer of powder belied her age. "He's drawn tae the prettiest woman in the room—that he hasnae seduced yet."

Gavin not so gently removed her talons from his arm. "Natalya love, there is no excuse for catty behavior." He half-bowed to Paislee and moved off to speak with Lydia, Grant, and the ad execs.

Paislee wasn't sure what to expect now that she and Natalya were alone, but the predatory look left her gaze and she bumped her arm into Paislee's as if they were confidants.

"You seemed like you needed saving," she said. "Unless I was wrong?" Natalya gave Paislee a thorough going-over from Paislee's auburn hair to the borrowed heels. "I see why Lydia speaks so highly of you."

"She does? What do you see?" Paislee sipped from her flute.

"No guile. An acceptance of the world, both guid and bad, which is verra rare in someone so young." Paislee was tempted to duck, but her hair was up in a clip and there would be no hiding behind it. "Loyalty. If you are a friend, you willnae desert them. But you have few people in your inner circle."

Lydia joined them with Grant at her side. He was a smidge shorter than Lydia, but handsome and earnest with copper hair and emerald eyes. "Is Natalya telling your fortune yet?" Grant joked. "Give her another glass of wine—she's quite guid, actually."

Natalya didn't take offense. This was a woman sure of herself.

"She was just saying that I'm a loyal friend—I would like tae think so." Paislee held her champagne flute to Lydia's and clinked.

Grant chuckled. "Will Paislee have fame and fortune and be swept away by the love of her life?"

"I have the love of my life, thank you." So what if he was only ten?

At the same time Paislee spoke, Natalya said, "She has the love of her life."

*Wow.* Paislee proceeded to drink but her flute was empty. Lydia waved to Midge—the maid was the only female server—who exchanged it for a full glass. It was just her second but she wanted to keep her wits about her, especially if Natalya could read her mind.

"Who's the lucky man?" Grant asked.

"Behave," Lydia said to Grant with an eye roll at Paislee.

Natalya placed her fingers on Paislee's wrist. "You are blessed with a full life. You willnae have millions, but you have a skill that ensures you'll never starve. You're going through a rough time right now."

She thought of Cashmere Crush, and the years she'd spent building up her business. Shawn's eviction notice, and the threat of being sued. Paislee blinked and cleared her throat. "You're right." How could Natalya know?

Grant hummed a few notes as if danger was around the corner, and Lydia nudged his side with her elbow. "Sorry," Grant said. "I know you're having difficulties and I'm trying tae help, but the players make it complicated."

Natalya flipped a caramel lock from her face and focused on Grant with her laser vision. "How intriguing."

Paislee lifted her flute to her lips. Shawn was a key player in the sale of her building, and if Grant had discovered something to implicate her landlord, then that would be tough. Especially since she was a guest at his house.

"Mibbe the lass needs another hint," Natalya crooned.

Paislee realized why this wasn't the time. So much for being subtle.

Malcolm rang a brass bell in the doorway, breaking the tension. "We ask that you adjourn tae the dining room where dinner is served."

Natalya joined her husband and took his arm. Lydia and Paislee paired off, and Grant linked hands with a pretty girl with straw-berry-blond hair. Gavin followed with the ad execs and their wives. Without a date?

Paislee sucked in a breath of appreciation when they entered the dining room. The long wooden table had been covered in white lace and set with china and crystal. Bouquets of flowers were grouped down the center, not too high to interrupt conversation. Orange-yellow flames from silver candlesticks flickered.

"This is amazing—it's so beautiful, Lydia."

"'Tis," Lydia agreed, gray eyes shining. "Here we are. See your place card? Lady Leery writes each one herself in calligraphy."

"Do we get tae keep them?" She'd love a reminder of this magical evening.

"Why not?" Lydia whispered.

The people from the firm all found their assigned spots, ten guests on either side of the table. Mr. Silverstein and Natalya were in the center opposite Paislee and Lydia. Grant and his girlfriend were to Lydia's right, and Paislee's dinner companion on her left was one of the boisterous ad execs who was plying his attention on the female agent on his other side. The rest of the seats were taken by estate agents for the firm. The head of the table to Paislee's right was empty, as was the foot. Paislee noted that Shawn wasn't there— none of the family were. Had the Leerys changed their minds about joining the dinner party? Nobody would blame them.

A hidden door behind a tapestry opened, and Lady Leery entered with Graham Reid on her arm, her posture finishing-school perfect. They swept to the side-by-side chairs at the head of the table and sat in unison. Gavin was at Shannon's right-hand side, a wife of one of the ad execs on Gavin's right.

When Shawn exited from behind the tapestry, with Aila Webster, his half sister, on his arm, Paislee's wonderment dissipated. Neither made eye contact with the guests as they sank into the chairs at the foot of the table but kept their gaze centered on the ornate decorations and cutlery.

Aila was ethereal in her beauty—pale blond, slender, golden-brown eyes. Hardly the stereotype of a murderer.

Shawn looked as bad as he had on Wednesday, when they'd ushered him into the house to stop him from following Charles to the hospital. Bruise-colored shadows marked the bottom of his eyes, and his cheeks sagged, as if he'd suddenly lost a great deal of weight. His dinner suit was pristine yet baggy—even his brown hair seemed limp. His spray tan no longer hid his ill health.

Shawn was on Paislee's side of the table, but four people away from the end. She resolved to not being able to talk with him about the sale of the building during dinner. Lydia tracked her gaze and shook her head.

Paislee would search for an opportunity later in the night. Shawn waved to where Malcolm stood quietly near the rear of the room, and said, "Claret." Noticing Paislee for a moment, he moved a bouquet of bluish-white hydrangea, white snowdrops, and blue irises to block her view. *Rude.*

"Do you think you should?" Aila murmured.

"How else will I get through this nightmare?" Shawn didn't even pretend to be polite.

Aila shrank at his crudeness and stared down at the table.

Malcolm gestured for Midge to pour from a silver-and-glass carafe. The maid attended to each person's glassware. Paislee nodded her thanks.

Lady Leery stood. She was seventy-three but could have been fifty. Her face seemed as smooth as the porcelain dishes before them. She'd accessorized her blue lace cap-sleeved dress with a lace scarf that floated around her neck. Her sleek blond hair hung in a straight-edged bob to her chin. Slender, her makeup subtle, she was a confident and stunning woman.

Graham, to her left, had on a dark gray suit with a white blousy shirt. Paislee wondered if he had a closet of them. His dark honey hair waved loose around his face.

"He's delicious," Lydia said under her breath. They were shoulder to shoulder at the packed table. "And new. Shannon was with one of the valets the last time we were here. For Christmas."

"A valet?" Paislee whispered back, her lips close to Lydia's ear.

"Twenty, if he was a day."

Amazed, Paislee couldn't stop from peering Shawn's way. She shivered, catching his gaze on her. She averted her eyes.

"Good evening," Shannon Leery said. "I've met some of you before, but for those who are new friends, please remember our request for privacy."

A murmur of assent rounded the table.

Would the lady acknowledge the article in the paper this morning? Or that her daughter had been accused of murdering her cousin? No. This was an event, and they all had their parts to play.

"We will start with the soup course," she intoned. "Onion in a beef bone broth. We source most of what you'll be enjoying this evening from our own property, as we have done here for nearly two hundred years."

She sat down, and the waitstaff immediately brought out thin china bowls of clear brown broth.

Paislee draped an ivory cloth napkin over her lap, dipped her spoon into the broth, and sipped. She hadn't expected such flavor from a simple soup.

"Just wait," Lydia promised. "Each course gets better."

A spring salad with thinly sliced radish and sweet dressing was placed before her next. Paislee noticed that Shawn and Aila barely ate. This feast was probably nothing to them. She wondered if they felt on display.

Squashing feelings of pity, Paislee focused on her meal. There were two main courses—first the fish, caught from the Nairn River, then meat, a venison sausage that Lady Leery let them know was voted best in Scotland and available for purchase.

"I can't eat another bite," Paislee said, her hand to her stomach. Rubbing the hem of the soft napkin, smooth from many washes, she scanned the faces around the table, noting that everybody had slowed down. Graham had pushed his plate from him and was checking his phone messages. Shannon caught him and tapped her coffee spoon on his arm—much as Paislee would do to Brody. Not the fond actions of a lover.

"We will now enjoy a cheese-and-fruit plate," Lady Leery announced, getting her exercise by standing up to introduce each course. "Afterward, we will *all* retire tae the study for a dessert of *cranachan* and shortbread."

"Like guid trained monkeys," Shawn muttered and slumped back against his chair—drunk off the claret.

Aila's petite nostrils flared. "Will you grow up?" She covered her wineglass when Midge came around.

All was not well between the siblings. Paislee wondered if Shawn was jealous of his younger sister or if Aila wished that she were the heir to the estate. Throw in their mother's young lover and the household had to be chaos. Paislee peeped between the hydrangea blossoms like a voyeur. Aila engaged in small talk with her dinner companion on the other side, while Shawn glared into his cup. Twenty years apart and they each lived at the estate. Why?

Midge and three waiters in black brought out platters of cheese and fruit for their selection. Paislee chose a dish of balled melon and a small wedge of hard white cheddar with honey.

"These peaches have been soaked in brandy." Lydia gave Paislee a bite.

"Oh, yum. Do you think I could make that?"

"You can try, and I'll be your guinea pig, just like I was for your sweaters."

Paislee spoke quietly, for Lydia's ears only. "What do you think of Shawn? He and Aila have been barely polite tae each other. Have you met either of them at other events here?"

"I havenae," Lydia admitted, "but I wouldnae be surprised if she stabbed him with a fork. Discreetly, tae be sure."

Paislee remembered Charles falling dead through the hedges. The killer still on the loose. Could Aila have shot her cousin and fooled the DI somehow? She eyed the blonde between the flowers and noticed a grit beneath the glossy, socially correct veneer. You didn't have to be large to fire a rifle. "What if—"

"No!" Lydia shushed Paislee with a warning pat on Paislee's knee beneath the table.

The detective inspector had ruled Aila out as the shooter. Besides, the person she'd seen behind the hedge had been taller. "Fine."

"Please just enjoy your evening."

Conflicted on many fronts, Paislee kept quiet and watched Midge give Malcolm a message. The butler left his station by the dining room door and strode purposely behind Natalya and Gavin's side of the table to whisper in Lady Leery's ear.

Shannon's mouth thinned, but then she forced a smile and renewed her attention to Gavin, clearly dismissing Malcolm.

The head butler drew himself up, rebuffed, his jaw clenched. He turned abruptly and left the dining room.

Shannon rose fluidly. "Dessert will be served in thirty minutes—feel free tae linger here. Midge will be back around with coffee, or wine." She waved for Graham to stay seated and instead reached for Gavin's hand. "Gavin?"

Graham's expression hardened as his lady chose another, and the pair disappeared behind the tapestry. How many hidden doors were there in this house?

Shawn snickered from his spot at the opposite end of the table and raised his voice to say, "Get used tae it, pup."

Graham's face turned crimson.

Aila dropped her napkin over her cheese and glared at Shawn. "Excuse me," she said to the guests, then sailed out of the dining room, her head held high.

Paislee finished her melon, sneaking peeks at Shawn. His fake tan made her wonder where he'd been, or where he planned on going after selling the building.

The Caribbean? Florida? The Amalfi Coast?

She noticed what appeared to be scratches on the backs of his hands. She needed to get closer to see. He and his cousin Charles both had dark hair and were similar in height. Shawn's recent loss of weight had made him as trim as his cousin. He glanced at her as if feeling the weight of her regard; then he tossed his napkin to the center of the table to leave, but he stumbled once he stood.

Paislee leapt up. Now was the chance to save Cashmere Crush.

# Chapter 12

Paislee pushed her chair back from the Leery dining table where most of the Silverstein party guests lingered with coffee and conversation. Shawn Marcus teetered as if his legs were folding beneath him. The other diners hadn't noticed, and she hoped to not only save Shawn from the embarrassment of falling into his cheese plate but also to get answers at long last.

The thigh-high slit in her gown made it easy to maneuver as she hurried to the end of the table and slipped her arm around Shawn's waist. He was slender, but she hadn't noticed how thin until his bulky dinner jacket gave way. "I've got you," she murmured quietly.

His breath reeked of sweet red wine, but he straightened before he took them both down. "I can do it."

Stubborn and petulant. How had Shannon Leery raised such a spoiled man-child? Paislee led him out the same door Aila had gone through, which fed into the foyer of the front entrance. She aimed them both toward an upholstered green bench along the wall in the hall.

"Here you are," she said. Shawn sank back, his head resting against the faded wallpaper, the pink flowers almost invisible against the ivory. She stood, studying the foyer.

Antique light shone from a central Victorian chandelier with eight bulbs. A tall table next to the front door held a rotary phone, a guest book, and a silver pen. There was no sign of Malcolm, but he was probably dealing with Shannon and Gavin.

Buttery golden oak paneling complemented the Leery plaid, gilt picture frames, and brocade velvet upholstery. The staircase from the foyer was dark brown beech, with a crimson runner. The old railings were shiny from age and use. Everything was worn but quality. Genteel living, with an underlying layer of . . . She couldn't put her finger on it. Had they been rushed through here earlier to the drawing room for a reason?

From this position, she knew the kitchen and dining room were to her left, and the reception rooms all to her right. She wondered where they kept the gun cabinet. Was it locked away?

Shawn groaned and slumped forward.

Paislee helped him balance upright on the bench. "Would you like some coffee?" she asked, wanting him sober before she lobbed questions at him.

"No." He ran a trembling hand through his dark comb-over, barely threaded with silver. There were two deep scratches, and a web of finer ones, along the back of his hand. She recalled the thorns on the hedge catching the DI's suit jacket.

"How did ye hurt your hands?" Paislee had a sneaking suspicion. She braced herself to stop him in case he decided to bolt for the stairs.

"I didnae."

"The scratches."

"Oh, that, uh, gardening." Perspiration dotted his forehead.

She took a gamble and said, "I saw you behind the hedge that morning."

His face drained of color, turning his skin a sickly grayish orange. She was close enough now to see a hint of yellow on his neck near his collar that he'd missed. This was the reason for the spray tan?

She'd come here for answers and so far had only more questions.

He clutched his belly and closed his bloodshot eyes. "Help me tae my chambers."

"Are you ill?"

"Drunk," he slurred.

It wasn't just that—but she couldn't pressure him without possibly making things worse. "Och, Shawn." She put her hand on his shoulder to keep him straight. "Should I get your mum, or Malcolm?"

"No! No, help me upstairs," he demanded. "Trust no one here. Someone was in me room last night."

"Trust no one?" The man's mind was obviously muddled. Paislee was afraid to let him go for fear he'd topple to the floor. She eyed the steep stairs, having no idea where his room was—where Malcolm or Lydia, or even Midge, were.

"Please, Paislee?" He pleaded with her through bleary, bloodshot brown eyes.

"I'll try." She squeezed his frail shoulder with compassion, then crouched to slide her arm around his waist, slowly raising them both. Her feet wobbled in her heels. "Did you have a fever? Is that why you've been gone for the last month?" What caused yellow skin?

"No. I've been here. With Charles."

So he and his cousin were close then. Charles was a scam artist. Was Shawn doing something shady? Were the two things related? "You must be grieving. I'm so sairy for your family's loss."

Shawn leaned his weight against her, then straightened as if trying to rally. "Charles was an arsewipe," Shawn bellowed loudly. "Guid riddance."

Shocked, Paislee tightened her grip on his waist. Surely that had to be the wine talking. She took a cautious step toward the bottom stair. Where had everybody gone?

"Why were you behind the hedge?"

Shawn lifted a scratched finger to his lips. "Shh."

Malcolm appeared suddenly from behind the stairs, moving silently in the dim light, no doubt from another hidden entrance. She sighed in relief, hoping the butler would help her.

"What is going on?" Malcolm demanded.

"Shawn is, er, tipsy. He'd like tae go tae his room. Would you mind helping?"

Malcolm crossed his arms, his posture bristling with indignation. "The master of the house can manage himself. If her ladyship wants tae coddle him, this is the result. It is not my job tae keep him sober." Stepping forward, he eased Shawn into a chair beside the foot of the stairs. "Damn you anyway. Cannae you behave for just one night?"

Shawn rolled and tipped, but between her and Malcolm, he landed with a crack as his head smacked the wall.

"Ouch! Be careful, man." Shawn rubbed his head.

Malcolm didn't appear the least bit sorry.

"What's wrong with him?" Paislee asked Malcolm quietly. "He's not well, and it's nothing tae do with dinner wine."

"Last year he had a kidney transplant," Malcolm said, scowling down at Shawn with disgust.

A kidney transplant? "I remember that he was sick—but then he'd gotten better."

Malcolm's mouth thinned. "One doesnae go aboot discussing such things outside of the family."

Well, now that she'd been put in her place, she thought with a spark of temper. "I'll go back tae the dining room."

Shawn reached out fast as a snake and clasped her wrist. "Stay with me. I want my room."

"Malcolm can help you—is there a service elevator here somewhere?" Paislee walked over and peered behind the stairs. A long open area shielded a closed door leading who knew where. There was a boot shelf for cleaning muddy boots, a coatrack with multiple hooks and jackets, and the gun cabinet, made of the same golden oak as the staircase.

A brass key ring hung from a hook beside it, but the cabinet was empty. She wondered if the detective inspector had taken the guns as evidence.

"Nothin' back there for you, Ms. Shaw," Malcolm intoned. "We have no elevator at the estate."

Shawn faux-whispered, once she returned to his side, breathing the stench of fermented grapes into her face, "Paislee. Dinnae tell anybody aboot the hedge. It's a secret."

"Well, you've just told the butler," she drawled, exchanging a look with Malcolm. Was this normal for the man?

Shawn belched and grimaced. "Malcolm knows everythin' that goes on in this pile of rock, don't ya? Has no problem listening at keyholes."

Malcolm wound up tighter, his body emanating anger, his cheeks flushed. "I would not go aboot accusing *me* of that, Mr. Marcus."

"Aila's the sneaky one!" Shawn declared. "She and Charles whispering secrets in the sunroom. You want tae know why I was outside that morning, Paislee?"

She didn't move, the object of Shawn's swaying attention.

He didn't wait for her to answer before shouting, "Following Charles after him and Aila had a hushed meeting."

The butler stepped forward, taking Shawn by the arm. "That's just aboot enough, Mr. Marcus."

Shawn prattled on, trying to shrug Malcolm off. "Aila was s'posed tae go tae the office with Mum, but she didnae. Charlesy went tae his room. I heard, I heard." He blinked. "Cannae tell you that, but I followed him behind the house tae see what he was up tae, double-crossing bastard."

Paislee's body lit with nerves. Had Shawn shot his cousin? How fast could the DI get here? Where were the security people Lydia's firm had hired?

"Is this a confession, *Shawn*?" Malcolm asked in a deadly quiet tone. "The entire household was privy tae you and Charles arguing the night before."

"I didnae do it." Shawn lifted his scratched hands to show Paislee. "But I tried tae pull Charles free from the thorny hedge. What if I was next? I ran home."

"Did you tell this tae the police?" Paislee sat on the bench opposite Shawn, her knees too weak to stand.

"That DI is an idiot. He's no respect for the order of things. Only his own agenda—like tossing a bloke in jail." Shawn, slouched in the chair, stretched his legs before him.

Malcolm scoffed. "Ms. Shaw, the family asks for your discretion in this matter. As you can see, Mr. Marcus isnae himself this evening. I'll go pull the lads preparing for dessert tae help Mr. Marcus to his chambers. Please stay here," the butler informed them both.

"Mum's cast-off windbag," Shawn muttered once Malcolm was gone.

The head butler acted very secure in his position with the heir of the household. She wondered if Malcolm was one of the lady's lovers. "What did you argue about with Charles?"

"Get me upstairs and I'll tell ye."

She doubted it. But she also doubted she would ever have another opportunity like this one. "Why did you sell the building on Market Street?"

His eyes widened with feigned innocence. "Why?"

"Yes!"

"For the money." He looked at her as if she were missing a few bricks. "Charles wanted a million pounds—dinnae tell Mum."

What a sum! "What happened tae it?"

"The sale fell through. Charles is dead. I've no bairns. I'm a disappointme—" He hiccupped. "A disappointment."

"Sh—" Paislee stopped talking when she smelled floral perfume and followed its scent upward.

Aila appeared at the upper landing of the staircase, her hand on the railing as she slowly took in Paislee and Shawn sitting below. Her blond hair was loose, her mouth glossed in pink. Her features were schooled into polite disinterest.

Shawn saw Aila and struggled to sit up. "Here's Mother Teresa now."

Paislee assisted as best she could, but he was heavy. She was embarrassed by his obnoxious behavior toward his sister.

"You didn't drown in your pudding?" Aila's tone held a mocking note as she turned her gaze from Shawn to Paislee and descended the stairs, possibly twenty of them. The gray of her sheath dress was nubbed silk, her legs in black hose and black heels. When she reached the bottom step, Paislee noticed that she gripped the railing so tight her knuckles were white. No scratches on her pristine hands.

Aila lifted her nose. "And who are you?"

"Paislee Shaw."

"With Mr. Silverstein's quarterly party. Shawn *would* have to behave so rottenly in front of Mother's favorite guests. Where is Malcolm?"

Paislee didn't mention that Shawn was also her landlord. "He went tae find somebody tae help Mr. Marcus upstairs."

Aila folded her hands before her and eyed Shawn like he was a bug specimen in a museum. "Not feeling our best tonight?"

"I'm sure he'll be right as rain after a good night's sleep." Paislee had no idea if that was true, but Aila's accusatory gaze made her protective of Shawn.

"Do you know who I am?"

"Aye, Aila Webster."

"I can see by your face that you read the morning paper."

Paislee felt a blush start at her throat and rise to her scalp.

"In the event you're wondering, I did not kill my cousin, Charles." She kicked the toe of her shoe against Shawn's calf, and he flinched. "Ask this one why the detective inspector arrived to search my room? I've never been so insulted. So taken advantage of—all by *Mr. Marcus* here."

"What do you mean?" But Paislee had a sick feeling.

"I've spent the last two years of my life wishing I'd never been a part of this family."

Shawn slid backward in the chair as he tried to glare up at Aila. "The perfect princess."

Had Shawn been the one to make the phone call to the station? Paislee covered her galloping heart with her palm and stared down at his gray-orange face. "Why would ye do that tae your own sister?"

Shawn got up and staggered, falling forward. His outstretched hand grasped the oak railing. He leaned against it, wearing a victorious grin, his eyes on Aila. "She talked Charles oot of giving his kidney tae me!"

Paislee, stunned, swung her gaze to Aila but then caught Shawn when he slid, her elbow around his waist.

Aila shook her head, her expression smug. "You're an idiot. You just confessed. Mother will have to realize how awful you are to me. And after everything I've done for you!"

Sibling rivalry? Paislee pressed her hand to her roiling stomach.

"Leave my mother oot of this."

"She's my mother too, and *you* are dragging her down! What did you expect her to pay Charles with?"

Paislee turned to the foyer. "I should go." She didn't want to hear any more dirty laundry.

Aila reached for Paislee with dismay. "Wait! My apologies. I'll go check on Malcolm." She fled down the hall.

Paislee whirled on Shawn as he collapsed into the chair. "Charles was going tae give you a kidney?" Was that why he'd been hiding for the last month?

Shawn's eyes were half-closed, his arms crossed over his knees. "Sell. The bastard was going tae *sell* me a kidney. Aila talked him oot of it."

"How do you know that?"

"I heard them whispering in the sunroom." He listed to the left, and Paislee righted him.

"What did you hear?" Could she get him to confess that Aila was a killer—but no, he'd played an awful prank on his sister. "Never mind. I can't trust you."

His bleary eyes flashed open. "You can! I heard Aila and G—"

Aila returned with Malcolm and Gavin on her heels. "What are ye saying, Shawn? Shut up!"

"Make me, princess. I know your dirty secret."

His sister jumped into the fray, jabbing her finger at Shawn's chest. "I did not collude with Charles about your kidney." She double-tapped, and Shawn winced in pain. "*You* were the one who argued with him the night before, Shawn. *You* messed up. And the entire household heard him yell that he'd help you over his dead body. Setting me up was ridiculous and childish and—"

"Enough!" Gavin announced, putting an end to the scene. "Shawn's had too much tae drink, and not well besides. Aila, please see tae your mother—not a word of this, understood?"

The young woman nodded tearfully but hurried off.

With a hand under Shawn's arm, Gavin steadied the man on his feet. "Malcolm, go see what's the holdup in the kitchen, aye?" The head butler strode purposefully down the hall to the left, past the dining room. "Steady now, Shawn, I've got you. Ms. Shaw, if you dinnae mind making your way tae the study? Follow the hall, and take a left at the nymph."

Paislee had no choice but to leave Gavin and Shawn. She glanced back and saw Gavin assisting Shawn up the stairs, murmuring what sounded like encouraging words.

She would never again think that having money and an estate was a recipe for a happy life. As she made her way down the hall, with gold-framed portraits and landscapes on either side, she tried to understand what she'd just learned. Could Shawn have killed his cousin that morning?

Laughter and happy voices filtered from somewhere at the very far end of the long hall. The last thing she wanted to do was rejoin the party, but this was about Lydia's celebration.

Passing a partially open door to her right, Paislee heard a sniffle. *Not your business. Keep going.* Her mother's heart urged her to stop and see what was wrong. One of the maids, perhaps?

She retraced her steps, knocked, and peered inside what had once been a Victorian telephone room, no larger than a closet. A young, narrow-shouldered woman leaned over a small desk. Pale blond hair cascaded to where stacks of files and a laptop computer had replaced where there'd been a telephone years earlier.

Aila. "Ms. Webster? Are you all right?"

Her head lifted, and she blinked damp golden-brown eyes in confusion. "I'm fine."

How often had Paislee said that when she wasn't?

"You must think me awful, hearing us fight." Aila lowered her lashes.

"I never had siblings," Paislee hedged.

"Me either. I thought I was an orphan all this time, and Shannon my kindly aunt who paid for my board and schooling." Her pretty pink mouth turned down. "What a fool I was—but honestly I was happier then. I could just be me."

"When did you discover the truth?" Paislee asked. "That Shannon Leery was your mother?"

"Two years ago, when Shawn needed a kidney." She drew in a breath, her eyes dry. "We have a rare blood type, and I'm a match. My price of admission to the family was a kidney for Shawn."

Paislee crossed her arms, her body chilled to the bone. It was like a Victorian drama. "You gave him one? So why would he need another from Charles?"

Her sympathies were torn between these siblings both wanting their mother's approval. Lady Shannon Leery was beginning to take on a darker role in Paislee's mind.

"He refused to take proper care of himself. He ate fatty foods, drank, and partied, until he collapsed." Aila got to her feet, smoothing her gray dress with a final sniff. "The spoiled heir suddenly realized he could actually die." Her posture grew rigid. "If they'd let her, Mother would split my remaining kidney, if she thought it would save her precious son."

"That's surely not true," Paislee said, unable to imagine such cruelty—and she didn't have a warm mum, either. "Your mother loves you."

"My mother resents me." Aila brushed her hands together. "God, what a melodrama. Shannon Leery prides herself on appearances, and if she found out that you were privy to the cracks in the family foundation?" She rolled her eyes. "She'd combust. Let's go. I'll walk you to the party."

"You don't have tae," Paislee said. "I can hear it down the hall."

Aila snorted indelicately. "And what then? Will I find you going through the guest book on Malcolm's desk?"

Stung, Paislee followed Aila to the study. "I only meant tae help Shawn, and then you. Not snoop."

"I know who you are. Everyone in town knows. You're the one who helped the detective inspector catch the last killer in Nairn."

Paislee was shocked that she'd be the subject of gossip in such a way. "I didn't really do anything."

"I don't believe you." After passing two closed doors, they turned left at a crossroads in the house where a two-foot-tall brass nymph held out a delicate, shiny hand.

Aila pushed open the third door, and Paislee heard cheerful voices. Pine-scented flames leapt cheerily in a large fireplace with a wood-carved mantel and a stag's head centered above it. People chatted on two sofas. A dozen wooden chairs upholstered in the green, blue, and black Leery plaid had been positioned along the wall. Those not on the couches held drinks and gathered in smaller groups in boisterous conversation.

Paislee perused the lively crowd for Lydia's red hair and spotted her laughing with Grant and a few of the other estate agents.

As rude as Aila was, maybe she knew something that would help Paislee with Shawn. Aila, realizing she still had Paislee's attention, tugged her by the elbow to the tea service at the far side of the study. From this position Shannon and Graham were in full view as they conversed with the Silversteins. Graham kept his hand on Shannon's back and passed her a filled flute.

Aila pressed her fingers to her side. "Mother is so beautiful. Men are drawn to her." She lifted a brow. "You know she's a crack shot? A survivor. Outlived her abusive husband." Aila poured hot tea into a thin china cup, the fragrant rose hips rising in the steam. "Is it a coincidence that Charles was shot? After refusing to give his kidney to Shawn?"

Was she insinuating that her own mother, Lady Leery, had shot Charles? Paislee's chest constricted. "I thought she was cleared of any wrongdoing."

Aila sniffed in disgust as Graham swooned over her mother.

Paislee cleared her throat. "I saw you all on the porch that morning after Charles was taken tae the hospital. What happened tae him? Was it possible for Shawn tae use the kidney?"

She bared her teeth in a grimace. "Oh, Charles got the last laugh. Shawn got screwed over in the worst way." Aila sipped her tea and chortled.

"What happened?"

Aila clicked her tongue and glanced at her as if Paislee were crazy. "I am *not* telling you that—I'd get sent right back to Switzerland, and I could kiss my job as head of the Lady Leery Feed the Poor Foundation goodbye."

Lydia spotted Paislee and motioned for her to join them.

"It appears your date would like some attention."

Tired of Aila's barbed comments, Paislee left the young woman to stew over her teacup and wandered through mingling groups to Lydia and Grant. "Hiya."

"There you are, love!" Lydia sloshed her champagne as she gave Paislee a hug. "Having fun?"

"How could I not?" Paislee countered.

Grant leaned toward Paislee to kiss her cheek, hitting her ear instead. "I havenae forgotten what Lydia asked me aboot."

Paislee knew now that Shawn'd sold the building because he needed the money for his health. This wasn't the time to share what she'd learned.

Grant held his finger to his lips and winked.

Gavin arrived, followed by Malcolm, and a second platter of desserts. Midge wandered through the room serving champagne flutes off a tray. Gavin joined the Silversteins, who greeted him warmly; Shannon provided a grateful smile. Was she aware that Gavin had taken care of Shawn for her?

"There's Gavin now," Grant said. "The man of the hour, for getting us into the estate. Silverstein had a huge crush on Shannon Leery back in the day, but she rebuffed him for the man she married."

George Marcus. "Does Natalya know that her husband admired Lady Leery?" Paislee homed in on the five people before the fire with as much interest as Aila had. Graham stuck to Shannon like a magnet.

"Natalya teases Silverstein aboot it, actually." Lydia finished her champagne. Midge arrived with a full flute.

Paislee declined another. The way this evening had been going, it was better to keep a clear head.

Natalya excused herself from the group by the fire, sipping her champagne, her long crimson fingernails shiny. She peered around the room and waved at Lydia, then sashayed confidently toward them. "Hello, darlings!"

Natalya plumped their trio to four and followed their glances toward where Lady Leery held court. "The queen," she drawled.

Gavin hovered attentively at Shannon's right. Silverstein rumbled something that made Shannon and the others laugh. Graham, brooding, nervously drummed his fingers on his thigh, less than a foot from the lady's side.

"How does she do it?" Lydia said with admiration. "Graham seems on the verge of a breakdown."

"Poor lad," Natalya drawled. "He's beautiful, but Shannon told me he bores her tae tears. He's a sculptor and can do marvelous things with his hands"—she paused dramatically—"but his conversational skills, well, they're not on par with Gavin's, or even Malcolm's."

"Why does Malcolm keep working for her? I mean, he's gorgeous." Lydia sighed. "I could think of many more things tae have him do than run me house."

Natalya laughed and shot Lydia a snarky look. "Shannon doesnae mind having her old lovers around. When they broke it off, Malcolm was the one who asked tae work for her, so that he could continue tae care for her."

"The perfect man?" Lydia teased.

"It speaks tae her vanity," Natalya said. "And he's loyal. Malcolm would do anything she asked without a second's thought."

Paislee recalled Shannon's dismissal of the butler in the dining room. Malcolm's assurance that he could speak how he pleased to Shawn. Would he kill for her?

Midge brought round a platterful of caramel squares decorated with the Leery Estate logo of the nymph and stag and offered them to their group.

"No, thank you," Paislee said. "I can't eat another thing. My thanks tae the chef, though." Midge walked away to the ad execs and Paislee said, "Oh! I should have tucked one in my purse for Brody."

Natalya chuckled. "You don't need tae skim the desserts into your bag—we can ask the chef. How old is your son?"

"Ten." Paislee was embarrassed to show her lack of social graces.

"Ask for two—your grandpa also has a sweet tooth." Lydia

swayed her hip into Paislee's, graceful even when tipsy. "I'm sure the boss's wife willnae mind."

"I dinnae," Natalya assured her. "You're a good reader of people, Lydia, which is why yer such a successful estate agent. You're an asset tae our agency, and don't think I havenae noticed, love." The older woman drifted toward her husband, who had left Shannon's orbit to flirt with both ad exec wives.

Lydia blushed, pleased. "Wasnae that nice? She'll take over the agency one day."

"She's right. You're talented and beautiful," Grant said. "You're sure tae win agent of the quarter." Grant left them to talk to Gavin, Shannon, and Graham. Grant's girlfriend joined him.

Lydia swiveled too quickly, her free arm through Paislee's. "There's Aila, standing on the edge of the crowd, alone. I feel sorry for her, having tae be here after that awful article in the paper."

Aila's slender shoulders were slightly bowed inward, her eyes shadowed even from across the room—her gaze didn't waver from her mother's group. Paislee's pride still stung from Aila's sharp comments. As if Paislee were snooping into the family's private business on purpose, when she'd only wanted to help. "Don't be fooled by the sweet exterior—she can hold her own."

"What happened?" Lydia demanded loudly—her brows rose as she realized how loud, and she giggled. "Oops, sorry. What happened?" she whispered.

Aila touched her side as she watched her mother, Gavin, and Graham laughing together, a wistful look on her face. Did she regret the loss of her kidney, or was it a fair price to be a part of the family? To run the foundation?

"I visited with Shawn after dinner. He wasnae feeling well. I'd hoped you'd pass by when you left the dining room," Paislee said.

"They took us a back way to view the formal portraits of the family. How'd it go with Shawn?"

"Awkwardly. Shawn and Aila argued—"

Lydia's gray eyes widened. "What has her fired up?"

Aila had gone from sad to angry in a heartbeat. Red cheeked, she stepped toward the group by the fire, but she was intercepted by two of the single estate agents, drunk enough to flirt with a possible murderess—at least according to the paper.

Aila had a temper. But was she guilty of killing Charles? The DI didn't believe so. Had Aila actually worked with Charles against Shawn? Perhaps she thought that if her kidney were cast aside, she would be, too?

In an instant, Aila's polite façade was back in place as she extricated herself from the men and joined the Silversteins, her mother, Graham, and Gavin.

Maybe she hadn't pulled the trigger on the rifle, but if she'd convinced Charles not to give Shawn a kidney, then Shawn might die.

Aila would have a clear path to her mother's love—and inheritance, with no blood on her hands.

# Chapter 13

Paislee couldn't erase the idea of Aila working with Charles to get Shawn out of the picture. Not giving a kidney was a very passive-aggressive action. While distasteful, it didn't mean the young woman had killed Charles. The pine from the fireplace was too cloying, the study too hot, and she couldn't catch her breath. Perspiration beaded her skin and nausea crept up her throat.

She needed some fresh air, quick. Paislee nudged Lydia toward Natalya and Gavin. "I need a minute—I'll be right back."

"Want me tae come with you?" Lydia asked, even as she swayed toward the others in full party mode.

"Naw. Have fun."

"The loo's tae the right." Lydia tottered off.

Paislee pressed her hand to her stomach to calm it. What she really wanted was to get out of this room and find Shawn. Would he be able to tell her exactly what he'd seen behind the hedge?

She stepped into the hall lit by wall sconces and electric candles. Left would lead to the main corridor and foyer; right, to the restroom and the back hallway of portraits Lydia'd said they'd been shown, which somehow connected to the dining room. She didn't want to bump into Malcolm, who guarded the front entryway like a Roman sentinel. Right it was. Surely a house this size had a back entrance.

The hall was cooler and less stuffy. Her body relaxed. She walked slowly, looking at all of the landscapes and paintings. Paislee passed several closed doors. There was the restroom to her right, and to the left was a wider corridor with chairs and potted plants along the walls. Images were framed in gilt. Shannon and Shayla as young blond girls, then Shannon and George's wedding. Shannon and Shawn. A formal portrait every other year until he'd reached his teens; then it was more sporadic.

The newest portrait was of Shannon, Shawn, and Aila, probably taken right after Aila had given Shawn a kidney. He exuded health; Aila, triumph; Shannon, benevolence. She recognized the mantel from the study as the backdrop for the family picture.

She kept on, trepidation tickling her nape. Paislee couldn't just dart upstairs and knock on doors to find Shawn's bedroom. Where was a way out of this manor? Just one cool sip of night air would clear her head.

The hall of portraits and paintings continued, though there was a blank space as if a picture used to hang there very recently. Farther down was a wall of glass that showed the shadows of beech and Scots pine lit with the pale red of landscape lighting behind the house. Was the hedge, and the path, visible from here? She fanned her warm face. Better yet, was there a door?

No. Paislee peered out the window into the dark night, clouds covering the moon and stars. She saw a masculine silhouette and her heart sped in her chest, but she stopped short of crying out when she realized the man was speaking into a radio.

Another security guard. Her tense shoulders lowered.

"Ma'am?"

Paislee squealed and whirled, the fringe on her dress shimmying. "Oh, Midge. Thank heaven. I'm lost. I was trying tae find a door, for a wee bit of air."

"'Tis a rabbit's warren, this house." The maid bowed her head, her white-and-black cap in place over her short brown hair. "I can take ye. Yer almost at the dining room."

"What's behind the house here?"

"Sharp's Park." Midge stepped away from the window. "This way, ma'am."

Paislee followed Midge's sturdy black-clad figure down another electric candlelit hall. "Midge, how is Mr. Marcus—have you checked on him since dinner? I'm worried for him."

Midge cast a glance over her shoulder at Paislee, her expression torn between being polite to a guest and guarding the family.

Paislee lowered her voice. "I know about the kidney transplant. If there is anything I can do?"

"M'lady will make sure Mr. Marcus gets what he needs."

Protective and loyal. "Midge, can you give Mr. Marcus a message from me? I'd love tae speak with him before the end of the night."

Midge's square shoulders stiffened as if what Paislee asked were in bad taste.

"I'm sairy. Forgive me if I've overstepped. We're . . . well, the truth is, he's my landlord at the sweater shop I own. Do ye mind giving him a note from me, wishing him well?"

She whistled beneath her breath, then glanced at Paislee. "I could pass him a note for the morning, but he needs his rest. Now, here we are at the dining room." Midge pressed a button, and a pocket door slid into the wall, revealing the tapestry the family had entered from at dinner.

The table had been cleared of all dishes and cloths, showing nicked edges and a bowed center leaf. The silver chandelier candles had burned down. Without the romantic glow of candlelight, the room appeared neglected. So dazzled at the time, she hadn't realized that some of the chairs were mismatched.

"This way tae the front door. Will ye be awright?" Midge brought Paislee to the foyer.

"Aye, thanks. I just need tae clear my head—I'll write that note before I go." Paislee's gaze was drawn to the green bench on the other side of the staircase as if Shawn might still be there somehow. Of course it was vacant, as was the chair.

"Follow this hall tae the nymph and go left tae the study—ye can't lose yer way." Midge disappeared behind the stairs. Did the door by the gun cabinet lead to the kitchen?

Paislee gazed at the landing upstairs. No Shawn there, either. She turned to the front door and twisted the old brass knob. Locked.

Perspiration dampened her skin.

"May I help you, Ms. Shaw? Why are ye not with your party? Again?" Malcolm drawled. His dark eyes glowered at her.

"I'd like some fresh air."

He stared at her, unmoving. Paislee kept her hand on the knob, anxiety making her pulse skip.

"The gardens are closed," he said sternly. "'Tis not a good idea tae wander aboot, and you know well why. A man was killed."

"I'll stay on the porch. Just a few minutes?"

Reluctantly, Malcolm took a key from a drawer in the tall table. "I'll keep it open a crack. Stay on the porch, for yer own safety."

They stood toe-to-toe in the foyer as he opened the door. Cool spring air brushed against her face, and her tension eased, but she realized just how cold it was and rubbed her bare arms.

"Ye'll need your wrap," he murmured with a disgruntled huff.

She'd noted the jackets and coats behind the staircase, out of sight. "If it's no bother?"

The moody butler returned, removing a label with her name, and she snuggled the warm silver cashmere around her shoulders. "Thanks." Her tumbling thoughts settled. "How is Shawn?"

"He'll be fine, dinnae fash yerself." The regal butler kept his hand on the door for her to leave, but this was a great opportunity to ask about the guns.

"Malcolm, I noticed that your gun cabinet is empty. What happened?"

His brown eyes smoldered, and he tugged the front of his Leery-plaid vest. "The detective inspector confiscated them."

"*All?*"

"Aye. And some of 'em antiques, a hundred years or more in the Leery family. He's doin' his job, I ken, but those guns werenae used tae kill Charles."

"How can you be so sure?"

"I maintain the weapons on a weekly basis. I oversaw the constables as they packed the guns and could tell they hadnae been moved from when I'd cleaned them last."

Despite the cool air from the open front door, Paislee's skin heated. He'd cleaned the guns before the DI took them?

He exhaled at her reaction. "It's me job, Ms. Shaw. I wasnae covering a crime. I told the officers so."

"Sairy." Paislee had one more question for the butler. "That morning, on the path, you tipped Charles's body tae show something tae Graham."

His expression grew perturbed. "You see a lot."

Why was he bothered by that? Did he have something to hide? "There was no blood on the ground."

"Tae ease your mind, what I showed Graham was the bulge on Charles's back. He was shot, but the bullet didnae exit."

Not understanding, she shrugged.

"This could mean the bullet was one designed for hunting small animals." He sighed. "Not to be crass, but a larger caliber round would have been messier."

She'd wondered at that. "So why then does the DI still have your guns?"

His mouth thinned. "I'm sure I dinnae ken, Ms. Shaw." Malcolm opened the door all the way and gestured her to the front porch. "Didn't you require fresh air?"

Knowing she'd pushed as far as she could, Paislee stepped onto the wide stone porch. Cool night air revived her, and she breathed deep. Water from the fountain shot upward in burbling gold. She bent over the stone rail to see the slowly moving shadows of koi in the pond.

She wouldn't have been surprised to hear the door slam and lock behind her from the irate butler. He certainly seemed to know a lot about ammunition. Was it common knowledge for hunters? She could ask Amelia later.

Paislee leaned forward with her forearms pressed against the stone, the cashmere wrap protecting her skin. She looked to the lavender bougainvillea arch and the darkened gardens. A man had been killed there just two days ago. Who had done it? Paislee smelled spicy perfume as Shannon Leery suddenly joined her at the railing.

"You've caused my daughter and butler great angst," the lady observed dryly.

Paislee glanced to the entrance where Malcolm's profile was visible from the partially open door. The figure disappeared. She thought back to Shawn and his accusation of the butler listening at keyholes, his warning to trust no one.

Paislee faced the grand matriarch, wondering how much Shannon knew of Shawn's drunkenness and Aila's tears. "My apologies," she said. "Sometimes I leap tae help when none is needed."

Shannon curled her ring-covered fingers over the rail and peered out at the still night. Her designer dress was classic in style with its capped sleeves, but Paislee noticed the worn fabric around the pearl buttons at the bodice. It wasn't new, though the silk scarf at her neck added a modern twist. Her gold earrings were a knot-like style that had been popular fifteen years ago or more.

"A kind act can be forgiven." Shannon seemed polite. Just shy of friendly.

"Thank you. You have a lovely home." Paislee shivered and tightened her wrap as a breeze sprayed water from the fountain toward them. "My condolences, on your nephew."

The lady's eyes narrowed shrewdly. "You were here with Fordythe Primary when Charles was found?"

"Yes. My son, Brody, is in P6."

Her white brows drew together, though the Botox kept her forehead from furrowing. "I'm so sairy. How awful that the children might have been hurt." Lady Leery glanced away. "I wish Detective Inspector Zeffer would catch the criminal responsible so we may all be at ease." She eyed the security guard in the car park. "How are we supposed tae open the garden for tourists? I can't in guid conscious, until I know who is behind this."

"Tae be sure, this hasn't been an easy time," Paislee said softly. She chose her words carefully. "Shawn mentioned he has a rare blood type. Maybe I can ask Father Dixon at church tae spread the word, and see if we can find a donor?"

Lady Leery looked affronted and took a deep sigh, glancing to her diamond ring set in gold. The jewel glimmered in the lights strung around the railing. "We're on a donor list. I would give me son one of mine, but the doctors say I'm too old. I loathe those words. They're so limiting. I dinnae feel that way at all."

Paislee understood the heart a mother had for her son. There was nothing she wouldn't do for Brody. "And was Charles a match?"

The lady's body trembled—with anger, not sorrow. Her hands balled into fists. "Aye, but Charles had died by the time we reached the hospital. He'd left instructions tae cremate his body. He was *not* an organ donor."

Paislee gripped the edges of her shawl around her, her body chilled to the core. She remembered Aila saying that Charles had gotten the last laugh. "Oh!"

Shannon haughtily drew herself up and peered into Paislee's eyes. "Malcolm mentioned you've overheard a few private family discussions. I ask for your discretion. This is, after all, our family's business. I'm sure ye saw that ludicrous article in the paper this morning."

It would do no good to deny it. "Aye. I've never met your daughter before, but she seems"—temperamental was probably not the right word—"intelligent. She runs your Feed the Poor Foundation?"

"Aila does her best for me." The slight shrug suggested that it wasn't quite enough. Shannon folded a triangle of silk at her throat. "I regret not defying convention tae do as you did and raise her without a father, but as a peer in the community, such things werenae done."

Paislee was shocked. Her choice wasn't something she openly discussed . . . ever. "What do you mean?"

Lady Leery was not the least apologetic. "Malcolm runs background checks on everyone we invite into our home. We have hundreds of thousands of dollars in art and antiques. Yet there was a *murder* on the grounds." Her mouth twisted. "I know all aboot you and your sweater shop." Shannon caressed Paislee's wrap. "Did ye make this?"

"I did."

"It's verra fine."

"Thank you." Paislee couldn't tell if the woman was a friend or foe—drawing a conclusion was like trying to catch a raindrop in her palm.

"The point is, Aila isnae a killer any more than I am," Shannon said. "Thanks tae that article, and the DI calling my daughter down tae the station like a proper criminal, well, I daresay that I miss the old ways." She leaned forward and murmured, "A monetary 'donation' could set things right."

Paislee quelled a shudder, the story about George Marcus, dead after two years of a stormy marriage, hard to dismiss. With all his faults, Paislee doubted DI Zeffer, who followed the letter of the law, would accept a bribe of any kind. She heard Grandpa's reminder, that rich folks had different rules, like a cautionary voice in her ear.

Lady Leery clasped her hands before her and narrowed her eyes. "Did you see anything that morning? More than you're letting on?"

Paislee shook her head and shared her version of what had happened, including Graham and his knit cap by the floral arch. "Is there a way tae get tae the house from the maze without using the main path?"

"Yes," said Shannon, realization dawning on her face. "The trail behind the hedge leads from the garden shed tae the house. Graham and Charles must have just missed each other." She frowned. "He could've been shot. I didnae see Graham until the ambulance arrived—I assumed he was with the students."

Graham and Charles? And Shawn had been back there, too. Pretty crowded. "What did Shawn—"

Gavin barged out of the house, his hands open wide, cutting off her question. "There you two are! It's time tae hand oot the awards. Lydia's asking for you, Paislee."

They were ushered in, and Malcolm took her wrap as Gavin made jokes about them having a perfectly warm house to converse in—why the front porch?

The handsome accountant didn't expect an answer as he hurried them down the long corridor, past the nymph to the study. "I found them!" he announced.

"Ten minutes, please," Natalya called. "Then the ceremony will begin!"

Shannon pressed a thumb between her brows as if she had a headache but kept her smile. "I'll sit oot of the way, Gavin."

He immediately selected a cozy upholstered chair by the fireplace on the opposite side of the room where Mr. Silverstein and Natalya had piled a table with silver gift bags, shining gold tissue at the top.

Paislee was tempted to join Shannon out of the fray, but she hadn't been invited. Besides, she was here for Lydia, so she searched the room for her friend. Her cherry-red hair was hard to miss as she laughed with Grant.

Midge was quick to offer her a coffee, or raspberry cordial, and she chose coffee over the sweet wine. Her nose wrinkled as she sipped the hot and bitter beverage.

"Sugar and cream are by the dessert tray," Midge said, her eyes flashing with humor at Paislee's reaction.

"Thanks." Paislee crossed the room, drawn to Lydia as she sparkled like a diamond in her element. Grant appeared enthralled with her as he leaned in, nearly touching his glass to hers—Grant's date, not so much.

Aila, between Graham and the two flirty estate agents, showed more confidence with her mother to the side of the room. At the time when Lady Leery had been pregnant, having an illegitimate daughter would have been disastrous for her standing in Nairn, an old-fashioned shire. She'd sent Aila to private schools and cared for her as best she could within the confining circumstances.

How different would their lives be if the lady had been able to keep her daughter and raise her, despite what others might have said? Perhaps Shawn wouldn't have been the "spoiled heir" as Aila had called him.

Why hadn't he married and had children?

His job, it would seem, as next in line for the Leery Estate would be to have children of his own.

Paislee covertly studied Aila as the beautiful blonde tossed her head back and laughed. This was the friendliest she'd been all night.

Stirring more cream into her coffee, Paislee wondered why Malcolm and Aila had complained to Lady Leery about Paislee butting her nose where it didn't belong. Had they inadvertently told Paislee something she shouldn't know?

Shawn had said nobody could be trusted. Aila laughed again, leaning in to hear something Graham was saying. She had to get Shawn a note, but she had nothing to write with, or on.

Paislee placed her cup down and searched the tables in the

study, scoring a pen but no paper. A cocktail napkin would have to do. What to say? With little space, she kept it simple. "Shawn, I'm worried about you—please call me—Paislee Shaw." She jotted her phone number, then searched the room for Midge.

The maid was gone. Figured.

She sipped her creamy brew from the back of the loud study and wondered for the hundredth time *why* someone had killed Charles.

Did he have money, or property that would revert to the estate, and Lady Leery, upon his death? She'd seen firsthand that things were not as bountiful as first impressions indicated. Had he been killed for his kidney? She recalled her landlord's panic and determination when he'd wanted to reach the hospital and make sure that Charles lived.

What had Aila and Charles argued about that morning? Shawn had insisted his sister was talking Charles out of donating his kidney, but she'd denied it. Her test for gun powder residue had been negative, and the DI had ruled her out. Yet Paislee had seen the young woman's temper, how she despised her brother.

"C'mon, Paislee!" Lydia waved at her from the tall high-top table she, Grant, and two of the estate agents had gathered around.

"On my way." She lifted her cup. Time to join the party.

Graham, dark honey-blond hair to his shoulders, his gray suit jacket open, gestured for one of the estate agents also up for an award to come forward. The sculptor was charming. But what was his history before becoming Lady Leery's latest lover? Was he wealthy, or did he think that Shannon would pay his way? Had he seen Charles that morning?

Malcolm would do anything for Shannon. He was comfortable with a gun. He hadn't had the time to shoot a rifle and arrive at Charles's side. Shawn had lied about Aila to the police. All were covering up that Shawn had been the anonymous caller to the station.

For the first time, she actually felt a tingle of pity for the detective inspector. Not only was it hard to follow the facts, but you had to tell truth from lie.

Natalya stood before the fireplace and clapped for everyone's attention. "Mr. Silverstein would like tae say a few words before the awards are given."

The ad execs and their wives took seats on the sofas. Paislee set her awful coffee on a tray with other empty cups and joined Lydia. "Good luck!" she whispered.

"Feel better?" Lydia asked brightly.

Paislee nodded, and Mr. Silverstein (Paislee wasn't certain the man had a first name) faced his employees with a grin. White teeth, probably veneers, sparkled beneath his mustache. Thick silver hair had been styled back from his broad forehead, his face lined—he was seventy-four, and proud of it. "Thank you all for celebrating a very satisfactory quarter, eh, Gavin? You know you're doing well when your accountant sends you chocolate. And tae celebrate here at Leery Estate means so much." He patted his heart.

Applause sounded.

Gavin remained at Shannon's side, by the upholstered armchair. He lifted his champagne flute to Mr. Silverstein.

"I cannae do what I do without a solid team. Let's start oot with the first prize of the evening." The owner called the name of one of the men who'd been flirting with Aila. Natalya handed over a bag. They repeated this process until there was only one bag left. Lydia hadn't been called yet, and her friend, usually cool as ice, was a trembling wreck.

Paislee clasped her hand and squeezed.

"And the top earner of the quarter is . . . Lydia Barron!"

Natalya brought over the gift bag with a smile of pride. "Not only will she earn a wonderful bonus, and this plaque, but she also won a trip for two tae the Caribbean!"

Lydia's eyes welled. "Thank you so much, Natalya. You trained me, and I learned from the best."

The power ladies hugged.

The antique brass clock struck midnight, and Gavin stood next to Mr. Silverstein with more cheers of goodwill. "Thanks, my lady, for another magical evening at Leery Estate." Gavin bowed his head to Shannon. Graham stayed to the side, not seeming too perturbed by Gavin upstaging his position as host. He spread his hands out to the guests. "On behalf of Lady Leery and the Leery Estate, thank you. Take-out boxes with desserts have been made up for each of you."

Natalya winked at her, and Paislee mouthed, "Thank you."

Paislee caught up to Midge as the maid led everyone from the study toward the front door to give her the note for Shawn. Midge tucked it into her pocket like a disappearing magic trick but said not a word.

In the foyer, Gavin, Aila, and Graham shook hands with each guest as they left, offering a personal chat and a box of treats. Paislee noticed Malcolm overseeing everything from his post at the tall table. Shannon was nowhere to be seen. When it was her turn, Gavin held Paislee's hand and kissed her cheek a little too long. "Would ye like tae get a drink sometime?"

Paislee's smile wavered, not ready for the question that seemed out of the blue. Lydia thanked him again and pulled her by the arm to the waiting limo.

They got in and Lydia giggled, tipsy. "You are way too fine tae be a nun. Join me in the Caribbean. We'll have a blast. Bikinis and piña coladas."

"Grandpa and Brody can barely survive for a night without me there. A week isn't going tae happen." She slid along the leather seat, the treat box in her lap. "What's up with Gavin?" She got the feeling there was more to the man's offer than a date. Was she curious over what she and Shannon had discussed on the porch?

Lydia doubled over, laughing. "Just a drink!"

She nudged Lydia's shoulder. "Not interested."

"You're *never* interested!"

That wasn't exactly true, but she'd learned to squash amorous feelings. "Did you see the security guards there tonight? I—" Paislee stopped talking when she noticed the driver listening. She'd have to wait to share what she'd learned about the Leery family until they had privacy.

"I told you you'd be safe." Lydia put her dessert box into her silver gift bag. "So, what'd ye think aboot Grant? I asked if ye could tell yer business friends aboot the letters. He's so funny, and cute. All that ginger hair."

"What did he say? Isn't that his girlfriend?"

Lydia deflated. "He says they're on the rocks. But he's been saying that for a year."

"They were holding hands." Paislee had watched Grant, hoping he'd let her in on the certified letter, but an opportunity never arose. "What about telling the others?"

"You can but no details." Lydia's cherry-red hair seemed extra bright in the shadows of the limo. "Grant got a wee bit jealous when his date was talking with Graham—that man is a *flirt*. He's lucky Lady Leery didnae notice."

"Be careful, Lyd. Don't get your heart broken."

She laughed bitterly. "I don't have one. I aim tae be like our hostess one day. Surrounded by handsome young things ready tae cater tae any desire."

"Lydia, I'm not sure what tae make of her, but Lady Leery is not happy."

"How couldnae she be? She has everything."

Paislee glanced up at the driver, then whispered, "Shawn needs a kidney transplant."

"Crikey." Lydia slumped back against the leather seat.

"That's not all." She filled her best friend in on everything that had happened, how Aila and Shawn loathed each other, how Shawn said that nobody in the house could be trusted. How the DI had confiscated all the weapons in the gun cabinet.

She reached for her shawl against the chill and realized she'd forgotten it at the estate.

"Lyd?"

Her friend slumped against her, emitting an adorable snore.

# Chapter 14

When the alarm went off at seven Saturday morning, Paislee expected to step over her bestie, whom she'd made a bed for out of several thick comforters.

Instead, Lydia and her magic makeup case were gone, with a lipstick message on the vanity mirror. *xoxo, Lyd.*

Paislee stumbled down the stairs, her hand on the railing, her head pounding but not from overdrinking. Worry had kept her from sleeping sound. Her anger at Shawn had morphed into concern. The man was ill and needed a kidney.

She couldn't wait to offer a bit of hope to her business family this morning. Not that she had hard facts, but a hint of reprieve was better than none.

Grandpa sat at the table, nursing a mug of tea, but burst out laughing when he saw her. "Braw no more." He chuckled.

She ducked into the downstairs bathroom and groaned at her image. Her hair was plastered to the side of her cheek and mascara had clumped on her lashes. She quickly rinsed her face before joining her grandpa at the table.

The box of desserts from last night was on the counter, and he'd chosen a caramel square to go with his tea.

"Morning." She cleared her throat and poured herself a mug. "How were the ice-cream sundaes?"

"Sinful. Perfect fer me sweet tooth." Grandpa took another bite. "Brody was in bed at eleven thirty, after a wee bit of coercing. I heard ye later."

"Sorry if we were loud?" She'd had to assist Lydia up the stairs, and her best friend had found Wallace's pink nose poking through Brody's cracked-open door hysterical. Once Paislee'd gotten Lydia settled, she'd checked on her son. He'd slept like an angel—possibly conked out from too much sugar.

"I wouldnae suggest a career as a burglar, either of ye." He slurped from his mug. "Sounds like ye had a grand night oot."

"We did, thank you. The inside of the estate is lovely, but trapped in time a bit."

He stretched his ankles, his slipper dangling from the tip of his toes. "Did ye meet Lady Leery?"

"Aye, and had dinner with the family." Paislee sipped her tea. "With crystal and china for twenty-four. Lydia was in her element." She shrugged. "I felt like the odd girl out."

"Ye dressed up just fine." Grandpa nibbled a corner of caramel. "What did you think of the estate? Was Charles's murder a topic?"

"Not at first. Everybody acted like nothing had happened. Aila and Shawn do *not* get along. Grandpa, it was so sad. Shawn drank way too much. I found out why he had that awful spray tan—tae cover his yellow skin."

"Yellow skin?"

"Seems he needed a kidney transplant, which Aila gave him, but it didn't take, and now he needs another. That's why Charles was in town."

Grandpa removed his glasses and stared at her. "But then he was killed."

"You got it."

"Bad luck. Bloke shouldnae be drinking while needing a kidney."

"That was just one of the many things Shawn and Aila were fighting about."

"Do they ken who shot Charles?"

"No. Nobody in the manor seems tae mourn him, though."
Oh, to be a mouse in that house. She thought of Midge, the maid,
who probably heard everything that went on, including the fight
between Shawn and Charles. Had Midge given Shawn the note
from Paislee yet? It was probably too early to expect a call.

"If a man's family don't like him, what aboot his mates?"
Grandpa asked.

"Cohorts, more like, since Charles was a criminal." Paislee got
up and searched the counter by the home phone for a pad of paper
and a pen. "I'll make time after the meeting this morning tae research Charles in depth online."

Grandpa scratched at his trimmed beard in contemplation. "It's
not yer job tae find Charles's killer."

He had a point. "I have tae help if I can. Brody could have been
*shot* while at a school field trip, or Holly. Any of the kids, and we don't
know why. Nairn must be safe for the children." Paislee scrawled
*Charles Thomson* on the paper. Then *Midge*. "Before Shawn was
helped tae bed, he told me that nobody was tae be trusted."

"Pure mental, that. Docs probably have him doped up on med-
ication." Grandpa scooted his chair closer to the table. "For the kidney transplant."

"Maybe. I might be paranoid, too, if my home were filled with
hidden passageways and doors behind tapestries." Paislee got a whiff
of Grandpa's caramel, and her mouth watered. "You were right
about the peerage playing by different rules. Shannon admitted as
much last night on the porch. She said they used tae send a 'donation' tae the station and that would smooth things over. Can you
imagine DI Zeffer going for that?"

Grandpa snorted. "Never. Did ye find oot anythin' last night
that might help the detective? Mibbe ye could trade him for information."

She thought of all the folks in the house and drummed her pen
against the paper. "Shawn wanted Charles's kidney, and then he
was shot."

"Could Shawn have shot Charles to get his kidney? Mibbe he wasnae supposed tae die," Grandpa suggested.

Paislee considered this, the timing of the shot, and the three men on the trail. "I have tae talk tae Shawn. I hope Midge gives him my note."

Grandpa slid his glasses back on, his brown eyes thoughtful behind black frames. "Note? Who's Midge?"

"The maid. She helped me when I was lost searching for a back entrance tae get some fresh air. Never did find one, but I saw the path behind the hedge where Charles was shot. I need tae ask Shawn what he saw that morning."

Grandpa frowned. "From what ye've told me, your landlord has a lot at stake. If he's the killer, you need tae keep clear of him."

She got up and chose a dessert from the carton. "I'd love tae see behind the house in the daylight. Amelia said Charles was shot with a rifle. Where would Shawn have put it? Things happened so fast." She brought her caramel to the table. "Pretend this is Charles." She tapped the table to the right. "Shawn was here. The shot sounded. Charles crashed backward tae the path. Shawn said he tried tae help Charles out of the bushes but then realized he could be next so he ran. It all happened in minutes."

Grandpa studied the caramel square, then looked up at Paislee. "Shawn was too close tae be the shooter with a rifle—you'd have heard a louder bang, and there would have been a bigger wound."

"I didn't see one." Paislee bit off a piece of her treat and sat down again. "Malcolm explained that the bullet was inside Charles's body. Something about it being lesser weight for a smaller animal."

"So Shawn isnae guilty, and Aila isnae guilty."

"Shannon said last night that Aila was no more guilty than she was of shooting Charles." Paislee took a deep, mind-clearing drink of her breakfast tea. "But I can't say for certain. Shannon would do anything for Shawn. He has a rare blood type, which was where Aila and Charles came in."

Grandpa popped the last of the caramel square into his mouth. "Can ye put an advertisement in the paper for a donor?"

"Even quicker on the internet. All you need is money." Paislee rubbed her fingers together.

Grandpa chuckled.

"I don't think they're doing very well financially. The tablecloths and napkins were worn, and I noticed a painting was missing in their hall. Lady Leery made sure tae mention we could buy the Leery venison sausage. I'd bet the money she married for is long gone." It made Paislee sad, as if the estate were sinking into a bygone era.

"Paislee, that family has been a part of Nairn for two hundred years. They'll rally."

"I wouldn't be surprised if they did. Malcolm, the butler, runs a tight ship. Lady Leery is all about appearances—she expects Aila and Shawn tae fall in line and follow her wishes. She actually smacked Graham's hand at dinner when he was looking at his phone."

Grandpa laughed. "Manners are manners even for a boy toy, as ye called him. So what if she has high expectations? She's a lady, Paislee."

Paislee jotted down Gavin's name on her paper.

"Who's that?" Grandpa asked.

She left out how he'd asked her to get a drink. "Gavin Thornton is an accountant who works for both the Silverstein Agency as well as Lady Leery. He'd know the state of the family's finances."

"What difference does it make?"

"According tae Shannon's Wikipedia page, Charles has no heirs, just like Shawn. What if money reverted tae the estate upon his death?"

Grandpa frowned at her. "You think a woman of that caliber would shoot her own nephew for a few quid?"

"Who says it's just a few? I'm fairly certain that Gavin sets up these private parties for Shannon at the estate as a way to bring in money the property needs. I guess she and Gavin used tae be a thing. Her and the butler, too."

He whistled low. "What a lady."

Paislee leaned across the table and patted Grandpa's hand. "Listen, why don't *you* research Charles tae see if he had any other family while I'm at work today?" The computer at home in the living room was a desktop and the internet speed not as fast as at Cashmere Crush, but he should manage fine.

"I suppose." He eyed her keys.

"Ach! Grandpa, I'm sairy. I forgot you wanted the car today, tae drive tae Dairlee." And the storage unit. "Let me get Brody up and moving—unless you drop him at the shop on your way?"

"That's all right. I can do it another time."

"Are you sure?" She searched his face, but he gave nothing away. "We can go tomorrow. There's got tae be something fun tae do around Dairlee that you can show us."

He nodded but didn't answer one way or the other. So far he hadn't turned down a Sunday Funday.

"You want something besides caramel for breakfast?" Paislee got up to make fried egg sandwiches. "I appreciate you spending all of this time with Brody, so that he doesn't have tae be at the shop with me. This is more fun for him. I know at ten he probably doesn't need a sitter, but I feel better knowing you're here."

"Bored kids usually find ways tae entertain themselves that lead tae trouble," Grandpa warned. "We might make a kite today—that dragon pattern he was going on aboot."

"Sounds fine." She heated the pan and sprayed olive oil inside before cracking six eggs to fry. Her tummy rumbled with hunger as she toasted bread.

Five minutes later, they were enjoying a quick healthy breakfast. Wallace raced down the stairs on his short, furry legs, followed by a sleepy Brody. Paislee scratched behind the pup's ears and let him out the back door.

"Morning. Your sandwich is on the counter." She gave Brody a side hug and ruffled his wild auburn hair. Past time for a trim. Maybe when she dropped off Wallace next Friday? There was a barber on the corner.

"Mornin'. Did ye have fun with Aunt Lydia?"

"I brought you and Grandpa home dessert. I ate so much that I was too full tae eat it last night."

He glanced at his grandfather. "Grandpa made me go tae bed early."

"What are you talking about?" Paislee looked from Brody to Grandpa.

"He said I was mouthin' off and sent me tae bed after the movie."

"It was eleven thirty, and you were arguin' aboot brushing yer teeth after havin' sweets."

"Eleven o'clock is your bedtime on weekends, so it wasnae early." Paislee waited for Brody to face her. "You owe your grandpa an apology if you were being smart, especially after getting ice cream."

Brody brought his sandwich to the table in full pout mode. "I'm ten, Mum, not a wean."

"Do we have tae make it so that you can't have ice cream, pizza, *and* crisps on the same night? Bigger kids can handle stuff like that."

He sat, his pout nearly gone. "Sairy, Grandpa."

Grandpa Angus took a long sip from his mug. "Apology accepted."

Peace restored, she let Wallace back inside.

"Where are you going so early, Mum?"

"Oh sheesh, I'm supposed tae be at Theadora's for a meeting—I totally forgot." Seven forty. "I have tae shower the glitter out of my hair!"

She raced upstairs, taking them two at a time—when would she get ahold of her life, for heaven's sake?

After the fastest shower in history, she dressed in jeans and a white linen blouse, and slipped on her white leather sneakers. She rushed down the stairs, told Grandpa goodbye, kissed Brody on the head, and hurried out the door.

Paislee carefully drove five miles over the speed limit—relieved that even if she was late, Theadora couldn't give her detention.

# Chapter 15

Paislee parked in the alley behind Theadora's Tea Shoppe on the opposite end of the block from Cashmere Crush. She arrived at the back door at ten after eight and knocked before entering.

The first thing she smelled was sugary pastry and berries. Then strong coffee. She waved to the five business owners seated on plastic turquoise chairs in a circle at the rear of the bakery by the kitchen.

Toward the front a clerk ran the register, and three customers enjoyed pastries and drinks. A turquoise teacup clock on the wall confirmed her tardiness.

Dan pushed open the swinging kitchen door with a tray of blueberry muffins, which he placed on a table next to the urn of coffee. "Hi, Paislee." He greeted her with a shy smile—though average-looking, Dan had a wizard's touch in the kitchen.

"Morning, Dan, everybody! Sorry tae be late." For as demure as he was, Theadora, until a week ago, had been the bright and bubbly one, with bleached hair and turquoise streaks. This morning her hair was a beautiful golden brown, and she wore a loose, floral-pattern dress with ballet flats. Paislee hoped to hear good news about a pregnancy at last.

"Nothing new there, eh, Paislee?" Theadora glared at her as she hovered over the sugar packets and added one to her double-cupped tea.

Ouch. Someone was not in a good mood. Hormones? "Sairy."

"Dinnae mind her." Dan offered her a muffin. "Coffee or tea is on the table."

She'd already had tea, and breakfast, but this muffin smelled too good to pass up. "Coffee—thanks."

The others chatted as she doctored her coffee to make it drinkable. James Young patted the chair next to him. "I saved ye a seat." Older than Grandpa, James reminded her of an impish, aging leprechaun, and she adored him.

"Thanks." She sat with him to her right and Ned to her left. Jimmy and Lourdes were directly across from her, a vacant seat between Lourdes and Margot, and another between Ned and Jimmy.

Margot gestured toward Theadora with her blueberry muffin. "We're all on edge." She was bathed in her usual sandalwood oil, and her white lab coat hung over the back of the turquoise chair to reveal a blousy top and jeans.

"Theadora was joking," Dan said to the group as he sat by Ned. "Right, hon?"

"That's me, a laugh a minute." Theadora's mouth tightened and she blinked her watery eyes. "I'm sairy, Paislee." She skirted Dan's chair as if he had the measles, and plonked down next to Lourdes, with Margot on her other side.

It didn't take a detective to see that Dan and Theadora had been fighting again. She discreetly eyed Theadora's ankles for signs of swelling. When Paislee had been pregnant, hers had felt like they were the size of watermelons. Theadora's dress hid her legs.

"It's all right." Paislee lifted her coffee cup to her friends around the circle. "I have a great excuse for being late—I actually went out on a date last night . . . with Lydia."

Margot winked good-naturedly. "And here I was excited fer you!"

James grinned and propped his boot on his opposite knee.

"Heaven help us—where did ye two go? Dance clubs? Bars? The poor lads!"

Paislee blushed at his teasing. "The Leery Estate—for Lydia's quarterly party. She won a trip tae the Caribbean."

Her business family erupted with questions.

"The estate?" Jimmy asked. His ginger hair had faded in middle age, but his blue eyes remained very bright.

"Have they caught the murderer?" Theadora asked, her fingers kneading her double-cupped tea. Brick-red lipstick made a semismile on the rim.

Paislee shook her head. "Not yet."

"I cannae believe Lady Leery hosted a party!" Lourdes touched the gold chain at her neck. "Her nephew hasnae been dead a week."

"Lady Leery seems big on keeping up appearances." Paislee recalled the glitz that masked the worn tablecloth. "Also she didn't want tae let the agency down. Mr. Silverstein is an old admirer."

Ned finished his muffin and wiped his hands on a napkin. "What about our building?"

Paislee peered around the circle brimming with excitement. "As you know, Lydia's been checking every day for news of the property, and it hasn't shown up. Legally, we have thirty days from the date of the sale. Which hasn't happened."

"Nothing's changed," Ned groused. "Still kickin' the can down the road."

Nods went round the circle as they all watched her with anxious gazes. "I gave Lydia the certified letter that Shawn served us all with, and she passed it tae her legal department."

"And?" Margot breathed out.

"There's a *possibility* something is wrong."

Voices around her burst into louder questions. James put two arthritic fingers in his mouth and whistled for quiet.

"That's guid news, right?" Theadora's tea sloshed over the side of her cup when she scooted forward. "I just knew it would work oot."

"Lydia is well aware how much we want answers," Paislee said. "We're all under a lot of pressure, but there's hope."

James dunked a muffin in his coffee and took a bite. "If the sale does go through, I'll be retiring."

"You can't!" Paislee cried in dismay.

"No," Ned and Margot said in unison.

"Let's wait and see," Margot pressed.

"Truth is"—James put his coffee down to face them—"what if we keep the building? Well, our leases would all be up at the first of the year anyway. If not this sale, it might be another. Mibbe it's time tae put away me leather tools."

They shared a wall. She couldn't imagine trusting a neighbor as much as she did James—he'd helped her build her shelves and hang the lights. He had a key to her shop.

"You cannae retire." Ned exhaled sadly.

Lourdes exchanged a look with her husband, Jimmy. "We're thinkin' the same thing. We might let our lease go at the end of this year anyway."

"Why?" Margot asked. "Every time I step outside, you have folks in your shop."

"People *browse* cards, but they dinnae really buy. We'll be a lot better off with our day care idea that we can run from our house." Lourdes's voice was tearful but firm.

Jimmy nodded in support of his wife. "We have tae make a living. Our kids will be out of secondary school in the next two years. We need tae consider university costs."

"Kids *are* expensive," James agreed.

Dan sighed and leaned forward in his chair, his forearms on his knees. "Even trying tae have them has wiped our savings and profit. We're in the red. After all this time."

"Things are better now. We cannae give up." Theadora's whole being emanated desperate sorrow. Paislee knew she wasn't just talking about the bakery, but possibly babes as well.

Maybe even her marriage.

She stopped herself from getting up and giving Theadora a

hug—that would raise too many questions for the lass, who was trying to keep her composure. "I don't think any of us should give up. I was talking with Grandpa about this—if we were tae leave before our leases were up, out of fear, then *we* would be the ones breaking the lease, not Shawn Marcus."

"Do ye think that's what this is aboot?" asked Dan. "What kind of man would try tae *trick* us oot of our leases?" He glared at Theadora.

"That's really low," Ned huffed.

"He's a right bastard," James drawled. "Just for that, I'm not goin' anywhere. I'll protest and chain meself tae the door."

"I like that!" Dan and James high-fived. "I'll join ye, James. They can drag me oot of here by the apron straps. Why should the rich get it all?"

Paislee positioned her cup down by her feet. "Before we go all Robin Hood, let's be certain he was trying tae fool us. Has anybody talked tae Shawn?"

Noes sounded around the circle.

What could she share with her friends, while honoring the Leerys' request? "He was at dinner last night."

Theadora straightened fast.

"He was there?" Lourdes said, eyes shining. "What did he say?"

"Did ye ask him aboot the building?" James asked.

"He had tae explain why he's been avoiding us for almost a month!" Ned said.

Dan glowered. "I hope ye forced him tae admit that selling the building would be a mistake."

"And just how would she do that?" Theadora asked her husband, her cheeks red. "Besides, something else might save us."

His jaw clenched.

"It was a pure crazy evening. I barely had a chance for a coherent conversation," Paislee said. "Shawn was seated at the opposite end of the table, and went tae bed after dinner. He wasn't feeling well."

"Oh no," Theadora said softly. A golden curl slid over her shoulder.

"Is it the same thing he had before?" Margot asked. "What is it?"

Paislee shrugged. "I left a message for him tae call me today. He's been discovered, so I hope he'll stop playing games." She felt uncomfortable telling them about Shawn's illness until she'd talked to the man when he was sober.

Dan stood and crossed his arms, walking behind Ned and James, his throat ruddy. "So we're just supposed tae sit and wait? They drink champagne and eat caviar, and we have tae sit on our arses and twiddle our thumbs. They got the cash, they make the rules? That ain't right."

"Calm down, Dan," Theadora implored. She turned to the group. "I'm not the only uptight member in our family." Her voice trembled. "Waiting is torture."

Paislee had an inkling of what Theadora had at stake. She'd hoped that Theadora would announce wonderful news of a baby this morning, but it seemed they'd had crushed hopes again.

Dan rounded behind his wife and put his hand on her shoulder, giving it a squeeze. "We dinnae need their damn money."

Theadora looked down into her cup, ignoring his gesture. Dan returned to his seat.

"Was Lady Leery's daughter there?" Lourdes changed the subject. "Hidden away all these years! Do ye think she was the killer, like the paper made oot?"

"I met her." Aila had been an emotional mess and possibly hiding something. "I don't think she shot Charles, and neither does Detective Inspector Zeffer."

Theadora winced. "I dinnae believe the paper—that article was meant tae shock. I didnae even realize that Lady Leery had a sister, or a nephew. She's always just been the lady of the manor."

"The detective's sure in the hot seat," Ned said. "He dropped off his dry cleanin' yesterday. I asked him aboot the case, but he's not much of a talker."

"I saw the DI go into yer shop," James said to Paislee. "What did he want?"

She thought back to when she'd seen Zeffer last. It felt like years had passed, not less than twenty-four hours. "He had some questions about Charles's death."

"Shot, I read." Ned rubbed the back of his head where it was beginning to bald. "With a rifle. Who doesnae have one of those in the Highlands?"

"Me." Paislee drank her cooling coffee. "I don't know one end from the other. How about you all?" She'd been surprised by how many of the ladies in her Knit and Sip group were familiar with guns.

Theadora waved from her to Dan. "We have two rifles for hunting deer. Me dad taught me tae love the sport. And fresh meat supplements the grocery budget."

"One of six kids growing up," Dan said. "We had a vegetable garden, fished, and hunted everything from squirrel tae stag."

Jimmy put his arm around Lourdes. "We've got that old rifle from your grandpa in the attic. Forgot aboot it until just now." He sounded almost apologetic as he told the group, "I know fresh is better, but we buy our food already processed."

"It's healthier tae live off the land." Margot got up for a refill of hot water. "My ex used tae hunt—thought a good time was going tae the shooting range. I knew our relationship was over when I envisioned his face on the bull's-eye. Cheating bastard."

Dan glanced at his wife and blushed, then stormed into the kitchen, the hinges creaking as it swung back and forth before slowing.

Theadora kept her chin raised. "We got off track. What's our plan, then? Tae stay here and stick it oot?"

Paislee nodded. "According tae Lydia, we're entitled to stay until thirty days after the sale, which hasn't happened yet. So, yeah, we stay put. I plan tae to see if this was a calculated step by Shawn tae get us out."

Theadora burst into tears. "He wouldnae do that."

Margot stroked their friend's back. "Ah, lass, the medicine makes you emotional and weepy. It will pass."

The fertility medicine, Margot meant.

The door swung toward them as Dan returned from the kitchen, his face rugged with anger and defeat. "We're done. I'm callin' the clinic."

"Don't, Dan," Theadora pleaded, half-rising from her chair before dropping back. "I told you things will get better."

Margot rushed to Dan and held out her hand. "Let's talk aboot this later, after the meeting. Join us, please?"

Dan gulped and shifted to meet their eyes, darting a glance to the front of the shop and the customers. He allowed Margot to direct him to his chair. Once seated, his leg shook with emotion.

Paislee empathized with him and studied the others in the group. Everyone had grown quiet. Ned shifted in his chair, as did James. Jimmy and Lourdes continued to hold hands. Dan's jaw clenched tight and he studied his fingernails, his gaze on his wedding band.

The tension in the bakery was hot enough to fry dough. There was no way to fix this situation. She'd thought sharing what she knew about the leases would help, but things were worse.

Theadora glanced at the clock. "It's almost nine."

Dan rumbled, "This meeting is adjourned."

Paislee jumped to her feet with relief. Margot hugged both Dan and Theadora, murmuring to them. Dan yanked away to the safety of his kitchen. Out of habit, Paislee left the bakery through the front door, shoulder to shoulder with James.

"Something's up with the kiddos," the old man muttered once they reached the sidewalk. "Not lookin' guid."

Paislee agreed. "I'd hoped that I could help."

"They're yoked together. It's their journey tae find oot if they still work as a team—nobody can do it for 'em. We'll be there how we can."

She blinked away tears.

James kissed her cheek and unlocked the front door of his leather shop. "Stay in touch, lass. Soon as ye know for sure aboot the building."

"Aye." Paislee pulled her key from her pocket to open Cashmere Crush but then smacked her forehead as she remembered the question she'd had for Margot. She retraced her steps down the crooked sidewalk to the lab door and knocked.

The heavy wood door opened, and Margot smiled welcoming her in. The scent of sandalwood permeated the small space. The lobby of the lab was all white, even Margot's desk and phone. The only color was the silver computer. "Hey—didnae I just see you?" she teased.

"You have a second?" Paislee stepped all the way inside and shut the door.

"Sure. Have a seat." Margot gestured to a white metal chair. "Are ye here aboot Theadora and Dan? God, it breaks me heart. They love each other so much, but this situation—damn Shawn Marcus—will be the death of them."

"It's really sad," Paislee agreed. Shawn had no right to destroy others to save himself—she'd tell him so as soon as he called her back. Surely he'd be up soon?

Margot slipped into her white lab coat that was her office uniform. "Lourdes and Jimmy have tried tae counsel them, but . . ."

Paislee didn't want to hear too much and raised her hand. "Actually, that's not why I'm here. I'd like your expertise."

"Oh?" Margot sat down at her desk. "Are you all right?"

"Yes, fine." Paislee fiddled with her keys. "Is it possible for a rare blood type tae interfere with fertility?"

"You've got me thoroughly confused. I dinnae think Theadora and Dan have unusual blood types."

"No, not them," Paislee clarified. "I'm just curious and thought you'd be more reliable than Google."

Margot scratched the question on a pad of paper, her brow furrowed. "All right. Not what I thought then. Can rare blood type affect fertility? I have a friend at the clinic I'll check with."

"You do? In that case, what about rare blood types and kidney disease—would that make it difficult tae find a compatible donor? As well as affect fertility."

"What's going on, Paislee?" Margot searched her face, and Paislee looked away.

"I'll explain as soon as I can. Thank you, Margot."

Paislee's phone dinged a text, and she pulled the mobile from her cardigan pocket. It was from Lydia. Her smile fled.

*Gavin wants to meet.*

# Chapter 16

Paislee had no sooner unlocked the door to Cashmere Crush than she sent an urgent text back to her bestie—*I am not going out with a man who is twice my age, no matter how charming he is!*

*Chicken. What should I tell him?*

She halted in mid mental rant, tossing her purse on the shelf next to the cashmere vest, and reconsidered. Hadn't she just told Grandpa that Gavin Thornton, accountant for the Leery family, would know their true financial state? This might be the perfect way to find out about the Leerys' finances. Not just Shannon's, but Shawn's.

*I don't want to get drinks.*

Lydia texted back. *Lunch?*

Solving the money riddle might lead back to why Charles was killed. Gavin could tell her whether or not the Leery Estate benefited from Charles's death, if she asked the right way. She remembered Grandpa telling her to be subtle.

*Can't we just have a meeting at his office, without lunch? It doesn't have to be a date then. We can pretend a misunderstanding.*

*What are you up to?*

Paislee sent an image of an angel emoji. *I have a few questions, that's all. How about you and I have lunch after? Anything from Grant?*

*Not yet. You were the best date I've ever had* ♥ *I'll call Gavin TTYL*

Paislee put her phone away and prepared for a day at Cashmere Crush. She prepped the till, tuned into a soft music station on her laptop, and straightened the front of her shop to make sure that her bespoke sweaters and blankets were shown at their tempting best. She returned to her stool by the register and picked up her cashmere vest to complete three more rows. The project was nearly done.

Why hadn't Shawn called yet? Had Midge changed her mind about giving him the note? She'd text Hamish, who hadn't been in touch since yesterday. Her business phone rang, and she set the yarn aside. No wonder it took so long to get things done—there were constant interruptions.

"Cashmere Crush. May I help you?"

"Can I speak tae Paislee Shaw? This is Arran Mulholland."

The solicitor! Her body tensed. "This is she."

"Could you stop by for a few minutes around eleven? It seems that the Fisher family's attorney is approaching the idea of a lawsuit rather aggressively. I'd like for you tae file a statement."

"Oh—uh, sure. Of course. I thought we were meeting Monday for a consultation?"

"If we can counter their proposal today, we willnae need tae meet on Monday." His voice sounded confident enough. "See you then?"

"Aye. Thanks." She ended the call and nervously walked around her shop, taking inventory of her yarn and worktables, blankets and sweaters. Aggressive? Did that mean that they wanted all her assets?

An internal voice she liked to think of as Gran told her to calm down.

Her mobile dinged a text. Lydia. *Gavin says to be at his office at one then we can go to lunch after. I told him I had a file from Silverstein's to drop off. See you at quarter to one. This better be legit.*

*Any word from Grant?*

*PAISLEE!*

She spent the next thirty minutes with a customer, showing the differences between knitting needle sizes and what might be best for a beginner. She sold the young woman a book and some lavender yarn—the same color as the lavender bougainvillea arch at the Leery Estate.

Being busy distracted her from worrying about the meeting with Arran, which was in less than an hour. Fordythe was being sued because of her actions.

No wonder Hamish hadn't texted or emailed.

She'd run the scenario that day at the estate over and over in her head. She'd had to keep Holly safe, which meant not opening that door. Why didn't the girl's parents understand that?

Paislee called the Leery Estate for Shawn, but the phone kept ringing. Odd. Unless they were all outside? The property was vast.

It was early yet to call Amelia.

She sat behind the register and snatched the vest off the counter. In time, she hummed along to Belle and Sebastian as she slipped a loop of yarn over her wooden needles. *What should I do, Gran? I feel caught between a rock and a hard place.*

The front door opened. Paislee wasn't the least surprised, given how her day had been, to see the broad shoulders and russet hair of Detective Inspector Zeffer.

"Hello," she said.

The detective strode toward her, unsmiling. "How was the party?"

She lowered the vest and knitting needles.

Paislee knew that it galled the DI to even ask. "Interesting. The meal was a million courses long, and they use real crystal and porcelain china. Two mains. We had the Leery venison sausage. Very tasty. The chandelier is enormous. No wonder they have staff." Why hadn't Midge or Malcolm answered the phone?

He stared at her deadpan, and she held his gaze.

"You know I dinnae care aboot the fish course, right?"

She held his gaze. He wanted information. So did she. "Aye. I noticed all the guns in the cabinet were gone."

He half-smiled at that. "They're at the station."

"The butler told me. Malcolm." Paislee picked up her yarn and needles. "He seemed certain that none of them were the rifle that shot Charles."

Zeffer stroked his clean-shaven chin. "Perhaps. In any event, I willnae release them until the case is closed."

She didn't doubt the butler had a weapon hidden away somewhere. "Have you discovered more about Charles's mates from London? You said he had an arrest sheet as long as your arm."

"That's right, I did say that." Zeffer considered. "Two known associates of Charles bought train tickets from London tae Nairn. Bart and Joey Pickett."

"When?"

"Tuesday, before the shooting."

Her heart pounded. Why was he sharing this with her? "Can you arrest them?"

"If they committed a crime. We're searching for them now to ask a few questions," he said.

Paislee blew out a breath. "The Leerys had security guards around the house last night—I'm so glad. But with Charles dead, maybe those *associates* returned tae London?"

Zeffer drummed his fingers on the counter. "How did the family behave at dinner? Polite? Friendly?" He watched her face. "Angry?"

Her turn to give a little. "Shawn and Aila were like two cats in a bag, as Gran would say."

"Over what?"

"Aila accused Shawn of setting her up with the anonymous phone call, and he accused her of trying tae talk Charles out of . . ." Paislee trailed off. Did the detective know about Shawn's illness?

"Yes?"

She swallowed, her mouth dry. "None of the family liked Charles."

"If you know something that can help me find who killed Charles, you need tae tell me," he said stiffly.

"I know, I know. I need tae talk tae Shawn Marcus."

"Your landlord?"

"Aye." She crumbled. "What I'm going tae tell you needs tae be in confidence."

Zeffer raised his hands in frustration. "I'm an officer of the law. My job is tae catch criminals—in this case, a killer—I dinnae keep secrets."

"Shawn hasn't been in the best of health." The door to her shop opened, and her shoulders relaxed with relief at the reprieve. "I don't think they're related, but I'll tell you one way or the other later. I have a meeting with a solicitor at eleven."

"For what?" His brow arched.

She explained the lawsuit as a woman and her young daughter meandered in and browsed the sweaters. "I'm afraid of losing my shop in a legal battle. It's already under threat, as you know. Then I've a meeting with an accountant at one. I'll be in touch after."

Paislee slid off her stool and stowed her vest project under the counter, not giving him much choice but to end the conversation.

"If I dinnae hear from you, I'll track you down. Understand?"

She blew a tuft of hair from her eyes. "I said I would, Detective! Unlike you, who never—" Paislee bit her tongue.

The woman smiled at Paislee and the DI uncertainly. She had reddish-brown hair and round amber eyes. "Welcome tae Cashmere Crush," Paislee said.

"Hiya," she said, perusing some pattern books.

"I have tae go," Paislee murmured to the DI, who hadn't moved.

Zeffer's jaw clenched tight. He dipped his head to the woman and left without another word, banging the door closed behind him.

"Sairy about that."

The woman grinned. "Testy fella."

"He means well," Paislee said with a wrinkle of her nose. "Can I help you find something?"

"We just moved here from Inverness," the woman said. Her daughter was a mini replica, she would guess about six years old. "Is there a crime problem?"

"Not as much as a big city." She didn't share her opinion on the growing pains of Nairn.

"I know enough tae knit a blanket, but I'd hoped tae try something a wee bit more challenging." She lifted their joined hands. "This is Suzannah. I'm Blaise O'Connor. My husband is a golf pro at the resort. I discovered your shop online. It's really adorable."

"Nairn is a friendly town." Going with her instincts that this woman would be a good fit with the group, she said, "I offer a Thursday night Knit and Sip, where crafters of all levels get together." At least for the next month.

"Sip as in wine?" Blaise asked hopefully.

"Your beverage of choice," she said. "The ladies sometimes stop by during the week just tae chat."

"Once Suzannah is in class, that would be great. We plan on starting her next year at Tilda Swinton's school."

That meant money. Blaise and Lydia ought to hit it off. "Do you have a house already?"

"We're renting until we find the area we like."

"My best friend is an estate agent—let me give you her phone number. She's really terrific at matching people with their dream home." Paislee went back to the counter, retrieved her purse from the bottom shelf, and dug through her wallet for one of Lydia's business cards. "Here you are."

"Oh, she's lovely," Blaise said, admiring Lydia's smiling face from the glossy card.

"And nice. But she can't knit or sing, so we have tae love her anyway," she said with a chuckle.

"Well, I'd like this pattern on a knit cap with a hole for a ponytail, and some emerald yarn."

Paislee placed the items in a paper bag with the Cashmere Crush interlocking C's logo on the side. She gestured to the candy dish and waited for Mum's nod before offering Suzannah a piece of toffee.

"Thank you," the cutie said, making Paislee's heart ping.

She remembered Brody being so young and sweet. Now? "My son is ten and perfecting his pout."

"Oh, Suz is on her best behavior right now because I promised her a cookie from the bakery if she behaved."

Blaise and Suzannah left, and Paislee hoped she'd made a new customer.

She noted the time with a pang of alarm. Quarter till eleven! The lawyer—she absolutely *could not* be late. Paislee hung a Closed sign on the door and locked up, leaving out the back. She stopped on the stoop in a panic, staring at her empty parking spot in the alley. Where was her car? She expelled a worried breath and looked to the right. The tea shop!

Relief filled her. She hustled down the alley and hopped into her Juke, typing Arran's address into the GPS. Where was Dan and Theadora's SUV?

Minutes later, Paislee parked at Arran's modern brick building. She entered a white, glass, and chrome office, where a receptionist waited behind a pristine desk with only a phone and thin computer monitor on top. There were a water cooler and three white leather seats with decorative chrome bars.

"I'm Paislee Shaw," she said to the model-thin woman.

"Guid morning! Can I get ye something tae drink while you wait?"

"Naw, thanks."

"Mr. Mulholland will be just a moment."

Paislee hovered on the edge of the seat, afraid to break the artsy chair. She checked her phone. Nothing from Hamish. Should she text him that she was now at the solicitor's?

An office door painted glossy white opened, and Arran stepped out. He'd quit drinking, according to Mary Beth, and spent more time golfing which would explain his trim physique.

"Paislee—hello. Hold my calls, Cora."

Arran led her into the inner sanctum of his office, where dark wood–and–brass shelves lined the wall.

Photos of Mary Beth and his adorable twin girls added warmth to the room. A tall plant with green-and-orange leaves flourished in the corner, and two brown leather chairs faced each other.

He sat in one and gestured toward the other.

Paislee joined him and folded her hands over her lap, feeling way out of her depth, and nervous besides. "What's going on?"

"I know Hamish McCall from the golf club," he said calmly.

Her pulse skipped.

Arran leaned forward. "He mentioned this morning that his school was being sued. I told him right away that I had a meeting with a possible client Monday morning, and he suggested that if the client was you that we meet sooner, for your protection."

How awkward. And sweet. Mostly awkward.

"Tell me everything," Arran said.

Paislee briefly closed her eyes, caught in the surreal moment of when Charles had crashed through the hedge. She retold the tale to Arran as precisely as she could, and wet her dry lips when she was done.

Arran shifted, the leather chair creaking. "It sounds like you did everything right. Some people are sue-happy and think they're entitled tae money they aren't. They see a corporation, which is faceless, and want a piece of the pie. The Fishers are both unemployed, but Mr. Fisher was in Edinburgh Wednesday for a job interview. Mibbe this seems like an easier way tae bring in cash."

Money? She wasn't faceless. "I've lost my chaperone rights." To some it might not be a big deal, but Paislee had worked Brody's whole life to set a good example.

"We'll get those back." Arran gave her a blank piece of paper. "Can you write down what happened?"

"Sure. I already did this for the school, too."

"I'll contact Hamish—dinnae worry. I'll take on your case, pro bono. It's nice tae help the guid guys."

Her first reaction was to say no, that she was fine, but she had too much at risk. "What—Arran, I don't think . . ." Paislee blinked back grateful tears. He would take her case on without cost to her. Did she have a choice but to accept his assistance? She couldn't lose her business or house, and she wasn't made of money. "Thanks."

"Just write down yer statement."

Arran walked out of his office while Paislee wrote down what had happened, doing her best to be clear. Her mind kept going back to Graham's hat.

Ten minutes later, Arran ushered her from his building. "I'll be in touch. If ye think of anything that might help the case, the card I gave you has my mobile number."

"Thank you so much."

Paislee floated to her car—how kind of Arran to help her. Then again, he hadn't given her much choice. She'd ask Mary Beth what his favorite color was and make him a cashmere sweater.

She turned the engine on and let the car idle. Why hadn't Shawn called her back? Was Midge protecting Shawn by not giving him the note?

Paislee phoned the Leery Estate. This time she left a curt message, saying that she'd like to retrieve her shawl. She also wanted Shawn to call her. Right away.

Ending the call, she then focused on what she wanted exactly from the man. Stop the eviction, first of all—but she also wanted to know what Shawn had seen behind the hedge that day.

Shawn had been the last person to see Charles alive.

# Chapter 17

Paislee practically flew up the back steps and unlocked the rear entrance to her shop, tripping over her purse in her haste to answer the ringing phone—she lunged to reach it before the customer hung up. "Cashmere Crush!"

"Mum! It's your son, Brody."

She eyed the phone with a smirk. "I only have the one. What's up?"

"Edwyn invited me tae his house tomorrow. Can I?"

Sunday? Paislee bit her tongue before she reminded him that it was their day off to spend together. Of course he'd want to hang out with his friends. Tears threatened at his innocent request. She cleared her throat. "I'll have tae speak with his dad first." Bennett Maclean seemed like a nice man. He'd even chaperoned on the field trip to the Leery estate.

"I have Mr. Maclean's phone number." Brody's voice resonated with excitement. "I knew ye'd say it was okay."

"I'll call him after work today, all right?" Paislee still had to meet Gavin with Lydia. "I'm not sure when I'll be home. I have some errands."

"What aboot the kite?" His jubilant tone dropped like a rock. "We were going tae fly it at the beach! Grandpa helped me make the dragon teeth really sharp."

"Is it done already?" Paislee blew her bangs back and leaned her elbows on the counter. "Brilliant. I thought we'd take it out tomorrow."

"We should go today instead," Brody said. "You'll be able tae wash socks all day tomorrow without me gettin' in your hair."

"How thoughtful of you," she sniffed, half-annoyed, half-wistful. "I'll see ye later, love."

"But can I go?"

"Aye, if his dad says he really wants tae spend the day with you—should I warn him that you're a handful?"

"I'll be guid," Brody promised solemnly.

"You better be, or you won't be invited back." She'd make sure that during dinner tonight they discuss proper manners for a guest in someone's home.

"Thanks, Mum!" Brody hung up.

Paislee hunkered behind the counter with her knitting, managing another row on the cinnamon cashmere vest as she uneasily watched the time and formulated practice questions for Gavin in her head. She glared at both her mobile and then her shop phone, willing them to ring and give her answers. She'd texted Amelia, who wanted to talk later. Hamish, Shawn, Lydia, Grant—she'd welcome anybody. All these lines in the water and she was stuck in her shop.

When someone pounded at her back door, she nearly had a heart attack. She jumped from her stool and opened it, thinking it might be a forgotten wool order.

Dan's earnest face greeted her. "Hey! Have ye seen Theadora? She isnae answering her phone."

Paislee tugged him inside by the arm. "She's not here. Are ye doing all right?"

"After being such a jerk this morning, ye mean?"

Paislee bit her lip and didn't answer. "Things are very tense right now. For all of us."

"Have ye heard from Shawn Marcus?" His body bristled.

"Nothing. Not from Lydia about the letter, either."

"Thea's probably at the specialist." His shoulders bowed deject-
edly. "I know how much she wants kids. If we cannae do it natu-
rally, I'm happy tae adopt a dozen. Thea said she'd talked tae you
the other day. Was it aboot wanting tae be a surrogate?"

She thought of their emotional conversation about being pregnant. "No. A surrogate?"

"Just tae prove she can carry a babe." Dan's voice cracked. "I
ken how she feels. Like we failed somehow. But, I asked her—how
could she do that and not love that baby. It would tear her apart in
the end. Maybe even me, too."

Ah. Paislee lifted the jar of hard candy off the counter and offered it to him. "Why don't ye meet her there? Bring flowers, surprise her."

He exhaled. "Paislee, we've worked so damn hard on that tea
shop. Five years. It was our dream and now?" Dan chose a silver-
wrapped candy. "I'm scared I'm going tae lose her tae some jackass
with a Mercedes." He stuffed the uneaten candy in his front pocket.

He'd said the tea shop was in the red, which was hard to believe
considering their location. She imagined that their extra money
went to the specialists. "She loves you, Dan. Let her know you're
there for her, and she won't care about the rest."

"I'm such an idiot sometimes—thanks!" Dan hugged her, and
Paislee patted his strong back. He left out the front door in a rush of
energy, and Paislee said a prayer that he and Theadora would find
their way. All she could think of was how much Brody meant
to her.

Paislee picked up her knitting. Had Margot heard anything
back yet from her friend at the fertility clinic? It would just take a
minute to check. She put the project away and opened the door of
Cashmere Crush to see Dan running out of the florist shop across
the street with roses in his hand. *Good luck.*

She hurried a few doors down to the lab and went inside. It was
empty, though Margot sat at her desk, on the phone. When she saw
Paislee, she hung up.

"I was just going tae call you." Margot showed Paislee the pad of paper she'd taken notes on. The page was filled with scribbles.

"What did you find out?" She took a seat before the desk.

"Rare blood types *can* have a harder time with fertility—but like I told you, that isnae the case with . . ." Margot's nose scrunched. "People who are A positive, which is the most fertile—generally speaking." She dipped her head toward the bakery.

"And what if the person had kidney disease?"

She read her notes. "It would depend on the type, but it could be a factor. Is the person male or female?"

"Male."

Margot sat back and lifted a brow smugly. "Would this be the same male that we all noticed was so ill last year? And you say is not well again?"

Paislee's cheeks heated, and she was grateful nobody else was around. "Sh. You can't say anything, Margot."

"Why is it a secret?" Margot spread her hands to the sides.

"His family values their privacy. And with Charles being killed, the Leerys have enough tae deal with right now."

"Why is that?" Margot rounded the desk and leaned against it, arms crossed, her lab coat hanging loose. "Blood types. Family. Oh! Was Charles going tae donate a kidney tae Shawn? Oh no. That's terrible—Charles is dead. Or is it a lost cause? Was Charles a donor?"

"I can't answer any of that!" Paislee got to her feet in a rush.

Margot straightened and grabbed Paislee's wrist. "Why were ye asking?"

"Curiosity. Before Aila arrived on the scene, Shawn was the only heir." Paislee tugged free. "He should've married and had a child."

"Hmm. You're right. His duty would be tae carry on the Leery name. I never wanted kids. You ever think about having more bairns?"

"No!" Paislee's heart sped with panic at all that implied. "No, I need tae do a good job with Brody—that's enough for me."

"Shayla Leery and John Thomas only had Charles. Could be the Leerys just aren't a fertile bunch." Margot shrugged.

That made sense. "Shawn and Aila *are* twenty years apart."

"What did you think of Aila? From the grainy picture, she's pretty, but not like her mum."

Aila, always second best in the Leery family. Not a son, not first born, not as pretty. "I promise when this is over, we'll have a cup of tea and a long blether." Paislee inched toward the door before something escaped her mouth she'd regret. "Thanks!"

Paislee returned to Cashmere Crush. Margot's confirmation that Shawn would have a hard time reproducing not only because of his rare blood type but also his kidney disease offered an explanation of why he hadn't had children. What did he have against marriage?

Was Shawn's life at risk because of his illness? Had Shannon brought Aila into the family for dual reasons—first to try to save Shawn, second to inherit the estate?

And how did Charles fit in? If something had happened to Shawn *and* Aila, would he have been next in line? Would that be worth killing him over?

Paislee brought out her knitting project and completed another row.

What if she were to just drop by the estate to pick up her shawl? Surely Malcolm would have to let her in. Shawn might be there, or Shannon. At the very least she could talk to Midge. The maid had to know what was going on in the house the night before Charles was shot. Why hadn't Shawn called her?

She heard a little voice in her head say that when one barged uninvited to the home of a peer, one probably shouldn't go empty-handed, so Paislee chose a lightweight navy cashmere scarf in a lace pattern, wrapping it in tissue, and then a Cashmere Crush gift bag. She bagged a soft pink cap with a flower tassel, a pretty complement to Midge's brown hair, as a gift for the maid's kindness.

Paislee phoned Lydia as she locked up Cashmere Crush, leaving a note directing customers to her website. "On my way—do you mind if I drive?"

"Naw. See you in a few!" Lydia hung up before Paislee could ask her about Grant.

Fifteen minute later, Paislee reached the Silverstein Real Estate Agency where Lydia and Grant waited outside. They each wore a black power suit and were in an animated conversation. He waved at Paislee and ducked inside when Paislee parked her Juke.

Her eight-year-old car was a dinosaur compared to Lydia's sporty red Mercedes, but her friend just climbed in the passenger side, a black leather tote at her feet, and gave her a kiss on the cheek.

"Good tae see you—now, what's up?"

"What do you mean?"

"I know you, Paislee Ann, and you want tae visit Gavin for a reason."

"That's true—but first, what were you and Grant talking about just now? Something tae do with the letter?"

Lydia bit her lower lip. "Aboot that . . ."

Paislee stayed in park and stared at Lydia. "What?"

"Grant thinks they're fake."

Her stomach clenched. "Fake?"

"The eviction notice should be on file with a solicitor's office, but none is listed. Also, it should have been mailed to you in order for it to be legal. No postage on the envelope. I only thought of it because I had to sign for a certified letter the other day."

"Shawn hand delivered them." Paislee shook her head, not understanding. Her entire life had been turned upside down. Joy that her business was safe immediately soured as she realized what Shawn had dragged them all through. "That jerk!"

"I never questioned the validity of the sale." Lydia's mouth twisted in self-reproach. "My fault for not figuring this oot sooner."

"Here I was feeling sorry for him." Paislee smacked the steering wheel.

"Why would *you* feel bad?" Lydia demanded.

"He's sick."

"What?" Lydia tilted her head and leaned back in the passenger seat.

"Do you remember me telling you that Shawn Marcus needed a kidney transplant, on the way home from the party?"

Lydia's cheeks turned as bright red as her hair. "It's a wee bit fuzzy. He needs a kidney transplant? Your landlord? He was more drunk than me last night."

Five minutes later, and after many "Are you freaking kidding me?" outbursts, Lydia calmed down and gave Paislee Gavin's business address.

"So now what?" Paislee plugged it into the GPS.

"I dinnae ken. What do you want from Gavin? God, I'm glad you're driving. I might have two drinks at lunch. What a mess. *Why?*"

"I've been trying tae talk tae Shawn since last night, but he's not returning my calls. Shawn drunkenly told me he sold the building because he needed money. Charles wanted to 'sell' him a kidney for a million pounds."

"Awful. Gavin wants tae treat us tae lunch after I drop off the Benedetto file." She patted her tote. "I hinted that you really just wanted tae see his office—it overlooks the ocean with the best view. Flirt a little."

"I don't flirt, and now I don't even need tae make a reason up. Let's ask him, as the accountant for the Leerys, about the sale of the Market Street building."

"I don't know, Paislee," Lydia said. "Gavin is a verra important person tae the Silversteins and a cool guy. Let's tread carefully."

They reached the five-story cement building that faced the Moray Firth and scored a choice spot on the street. Salty ocean breezes ruffled Lydia's spikes and the hem of Paislee's white blouse.

Lydia pushed open the lobby door, and a rush of floral incense wafted toward them. A lone receptionist sat at a desk, typing away on a desktop computer. A bank of silver elevators was to the right.

"Good day," the receptionist said. "May I help you?"

"We're here tae see Gavin Thornton. I'm from Silverstein Real Estate Agency." Lydia walked confidently toward the elevators.

"I'll buzz him tae let him know you're on your way."

Lydia smiled and pressed the button. "Thanks."

The doors slid back, and she and Lydia stepped inside. "Let me take the lead, all right?"

"Sure." Would Gavin already know about the property? After a month of fearing the worst, she had no idea what to expect. Paislee swallowed nervously when the car dinged, and they got off on the fifth floor. There were three offices to the left with closed doors, and one to the right, the best of the lot. Gavin Thornton Accountant was etched in gold on the frosted glass door.

Lydia knocked and entered. "Gavin?"

Paislee followed on her heels.

Gavin stood in front of a large window that overlooked the water, a phone to his ear, his jacket off and slung over a black leather office chair.

"Malcolm, send me the bill. I'll take care of it—she doesnae need tae know."

Lydia knocked again.

Gavin whirled around and smiled when he saw them. "I have tae go. Mind what I said aboot extra security. The DI told me the Pickett brothers could be in town."

Bart and Joey Pickett? Charles's mates from London. She shivered, glad that Gavin had ordered extra security. How sweet of him to cover the bill—just as she surmised, this was not a prosperous time for the estate.

Paislee stepped into the fancy office decorated in steel and glass. Pictures of Gavin at the Leery Estate, of him with Shannon, and of him with Graham, Aila, and Shannon at an event were displayed on the glass shelves with pride.

He was the kind of handsome that bettered with age—his silver added to his distinguished look.

"What can I do for you ladies? Have a seat."

They did, and Lydia said, "You're going tae think I'm ridiculous—"

"Never," he assured her.

"Well, I sold the Benedetto property this morning." Lydia took a file from her tote bag and placed it on Gavin's desk.

"That was asking price five million—what'd ye get for it?" Gavin crossed his arms.

"Five million pounds."

They slapped hands. "Well done, you," he said.

"So I just wanted tae make sure their financials were all in order?" Lydia sounded uncertain.

"Spending your commission already?" Gavin chuckled.

Lydia gave a little shrug. "I want tae make sure I'm not dreaming—last night was brilliant, and it could've been the champagne."

"It was a magical evening—congratulations on your win. What does that make for you? Four times?"

Lydia blushed, and Paislee couldn't be prouder of her as she said, "Natalya has been an amazing mentor."

"She thinks very highly of you, too. Did you enjoy the celebration at the estate, Paislee?" Gavin's kind expression was that of a fond uncle, not someone desiring a date with a single mom. So, what did he really want from her?

"Very much—though I left my shawl there. I plan tae stop by and pick it up later."

"Mibbe call first?" Gavin suggested. "The family's been oot of sorts with Charles's death hanging over them."

If she waited for someone to return her call from the estate, it might never happen. She didn't commit one way or the other but walked to the glass shelves, lifting a steel-framed photo of him and Shannon Leery from about twenty years earlier. The array of pictures revealed his affection for the woman. "This is lovely."

"I keep that one close as a reminder." Gavin rubbed his chin, his manner self-mocking.

"Of what?" Love, Paislee thought romantically.

"That was the night I asked Shannon tae marry me. I promised tae love and cherish her, tae give her my fortune. She broke up with me the next day."

Paislee set the picture down in surprise. "But why?"

His green eyes shimmered. "She loved her first husband—but he was awful tae her, so she decided never tae marry again. Love, yes, but on her terms—and nothing permanent."

She must have passed that attitude to Shawn.

"Did you know her when she was married?" Paislee returned to her seat.

"No. I met her later. She'd already built a pretty fantastic reputation by then, and I was halfway in love before our first kiss."

"That's terribly romantic," Lydia said. "And tragic."

"Crossed stars, I suppose, but I dinnae regret a thing." He sank into the leather chair behind his desk, exuding confidence.

"Malcolm also cares for her with that devotion," Paislee observed. "And Graham."

"Shannon requires it. She won't give you her heart, though she demands yours. Isnae fair, but it's the price of being part of her life." Gavin gestured at the display. "I have no regrets—she's the love of me life. I only wish she'd let me do more for her."

Was he alluding to Shannon's financial situation? Would he know if Charles had heirs? Did he know about the sale of the building?

Paislee was on the verge of asking about Charles when Lydia leaned forward, her hands clasped in her lap. "You know that Paislee is a client of mine, as well? She owns a custom-sweater business on Market Street."

His brow furrowed. "A row of businesses—historic brick building?"

"Yes." Paislee pressed her palm over her trembling knee, suddenly anxious at possibly getting answers. "Cashmere Crush is on the corner across from the Lion's Mane pub. Opposite end from Theadora's Tea Shoppe."

"Isnae that block owned by the Leery Corporation?"

Lydia exchanged a look with Paislee. "Well, the building was supposedly for sale."

Gavin straightened from his relaxed posture. "Oh?"

Lydia gave Paislee a nod. "Go ahead. Tell him what's happened."

At last! "Twenty-eight days ago, Shawn Marcus—he's my landlord—handed 'certified' letters tae each of the business owners there, giving us thirty days tae leave. We were told the building had been sold, and that nullified our leases."

Gavin turned a shade of off-white, and his friendly expression darkened.

"I don't know if you realize how important foot traffic is tae all of us on that strip, but we were devastated." Paislee paused for a calming breath. "We tried tae locate Shawn—Mr. Marcus—but he'd disappeared. He wasn't returning our calls—he still isn't."

"I see," he said between gritted teeth.

"So I told Lydia." Paislee motioned to her best friend.

"There's no record of a sale online," Lydia explained. "I checked daily, and finally I gave the document Paislee and the other businesses received tae Grant in legal. The certified letter appears to have been a . . . fake."

Gavin dug his fingers into his thick silver-gray hair. "Shawn. That bastard."

Paislee couldn't agree more. "Last year we'd noticed that Shawn wasn't well, and at the party I found out about his kidney transplant from Aila, how it didn't take, and that Charles was going tae donate one, for a price, but then he double-crossed him, according tae Shawn. He believes Aila and Charles were working against him. I've been calling him all day, and he's not returning my messages."

"What a can of worms." Gavin exhaled and leaned back in his chair, swiveling to look out his window at the ocean. He glanced at Paislee. "You havenae moved?"

"No. I had the worst thought that if we'd have moved, *we* would have been the ones tae break the lease."

"Dinnae move. None of you should move. Good God. Let me do some poking around."

Paislee released a pent-up breath.

Gavin tapped a calendar on his desk. "The last thirty days, Shawn and Charles were working with a transplant team tae make sure the living donation for the kidney was a success. These things are rather complicated. And expensive, if ye want it done right."

Medical issues had kept Shawn out of sight.

Gavin pursed his lips. "I won't speak ill of the dead, but I'll tell you this—I dinnae blame Joey and Bart Pickett for shooting Charles. My only regret is it was done on Leery property."

"They did it?" Paislee asked. The DI hadn't been so sure.

"I spoke with Detective Inspector Zeffer an hour ago, and he seemed tae believe it likely." Gavin scowled with distaste. "Charles had let the brothers take the rap for his insurance scam, fleecing old folks out of their retirement. Can you imagine?"

"Awful!" Lydia exclaimed.

Paislee inhaled slowly to quell her anxiety. Shawn was no peach, either. Two genetically sour peas in a pod. "Shawn said that Charles was *selling* him his kidney—for a million pounds. He tried tae sell the building, but the buyer fell through."

"His mother footed the bill. Auctioned off an Impressionist painting worth quite a bit of money tae do it." Gavin shot to his feet, his hands to his sides. "How could he go behind Shannon's back like that? She's done so much for him. Aila too."

"Shawn thinks Aila convinced Charles *not* tae give him the kidney," she said.

"I doot that. Aila wouldnae risk making Shannon unhappy." Gavin strode toward the window to look out at the Moray Firth, then turned back to them with concern. "Listen, ladies, do ye mind if we do lunch next week? I'd like tae dig into this building situation. Shawn's been oot of touch today, but if you hear from him, have him call me? It's urgent."

Paislee brought her purse strap over her shoulder. She was so mad at her landlord yet worried, too. "Gavin, will Shawn die without a new kidney?"

Lydia gasped at the blatant question.

"Och, no. Shawn's spoiled, lass." Gavin stepped to his desk and his phone. "He expected everything tae be handed tae him. He's got a head for business but prefers his whisky."

Shawn had proven that he was willing to cheat the system with his fake eviction notices, and frame his own sister for murder. He'd discovered he couldn't shortcut his health.

"There are other options available tae someone with kidney disease. They're not as pleasant, but he'll be alive." Gavin shrugged, his expression doubtful.

Paislee rose. Shawn didn't have an immediate death sentence, unless he chose to ignore the doctors. "Thank you." Her gaze landed on the picture of Graham, Shannon, Aila, and Gavin. All four exuded love centered around Shannon. Shawn wasn't in it.

The phone in his office rang. Gavin held up a finger and answered it. "Excuse me. With the Pickett brothers on the loose, I'm trying tae get new security installed at the estate. Shannon's fighting me every step."

# Chapter 18

Paislee and Lydia hadn't gone two paces from Gavin's office before the accountant opened his door. "Paislee!"

Paislee stopped and faced him. "Yes?"

"Shannon wants tae know if you can visit her for tea at the estate right now? Since we've missed lunch." He glanced at Lydia. "I'll owe you one, love."

"A favor owed from Gavin Thornton? I'll take it!" Lydia blew him a kiss and walked the few feet to the elevators, pressing the call button.

"She doesn't have tae go tae all that trouble," Paislee insisted. "I can get a sandwich later."

"You willnae want tae miss out on Shannon's basil scones. Besides, you need your shawl." Gavin resumed talking into the phone and shut his door, his shoulder visible through the frosted glass.

"Wow," Lydia murmured when the elevator arrived. "A private tea with Lady Leery. Look at you, Ms. Shaw."

Not as exciting as it would have been before Wednesday, and dead Charles. "What if the Pickett brothers are around?"

"Gavin's taking care of security. It doesnae make sense that they'd want tae harm anyone at the estate. Charles was the one they were after, and they got him."

Once Lydia was in, Paislee pressed the button for the lobby. "I wish Shawn would just call me already!" She clenched her fist. "I hope he's at the estate for tea."

"You deserve to rake him over the coals. Twice."

"Shawn must've seen the Pickett brothers. He was back there at the same time Charles was shot." Something about them being responsible just didn't sit right. "I'll feel better when they're caught. The rifle found. All that."

"Proof?" Lydia teased. "The DI is rubbing off on you."

"Don't tell *him* that." Paislee bowed her head and laughed. "I'd never live it down."

They exited and strolled through the marble lobby, waving goodbye to the receptionist.

"Gavin Thornton does very well." Lydia gestured to the ocean view from the sidewalk. "It wouldnae hurt tae get a drink with the man."

"He's just admitted he's in love with Shannon."

"Excellent point. Why ask you then?"

"My guess? Shannon told him I was being a snoop, and he wanted tae learn more about me."

"That's devious." Lydia opened the passenger door to Paislee's Juke and got in. "I'd feel bad except we were also there under false pretenses."

Paislee started the vehicle. "We learned that the Leerys are having financial difficulties. Shawn's illness, Charles's demands for money. Gavin's love for Shannon. What wouldn't he do for her?" She'd forgotten to ask if Charles had any heirs, or if his assets would go to the estate, if he had them.

"Tae inspire such devotion." Lydia sighed.

"Y'know, I blamed forgetting my shawl on the champagne, but what if it's another setup?"

"Why?"

"I guess I'm about tae find out."

"You're pretty guid at getting tae the bottom of things—but no trouble, awright?" Lydia poked Paislee's shoulder. "You better at least text me on yer way home."

"Hey, since I'm driving, will you Google Bart and Joey Pickett? I want tae know what they look like, just in case."

"Guid idea." Lydia's fingers tapped on the mobile screen. "Oh—they're kinda cute. What does that say aboot me tastes these days?"

Paislee didn't comment. When she stopped at a red light, Lydia handed her the phone. The brothers could be twins with dark brown hair, brown eyes, sloped noses, and shady but charming grins. "There should be a law against bad guys being attractive."

"That would save a lot of heartache." Lydia took back her phone.

Should she ask about Grant? Or give Lydia time to sort it out? The light turned green, and Paislee pressed on the gas. "Oh! I met an interesting woman today named Blaise. She and her husband just relocated from Inverness, and they're looking for a house tae buy."

"She called already—thanks for the referral. Blaise seems all aboot community, so they should be a guid fit for Nairn."

"That's what I thought, too." They exchanged smiles.

Paislee parked in front of the Silverstein Real Estate Agency. "Wish me luck."

"Luck." Lydia climbed out. "I totally support you letting Shawn have it—and I've got bail money if ye need it." She shut the door on a wink.

Paislee used her Bluetooth to call home and check in with Grandpa as she drove to Leery Estate. If she went straight home after tea, they might be able to fly the kite before it got too late.

Brody answered. "Mum! Where are ye? Can you bring home pizza?"

"You are not getting pizza two nights in a row. Let me talk tae your grandpa."

"Aren't ye coming home yet? You *promised*. It's the best dragon, with a long red tail. Wallace keeps trying tae eat it."

"It sounds fine, Brody." Wallace would love to chase it on the beach. The dog was a lolling-tongue menace to seagulls everywhere.

"Where are ye?"

"I have an appointment for tea with Lady Leery. I'll try tae be home after that. Where's your grandpa?"

"He's in the bathroom. He's taking for . . . ev . . . er."

"Brody, it is not polite tae tell someone that another person is in the bathroom."

"Why not? He is."

"It's bad manners."

"So what do I do, lie?"

"You don't *lie*, so much—"

"What am I s'posed tae say?"

Paislee was sorry she'd even brought it up. "Be verra nice tae your grandpa. He didn't have tae help you with that kite."

"I know, Mum. Dinnae forget ye have tae check in with Edwyn's dad. He called tae talk tae you. What if he changed his mind?"

"If Mr. Maclean invited you, then you're fine. If it's something you and Edwyn cooked up on your own, well, then, you'll be staying home. In your room. No kite."

"Why are ye being *so mean?*"

"I am not mean, I'm your mother."

Rather than risk more details about Grandpa's bathroom habits, she said, "Tell Grandpa I'll be home after tea, okay? Text if you need something, but don't call."

"We can't text, Mum. I dinnae have a mobile. Mibbe I should get one."

"Nice try, lad. Love you!" Just in time. There was the wooden sign that read Leery Estate. She turned right down the dirt path and stopped at the closed iron gate. A dart of apprehension shot across her senses. A murder had occurred here. She'd witnessed a man's last breaths.

The gate allowed a false sense of security—you could jump over the fence around the horse pasture or climb up the incline by the stream. She rolled down the window and pressed the intercom buzzer.

"Name?" A man—it sounded like Malcolm—asked.

"Paislee Shaw."

The gate opened slowly, and she followed the narrow dirt road, parking next to the fountain in the gravel lot. She noticed there were only three cars beneath the shelter. The silver Mercedes was missing. She brought out the gift bag for Lady Leery but left the one for Midge in the Juke. The fountain had been turned off, leaving the nymph without a job as she pursed her brass lips. The koi swam in brackish water.

Paislee climbed the porch steps, and Malcolm opened the heavy wooden door before she knocked. "Guid day," he said. The butler had on casual attire of black denim and a sage-green sweater.

"Hello. Is Shawn in? I'd like tae speak tae him."

His brow lifted. "*Lady Leery* is expecting you in the sunroom. A light lunch will be served."

"That sounds wonderful, thank you—but still. Might I speak with Shawn first?"

Midge popped out from behind the stairs, a feather duster in her hand. "Mr. Marcus isnae in his room—I just tidied it." Her uniform consisted of black slacks and a black shirt. Her short brown hair was bare.

"He's not?" Malcolm asked. "Have *you* seen him, Midge?"

"No, sir." Midge kept her gaze on the plaid area rug at her feet rather than acknowledge Paislee. Had she given Shawn the note? "Not since the family meeting this morning at breakfast."

Malcolm clasped his hands behind his back. "It seems Mr. Marcus isnae here right now. Let me show you tae the sunroom."

The butler led the way to the right side of the house away from the family's private quarters. They passed the old Victorian telephone room where she'd stumbled upon Aila crying last night.

In the light of day, it wasn't hard to notice the worn spots in the carpet runner or the water stains on the ceiling. The house, not unlike Lady Leery, had begun to show its age while retaining an elegant beauty. She followed Malcolm to the two-foot brass nymph in the hall, but rather than go left to the study, he continued straight, until they reached a slightly ajar door. Malcolm knocked and entered.

The sunroom had originally been a porch that had been enclosed with glass walls. Potted palms and fragrant gardenias added lush greenery. A round wrought-iron table, painted white, with six cushioned wire-back white chairs, was tucked in the farthest corner. The lady of the manor, elegant in a dove-gray sweater and pearls, wrote in a journal.

Lady Leery set aside her pen and rose at Paislee's entrance. "Welcome! How lovely tae see you again."

"I'm so sairy for leaving my shawl here." The woman's smile didn't slip. Paislee lifted her Cashmere Crush bag. "I brought a thank-you gift, for such an amazing evening." She handed her the bag.

"Not necessary," Lady Leery said, though she accepted it eagerly. "Call me Shannon. Have a seat." Paislee sat, and Shannon turned to Malcolm. "Tea, please—and bring the cock-a-leekie soup and basil scones." She turned to Paislee. "Gavin tells me you havenae eaten."

"Please don't go tae any trouble." Gran's chicken and leek soup had been very tasty, and her mouth watered at the memory.

"I havenae lunched yet, so 'tis no trouble. Malcolm, see if Aila can join us? Graham's in the workshop, sculpting." She murmured to Paislee, "No need tae bother him if he's under the spell of a different muse." Shannon raised her face to the butler. "Invite Shawn to tea?"

That would be wonderful, Paislee thought.

Malcolm's jaw tightened. "He isnae in his room, m'lady. I'll look again. I believe Aila went riding."

"Just the two of us, then. Is that all right, Paislee?"

"Aye." Shawn's absence allowed Paislee to connect with Shannon, set her at ease, and find out her version of what happened to Charles.

Malcolm left, leaving the door slightly open. Shannon adjusted herself daintily on her seat and peeked into the bag. "It's poor manners tae open this right now, but do you mind? I cannae imagine what you've brought!"

Paislee laughed and hoped Shannon enjoyed the gift. "Just something from my shop. I noticed you like navy blue? It matches your slacks."

"It's me favorite hue of the Leery plaid." Shannon gently pulled the delicate knit lace from the bag. "This is heavenly," she exclaimed, bringing the soft yarn to her cheek.

"There's nothing like cashmere."

Shannon folded the scarf in her lap. "Gavin told me of the *misunderstanding* regarding the sale of the building where you have your lease. I cannae imagine what Shawn was thinking."

Paislee shifted on the thin cushion of her wrought-iron chair. He'd wanted a kidney, obviously, and Charles had demanded extra payment. "I've been trying tae talk tae Shawn since last night, when he told me of his illness. Was he raising money for that?"

"Aye, that could be, but I was already taking care of it." Shannon's gaze narrowed.

Gavin had said the same. While she empathized with Shannon, that didn't change the pressure they'd all been under on Market Street during the last month. "Can I let the other businesses know that it was a false alarm? It's caused quite a bit of stress." Theadora would be her first call.

"Aye. Rest assured that the building will not be sold." Shannon offered a heartening smile, but her golden-brown eyes held worry. "Gavin said your leases are all yearly? We'll extend them tae two years, tae make amends."

*Perfect.* "That's wonderful news, thank you."

Malcolm knocked and widened the door, his nostrils flared as if perturbed. "M'lady, Shawn isnae answering his mobile, and his car is gone."

"Thank you," Shannon said. Malcolm hovered, one hand on the knob. "Anything else?"

He cleared his throat and glanced at Paislee.

"Just tell me, Malcolm!"

"Father Dixon called."

Shannon's mouth firmed. "Aboot a memorial for Charles. I'll make a decision this afternoon. Thank you, Malcolm." She dismissed him, then scrutinized the door as if to make sure the butler was gone.

Paislee glanced over her shoulder, too. No Malcolm.

"I would just as soon not have one, but folks would find it odd." Shannon stroked the soft scarf like a navy-blue kitten. "Last night after the party, I went up tae Shawn's room."

Paislee remembered that Shannon hadn't been in queue to say goodnight.

"I asked him tae explain what he'd told you . . . that Charles had double-crossed him?"

"That's right."

"Stubborn man didnae want tae tell me, but I already knew aboot the argument between him and Charles. My servants are loyal."

She'd seen that of Midge, and Malcolm, for herself. "What did he say?"

"Shawn said he wanted tae apologize tae Charles and accidentally overheard Charles talking on the phone that morning with Bart tae arrange a meeting in Nairn."

Accidentally? She'd bet everything in her account that he'd been snooping after hearing the fight with Aila. "Bart? As in Bart and Joey Pickett?" Paislee tucked her hair behind her ear. That was confirmation of what the DI had told her. Tuesday night they'd arrived by train, and Wednesday, Charles was dead. "Was Charles still working with them?"

"My *guess* would be that he owed them something. I'd just paid him a quarter million pounds for Charles's kidney—Charles was going tae start over in America."

Paislee couldn't comprehend that much money. Her savings were at the low end of three figures. "What happened tae the cash?"

Shannon put the scarf in the gift bag, and the bag at her feet. "I transferred it tae him—but Charles never had the chance tae meet up with his cohorts." She focused her intense gaze on Paislee. "That's why I dinnae believe the brothers are behind the shooting."

Understanding dawned and Paislee relaxed against the chair. "They'd want their money first!"

"Exactly." Shannon glanced at the door, then leaned toward her. "Shawn swears that someone pushed him down the stairs last night."

Shawn had been very intoxicated, but Paislee didn't want to be rude and point that out.

"I asked him who, but he said when he brushed himself off tae look, nobody was there. Also, he believes someone was in his room . . ." Shannon eyed the door. "Malcolm?"

It opened with a shove, and Malcolm appeared at the threshold. "M'lady."

He'd obviously been listening to their conversation. She'd have to give Shawn credit for being rightly suspicious.

The lady of the house peered over her lifted nose. "I've asked you tae announce yourself, Malcolm."

"I did, m'lady," he said without remorse, wheeling in a cart with two soup bowls and a ceramic tea service. "Should I stay and pour?"

She shooed him away. "I can manage."

He left slowly, practically dragging his feet.

"You may shut the door, Malcolm, thank you." It clicked closed. "Servants," she snapped.

Servant, aye, but also once a lover. The role must be difficult. "How long have you and Graham been together?"

Her lips tilted in a half smile. "I love art but have no talent. Graham is verra gifted. Hmm. A year? We've been serious for the past few months. He's from a poor fishing family in Inverness. I hope tae help him reach a wider audience for his sculptures."

"The stag is beautiful." From what she'd seen in the brochure. "And the benches."

"Aye." Lady Leery lifted the ceramic pot and poured two cups of fragrant tea. Basil scones had been arranged on a tray. She handed Paislee a cup on a saucer, with two square pastries on the porcelain edge. "Sugar? Lemon?"

"None, thank you." Paislee settled the saucer before her and breathed in the fragrant steam. Scottish Afternoon Tea—she'd recognize the familiar blend anywhere.

Shannon passed a bowl of chicken and leek soup, the broth creamy. "This is one of my favorite comfort foods."

Paislee dipped her spoon into the bowl and tasted the savory soup. "Delicious. Gran used tae make this." Lady Leery's was almost as good. "Have ye told Detective Inspector Zeffer why you don't think the Pickett brothers are guilty?"

"No. I dinnae like the man. Inspector Shinner would have shown a great deal more respect with this situation." Shannon looked up from her bowl. "Rumor has it that you helped him in his last investigation?"

She swallowed her spoonful quickly. "It wasn't like that."

"I've seen ye ask questions here in me own home." Shannon

laughed. "I want you tae help me find who killed Charles, and who is after my Shawn."

Paislee's knee shook under the table. "That's not, I mean, I have a custom-sweater shop. I knit."

"What if your son was in danger?" Shannon leaned over the table to lock Paislee in place with her gaze. "Forgive the subject matter over soup, but Charles's kidneys are only guid for up tae seventy-two hours. Anything after that and the chances of a successful transplant diminish. Charles's body is on ice, of course, because of the investigation."

Her stomach rolled. "I–"

"I've got calls in tae the best solicitors in the country tae see what can be done, but the paperwork he'd signed was tae be a *living* donor—now Charles is dead. If this case isnae solved immediately, then it won't matter for Shawn anyway." Her lower lip trembled, but she tried to hide it by peering into her soup bowl.

The clock was ticking for their family. "Tell me more about Charles."

"I tracked him down, for Shawn's sake, and invited him here. Charles wouldnae even agree tae a blood test until I paid ten thousand pounds. Everything since has been a bloody negotiation." Her cheeks flushed.

"You had tae, as you said." Paislee nodded in understanding.

"You're a mother, too, Paislee, a mother of a son. They hold your heart."

Paislee held her palm to her chest in agreement.

Shannon's mouth pursed in displeasure. "Charles had scammed a lot of people and was wanted by the police. I rescued him from being arrested in London, where I found him sharing a flat with two other men—the Picketts." Her face reddened with anger. "I believe that's why he wanted tae stay at the estate, tae be out of the public eye. I didnae ask."

Paislee drank her tea, the brew quieting her tummy. "He and Shawn fought while Charles was here?"

"Aye, like two cocks in a yard. Shawn thought Charles should just donate a kidney out of familial duty. Charles wanted recompense. Once Charles realized how desperate we were"—her voice pitched high—"well, he upped his price."

And then demanded even more from Shawn. "How did Charles and Aila get along?"

"Toward the end of the month, things were especially tense between them. I've asked Aila why, but she says it's nothing." Shannon finished her soup. "Both of my children are lying tae me." She nudged the bowl back. "Who are they trying to protect? I *will* get tae the bottom of this, never fear."

"I believe you." The woman was very determined to save her family.

Shannon dabbed her mouth with her napkin and looked around the sunroom, the scent of gardenia nature's perfume. "This is my favorite room in this gloomy old house. I try not tae notice the cracks."

"I know what you mean," Paislee commiserated. "Not on such a grand scale, mind, but my house is a hundred years old. What gets repaired first is based on function, not appearance."

"You do know, then!"

"I dream of a brand-new kitchen tae replace my old cooker and fridge."

Shannon laughed softly. "It costs even more tae bring an older property into the twenty-first century. We'd transformed the shed into restrooms that had tae be handicap compliant in order tae get funding from the bank for a loan. I plan tae be open more hours, tae bring in more income." She drank from her teacup.

"It's a race—us against our houses. I thought once that if things got too tight, I could rent out Gran's rooms." Now, that was no longer an option.

"You're resourceful, and I like that. Can ye help me?"

"I'll try, but I don't know where tae start." Well, not true. She wanted to question Shawn about what he'd seen behind the hedge that morning.

"Not with the Pickett brothers, like that detective thinks." Shannon brought out a silver flask from behind the teapot and added golden liquid to her tea. "A drop of whisky?"

"No thank you." She smiled. Grandpa and Shannon would be bosom buddies if they ever had the chance to meet.

Shannon closed her eyes for a moment and took a deep drink. "I, we . . ." She cleared her throat and sipped again. "The Leery line isnae strong."

Paislee added more tea to her cup. "You have two children." She thought of what she'd found out from Margot. Between Shawn's kidney disease and rare blood type, it would have been a bloody miracle if he'd had children.

"Twenty years apart." Her white brow arched high. "And Aila was a surprise, I can tell ye that."

"She's beautiful." And angry.

"Aye." Shannon nibbled a corner of her scone. "I've got tae find the lass someone suitable—someone tae strengthen our family tree."

Paislee straightened. "That seems old-fashioned."

"It's necessary tae continue the Leery line. Wealth will be a factor. I've spoken with Aila regarding her duty, but she went on aboot love. Love, I told her, will not maintain the estate. I did it and survived. She will, too."

Paislee lifted her cup to her lips to hide her dismay at the archaic decree.

"Dinnae act so shocked." Shannon fluttered her fingers. "Yer just like Aila. I thought you much more sensible, Paislee."

"I am, but, well, this is the twenty-first century. Things are changing. Even in Nairn."

"Not in this bloody estate," she said coolly. "I had tae *beg* Shawn tae go tae a specialist and see if they could do anything at all for a viable sperm—just one tae ensure the line." She eyed the ceiling of the sunroom, and Paislee did, too, noticing a watermark in the corner where the glass joined. "Didnae work."

"Why didn't he marry?"

"My fault, I s'pose. There was never a woman guid enough. I thought we had time, and now it's too late." Shannon choked up.

Paislee reluctantly felt empathy for all of the players in this drama.

"Damn Charles for dying. It's ruined everything. Shawn was tae have another chance. And now someone could be trying tae kill him next?"

Paislee reached for her hand but then drew back. She wasn't convinced that Shawn was in danger from anybody but himself, but she would help. "Surely with your resources, and the internet, a compatible donor can be found?"

Shannon raised watering eyes, suddenly looking her age. Grief shadowed her gaze. "My hope is dead. As dead as Charles—and possibly Shawn." She poured whisky from her flask into the empty teacup, sipping delicately. "Call me the minute ye find oot who killed Charles. Who is after Shawn. Malcolm has your shawl."

Dismissed. "Thank you." Paislee gathered her things, feeling with certainty that Shannon had Malcolm take her shawl last night.

No doubt the woman had also asked Gavin to invite her for a drink. To gather information. Paislee couldn't ask as the lady had turned away to stare out the window, her shoulders trembling.

Once again at odds with what she felt regarding the lady of the manor, Paislee left the sunroom for the hall, where Malcolm waited. How much had he heard?

"This way," he said.

They reached the foyer without a word, and he retrieved Paislee's shawl from the hooks behind the staircase. "Is Midge here?"

"She's working. There ye are—my apologies for any inconvenience."

"Why didn't you give me my shawl last night?"

His jaw tightened. "I dinnae ken what you mean."

Paislee accepted her soft wrap and studied Malcolm. "Do *you* think one of the Pickett brothers shot Charles?"

He bowed his head stoically. "My opinion on the matter is of no importance."

"I know you're helping Gavin with security on the estate, because of Charles's old mates being seen in the area. Yet your lady doesn't believe Joey and Bart are guilty, which is why she's fighting Gavin about the added expense."

Malcolm braced his shoulders and stared down his nose at her. "You seem tae know so much—why don't *you* tell me who shot Charles?" His tone was heavy with sarcasm.

She sighed. "Why were Aila and Charles arguing that morning?"

"Were they?" He walked toward the front door and motioned for her to follow.

Paislee refrained from rolling her eyes. "Do you know where Shawn might be?"

Malcolm took several more steps. "Probably holed up somewhere figuring oot how tae get his hands on Charles's kidneys. Time's up today."

She walked after him, imagining Shawn creeping around town in a hat and trench coat, with a cooler in one arm. "He wouldn't!"

"Shawn Leery is heir tae the estate," Malcolm said bitterly. "He's always thought he could do as he pleases. I wish he'd quit causing his mother grief. Charles was bad enough, until we were rid of him."

It was believable to Paislee that if Malcolm thought Shannon was being taken advantage of by Charles, he'd protect his lady. Shawn was also protective of his mum. Aila would want to guard the estate that was her home. Neither Graham nor Malcolm would have been upset if the body had been Shawn's, rather than Charles's. And would Shannon get the money back from Charles now that he was dead? By outward appearances, the estate could use that quarter million pounds. They all had a motive, and the thought of it made her head spin.

She passed him over the threshold to the porch. "When Shawn returns, please have him call me. Shannon wants me tae help."

Malcolm slammed the door behind her.

# Chapter 19

From the front porch of the Leery manor house, Paislee gazed out at the car park and the lavender bougainvillea arch that led to the path where Charles had died.

Laughter sounded from the stables on the far side of the property as Aila, in riding breeches and fitted coat, dismounted from an ebony horse. She stumbled, but Graham steadied her while Midge patted Aila's back.

The three trudged across the lawn. Paislee slowly descended the steps, lingering to give Midge her gift of the knit cap and perhaps have a private word regarding Shawn.

Aila's smile fled when she spied Paislee, and she murmured to Graham. The sculptor tucked his hands in his denim pockets when they reached the gravel car park and ambled around the side of the house between the kitchen and the arch. She noticed a narrow path. Is that where he'd lost his cap Wednesday morning?

Midge and Aila kept on. The maid adjusted her cardigan as if she felt a breeze. Paislee opened the back seat of her Juke for the gift bag.

"Good afternoon, Paislee," Aila greeted her politely but continued speedily up the stairs in obvious avoidance.

"Hello," Paislee said. "Midge?"

The maid stopped before she reached the stone steps and turned as Aila disappeared into the house. "Aye?"

Paislee held out the bag. "I wanted tae thank you for your kindness last night. Not only about the note."

"I gave it tae Mr. Marcus this morning with his scone and jam."

"Thanks. You helped me when I was lost."

Midge's rosy cheeks turned scarlet as she accepted the gift. "You dinnae have tae give me anything."

"It's my pleasure," Paislee insisted.

She peered inside the bag and grinned wide. "How braw. Pink's me favorite."

Paislee shifted, the gravel scrunching beneath her shoes. "Midge, Lady Leery is worried about Shawn and asked me tae help. She said he thinks he was pushed down the stairs?"

Midge glanced up at the front porch of the house, then back at Paislee. "He was, ma'am. Twisted his wrist. He's worried whoever killed Charles is after him. Someone was in his room, too, holdin' a pillow."

"Do you know where he is, Midge? He seems tae really trust you."

The maid's entire face flamed. "Aye. I mean, m'lord knows he can count on me." She twisted the button of her shirt over her heart. "He's scared tae be in the house so he's lying low on the property." She gestured toward the land beyond the maze. "Had a trashy blonde keepin' him company, but she's gone now."

Her pulse sped as she processed the information. "You can reach him?"

Midge held up her hand to stop Paislee from racing down the garden path. "I'll relay the message that ye want tae help, but that's all."

"What did he say about my note?"

She shrugged and averted her gaze.

Nothing polite then.

Malcolm opened the front door. "Midge? You're needed in the kitchen. Now."

The maid rushed up the stairs and brushed by Malcolm.

Disappointed, Paislee drove home with the butler's glare imprinted on her mind. She phoned Lydia and told her about the meeting, but her friend was showing a house so they didn't chat. Ten minutes later, Paislee parked in her driveway and got out of the Juke.

Wallace barked at the front door, announcing her arrival before she entered the tiny foyer. Her home seemed like a hut compared to the Leery Estate. It was hard to believe that she and the lady of the manor had just shared cock-a-leekie soup.

Her pup jumped up on her leg, and she scratched behind Wallace's ears.

"Mum!" Brody raced down the narrow hall and grabbed her around the waist. Had he grown? She ruffled the hair atop his head, which now reached the middle of her rib cage. She'd bet a new stainless-steel fridge that he had.

Grandpa opened the door of his bedroom at the noise. He wore his flannel shirt untucked over khakis, his black glasses nestled in his silver hair. "Hiya, lass. Tea with Lady Leery?"

"Yes—what an odd day it's been."

"Can't wait tae hear all aboot it." Grandpa left his room. "We finished the kite."

"It's still early, Mum. Can we go tae the beach?"

It wasn't even four yet, but she was emotionally beat. Paislee wanted nothing more than to sit down and put her feet up on the back porch with a mug of strong tea, but that would have to wait.

She'd promised. "Aye—let's see this beauty fly." Paislee followed Brody down the hall to where a red-and-white dragon proudly covered the round kitchen table. The puzzle had been moved to the counter.

Brody lifted the work of art carefully for Paislee to admire. "Look at the tail, Mum!"

"This is really fine," she said. "You did this?"

"Me and Grandpa," he said proudly.

"Without killing each other?" She glanced from Grandpa to Brody, both brows raised—half-teasing, half-serious.

Brody snorted. "Almost."

"Oh?" She bit her lip to keep from laughing. "Grandpa?"

Grandpa crossed his arms over his narrow chest and winked. "Things were a wee bit tense when gluing in the teeth, but we worked it oot."

Wallace nudged her hand with his nose for another scratch, and she obliged. "I'm very impressed, Shaws. Should we bring snacks tae the beach with us?"

Brody handed her the house phone. "Mum, dinnae forget tae call Edwyn's dad."

"All right, all right." She took the phone.

He'd already punched in the number. "Just press the button."

"I can handle making a phone call." She rolled her eyes at Grandpa while smiling. "You'd think it's Christmas."

"Better than Christmas. We get to spend all day reading comics and playing video games."

A male voice answered, "Hello."

"Hi, it's Paislee Shaw, Brody's mum. Bennett?"

"How are ye?"

"Fine." She pulled up the image of Bennett Maclean. Tall, blond shaggy hair, jade-green eyes, and stunning. Perfect for her friend Lydia, but she'd said she'd reached out and Bennett hadn't returned her call. Maybe there was something she could do to help them along. "Brody said he was invited tae spend the day to-morrow?"

"Aye. I'll be at work with the boys. Having a mate keeps Edwyn oot of trouble."

"I understand that." Before Grandpa had arrived, she'd quit work by four, or else bring Brody to the shop to do his homework.

"So drop him off any time after ten—we'll be at the store."

"Does he need anything? A change of clothes?"

"What? Uh, nooooo. Unless he's a messy eater or something."

Brody glared at her.

She shrugged. This would be the first time at a friend's for the day. There'd been other playdates where she and a few mums got together in the park for football, or swimming indoors at the community pool. This time she wouldn't be involved at all.

Bennett cleared his throat. "Have you heard anything more about that shooting?"

"Nothing tae speak of." That she could share.

"Okay, then," Bennett said. "See ye tomorrow."

"Cheers." Paislee hung up.

Brody looked mortified. "I'm not a baby, Mum."

"I know. Sorry about that."

Grandpa held up a spool of twine. "Is the hamper packed, Brody? I've got extra in case our string breaks."

Brody shoved fruit and a tin of crackers into the basket. "All done."

Paislee clipped on Wallace's leash, and they all piled into the Juke for the short drive to the beach. The light gray sky was streaked with pale blue, and while windy, there wasn't a drop of rain. She parked and they all climbed out. The salty breeze fluttered her hair. Wallace strained against his collar, wanting to chase after the birds on the dune. Folks scavenged for shells on the hard-packed sand. Nobody was brave enough to swim in the cold sea.

Brody held the dragon kite very carefully and showed her where the strings were attached and how the tail was going to move in the wind. She prayed the amateur construction was up to the heavy gusts. "Perfect kite weather, Brody."

Brody raced forward. "I know!"

"Careful now." Grandpa jogged and lifted the tail's red paper scales. "Awright, lad."

They walked together past dunes and seagrass toward the Firth on the other side. The afternoon sun occasionally broke through the gray and shined golden rays on the blue-gray surface of the water.

Paislee shook out the beach blanket from the hamper and smoothed it on the sand, anchoring it at one corner with the basket and a rock on another.

Brody and Grandpa worked in tandem to get the kite into the air. If someone would have asked her two months ago if this was even a remote possibility, she would have denied it with her last breath.

Grandpa's arrival had been a complete surprise, and one she hadn't welcomed. Paislee grew to appreciate him more with each passing day.

It was a miracle, and one sent by Gran, she had no doubt.

Wallace barked at the dragon soaring through the sky as Brody and Grandpa each held on to the string and handles—it took both of them to make it fly. Brody had the head and Grandpa the tail.

Paislee snapped pictures with her mobile, and then captured the scene with video. "Woo-hoo!"

Brody laughed like she'd never heard before, and sheer joy filled her heart.

Joy, yes, but bittersweet because these moments were numbered.

He wouldn't be a boy forever—she'd be lucky to have him be a "boy" for the rest of the summer.

The tail on the kite loosened, driving the dragon toward the ocean and swooping over a tourist's head. Thank heaven the man ducked out of the way with a chuckle. The broken kite fluttered.

Paislee called out, "Careful!"

"Did ye see how high it flew, Mum!"

"Bring it down or lose the rest," Grandpa shouted.

Grandpa's heels were dug into the sand, when Brody released his handle in excitement. The yellow plastic whipped back and knocked the green tam-o'-shanter off the old man's head.

"Brody! What did I say aboot hanging on, lad?"

With nervous laughter, Paislee jumped up and ran into the fray to catch the wildly dancing handle. Once she had it under control, Brody helped and they brought the dragon to the sand.

"Teamwork!" she said, catching her breath.

Brody grabbed Wallace's leash—the pup had snapped up a loose dragon scale. "Give it, boy."

Wallace released the damp paper with a playful growl, his tail high.

Paislee walked slowly back to the blanket, out of breath in a good way. "Ready for a snack?"

"Naw!" Brody raced with Wallace down the strip of beach, the dog and boy running in and out of the surf.

Grandpa gathered the pieces of kite and stashed them by the blanket. "I'll have some crackers and cheese." He eased himself onto the black-and-red-checked blanket and crossed his legs.

"I'm hungry, too. I had a bowl of soup with Shannon Leery. She made cock-a-leekie, like Gran—almost, but not quite as good." Paislee stretched her legs before her to get comfortable, then chose an apple from the hamper.

Grandpa dug into the tin and pulled out a cracker. "So why the special invite tae tea? Did she ask aboot Charles's death? I searched for any heirs, like ye asked, but couldnae find anything. No record of being married, no known children."

"Thanks for trying. She wanted my help."

Grandpa snapped a square cracker in two. "What on earth with?"

Paislee watched his face at her news. "Shawn faked the certified letters evicting us from the building."

Grandpa inhaled his cracker and coughed. "What?"

"I've never gotten one before and didn't know it had tae be mailed. Lydia just saw the letter." Paislee polished the apple on her pant leg and filled in the details of the miracle. "We're tae sign two-year leases."

"Congratulations, lass."

Saying the words to Grandpa was the first time she truly under-stood they'd get to keep Cashmere Crush on Market Street. Her shoulders lightened.

"Didn't I say Shannon Leery was a fine woman?"

"Ye did."

Grandpa curled a fist. "But I'd like a word with your Mr. Marcus for all his trouble."

"We'd have tae find him first. Shawn is very ill, but the time is up for a successful kidney transplant from Charles." She bit into the crisp, sweet apple. "On a high note, I get tae tell the business own-ers that we're saved."

"Will ye hold a meeting?"

"No—it would be cruel tae make them wait any longer. I'll call."

"Go ahead." Grandpa stood up and brushed sand from his bum. "Gonna comb the beach for driftwood. I used tae whittle, you know."

She didn't know. He walked briskly down the beach, searching the seagrass and sand dunes in the opposite direction of Brody and Wallace chasing waves.

Paislee started her list of good cheer with the bakery. Dan an-swered. "Theadora's Tea Shoppe."

"Hi, Dan! It's Paislee." Had it just been that morning he'd stopped by upset with himself for arguing with Theadora? And now the couple would have something tangible to celebrate—she was so excited her fingers shook as she held the mobile. "Did you ever catch up with your wife?"

"Aye." He didn't sound happy.

She cleared her throat. "Well, I have amazing news about the shop—the building is not for sale, and our leases are now good for two years."

"Shawn Marcus can shove the building up his rich arse." Dan hung up.

What? After that, Paislee wasn't sure she wanted to call any of the others—but she had to. They deserved to know. There was no answer at the office supply shop, so she left a message for Jimmy and Lourdes. Next was Margot.

"Medi-Lab, Margot speaking."

"Hey, Margot—It's Paislee. I have good news." Margot reacted with a happy shout more in line with what Paislee had been expecting.

"That's just brilliant," Margot said. "I might close early tae celebrate."

Paislee called Ned, who was pleased, as was James. Good deed done, she stood and stretched, breathing deep the salt air. Brody had convinced Grandpa to play ball with him, and the two tossed it back and forth while Wallace chased it, pink tongue to the side, tail wagging as he barked, in dog heaven.

Paislee ate a cracker, then another, but her stomach growled. After a few more minutes of watching them, she called, "Who's ready for dinner?"

They carefully packed the kite into the back of the Juke. Wallace jumped up on Brody's lap while Grandpa climbed into the passenger seat. Paislee passed Grandpa her phone, and he and Brody watched the video she'd taken of them flying the dragon. Grandpa offered pointers for their next kite.

"Can the tail be fixed, Grandpa?"

"I think so, lad. We can certainly try."

The sun lowered in an orange-and-yellow sky as they reached home. She hadn't heard back from Lydia or Hamish, or Shawn, despite Midge's promise.

She perused the freezer for something that might magically appear for a healthy supper. There wasn't even a frozen package of peas.

Why couldn't there be more hours in the day? She had an obligation as a mother to feed her offspring—but she really didn't have the energy to go shop for groceries right now.

Paislee checked the pantry and lucked out with a few potatoes.

Flour. Applesauce. Can of beans. "Breakfast for dinner, anyone? Tattie scones, and I think there's some bacon left in the fridge."

While the meal wasn't as grand as anything at the estate, it was tasty, and they filled their bellies. "Write out what you want for the week, and I'll shop tomorrow." Sunday stretched before her without a plan.

"Orange marmalade," Brody said right away. The child slathered the jam on everything from toast to crackers. "Can I be excused? I want tae watch telly."

"Aye, but bring your plate tae the sink please." The clock above the cooker read seven. "Only for an hour, and then it's time for your bath. Can't go tae Edwyn's all stinky, now."

He stepped away, but she pulled him back, refraining from mussing his hair—but just barely. "Did ye have a good day?"

"Aye, but I cannae wait for tomorrow. Edwyn's got the new DualShock game controller. It's supposed to be *sonic*!"

"Mind your manners, like we talked about."

"Please and thank you, open the door for others, don't slam it"—he rolled his eyes—"and dinnae be a messy eater. Clean up after meself."

She let him go with a grin, and he dashed to the living room. "So, Grandpa, can I interest you in a trip tae the grocer's tomorrow?"

Grandpa finished the last tattie scone. "I'd like tae go tae Dairlee. It's time tae pay for the storage unit."

"I can drive you. My day is disturbingly empty."

His shoulders lifted, and he lowered his voice. "I dinnae need a keeper."

"I didn't say ye did." What was his problem all of a sudden? "But I'll need the Juke to pick up Brody. I'll go wherever you want." Maybe she should consider a second mobile? She winced at what that might cost.

Grandpa glanced away. "I never knew Craigh when he was

small, but Brody reminds me of yer da." He wiped his bearded mouth with a napkin. "I have tae find him."

What was it with sons? Lady Leery's sorrow over Shawn at tea earlier hadn't left her heart. It made Paislee want to keep Brody close at all costs. She could raise him just fine, and then what? Send him out to the world where she couldn't protect him?

Her throat ached so she sipped her water. "I'll help—we've done everything you've suggested so far." And the plan was to wait a month.

He squeezed the bridge of his nose. "I can handle it."

"Maybe we can save some money by emptying out the storage unit and bring your things here? We'll make room in the garden shed," Paislee offered.

His face turned the color of the old bricks on Market Street, ruddy at the cheeks. "I dinnae need your pity." His voice rose. "I'm only here until we find Craigh."

Paislee sat back. "Keep your storage unit then! I'm just trying tae help."

"I don't need it."

She cocked a brow. "Really? I seem tae remember things a wee bit differently when a certain detective inspector caught ye sleeping in the park."

He pushed back from the table, scuffing off to Gran's room—his room, now. She started to apologize but then swallowed the words when he slammed the door.

He'd been upset about his son, understandably so. Craigh was missing or maybe even dead. Worse than that would be if the man had abandoned his own father. Paislee brought the dishes to the sink.

All the talk about Shawn missing must have stoked his worry over Craigh and there was nothing else to do, until another month passed.

She knew his foul mood stemmed from fear.

When the dishes were done, she brushed the sand from Wallace's fur and then coerced Brody into the tub. "And wash behind your ears—ye can't embarrass me now."

"Mum, I'll do it—ye don't have tae make sure."

After leaving Wallace to supervise Brody in the bathroom, she walked to her bedroom and sat at the desk to go through her bills. She was grateful that Arran hadn't charged her for the visit. He'd seemed certain that he could help her but how could she help him? And Hamish? The Fordythe Primary headmaster was all about rules, making the parents sign in triplicate.

Wait.

Sign.

Hadn't she signed something about Brody being able to take a Fordythe field trip?

"Oh, please, please, please let me have saved this." She opened the drawer of her desk and rifled through the school papers for this year. There it was—the hated school rules sheet that she'd signed and dated, and yes . . . she'd signed a waiver about not holding the school liable for incidents that happened on a field trip. Acts of God—a random shooter might not be godly, but it was certainly out of their control, right?

She snapped a photo of the paper, and her signature releasing Fordythe from liability, then sent it to Arran. She included Hamish in the message.

"Mum—I'm done!" Brody's shout was followed by the sound of the plug releasing the water into the old pipes.

The gurgle and chug reminded her that her home's plumbing was on borrowed time. Replacing the pipes would cost a small fortune. She empathized with Shannon Leery trying to hold her house, fortune, and family together while harboring a scam artist like Charles Thomson. The man had demanded money from his ill cousin, as well as Shannon, who was only trying to save her son.

Paislee tucked Brody in bed, allowing him to watch a movie on his bedroom TV—last year's Christmas present from Lydia.

"Love you, hon. Sweet dreams."

"Night, Mum."

Wallace curled up at Brody's side and gave her a tail wag, then lowered his silky black head. Before returning to her room, she partially closed the door and asked Gran to keep watch over them.

There were no messages or texts on her mobile. She called the estate number, and Midge answered.

"Hi, Midge, this is Paislee Shaw—is Shawn Marcus available?"

"No, ma'am." The maid's voice lowered, and Paislee imagined her hunched over the phone. "I went tae where I thought Mr. Marcus was staying, but he ain't there. The whole house is in an uproar. M'lady is worried that something bad's happened tae him."

# Chapter 20

Paislee pulled the phone back from her ear as Midge ended the call and a harsh ring tone sounded. Shannon had asked her to help, and Paislee had gone to the beach. Guilt filled her. She realized that she hadn't been in touch with the DI, either. Being a mom had taken precedence. She wasn't cut out to be a sleuth.

She dialed the detective, but it went to voicemail, so she left a message for him to call her. Nervous energy filled her. Surely, if Shannon was that worried, she would call the police.

Overwhelmed, she lay on her bed to think of a plan. Who killed Charles? Where was Shawn? Her eyes drifted closed.

Next thing she knew, it was six thirty in the morning and her bedroom light was still on. She tried to go back to sleep but eventually decided to get up and do laundry rather than toss and turn, fret over her son growing up, and whether or not Shawn's life was in danger. In her dream, she saw Charles on the path, but it changed to Shawn, and then back to Charles.

Wallace scratched at Brody's bedroom door, and she widened it to let the dog out. Brody was fast asleep on his back, his arm over his head. *Sweet.*

"I'm not the only one up early, huh, pup?" Wallace raced down the stairs before her. She heard someone in the kitchen.

Grandpa had already gone out to shop, and cloth bags filled
with groceries lined the counter. "Mornin'. Hope ye dinnae mind I
borrowed the car?"

She crossed through the kitchen and opened the back door for
Wallace, who immediately barked at a robin in a flower pot.

Green buds dotted the trees and tufts of grass poked through the
wintery lawn. Taller sprouts surrounded the T-shaped metal pipes
of the clothesline. Blossoms colored the trees. Spring had arrived in
their narrow back garden.

Paislee shut the door and faced her grandpa. Was this his way of
apologizing for his short temper last night? "Shopped, too. Let me
know what ye spent, and I'll get cash for you."

"I can do me part." He'd slung his sweater over the back of the
dining room chair and rolled up the sleeves on his collared pale blue
button-down. Faded but clean, as were most of his things.

"Well, then, thanks. I hope ye remembered the marmalade,"
she said with a laugh, not wanting to poke his pride.

"Aye, it was on special even, so I bought two jars."

"Let's hide one or it'll be gone."

"Smart." Grandpa put one jar in the fridge and the other on the
top pantry shelf next to the bottle of Scotch.

Paislee folded the cloth bags and stowed them on the bottom
shelf.

"I thought I'd make an egg-and-potato casserole for breakfast,"
he said. "Why don't ye relax on the porch with a mug of tea? The
newspaper's on the table."

"I was going tae get the laundry started before we go tae Dairlee," she said. And try to form a coherent plan to help Shannon.

His shoulders tensed. Had he hoped to butter her up and get
the car to go on his own? She wasn't that soft, thank you.

She opened the newspaper and was greeted by Charles's picture
on the front page, the headline reading "Unsolved Murder." Her
stomach tightened at how similar he'd looked to Shawn. No wonder she'd dreamed about it.

Paislee checked her phone, but there were no messages—she

knew the DI would have plenty to say to her when they finally connected, but she had information that would hopefully make him forget he was mad at her.

She plugged in the electric kettle for tea and read the article at the kitchen table. Grandpa brought out the tin of Brodies Scottish Breakfast Tea and two mugs, pouring hot water over the tea bags.

"Listen tae this," she said. "Lady Shannon Leery is putting up one hundred thousand pounds for answers leading tae the capture of Charles's killer." Where was Shannon finding the money? "She told me yesterday that the kidneys are only good for so long, and that time has passed." Shawn couldn't use them now.

Grandpa leaned his hip on the table and read over her shoulder. " 'Joey and Bart Pickett, known associates of Charles Thomson, were seen in the Nairn area'—there's a number tae call if ye know where they are."

The images of the brothers were the same ones that Lydia had found online. She shivered at the evil she sensed behind their charming smiles. "Shannon doesn't think the Picketts are guilty."

"Why not?"

"Shawn supposedly 'overheard' a conversation Wednesday morning where Charles was going to meet with the brothers and give them money. Why would they shoot Charles before getting it?"

"Logical."

"Last night when I called the estate tae speak with Shawn, Midge told me they can't find him. Shannon is worried he's in real danger. She asked me tae help, but I didn't—and now I feel terrible."

"You were taking care of your own son, lass," Grandpa said. "Where is she getting her funds?"

"Shannon sold a painting tae pay Charles a quarter million pounds for one of his kidneys."

Grandpa smacked the table and sat down. "That's a fortune."

"Yeah. Now that Charles is dead, do you think she'll get it back?"

"I hope so. Her nephew was a real wanker."

"Seven is too early tae call the estate, but I've got tae know if Shawn's home in bed, or if I need a plan tae find him."

"I know her pain, her son missing." His voice lowered. "I'll help, too, lass." Grandpa got up to check his casserole, which tempted with baked onion and garlic scents.

Wallace scratched at the door to be let in for fresh water and kibble, and Brody slowly descended the stairs.

"Morning," she said. The legs of his pajamas were hiked up to his shins; the snug top showed an inch of midriff. "Last time for those pj's, laddie. I want them in the donation box."

She pointed to the cardboard box of clothes and knickknacks they no longer wanted on the far side of the kitchen by the indoor clothes-drying racks. Their combo washer-dryer didn't work well, so she used the drying racks through winter, and the outdoor clothesline for the rest of the year. To her, there was nothing better on a summer's day than crisp clean clothes in from the line.

"But these are my favorite, Mum." He patted the very faded Scottie dog on his top.

"We can see about getting another pair."

He looked uncertain—which was how she felt. He was too grown-up now for pj's with puppies.

No wonder he wanted to keep them. She heard Gran say, *Pick yer battles, lass. There will come a time when he can't wear them at all, and nature will take its course.*

"Grandpa's baked a casserole. Thirsty?"

He nodded, his auburn hair a mess.

"I'll get it." Paislee poured him a glass of orange juice.

Brody collapsed into his chair at the table, lifted Wallace onto his lap, and glanced at the paper. "Who's that, Mum? Looks like your landlord."

"That's his cousin Charles." She set the glass on the table.

"The one who was killed on our field trip?"

"Aye."

"They havenae caught who did it?" His nostrils flared with worry.

Brody was the most important person in her world. She knew from speaking with Shannon Leery that Shannon felt the same about her son, too.

Was that why she offered a reward, one she could ill afford, to find the killer?

"Mum!" Brody waved the paper before her eyes. "I asked you if they caught the bad guy?"

"Not yet. They will."

He leaned over Wallace, who covered most of his lap, and picked up his juice to drink. When he was done, he licked an orange ribbon from his upper lip. "I hope so. It's all they talk aboot at school. Holly's an attention hog, and nobody likes her anymore."

"Why not? It's not her fault that she was in the bathroom when it happened."

"You were there, Mum, keeping her safe. She acts like you locked her in on purpose." His brown eyes hardened with Shaw loyalty. "I know ye didnae."

"Holly said I locked her in?" The girl was telling lies in the schoolyard. "There was no outdoor lock, Brody. I held it from the outside, so she didn't see the bod—" She pointed to Charles's image. "Charles."

"Nobody will play with her—she's made all the kids mad."

"Have you talked tae Mrs. Martin about this?"

"No, but Britta did."

The sweet blond girl from her chaperone group. Despite Holly's behavior, Paislee couldn't condone bullying. "Just be fair, all right?"

"Nobody's mean. We just dinnae want tae listen tae her pretend cry."

It was a jungle out there—hopefully Holly would learn her lesson, and her friends would forgive her being dramatic. She was only ten.

"I'm sure she'll calm down, once she realizes the consequences of her actions."

Brody finished his juice and set the empty glass down. "Edwyn thought she was cute, but not anymore. I'm glad—I'd rather play football than talk aboot girls."

Paislee sighed. He wouldn't think that for much longer.

Charles's image stared up at her from the newsprint, next to the faces of the Pickett brothers. Guilt prodded her to locate her purse and find Detective Inspector Zeffer's business card for his office line. It was Sunday, so she wasn't even sure the station would be open, but she hoped to leave another message.

To her surprise, the detective answered.

"Detective? It's Paislee Shaw."

"Ah . . . the same Paislee Shaw who made a rather snarky promise tae call but didn't?"

Her cheeks flamed, and she walked from the kitchen to the foyer. "I left a message."

"Late last night."

"Sairy." She sat on the middle step of the narrow staircase. "I was wondering if I could have a word. In person." She owed him an update, and could make her point better if they were eye to eye.

"I'm here for the next fifteen minutes. If you're not, I cannae wait."

"I'm on my way." She hung up to find both Brody and Grandpa watching her. "I'll be right back, I promise—I know how important today is."

"Why are ye going, lass?" Grandpa asked.

"I think the DI should know *why* Shannon doesn't think these two jokers killed Charles."

Grandpa tugged his beard, his expression uncertain. "Subtle might not work with the detective, lass—guid luck."

"Hurry back, Mum," Brody said.

"It's not even eight yet!"

Paislee stuck her hair in a quick braid, grabbed her keys, and headed out the door. She arrived at the station ten minutes later with her conversation prepared, at least in her mind.

Zeffer paced the station in an unlit lobby. She knocked on the door, and he opened it, then locked it behind her. Today's blue suit was darker than most, nearly black. The only light was from the windows on either side of the building. The two reception desks were empty, phones blinking as if they held messages.

"Thanks for seeing me." The lobby had four chairs for visitors, but Zeffer didn't suggest they sit. She stuck her hands in her cardigan pockets.

"Today's reward in the paper is goin' tae make this place a zoo with Pickett brother sightings. I plan on being anywhere but here. What's up?"

"I had tea with Lady Leery yesterday. She doesn't think the Pickett brothers are guilty of shooting Charles."

He crossed his arms. "And why's that?"

"She thinks Charles was on his way tae meet them that morning for a payoff. In order tae get the money, they'd want him alive, right?"

He leaned back against the empty receptionist desk that Amelia sat at during the week. Blast! She still owed her friend a call. "And you care why?"

She gritted her teeth at his rudeness. "I'm trying tae help you, Detective, so that you aren't wasting time searching in the wrong direction. Shawn was the man behind the hedge—remember I thought I saw something?"

Zeffer stood instantly. "Explain."

Paislee pointed out, using her own hands, where she'd seen the red cuts. "I saw scratches and asked him about it—he admitted tae being behind the hedge. He'd followed Charles, wanting tae negotiate after an argument, and tried tae help him from the bushes—then he realized he could be a target and ran into the house."

His jaw tightened. "I need tae speak with him."

She shuffled her feet. "Well, the thing is, he believes his life is in danger, too."

"Uh-huh. Where is Mr. Marcus?"

"His family hasn't seen him since yesterday after breakfast. He's an ill man."

Zeffer chuckled without humor. "He's a *wanted* man."

"Grandpa and I were discussing where Shawn stood that morning, and where Charles had crashed through the hedge. The sounds I heard. Shawn couldn't have shot Charles that close with a rifle without it being louder and, as Grandpa put it, messier." She didn't remind him that there'd been no blood on the path.

"We have video footage of Shawn Marcus trying tae break into the morgue. He fled the scene and is now wanted for questioning. Any idea what he may have been after?"

*Ew.* "Kidneys."

"Excuse me?" Zeffer tugged his suit jacket lapels.

"He has a kidney disease. Charles was at the Leery Estate because he was going tae donate a kidney tae Shawn—only, Charles wanted money. A million from Shawn that he never got, and a quarter mil from Lady Leery that she paid."

He raked his hand through his russet hair in obvious frustration. "I know aboot the transplant from the interviews we did the first day. Not aboot the money—hardly a close family, eh? That doesnae explain why Shawn was trying tae steal kidneys."

"He has a rare blood type, and there's a limited time span for kidney transfer. Charles would have been a perfect match."

"Huh. Anything else you want tae tell me aboot? Like your visit with the solicitor?"

"Well, it seems I'm being sued for what happened that day, for not letting Holly Fisher out of the bathroom. Arran Mulholland is going tae take my case."

His seafoam-green eyes narrowed. "Her parents have been . . . difficult."

She took her hands from her pockets. "I'm sairy for not calling you yesterday, but I really was just busy. It wasn't intentional."

Zeffer relaxed his shoulders a fraction. "The Pickett brothers are persons of interest."

"You don't think they did it?"

"I dinnae ken, Paislee Shaw. But we should have answers within the hour. Idiots used one of their old aliases, and I'm off tae meet Constable Payne right now at their hotel room."

"I'll head on home then."

He unlocked and opened the door for her. "The station thanks you for being a concerned citizen."

Paislee's pride stung from the sarcasm layered in each word. She drove back to her house, where Grandpa fed her potato-and-cheese casserole. Afterward, Brody gave her a chocolate biscuit while she nursed her self-respect.

"I was only trying tae help," she lamented. "He didn't know about Shawn being behind the hedge, or that Charles was 'selling' his kidney."

Paislee dialed the Leery Estate, hoping to get Midge, but Malcolm answered. "Is Shawn home yet?" She prayed the butler would answer in the positive.

"No."

"May I speak tae Shan—" She glared at her mobile. "He hung up on me." This was just not her day. Her phone dinged a text, and all three Shaws read whom it was from. Hamish.

*Thanks for sending the document. I already have both on file—that doesn't stop the lawsuit. I've scheduled a meeting Monday morning at nine a.m. Please don't be late.*

She didn't answer but rinsed out their teacups, feeling slightly sick. Those forms were supposed to protect them, she thought. "Ready tae go, Brody?"

Between letting Wallace out one last time and getting Brody's favorite comic book, they arrived at the comic book store at half past ten. Edwyn waited outside for them. She parked, leaving Grandpa and Wallace in the Juke, and walked in to greet Bennett.

This was not just a shop where comics were sold—this was a boy's Adventureland. Life-size posters of comic heroes lined each wall, from Ant-Man to Spider-Man. In the center was a foosball table, and arcade games lined one entire wall. There was a pinball machine and a huge TV playing some sort of superhero movie she didn't know. Beside a large sectional couch and table, there was even a popcorn machine. The entire store smelled like greasy buttery goodness.

Bennett, tall and blond, met her at the front door.

"I think I've just lost my son tae you, Bennett. He's not going tae want tae come home after this. Morning, Edwyn."

Bennett laughed and kissed her cheek. "Paislee. Hey, Brody. He's welcome."

"I'd miss him."

"She says she's gonna sell me tae the gypsies," Brody said. "Mibbe I could stay here instead."

"Edwyn gets threatened with being sent tae sea for the sailor's life. Guess we all have our limits."

She really liked this guy. He'd be great for Lydia. Paislee wondered if there was a way to bring her best friend up in the conversation. Bennett smiled at her politely. "So what are you going tae do with your free day?"

"Socks," Brody said with assurance.

"Ha—just so you know, I'll be driving tae Dairlee with your grandpa."

"Pretty coastline there. There's a tidy little diner on the pier that serves great crab cakes," Bennett said. "It's a local hangout, left-over from the treasure-hunting days."

"There were real pirates in Dairlee?" Brody asked, wide-eyed. "Maybe Craigh was kidnapped."

Bennett looked at her in alarm.

"It's a long story for another day. Nobody was kidnapped. Brody, have fun, okay?" Paislee pulled him in for a side hug, which he briefly allowed before tugging free. "You have my mobile number if you need me. What time should I pick him up?"

"We close at five, but whenever. We live behind the shop, if we're not here."

"Perfect. See you later."

She was tempted to stay and play a game of pinball but headed out to the Juke. Lydia had to make a move on this guy—they could raise beautiful children and have a fun-filled life.

Grandpa sat in the front passenger seat, his green tam pulled over his forehead, and Wallace sprawled on his blanket in back.

The old man's mood was pensive and gloomy, and she was reminded of when she'd first met him, and they'd gotten bacon butties for breakfast. It would be a month tomorrow.

Where had the time gone?

She paid him for twenty hours a week at the shop, and he helped with Brody on Thursday and Saturday nights. Sundays they'd spent as a family, getting to know one another. Likes, dislikes.

Grandpa knew that Brody liked a cheese sandwich with two pickles better than the school lunch. Grandpa preferred sugar in his tea, and sometimes milk and lemon.

Someday she would discover what had happened between Gran and Grandpa, how they couldn't find their way back together. All her life, Gran had refused to discuss it. Paislee hadn't pushed—her grandmother had meant the world, and her passing five years ago had left a huge hole.

She'd never dreamed it might be filled by the grandfather Gran had kicked out of their house when she'd found out about his illegitimate son, Craigh.

Paislee followed the coastal road through heavier-than-usual Sunday traffic from Nairn to Dairlee. To their right, in between businesses, the gray-blue water of the Moray Firth beckoned.

"What's it called?" Paislee asked.

"Dairlee Ship and Store—turn left at the light, then right."

Paislee followed Grandpa's directions and parked before a single-

story building with thousands of storage units fenced and locked behind it.

"I'll just run in and pay," he said. "Then we can drive back tae
my unit."

"All right." Would he finally stop being so secretive?

He was out within ten minutes—snugging closed his cardigan
sweater with one wrinkled fist. The morning light glinted off the
black frames of his glasses as he got into the car.

"No word," he said.

"Were you expecting something? A message?"

"Hoping, more like. I forwarded the mail from our flat tae
here—for a fee, tae be sure. But there's nothing from Craigh."

"I'm sairy, Grandpa."

"Me too, lass." He eyed the metal gate, and she moved the Juke
forward. Paislee rolled the driver's side window down, and Grandpa gave her the code to punch in. They drove inside, and the gate
closed.

"Very last row," Grandpa said.

She drove slowly. There was barely enough room. She couldn't
imagine trying to bring a trailer here. "How did you get everything
inside?"

"I managed. Rented a truck. Our flat was furnished—verra
nice, but it wasnae ours. There wasn't much tae take. Just some of
Craigh's boxes."

"Did you go through them?"

"Of course not. They were sealed and marked private."

"There could be answers in there."

"I'll know when tae open them," he groused, his entire demeanor defensive. "Stop."

She hit the brakes and winced. Unit 857. The space was half the
size of their garden shed, and she recalled Grandpa mentioning that
he'd spent the night inside a few times. He wouldn't have been able
to lie down.

Paislee turned off the engine. Grandpa climbed out and went

around to the front of the car, his shoulder to her as he tried to open the lock with a key from around his neck.

Wily old man.

A survivor.

He hesitated, and she rolled the window down. "What's wrong?"

His narrow shoulders tensed. "I'm not sure."

He yanked the lock open, pulled the shed door up, and peered inside. Sun briefly broke through the clouds and illuminated a row of boxes, blankets, a pillow, and a suitcase.

Grandpa let out a curse, then slammed the door closed, locked the shed back up, and got inside the Juke.

"What is it, Grandpa?"

"Someone's been inside that unit." He tugged his beard, a quaver in his voice.

"Is something missing?" Everything had been neat and labeled.

He glared at the unit, then at the dashboard. "I dinnae ken— but the boxes have been moved."

She hated for him to be taken advantage of, when he had so little. "Let's file a complaint—ask tae see the security footage. Grandpa, let's at least load the boxes into the Juke and take them home."

"Lass, I'll ask ye tae stay oot of this and mind yer own business." He kept his heavy gaze on her until she nodded.

He clamped his jaw tight and didn't say another word. Paislee put the car in gear and left the storage facility, heading back toward Nairn. It was obvious that he was worried, and just as clear that he didn't want to talk about it. His slouched shoulders and green tam tugged down on his forehead were signs a blind man could read.

While he stewed, she thought of where Shawn Marcus might be after his failed attempt to break into the morgue. He wasn't physically well, or mentally, if he thought *that* was a good idea. What was he going to do, cut out the kidney himself?

"What are ye thinking that has ye glowering so? I'm sorry I snapped at ye."

"It's all right. Just trying tae figure out where Shawn might be.

Malcolm told Shannon yesterday that Shawn's car was missing—I noticed a new Mercedes gone from their carport. He's got access to money. Does he even need tae come home?" She kept her eyes on the taillights of the van in front of her. The sky grew dark as if ready to rain.

"What aboot for medicine?"

"That's a good thought." Paislee glanced at Grandpa. "Midge said that Shawn sometimes stays in one of the other buildings on the property, but he wasn't where she thought he'd be last night."

"I remember a hunting lodge, and a cottage." Grandpa crossed his ankles. "I'm sure they've checked those already."

"Midge seemed surprised he wasn't there. What if he returned between then and now? The DI is looking for him, so the safest place he could be is out of sight yet hidden on his family property." Motivation to find Shawn filled her. "I just need tae ask him what he saw that day. What if it was the Pickett brothers, and Shannon's theory is wrong?"

Grandpa leaned his head against the seat, squishing his green tam. "I know a back way onto the property—or I did, aboot a dozen years ago. We used tae do some fishing. Huge sea trout, and tasty, too." He smacked his lips together.

"Isn't that *trespassing* on Leery land?"

"We had unspoken permission so long as we respected the grounds." Grandpa gestured back to the dog. "We'll bring Wallace. If busted, we claim we're lost. It's a thick forest with lots of beech and pine trees, right across from Sharp's Park."

"I don't know. . . ."

"Do ye think that butler is going tae let you in the front door?"

"No." Malcolm didn't like her much.

"Didnae Lady Leery ask ye tae help?"

"Aye." Paislee couldn't forget the trembling of Shannon's shoulders in the sunroom. "Shawn thinks that someone pushed him down the stairs in his own home, and he said tae trust no one. Even if we were allowed in, it might alert the wrong person."

"Who was in the house?" Grandpa asked.

"Shannon. Aila. Graham. Malcolm. Midge. Shawn."

"Why would Shannon push her own son down the stairs?"

Paislee shook her head. "She wouldn't. Aila? She resents Shawn. She might want tae pay him back for setting her up with the police."

Grandpa turned toward her as she drove, but she glimpsed excitement on his expression. "Graham."

"Shannon's lover? I don't know. I've never seen him and Shawn interact. Graham is from a poor fishing family. Jealousy?"

"Mibbe. What aboot that butler?"

"Malcolm is protective of Shannon—but he knows how much she loves her son, so I don't think he'd hurt Shawn."

"Midge."

"I think she's got a little crush. And we can't rule out Shawn falling drunk down the stairs and being his own worst enemy."

"Well, lass?"

Paislee tightened her grip on the steering wheel. "All right. Let's find Shawn."

# Chapter 21

Paislee drove down the highway toward Nairn. She had to find Shawn—if he wasn't there, then maybe she'd discover a hint to where he might be hiding out. It made sense to her that he'd stay close to home because of his medical needs. The time on her dashboard read 11:55. Drizzle—part rain, part mist—coated her windshield. "Tell me which way tae go, Grandpa."

"Toward Sharp's Park, but the other side." Grandpa's good spirits seemed to have been restored at the idea of tramping through the woods on a secret mission. "Turn here."

She left the highway for a two-lane road, and after a mile or so the low shrubs along the coast grew into taller trees and woods. Mother Nature was at her lush, green best. "Where should I park?"

He straightened his glasses and gestured to a stand of pine trees so thick it was hard to see inside. A ditch dipped between the road and forest. "Anywhere along here. There's the path."

She'd spent the last ten years of her life not breaking a single law. "I'm only okay with this because of Shannon's request. There might be security guards. I heard Gavin tell Malcolm tae hire some, but Shannon was against it."

"If anybody questions us, we're just hiking through the beautiful woods, taking our dog for a walk." Grandpa pushed his tam back and held her gaze, his voice strong. "My son is missing, and I don't even know where tae look. How can I not help Shannon Leery?"

Paislee hitched Wallace to his leash, making sure she had treats to distract him if he started to bark. "You sound beholden, but you don't really know her."

"Shannon is our lady in the shire." His tone was wistful. "In the old, old days we had free run of the woods. Even twelve, fifteen years ago, so long as we took care not tae disturb the property, she looked the other way."

"She knew you'd come out here?"

"Her and her family. This stream has the best fish," he said with a shrug. "It's not like we were poaching deer."

Poaching! Like a medieval castle? "That sounds archaic."

"That's me. Archaic." Grandpa climbed down the side of the gravelly ditch as nimble as a goat—hardly an old man of seventy-five.

Paislee and Wallace followed more cautiously. Wallace eagerly sniffed every new scent with his head down and his tail wagging.

They jumped the trickle of a stream at the bottom of the ditch. The shade of the forest was cool and the air damp. She was glad to have dressed warmly in boots and jeans, a thick sweater, and a knit hat.

"This way." Grandpa ascended the other side of the ditch with the same agility as he'd gone down it. When he disappeared between the pines, she felt a moment's panic that she'd be lost.

"Wait for me," she called, reaching the narrow path.

He stopped and rubbed his hands, a man in his element. "Gets the blood pumping. Now, if we're caught, we're just—"

"Taking the dog for a walk," she recited. Her secondary plan was to call the house and speak with Shannon.

They tromped in about half a mile, before the trail curved to the left.

"Hear that?"

She listened. Gurgling. A brook perhaps.

"Over here!" He bent back a few branches for her and Wallace to follow him off path. They tread over pine needles and brush for another quarter mile.

Grandpa presented the fast-moving stream with pride. "In the Highlands, even a poor man can eat like a king—something my da used tae say. He taught me tae fish using a reed. I'll show Brody."

She smiled at his enthusiasm. "He'd like that. Is this the same stream behind the estate?"

"Aye." In the shade of the glen, clear water bubbled through river grass over mossy rocks and stones. "We'll follow along—the hunting lodge is first, then a cottage, and finally the estate—all told, less than a mile."

Wallace lapped water from the stream, his whiskers sparkling with droplets. It was so beautiful it was hard to believe something as sinister as murder could happen. Paislee searched the woods for danger, like the Picketts, but all she heard were squirrels.

"Ready?" Grandpa brushed his hands against his khakis. "The hunting lodge is a hundred and fifty or more years old. If Shawn isnae there, we'll try the cottage. For all I know they've added more tae the property." Grandpa swiveled on his bootheel and spread his arms. "He could pitch a tent and be anywhere."

"I don't think Shawn's the tent type." Paislee prayed they'd find Shawn warm and safe. Then she'd drag him to his mother's house, get him medical treatment, and call the DI so Shawn could explain his actions. Completely mental!

Grandpa traipsed on and Wallace raced after him, tongue out, brambles in his silky fringe.

A doe with her fawn darted in front of them. Wallace stopped and growled a warning at an animal he'd never seen before.

Ah, protective! "Thanks, pup." She scratched his ears, and they marched on.

Grandpa turned to the right, and she saw a tall stone house with a chimney, the wooden shingle of its roof covered in dark green moss. A wooden door with leather hinges was closed but hung askew as if the boards had warped from years of weather.

"It's like a fairy tale," she said in wonderment. "I wouldn't be surprised tae find seven dwarves inside."

Grandpa chuckled and leaned back to eye the smokeless stone chimney. "Let me go first and make sure it's sound."

Paislee hurried to catch up with him on the wooden stairs. "Don't go all the way in—let's just look from the door." She wouldn't want to explain to Shannon Leery that they'd broken into her hunting lodge. The woman had enough on her plate.

Grandpa gingerly twisted the knob and pulled it open. Light spilled between broken slats of the mossy roof to a cement floor. Wooden furniture—thick and well made—waited to be used again.

Cobwebs dangled from the corner eaves and stretched across the fireplace. Paislee got the sense that nobody had been here in some time. "No Shawn. It's been forgotten," she said.

"Well, let's hope for better luck at the cottage."

They strolled another quarter mile and stopped before a two-story wooden cottage overlooking the stream. The door had been painted a dark green to match the pine trees and had two steps leading to a long porch that held two rocking chairs.

Paislee tugged Wallace back on his leash. He strained to smell the steps and the daffodils at the base of the house. "This must be where Midge thought Shawn would come." Was he inside? Was he all right?

Curtains had been closed behind square, clear-paned windows. After a moment of indecision, Paislee stepped toward the door, Grandpa at her side. He knocked. When there was no answer, Paislee twisted the knob and opened the door.

"Fresh flowers, shortbread cookies. Apples. Paper cups. The blanket on the bed folded back." Grandpa waggled his bushy brows.

Paislee handed Grandpa Wallace's leash to keep the muddy pup outside and to get a better look. The daybed before the window had the covers kicked aside as if slept in. "Two someones," she said. "Two turquoise paper cups." Her heart dropped to her stomach. Paper, double-cupped, one with a brick-red smile. She didn't want to believe it, but couldn't deny what she saw. She reached for one—cold to the touch.

"Good eye." Grandpa grinned. "Maybe Shannon and her man, what was his name?"

"Graham." She pressed her hand to her stomach as disappointment, shock, and sorrow collided, making her slightly ill. "Grandpa—those cups are from Theadora's Tea Shoppe." That shade was Theadora's lipstick.

"A love nest—but for Shawn? And Theadora? Isn't she married tae that baker fellow?"

"Dan." Paislee closed the door, wishing she'd never opened Pandora's box. What had Midge said about him being with a trashy blonde? "We should go. I'll call Theadora." And say what? Caught ya? She stepped down to the grass, not wanting to think about ramifications. Then again, maybe Shawn was with Theadora *now*? Or she could know where to find him, and that was most important for Shannon's sake.

"Ye don't want tae meddle in a marriage," Grandpa said sagely.

Paislee didn't want to "meddle" at all. "What if she can find Shawn?"

They heard the sound of sticks snapping as something moved toward them through the trees. Wallace growled and stared toward the path.

"Hush, boy." Paislee quieted him with a piece of bacon-flavored kibble.

Grandpa tugged her behind the cottage and out of sight.

Graham cantered past them on a black horse, dark honey hair loose down his broad back.

"Who was that?" Grandpa murmured.

"Graham Reid. Sculptor who designed the metal stag for Shannon, and her latest lover."

Wallace gave a warning growl and his ears laid back. Someone was in the pine and beech between them and the manor. Not another horse, or a deer. "Shh." She gave Wallace a look to hush.

Someone who whistled as they walked. A woman or man? Whoever it was made their way after Graham, thick green fern concealing them from view. Could it be the security Gavin might have hired? Where were they going?

Paislee got her bearings—the stream to her left, the house ahead. "The stables are tae our right," she said softly to Grandpa.

After waiting a minute, she and Grandpa followed, staying on the same path Graham had taken. The trees thinned, and she saw the blue roof of the restrooms ahead through the pines, which meant the maze and the picnic area were between them and the manor.

"There's a path tae our left," she told Grandpa, "that goes behind the garden shed. The hedge provides privacy from the park across the stream. It's where Charles was shot and fell through the brush. Shawn was there, and Graham, supposedly." Her pulse sped as she recalled the danger that morning.

Grandpa held her arm. "Going closer tae the house might get us caught."

Wallace pulled on his leash toward the whistler, who remained hidden by a patch of green fern. The whistling stopped abruptly. Wallace chuffed, and Paislee quickly picked him up to ensure he didn't bark. "Hush now," she crooned to the pup.

A male and female voice drifted toward them in conversation. She hoped it would be Shawn so she could confront him about the hurtful game he was playing.

Holding her dog's snout, she brought her finger to her lips. Grandpa's gray brow arched. A layer of thin mist covered everything.

The woman's voice was younger than Shannon's—Aila's. She recalled her riding the other day. Paislee couldn't make out the man's voice.

"I'll meet you in an hour," Aila said. "I have to calm Mother down. Her precious Shawn could be dying somewhere—what a break that would be, aye?"

The man said nothing, but there was the sound of lips pressed together, kissing—then horse hooves. She assumed it was Aila leaving. Horse hooves slid on the damp grass. After a pause, whistling.

She and Grandpa stayed behind the maze until there were no more noises and then walked to the far end of the hidden trail where she could see the place Charles had been shot. Across the stream and ten feet up the bank was Sharp's Park. Beside a cluster of pine trees and a boulder the size of her Juke was a wooden picnic table.

Anybody could be over there, on public land. It had a clear view of the trail the family would use to be screened from tourists on their property. Hadn't she and Grandpa just proved that privacy was an illusion?

"Could someone shoot from over there"—she pointed to the boulder—"and hit their target, here?" she whispered.

"Easy." Grandpa spoke in a low murmur. "I could throw a rock from that boulder tae the hedge. A rifle would be no problem."

Being close to where Charles had died brought a queasy feeling to her stomach. "Let's go before we're caught." The mist had thickened to drizzle.

"Got the willies?" Grandpa adjusted the green tam over his silver hair. "Me too. Makes ya wonder if there really are ghosts."

Paislee cast a nervous gaze toward the slate roof of the estate visible over the hedge. She wouldn't want to meet up with Charles's ghost. Would he think she owed him for being witness to his passing? Goose bumps trailed up her spine, and she shivered.

"Hurry." Stepping away from the stream, Paislee let Wallace

lead them down the path to the cottage. She hated to think it, but an affair would explain why Theadora had burst into tears at Shawn's name, why she and Dan were fighting so badly. Theadora had changed from her white-and-turquoise hair to the conservative golden brown. Was she thinking she could do better with Shawn, as Dan feared? Hadn't she known about his illness?

She thought of collecting the cup with Theadora's lipstick on it but decided to leave it at the cottage. She didn't *want* proof of Theadora's affair with Shawn Marcus. She glanced back at Grandpa. "We know that Shawn is still missing, and that Shannon fears for him. Our next step is tae contact Theadora."

"Call her from the Juke, lass."

"I don't have her mobile, only the store number." She'd hate to reach Dan by mistake.

They followed the stream upriver and passed by the cozy cottage. Even Wallace seemed to have a sense of urgency as he sniffed their previous trail toward the car.

Malcolm rounded the two-story home and narrowed his brown eyes with anger. He folded his arms over his sage hunting jacket. "What are you doing here, Ms. Shaw?"

Her cheeks flamed as she pointed to Wallace. "Just walking our dog."

Grandpa averted his gaze.

Malcolm stepped menacingly toward them. "I've heard better excuses from me four-year-old niece."

"Hey now," Grandpa said. "Yer talking tae a lady."

"A trespasser. As are you." Malcolm turned on Grandpa. "What are you doing here? Who are *you*?"

"We're walking the dog, as we do on a Sunday," Grandpa said in a reasonable tone. "I was showing me granddaughter where I used tae fish as a lad."

"That would have been quite a while ago." Malcolm scoffed. "This is private property."

"We saw no fence," Grandpa said. Which was true. He'd found an opening that wasn't marked. "And the lady used tae allow us use of the stream. We meant no harm."

"I'll walk you oot," Malcolm said gruffly.

"That's not necessary," Paislee said.

"Och, but it is. As you well know, Ms. Shaw, there's been a murder on our property and the killer is still at large. Two known criminals acquainted with Charles Thomson have been spotted in the area. Should I call the police?"

Paislee sucked in a breath. "That's not necessary."

Grandpa stayed at her side, and Wallace growled at Malcolm.

"Well?" the butler asked, stepping back from the dog. "Go on."

"Has Shawn been found?" Paislee didn't move and inwardly cringed at being so forward, but she had to know.

"You have some nerve." Malcolm shook his head in disbelief. "I dinnae understand what m'lady sees in you."

He listened in at doors and knew Shannon had asked her for help. "Are you searching for him, too? We saw Graham on horseback." Headed toward the stables.

"You should be hightailing it oot of here." Malcolm stuffed his hands into his jacket pockets. "Shawn likes his luxuries—he'll turn up when he runs oot of money. Nobody pushed him down the stairs. He's a drunk."

"Is that why you don't care for him?"

"I *despise* him because he isnae guid tae his mother," Malcolm said flatly. He ushered them toward a narrow trail that led toward the hunting lodge and exit. "Go. The only way you may return is if you've purchased a ticket tae the grounds, once we open up again."

Grandpa tipped his tam at Malcolm. She peeked back to see Malcolm staring at her, arms crossed. She didn't observe a gun, but it wouldn't have surprised her. Their departure through the forest was somber, and she exhaled with relief when they reached its edge and the road where her car was parked.

"Glad he didnae call the coppers." Grandpa opened the side passenger door while Paislee brushed most of the mud off Wallace before putting him on his blanket, then slid behind the wheel.

"When I met him, he had a gun in his pocket. Told the DI it was tae shoot pests." Paislee checked her rearview mirror, expecting Malcolm to burst from the trees after them, but the forest was quiet. She turned the car around and headed to the main road.

"Did ye see a weapon?"

"No."

"Guid." Grandpa brushed his hands together. "Now, what did we learn?" He lifted a finger. "Shawn and Theadora are doing the midnight tango."

"Hey!"

"Shawn is still missing from the house. He might be with Theadora, but ye dinnae have her mobile. Can we swing by the bakery?"

"Aye, but I'd hate tae see Dan. What would I say? What if we're wrong?" She hoped their marriage would matter more than an indiscretion.

Her phone rang, and she realized the time when Brody's face lit up the screen. How had it gotten to be five? She and Grandpa exchanged a look.

"Brody!" she said over the Bluetooth speaker. "We're ten minutes away, love. Are you having fun?"

"Aye—I hoped you'd be late. Guess what I'm having?"

"What?"

"Pizza!"

Grandpa chuckled.

"You're going tae turn into a pepperoni."

"Am not. Come tae the back of the shop, okay? I'll look oot the window for you."

"See you."

She ended the call and glanced at Grandpa, her mind still on the angry butler. "One thing that has always bothered me is why there was no blood, or exit wound, on Charles's body. Malcolm explained about bullet weights—do you know about that?"

"Sorry, lass. I'm more of a fisherman than a hunter."

She tossed her knit cap to the back seat by Wallace. "Who was Aila talking tae? Malcolm? He was out there at the same time." And who was the whistler?

"That makes sense. But Malcolm and Aila kissing?" Grandpa scratched his beard. "What would Shannon think?"

Paislee parked behind the comic book store in front of a cute bungalow. "She has plans for Aila tae marry someone with a title and wealth." Not a good situation for Aila, who wanted love. But with the butler? "You want tae . . . ?"

"I'll stay with Wallace in the car."

She hopped out, then walked the twenty steps to the front door and knocked.

"Paislee!" Bennett answered on a wave of garlic and tomato. "Can we tempt you with a slice?"

"No. Sairy about the time." Paislee's stomach rumbled at the savory smells.

Brody grinned at her from next to Bennett in the foyer, sauce on the corner of his mouth. "Dinnae worry, Mum. I told him yer always late."

"Not always," she said defensively.

Bennett's jade-green eyes glimmered with mirth. "It's been great getting tae know Brody, and you, a bit more."

She couldn't help thinking how good this man would be for Lydia. Funny, kind, handsome. And then an adorable blonde poked her head from the kitchen, carrying a slice of pizza on a plate. "Yer sure you willnae stay for a wee bite?"

Bennett held out his hand toward the cutie. "This is Alexa. Alexa, Paislee."

"Nice tae meet you—another time, maybe? My grandpa and dog are in the car."

Edwyn and Brody darted outside between them. "Wallace!"

"You've got tae be exhausted," Paislee said with a laugh. "Have they been on hyper mode the whole time?"

"We're used tae it," Bennett said. "Edwyn is constantly on the move."

"True." Alexa bit off the pointy end of her pizza slice.

"It was nice for Edwyn tae have someone tae hang oot with." Bennett looked at Alexa, then Paislee. "Maybe we can steal Brody next weekend, too?"

"We'll see. It should be my turn tae have Edwyn over." She could have kicked herself for saying those words. What did she know about entertaining two rowdy boys?

The couple jumped on her offer.

"That'd be great," Bennett said.

"Let's confirm at the end of next week." Alexa grinned up at him. "A romantic getaway, just the two of us?"

And now she knew why he hadn't called Lydia. Paislee forced a smile. "Sounds great. I'll be in touch—thanks again for having Brody stay."

The three adults ambled toward her Juke, where the boys were in the back seat, petting Wallace. The pup soaked up the attention with quick licks of appreciation.

Grandpa had his tam pulled low as if to drown out the boys' chatter.

She made the introductions.

"We'll see if Edwyn can spend next Sunday with us," Paislee said. The boys erupted with cheers and high fives.

The look of dismay on her grandfather's face was priceless.

The whole ride back to their house all Brody could talk about was the fun that they'd had, the pizza he'd eaten, the games they'd played. And now Edwyn would get to come to his house?

"We can go tae the beach, right Mum, and fly kites?"

That sounded fine to her—outdoors where they could be as loud as they wanted. "We'll see. You have tae make sure you're good all week."

"I promise, Mum. I'll even help you fold the socks."

Paislee nodded. This playdate thing just might have a few perks.

# Chapter 22

Paislee half-listened to Brody as he went on during the ride home from Bennett's house; the other part of her brain wondered what to do about Theadora. Would she know where to find Shawn? Could she ask Theadora to have her lover call?

She parked in her driveway beneath the carport and turned the engine off. "Home sweet home." Thanks to Grandpa's early-morning grocery run, they had roast chicken for dinner. A blue SUV pulled up behind her. Dread rushed through her system. What could the DI possibly want? It was never good when he showed up.

She, Brody, Wallace, still leashed, and Grandpa all got out of the car. They gathered at the steps of the house—a united front against the detective inspector.

"Detective Inspector Zeffer," Paislee said stiffly. She hadn't forgotten his sarcastic "Thanks for being a concerned citizen" earlier that morning.

"Shaw family." The DI raised his palm. "How is everyone?"

Wallace wagged his tail but kept his ears lowered—not quite sure if the man in the blue suit was friend or enemy. That was often how Paislee felt about DI Zeffer, too.

"Great, thanks."

"I'd like a word?" He tilted his head, the russet locks sliding stylishly across his forehead.

There was little chance of not inviting the man inside. She didn't want to be rude or give the neighbors an eyeful.

"Sure—excuse the mess." The dishes were done, but had she finished the laundry? "We werenae expecting company."

Grandpa, who now had his own key, unlocked the front door, and he, Brody, then Wallace tramped in, followed by Detective Inspector Zeffer, with Paislee bringing up the rear.

She closed the door firmly, wondering if Zeffer would stay in the foyer to talk with just her, but no. He gravitated toward the kitchen table, where the morning newspaper lay open with Charles's and the Pickett brothers' pictures.

"Grandpa, will you clear the table? Can I get you some tea, Detective?"

"I'd love a cup, ta."

Paislee was completely thrown off stride. Brody stayed at her side as if he feared the DI might haul her off to jail. Grandpa stuffed the paper on top of the laundry basket with the clothes she'd intended to fold when she had a minute.

She got down three mugs, while Grandpa set a tin of tea in the center of the table.

The kettle clicked off, and Paislee brought the hot water over, placing it on a trivet.

Handing out mugs to Grandpa and the DI, and one for herself, she asked, "Brody, did ye want tea?"

Her son shook his head, eyes wide.

His fear in their own home made her protective and defensive. She directed Brody by the shoulder to a seat between her and Grandpa.

Paislee studied the detective and decided to get straight to the point. "Detective, why are you here?"

He winced, the skin around his mouth tightening before he gave a nod. "I thought about calling first but decided tae stop by."

"Regarding?"

"An unofficial complaint made by Gavin Thornton."

Shoot. Malcolm had blabbed about them being on the property.

Grandpa poured hot water over a tea bag, then dunked it. He lifted the pot toward the detective.

The detective nodded.

Grandpa put a bag in the mug for the detective and repeated the process with the hot water. "Sugar? Milk?"

"Neither."

Her grandpa was stalling to give Paislee time, but she decided to stick with the story they'd been using.

"We bumped into Malcolm when Grandpa was showing me his old fishing hole today. I'm surprised it was Gavin tae complain—we spoke tae the butler."

Zeffer let out an exasperated sigh, as though he knew this was a whopper. "Tell me what happened."

Brody scooted his chair closer to her and picked up Wallace. The dog sprawled across his lap.

"We often hike the trails around Nairn, and Grandpa told me about the amazing fish he used tae catch—we happened tae be in the neighborhood, and he offered tae show me." She skirted the truth as best she could. "Took Wallace with us, tae burn off some of his energy."

Wallace was limp as one of the socks hanging on the dryer rack, his head lolling off Brody's knee, so it was hard to believe how much energy the Scottie had. The detective glanced at the black pup with doubt. "And your son?"

"Brody spent the day with his friend Edwyn Maclean."

"We ate pizza and played video games. Mum, why'd ye go hiking without me? I thought you wanted tae go tae Sharp's Park?"

Bless her son for paying attention. "Grandpa showed me where he used tae fish near there."

"And it didnae bother ye tae be trespassing?" DI Zeffer sipped from his mug.

"We saw no signs or fences." Paislee played innocent with her chosen words.

"Back in my day, the open fields were free tae everyone," Grandpa said. "So long as ye did no harm."

"Times have changed, Angus Shaw. Times have changed." Zeffer took in her grandfather from boot to silver hair. "And how have ye been?"

Grandpa shifted on his chair—in the hot seat. "Fine, fine."

"Any news on your missing son? Craigh, was it?"

"None."

Paislee wondered if Grandpa would mention their drive to Dairlee and the break-in of the storage unit, but he merely tugged at his beard. She cleared her throat. "Malcolm asked us tae leave the property, so we did."

"That simple?" Zeffer's russet brow lifted.

"Well, he asked us not tae come back."

Brody watched the detective warily, petting Wallace beneath the chin. "Ever, Mum? What about field trips?"

She knew that Hamish had cancelled the field trips for the rest of the year in exchange for golfing but didn't bring that sore subject up. "I meant," she clarified, "without a ticket."

Grandpa slurped his tea.

The detective cupped a hand around his mug. "So, did you happen tae find Shawn Marcus while you were taking the pup for a walk?"

Ah. The detective knew what they were up to. She maintained her bluff. "No. I hope the family's filed a missing person report."

"They have not, which leads me tae believe they know *exactly* where Shawn Marcus is at and they're covering for him."

Midge had hinted to Paislee that Shawn often hid out on the property, so the DI wasn't too far off. "This time is different." She glanced at Grandpa, then her son. "Brody, hon, why don't you go watch TV?"

Brody shuffled off with Wallace awkwardly in his arms, the pup licking the boy's face.

The detective almost smiled. "I never had a dog, growing up."

Explained a lot. "Why's that?"

"Our family traveled quite a bit." His expression flattened. "Now, what is different for Shawn?"

She waited until Brody turned on the television in the living room before murmuring, "Shannon told me over lunch yesterday that Shawn believes someone is trying tae kill him."

Zeffer nostrils flared. "He's wanted for questioning regarding his whereabouts during the shooting. For his attempted break-in at the morgue. He can tell me all aboot it from the safety of the station."

"I told you this morning why Shawn couldnae have killed Charles." She leaned in. "When Grandpa and I were on our . . . walk . . . with Wallace, we saw the park across the stream. It makes more sense that someone shot from there. Shawn was right by the hedge. The paper said the weapon used was a rifle and—"

His fist curled around his mug. "You're right."

"I am?" She'd expected more of an argument.

"I dinnae mind telling ye since my team has already been over every pebble. We have a partial boot print by the boulder."

Paislee straightened. "You'll be able tae match that tae what the Pickett brothers are wearing. Did they confess?" He'd been on his way to arrest them earlier.

Zeffer shifted as if the seat had grown thorns. "I have Bart Pickett in custody. Joey wasnae at the hotel."

Paislee sipped her tea. This meant the DI knew Shawn hadn't shot Charles and he was looking for Joey Pickett.

Zeffer jabbed his pointer finger onto the table. "I've been tae the estate. I've got a unit patrolling around the morgue as well as the hospital. I've been in touch with Shawn's doctors. He's disappeared."

She knew well the detective's frustration. "If by some miracle Shawn contacts me, I'll pass on your message."

"Ms. Shaw. Paislee." Zeffer looked her straight in the eyes. "This is verra important. Bart hasnae confessed tae shooting Charles."

She lowered her mug.

"He claims that Shawn Marcus was physically fighting with Charles right before the man died."

She sucked in her breath, recalling what had happened. She'd seen the scratches on Shawn's hands. He'd claimed to have pulled Charles from the hedges—which she'd told Zeffer. "But—"

Zeffer held up his palm. "Aila Webster confirmed what you told me, that Shawn and Charles had shouted angrily Tuesday evening. Charles informed Shawn that he would get his kidney"— the DI pulled out his black leather notebook from his suit pocket and read—"*over my dead body*. Shawn knows more than what he's let on. You understand my concern?"

Why would Aila tell that to the police? Revenge, of course. Paislee'd heard Aila's hatred for Shawn earlier.

Grandpa dunked his tea bag like it was a bloody yo-yo.

"I do." She would get better at this game. Give a little, take a little. "We overheard Aila talking with someone—we didn't see who, but then later Malcolm was by the cottage. Maybe him?" She shrugged. "Aila said she had tae go comfort her mother over Shawn being gone. I don't think they're covering for his absence."

"With that kind of family, who needs enemies?" Zeffer's jaw clenched. "Anybody else?"

"I think Graham was out looking for him, on horseback, and there was another person, too."

"A whistler," Grandpa chimed in.

"Did they hire security for the property?" Paislee asked. "We thought it might be a guard."

"I didnae see any, and I was just there." Zeffer tapped the side of his mug in thought. "Bart's a con artist. He had on sneakers, not boots. No gun in the hotel." His eyes widened as he realized what he'd just told her.

She didn't show a reaction, but she was elated that he'd let down his guard. "Maybe Joey stashed it? When ye find him, then you'll have the gun and the boots." Then Nairn could return to normal.

Zeffer's gaze narrowed, and he drummed his thumb against his notebook. His phone rang. "Hang on. This is Zeffer," he said, answering. His mouth firmed. "Uh-huh. I'll be right there."

He stood quickly, and his chair snagged on the braided rag rug, almost tipping over before he caught it. "Joey Pickett just evaded capture—he's after Shawn for killing Charles."

"But he didn't!"

"I dinnae think the man is listening tae reason. We need tae find Shawn before Joey does."

Grandpa cleared his throat and pursed his lips in a smooch.

Paislee thought of the cup with the brick-red lipstick and blushed. "This isnae a sure thing," she hedged, not wanting to repeat something awful—but if it saved Shawn? She had to try.

The detective crossed his arms, his keys in his hand. "What is it?"

"When we were on the property, we stumbled across two paper cups in the cottage by the stream, where Shawn was hiding out."

"And," the DI said impatiently.

"One of the cups, I'm pretty sure, belonged tae Theadora Barr. It was her shade of lipstick. The same little smile shape on the rim."

His shoulders dropped in disappointment.

She hurried on. "Theadora and her husband own the tea shop on the corner of Market Street."

The DI quickly put the scenario together. "*If* it is Theadora, she was with Shawn, not her husband, in this cottage? Mibbe together now. How can I get ahold of her?"

"I don't have her mobile number, just the shop's." She held her hand out to Zeffer, feeling terrible. "Please be kind if you question her—they've been trying tae have a baby, and with the threat of the sale of the building, things have been very stressful." Paislee got up and wrote the number on a piece of scrap paper by the phone.

The detective blew out a breath of exasperation. "I have nothing tae question her aboot except tae see if she knows where Shawn is. Lipstick on a cup? A cup I havenae even seen for myself?" He dragged his hand through his styled hair, his expression tormented. He took the paper and turned to go.

"You could ruin a marriage if ye don't take care," she said, her heart burning that she was somehow betraying her friends.

"Sounds broken already," Zeffer remarked. "Let me know aboot Shawn—we'll get him in protective custody."

He lifted a hand and hurried out their front door. Paislee followed and locked it behind him.

Heart thudding, Paislee hoped the DI found Shawn before Joey Pickett killed him.

# Chapter 23

"Well," Grandpa observed when Paislee returned to the table. "I think you got under the detective's skin, lass."

She sank to her chair. "I hope that wasn't a mistake. What if there was a perfectly good reason for her and Shawn tae be together?"

"Hiding oot in a love nest?" Grandpa queried doubtfully. "The covers kicked back? You'd planned on contacting her yourself, for the same reason, tae find Shawn. Now Joey is after him. Ye did the right thing."

She reached for Grandpa's hand. "Thanks." Then noticed the time. Half past six on a school night and they hadn't had dinner yet. Her pulse skipped as she searched for where to begin her routine. "Brody—have ye done yer reading for the day?"

"Mum!" The telly clicked off, and Brody dragged his feet to his backpack in the closet by the stairs. Wallace barked at his heels, wanting to play. She triple-checked the lock on the front door, and then the back as well. The windows, too.

A killer loose in Nairn, searching for her landlord. She'd been so sure that it hadn't been the Picketts that she'd hiked around the Leery property without a care. Yet Bart claimed not to have done it. "Grandpa—do you mind researching why a bullet might not exit the body? Specifically something about the weight." She wanted to better understand what Malcolm had told her.

Grandpa fired up the desktop computer in the living room while she cooked the chicken and veg. Thirty minutes later, they were eating together as a family; then she sent Brody to the tub for his bath. She did a load of laundry and started in on the dry clothes that needed to be folded. If Grandpa didn't find a good answer, she'd then ask Amelia. They'd been playing phone tag.

Grandpa waited until Brody went to bed before sharing what he'd found online. "Bullet weights for small deer or fox are less than standard weight, so as not tae tear apart the animal."

She and Grandpa exchanged a look. "Which means that whoever shot Charles used a small-deer hunting rifle?"

"I dinnae know all the particulars—as I said, I'm a fisherman." Grandpa headed toward the kitchen and put the Big Ben puzzle on the table. "Another reason listed was the bullet got stuck by a bone."

She hadn't seen an entrance point. Paislee retrieved the Scotch from her pantry. "We've earned a dram, I think." She poured them each a wee bit into their tea mugs, then leaned back against the counter, her arm curled over her waist as she sipped.

"It's been an interestin' day." Grandpa clicked Paislee's mug.

"Shawn claims tae have been hurt inside his own home. I think Malcolm would have noticed if the Picketts had broken in, don't ye think? Or Midge."

"What are ye gettin' at?"

"Bart was wearing runners, not boots." She crossed him off her mental list. What about Joey? "I think whoever shot Charles didn't plan it out."

"Why?"

"Otherwise they wouldn't have used that particular rifle but a weapon meant tae kill a *man*. The Picketts took a train from London tae Nairn. A planned action, not impulse."

"Another logical point against the Picketts," Grandpa said. "So Aila isnae the shooter."

"Though she hates Shawn. Neither is Malcolm. Or Shawn."

"Who does that leave?"

"Graham . . . but why? He's living the high life. Should we toss Gavin into the mix? He's always at the manor with Shannon. Unrequited love. Midge. I think she's got feelings for Shawn. He's a lord, and she's just the maid." She tilted her head back and growled her frustration.

"Right now it's all muddled." Grandpa drank deeply of his Scotch tea, one silver brow arched. "It's a different kind of puzzle than Big Ben here. Keep at it, one piece at a time, and ye'll find the solution."

His companionship had come as a pleasant surprise. "Why didn't you tell the detective that we were in Dairlee today, or about the break-in?"

"That DI hears too much as it is." Grandpa clicked his tongue behind his teeth. "No wonder he's taken tae dropping by. You do all his work for him."

She snorted. "That's not true. Although it's his own fault he made the Leerys angry, trying tae draw a line of equality in the sand. He'd have been better off treating Aila with kid gloves."

"I think he's realizing that. He's an odd man. What with his styled hair and blue suits. Not a local lad, that's for sure."

"So why didn't you tell him? Maybe he can help you find Craigh."

He cleared his throat, drained the mug, and poured a second all-whisky cup. She sipped hers, needing a clear head tomorrow for her appointment with Hamish in the morning about the lawsuit. There'd been no other word from Arran.

"You're still working in the morning for me at Cashmere Crush, don't forget."

"I can handle me whisky." He scoffed.

"Didn't mean tae say otherwise. Whatever is bothering you, I'm here tae listen. Or help—whatever you want."

"Thanks." He stroked his beard. "It's just, a man wants tae be proud of his son, ye ken?"

She remained by the counter, afraid that if she joined him at the table, he'd spook. "A woman, too," she said, thinking of herself and Shannon Leery.

"Aye, aye. But I didnae meet Craigh until he was an adult, and it caused a rift between your Gran and me. My feelings toward him were . . . conflicted."

She nodded—biting her tongue to keep from asking questions.

"So I looked the other way more than once. I'm not sure Craigh's job was on the right side of the law." His shoulders were stiff and defensive. "Craigh felt like I owed him a better life—and I suppose that I fell into the guilt trap. I did me best for him, but he wasnae always forthcoming aboot what he was up to."

Oh. She straightened. "You think what he's doing might be illegal, and that's why you don't want tae involve the detective?"

He stared moodily into his mug. "I've an idea who broke in. I'll wait until the date he was supposed tae return, and then, if there is no word, *then* I'll open his private boxes."

"What if *someone* breaks in again?"

"What if it was Craigh, eh?" He raised his anguished eyes to hers. "I cannae tell the police my suspicions, but I want me son back. Craigh wasnae a bad man, just a wee bit shady, thinking that I, and the world, owed him."

He thought his own son was the one who'd been in the storage unit. Grandpa truly believed Craigh was still alive.

"His stepdad raised him, after Noreen, Craigh's mother, died. He believed in the 'spare the rod, spoil the child' method of child-rearing." Grandpa's fist clenched. "He's already dead, or I'd a had a word."

"You didn't know."

"I've been trying tae make it right. How can the police tell me that the oil rig he's supposed tae be on doesnae even exist?" His voice deepened. "What if Craigh was tired of living with his old man, so he emptied the accounts and vanished?"

"Oh!" She put her hand to her heart. "Surely not."

"I dinnae want tae think that. Nor believe he was a bad man."

She pointed to the calendar hanging on the wall next to the refrigerator. "Another month before the *Mona* is supposed tae return, and Craigh. I understand now why you want tae wait for the boxes."

"You do?"

"Aye. If Craigh returns, then you honored his wishes and didn't break his trust in you. You're trying tae build a relationship with him. I get it."

Grandpa drained his mug. "That means a lot, lass. I havenae had someone on my side since, well, yer grandmother couldn't quite see tae forgive my madness before the wedding. Too much tae drink was no excuse, and she was right. I loved her as I loved no other."

Paislee joined him at the table and squeezed his hand. "I wish she could know that."

"I tell her every night."

She blinked to hold back tears. "Och. That's the sweetest, saddest thing I've ever heard."

Grandpa chuckled and brought his mug to the sink to rinse it out. "On that note, I'm tae bed. Night, lass." He closed his bedroom door, though it was only nine. The Scotch and the confession, combined with their hike, must've tuckered him out.

Paislee stayed up to finish folding laundry, texting with Lydia. They made a date for coffee after the meeting with Hamish and Arran. Texted Amelia, who was glad she was all right.

Laundry done, Paislee wrote a list of questions about the Fishers' lawsuit. Hamish didn't seem certain that the signed paperwork would be enough, but if it was, she'd no longer make fun of his forms. To regain her lease, only to be sued and lose her business assets, didn't seem fair.

Why would Joey think that Shawn had killed Charles? What had he seen? If Shawn would just call her! She realized he was scared for his life, and he had reason to be. Hopefully the DI would have luck with Theadora in finding the man.

At nine thirty, a soft knock sounded on the front door. She hurried before it woke Brody or Grandpa. She peered through the peephole, expecting to see Detective Inspector Zeffer with news of Joey's arrest.

But no, it was Gavin Thornton with a giant bouquet of flowers.

She opened the door, and he waltzed in, giving her a cheery wink. "I'm here tae apologize. I explained what'd happened tae Shannon, and she assured me that she'd always allowed the gents tae fish on the stream—she was verra put oot with me for telling the detective you were on the property."

Paislee hadn't expected an apology. Wallace chuffed from the top of the stairs at the unknown visitor. "It's all right, pup. Come on in, Gavin." She accepted the fragrant lilies and gestured for Gavin to join her at the kitchen table. She filled Gran's crystal vase with water.

Gavin scanned her kitchen and living room, then the back door and the porch, before returning his focus to her. "Have you seen Shawn, by chance?"

"Why would he be *here*, and this late?"

He smiled charmingly. "We discovered that Shawn has a lady friend. I wondered if it was you who'd met him at the cottage earlier."

"And I brought my grandfather and dog with me?" Paislee crossed her arms. "That's ridiculous."

"It was a guess, that's all." Gavin held up both hands.

The nerve of this guy! "We heard Aila talking with someone, and we saw Malcolm. No Shawn." She didn't tell Gavin that she knew the identity of the lipstick wearer, or that Aila had been kissing her mystery man.

Grandpa's door opened briefly, then closed. Gavin whirled at the sound.

"I hope you haven't woken *Grandpa*." She arranged the lilies in the vase and placed the bouquet on the counter since the puzzle was on the kitchen table.

Gavin flexed his shoulders and put his hands behind his back. "Shawn takes medicine for his kidneys, but he hasnae been home since yesterday morning. Shannon is, understandably, worried for her son."

"The DI is looking for him, too."

"Zeffer was at the manor already, aboot the morgue incident. I assured the detective that Shawn's medicine can make him a wee bit mental."

How clever of the accountant to think of an excuse that a good solicitor might use to get all charges dropped. "Did he tell you that Joey Pickett's after him?"

"Aye." His green eyes flashed with remorse. "Shannon told me that Shawn's had at least two attempts on his life. An incident in his room, and the stairs?"

Gavin waited to see if she would invite him to sit, but Paislee took a step toward the hall. "Thank you for the flowers. Send my regards tae Lady Leery. How is she holding up?"

"Charles's murder, Shawn's health, they're tearing her up inside. The family doctor prescribed sleeping pills, so she's resting, against her will."

Paislee quickened her steps to the door. "If I hear from Shawn, I'll let ye know. I would appreciate the same courtesy."

Gavin shrugged and gave a disarming smile. "You have a cozy home, Paislee. It's warm, like you."

She blushed and opened the door—Wallace was curled up on the top step of the landing and now rose, tail wagging. "Thank you. Good night."

He waved and hopped into a bronze Audi she hadn't seen before.

Paislee locked up behind him and turned in the foyer. Wallace was gone, probably back to bed with Brody. The light beneath Grandpa's door switched on; then he cracked it open, eyes large and brown in the dim hall light. He wasn't wearing his glasses, and had on a pair of sweatpants and an old sweatshirt. "Who was that?"

"Gavin—Shannon's accountant. He dropped off some flowers of apology."

His hair stuck up on one side. "I'll put on the kettle."

Her heart panged. That was exactly what Gran would have done if woken in the night.

"No need, Grandpa," she said in a thick voice. "I'm headed tae bed. It's a big day tomorrow. Shawn is still missing—Gavin was checking the house tae see if he could be hiding here. Can you believe it? Shannon sent him."

"Well, now," he said, eyes sparkling. "She's a lovely woman—but had nothing on your grandmother."

"Good night, Grandpa."

*Gran, I hope you know how much he loves you, and that you can find it in your heart to forgive him.*

Paislee climbed the steps slowly to her room, careful of the creaky ones, slipped into pj's, then crawled beneath the covers of her bed, the whisky easing her into much-needed sleep.

# Chapter 24

Paislee dreamed of warm raspberry scones straight out of Theadora and Dan's bakery oven, with a piping hot cup of tea—then she was racing toward Fordythe in a panic at being late, only to discover she'd forgotten Brody at home. What kind of mum did that?

She was stuck behind an old woman driving slow as molasses round the traffic circle. Paislee honked. She had to get home to Brody! They were going to be late!

Her brain scrambled to piece together the noise she heard—was it a flat tire on the Juke? That had happened before. No, the noise was real.

She scrubbed the grit from her eyes and sat up. The pounding sounded from downstairs, from the front door.

Why wouldn't Grandpa answer it?

She hurried out of her room and flew down the stairs—Wallace at her heels. He barked. "Hush." He barked softer, excitedly wagging his tail.

Another knock.

She peered through the peephole in the wooden frame, and a distorted image of an orange-skinned man with brown hair and sunken cheeks blinked back.

Was she still dreaming? She pinched her wrist in disbelief. The shower from the downstairs bathroom gurgled through the pipes. Grandpa.

A knock thudded louder.

Paislee opened the front door a crack. "Shawn—what are *you* doing here?"

"Let me in!"

"No!"

He seemed surprised at her reaction, but she had to protect her family. Though the man wasn't well, he was being hunted by a killer—and the police.

Wallace, needing to relieve his bladder, darted outside, nearly knocking Shawn over. He grabbed the wall of her stone house for support.

She slipped outside and shut the door behind her, keeping it at her back. "Where have you been?" His lightweight jacket had grass stains and dirt on the elbows, his khakis were torn at the knee, and he wore a polo shirt with the local golf club's insignia.

Wallace watered the grass, lifting his leg at the rose bush, before he trotted back to her. The spring morning had a bite, and she curled her toes on the cement step, her flannel pajamas not quite warm enough.

Shawn had parked his Mercedes in the driveway at a slant behind her Juke.

"Are you drunk?" she demanded.

"No, no." He half-closed his bloodshot, jaundiced eyes. "I tried tae get drunk, but the bartender cut me off."

"Where have you been?"

"I slept in me car last night."

"Everybody is looking for you. The DI, your mum, *Joey Pickett*."

"I know," Shawn said, glancing behind him. "At first I thought I was being paranoid, but no. Someone wants me dead. Not just Joey. He almost caught me at the golf course, but I lost him." He tipped sideways.

Paislee slipped her arm around his too-thin waist so he could stand upright, reminding her of his inebriated state at the party. "Listen, I know you didn't shoot Charles. If you can explain tae Joey—"

"You dinnae explain nothin' tae a creep like that. He thinks *I* shot Charles?" Shawn scowled. "It wasnae me. And I didn't see those two good-for-nothings that morning. I was having it oot with Charles, thinking if I offered him more money, he would sell me his kidney. I don't want dialysis for the rest of me life." He broke down in a sob.

"Oh, Shawn. Hush, now."

He hiccupped and scanned the neighborhood with a panicked expression, but thankfully nobody else was awake yet. She didn't see Joey, either.

"The DI knows you were fighting with Charles." Paislee tucked her toes beneath Wallace's warm fur as she shivered. "Running only points tae guilt."

"Ye think I don't know that? It isnae logical for me tae kill Charles—a live donor has a much higher success rate." He placed his hand to his side. "And since me body rejected the one from Aila, I have tae be careful."

Running around all night and breaking into a morgue didn't sound like he was being cautious; neither did drinking like a fish. She caught a whiff of gin on his breath and leaned back with a scowl. "So, what did you see that day behind the hedge?"

"Nothin'!" He reached for her with trembling hands. "I think it's someone in the house, Paislee. Someone I know." His shoulders bowed.

She wiggled her toes. "I've ruled out a few people."

"Who?" His voice wobbled.

Starting with the easiest, she said, "You."

He rolled his eyes, not amused.

"Malcolm."

He swayed with his nod. "Aye. He's a bruiser, but he wasnae behind the hedge."

"Who did you see? Was Graham there?"

"No." Shawn pointed his finger, off on a tangent. "I followed Charles. He was a scam artist. Ripped off old people. A leopard doesnae change his spots, does he?" He brought his knuckles to his mouth. "At the beginning he acted like he was going tae walk on the deal—until I promised him a million pounds. Me mum doesnae have that kind of cash. That's why I had tae sell the building."

"You should have told her."

"I know." He coughed into his hand and nervously looked behind him. "Mother already helped me, but Charles demanded even more. We fought. Then, bam, he's dead."

Paislee massaged the goose bumps from her arms. "Was Charles conning someone else? He'd told your mother he wouldn't help you unless he stayed at the estate and she paid him. He wasn't going tae help you unless you paid him extra. What about Aila? Maybe their whispers weren't about your kidney, like she said, but something else?"

"Aila's a right bitch." He fumbled with his jacket packet and pulled out a cheap black mobile.

She'd assumed he'd have the latest and greatest in mobile service. This was plastic. "Where's your phone?"

"I smashed it. Gavin has us all on the same plan. I'm sure he's tracking me."

"Gavin?" She thought of the handsome accountant who'd brought flowers to her just last night. To find Shawn . . . Her body froze. She'd tossed his name onto the pile of suspects with Grandpa. Had her subconscious picked up on something off?

"Thursday night, I woke tae someone in me room with a pillow. I shouted, and they left." Shawn stroked the back of his head. "Then Friday night after the party, someone shoved me down the stairs. If I hadnae been drinking, I'da broken me bloody neck. I had tae leave."

"Go tae the police," Paislee said. "The DI will protect you from Joey, and whoever else, so long as you're innocent. I know you didn't shoot Charles—so does the detective."

Shawn ignored her advice and tapped his temple. "I've been thinking aboot it."

Annoyed, Paislee snapped, "Between drinks?"

His threw up his hands and stepped away. "Never mind then. Midge said ye wanted tae help."

He was like a petulant child rather than a grown man. "Why did you set Aila up? Revenge has tae be why she told the detective about you and Charles fighting the night before he was shot."

"I was jealous"—he pinched the bridge of his nose—"at how well she fit in with our mother's world. She runs the Feed the Poor Foundation like she's done it all her life."

Paislee felt her patience dwindling. "So you thought, hey, I'll send her tae jail?"

He raised his palm but skipped back a half step, unsteady. "Not my finest hour, I admit. Aila wouldnae have been arrested. I tried tae follow her after I found her and Charles in the sunroom, heads together, but she disappeared on me. Probably used one of the servant's halls. I went up tae my room tae figure oot what tae do next, and that's when I heard Charles talking on the phone with Bart. He was arranging some kind of payoff at Sharp's Park. I followed him, to renegotiate, around the back."

Paislee pictured the scene. "Where was Graham—did you see him on the trail?"

Shawn stuck his hands in the pockets of his jacket. "No. He wasnae there."

"Your mother?"

"In her office, waiting for Aila tae go over the accounts. Gavin was supposed tae be there." Shawn shrugged. "He hates me."

She thought back to how gentle Gavin had been with Shawn when he'd walked him to his room the night of the Silverstein party. "Maybe he's simply frustrated with your behavior?"

"He's not me da, is he?" Shawn shouted.

"No." Shawn hadn't had a father.

"I trust me mum completely, but Gavin is like poison in her

ear." Overcome, Shawn started to weep. She awkwardly patted his arm.

"You should go home and rest. I can contact the DI for you and have him meet you at your house. Then you can explain what happened." Shawn was in no condition to drive. But she couldn't invite him in. Maybe she could walk him around the side of her house to the back porch, give him strong tea, and call the detective.

"I cannae go home." Shawn stopped crying and garnered the strength of the inebriated self-righteous. "Someone is trying tae kill me, just like they killed Charles. Who can I count on?" He pleaded with her.

Had Theadora understood that Shawn had a serious disease? It wasn't like he could hide it. The fake tan made his illness more obvious. "What about Theadora?"

Shawn stepped back with an upper lip snarl. "What are ye talking aboot?"

She grasped him by his wrist. "Theadora Barr?" Was he so drunk he didn't remember? "Your paramour?"

He snorted. "That's not what ye think. We met at the fertility specialist and . . ."

"Fell in love?"

"God, no—with that tart? Me mum wants an heir. I offered Theadora fifty thousand pounds if she'd carry me babe."

Shocked, Paislee leaned her body back against the door, her knees shaking. Dan's words about Theadora considering being a surrogate poured over her with cool clarity.

"Theadora is a tough negotiator. I shoulda had her help me with Charles."

"But she can't, I mean, they're trying."

"Nothing wrong with her parts," he said with assurance. "Mine, not so much. Tests came back with very *very* slow swimmers."

"How was she a good negotiator if you can't, uh, do your part?"

"I promised tae pay her fifty thousand pounds no matter what—and drop the sale of the building."

Paislee crossed her arms in disbelief. "The sale had fallen through already!"

"Aye." He chuckled. "But she didnae know that. And with Charles dead, the building is safe. All's well, Paislee."

"It's not, either! Your mother is furious at you putting it up for sale."

"She didnae know that Charles was triple-crossing us. Bastard. Mother is a saint. Anyway, Theadora's a good sport, but not me type."

Paislee couldn't imagine Shawn's "type."

She'd jumped to the wrong conclusion about Theadora and Shawn. What had the detective said to the Barrs? Paislee prayed that she hadn't caused a divorce.

"Shawn, listen. This is very important. Do you think that Joey Pickett shot Charles? Is that why he threatened tae kill you? Tae frame you for the murder?"

Shawn swayed again but held the lapels of his stained jacket like a lord addressing his servants. "Enemies come with the title. People ashume—assume ye have more money than you know what tae do with. Not true." He sniffed. "Mother sacrificed tae keep that pile of stones running. I should have had an heir for her, but I didnae. I couldnae." He closed his eyes and expelled a ginny breath. "I failed her."

Paislee felt compassion for his situation, but that wouldn't keep him alive. A car engine revved two houses over, and Shawn jumped.

She held out her arm. "Let's get you tae the porch and have a cup of tea. We'll call the detective, and he can help you, Shawn. You have tae stop running. We know that Malcolm isn't guilty. We know that Aila isn't guilty. We—"

"Wrong!" His brown eyes turned crafty as a wild fox. "When I was searching Aila's room for proof of her and Charles working to-gether, I found a stash of love letters, tied with a red bow." He wiped his nose with the back of his hand. "They were signed from someone with the initial G. I heard Aila coming, so I didnae have time tae see who they were from exactly."

"Shawn! What is the matter with you, digging into other people's things? Besides, she's single and can see who she wants." She thought of Aila and Malcolm and the kissing sounds at the picnic table. It wouldn't be what Shannon wanted, but they did no harm.

Shawn lifted a trembling finger. "Then why hide having a boyfriend?"

"Aila didn't shoot Charles, but you think she's trying tae kill *you*?"

"She would automatically become the heir if something happened tae me."

A cold knot formed in her stomach. Malcolm. Gunn.

"She coulda had an accomplice. You know who wasnae with Mum that morning? Gavin." His voice rose. "Gavin is always around, so where was he then? Huh?"

She pulled her mind from picturing Malcolm as the killer and fit in the accountant's image. Gray hair, masculine, green eyes, confident. "Shawn, why would Gavin want you dead?"

His bloodshot gaze sharpened. "He and Aila work together all the time because of the Feed the Poor Foundation. Maybe they fell in love while going over the books, I dunno."

She recalled how Gavin had given her home a cursory search for Shawn last night. Perhaps not to appease Shannon after all. Maybe he wanted Shawn out of the way? "That's not proof."

Shawn waggled his brows at Paislee. "Gavin gave her a ride home last week and they were late. Mum was worried. He said they had a flat, but did they?" His tone sounded highly doubtful.

"Stay focused on what we know, all right?" Paislee stepped away from the warmth of Wallace's fur on her bare feet to help Shawn, hooking her arm around his waist. "We can tell it all tae the DI."

He yanked free from her and toppled a step backward. "It's Monday. Gavin will be there tae go over the household accounts. They have tea and scones." His tone turned bitter. "When Mum discovers that Gavin, her ex she keeps on a pedestal, is in love with her daughter? Aila and Gavin will both be oot." Shawn rubbed his hands together gleefully.

"Shawn—that will break your mother's heart. And I don't know if that's true." She couldn't see Gavin's face, but Malcolm's.

Shawn was too wound up to listen. "He thinks he's family, but he's not. He's the damn *accountant*. Leery Estate will be mine one day, and Gavin oot of a job. He should think of that before crossing me."

She realized that for just those reasons, Gavin had a motive to want Shawn out of the way. If Shawn was "removed" from the picture, then Gavin would have full sway over the estate through Aila. Poor Shannon!

Shawn's clouded gaze cleared briefly as he saw understanding on Paislee's face. "I'll haul his ass off the estate for guid—by shotgun if necessary. I keep a loaded one hidden at the hunting lodge."

"No! No guns. Call the police." Paislee clasped his wrist. "You look awful, Shawn. When did you last take your medicine?"

"I feel like hell." Perspiration beaded along his forehead and across his nose. "I'm gonna confront Gavin. I'm a crack shot, y'know. Just like Mum."

He stumbled down the two steps to the grass and his car, opened the door, and got behind the wheel.

Paislee picked up Wallace so her pup wouldn't chase after him. "Don't go. You're in no shape tae drive."

He peered at her through the streaked windscreen and revved the engine. "Dinnae tell anybody you've seen me."

"I'm gonna call the DI." The man was crazy if he thought she'd keep his visit secret.

"Not my mother. She's under Gavin's spell. They all are. He cannae kill me. By God, I'll kill him first."

"Don't do anything stupid, please. You're not well." She ran to the driver's side of his Mercedes, the window down. "Let me drive you."

"You cannae trick me, Paislee." The car jerked backward as

Shawn confused the brake with the gas. She barely got out of the way. "I'm calling my own damn family meeting!" he shouted as he sped away.

Thankfully nobody else was on the road.

Going back to the Leery manor was suicide.

She ran inside, found her mobile in the pocket of her purse, and called the detective. He didn't answer. "Shawn Marcus just left my house, not well at all," she said in a message. "I'm following him tae the estate—he thinks Gavin Thornton is trying tae kill him."

She grabbed her keys as Grandpa hurried out of the bathroom, water dripping from his hair around his face.

"What's going on, lass?"

Shawn was going to kill Gavin, but was he actually guilty of murder? Who else had been at the estate? Who else would Aila kiss?

Graham Reid. Sexy sculptor. From a poor fishing family—perhaps he considered Aila a better bet to hold the Leery title?

"Grandpa, please get Brody ready—I have tae stop Shawn Marcus from making a terrible mistake!"

# Chapter 25

Paislee was one bare foot out the front door with her keys, determined to stop Shawn from harming Gavin. Grandpa raised his voice to get her scattered attention. "Yer in your pajamas!"

She eyed her light blue flannel pajama bottoms, sleep tank, and button-up flannel shirt and returned to the foyer. Paislee bumped the door closed with her hip. There was no time to change. "Shawn's lost his mind. He thinks Gavin is trying tae kill him. He claims tae have a gun!"

"Gavin? The accountant that brought ye flowers?"

"Exactly! Shawn thinks Aila and Gavin are having an affair and colluding tae kill him."

"But we know she was kissing the butler!"

No, not Malcolm, either. Malcolm had come from the other side of the cottage closest to the hunting lodge. Midge was the whistler—she'd been with Graham and Aila before, at the stables. *Graham* had been on horseback that day, and hadn't she heard more than one set of hooves? It had been Graham's hat out of place, where it didn't belong.

"It's *Graham* having an affair with Aila." But Graham had not shot Charles—who had?

"Graham," Grandpa repeated with confusion. "The sculptor—ah, a boy toy." He nodded wisely.

She palmed her keys, eager to leave and save both Shawn and Gavin from heartache. "Grandpa. We're looking for two different criminals. Whoever killed Charles is not the same person who is trying tae kill Shawn." Her pulse raced.

Grandpa slung his damp towel over his shoulder. "I told ye, you're guid at this. One piece will lead tae the next."

Paislee gripped the knob of the front door—anxious, worried and fearful. "I don't know who did what, but Gavin can't die. I'll be back."

"Dinnae go inside after Shawn—wait for the police. I'll phone them."

"I left a message with the DI, but that would be great, Grandpa. Call me with news." She shoved her feet into a pair of pink and purple wellies by the door and rushed out. Her hands shook with adrenaline as she got behind the wheel of her Juke.

Checking the rearview mirror, Paislee reversed from the driveway and then raced down the street. Mrs. Carlisle, dressed in her pink satin robe, picked up the paper and waved from the corner.

Paislee reached for her phone to activate her Bluetooth and realized she'd left her purse and her mobile by the front door. Exhaling with regret, she stepped on the brake to go back.

At least ten minutes had passed since Shawn manically left her house.

Anything could happen, especially if Shawn had a gun.

Paislee said a prayer that she wouldn't be too late and kept going. Every red light, every traffic circle, made it seem an eternity.

She'd thought that Graham and Aila had been an item that Wednesday morning on the porch. She'd witnessed Graham gently helping Aila from her horse.

Graham definitely started with a G.

She was on the very edge of her seat as she drove, both hands on the wheel. Perspiration trickled down her back. Why would Graham want Shawn dead?

Did he hope to marry Aila and become Lord of the Manor? A big reach for a lad from a poor fishing family.

At last she saw the wooden sign that read Leery Estate. She slowed and turned right, down the narrow dirt road.

Her slick palms slid on the wheel.

The wrought-iron gate was closed. Tempted to drive around and right through the pasture, she got as close as she could with her car and nudged the gate.

It opened, slowly.

Not latched.

Another illusion of safety.

Paislee swallowed, her mouth and throat dry. She crept through the gate, and the house came into view. Pink and gray swirls of dawn hovered over the slate roof. The chimney didn't smoke, giving the manor an empty feel. The green gardens stretched to her left, the carport to the right.

Before her, Shawn's silver Mercedes was parked crookedly— the back tire in the fountain with the koi, the nymph falling forward. The driver's door was open.

Should she wait for the police?

Should she just go in?

All she had to protect herself was her keys. Not for the first time, she cursed her landlord's name. She realized that there were more cars in the lot. She recognized Gavin's Audi. And . . . a dark gray SUV. With a Theadora's Tea Shoppe sticker on the back window.

Had Shawn lied to her, and Theadora *was* his girlfriend?

Her stomach knotted and she exited her car to peer in the window of the SUV. No baking goods. Or tea supplies.

A box of bullets was open on the passenger seat. Paislee recalled Theadora proudly stating that she hunted with her father. Had something gone wrong in their negotiation? Maybe she'd had feelings, and Shawn had not?

Paislee rubbed her hand over her cheek and stared at the front door of the house. She had to go in and stop whatever it was going on.

Gathering courage, she ran up the stairs and halted before the front door. She started to knock but pulled her hand back. The noise might startle Shawn and cause him to react in a rash manner. Stealth could be a safer plan.

She twisted the knob and hoped it would be open like the gate had been. It was locked.

She blew out a breath, warm even though she was in only pj's, and wondered where else she might get inside. She recalled that Graham had disappeared on the side of the house.

Paislee clomped down the stone stairs in her boots, her keys in her fist, and followed the very narrow dirt path between the bougainvillea and the stone manor. She noticed a wooden door, and long, low windows. The kitchen!

The door was unlocked, and she hurried inside. Old appliances, older than hers even, took up an entire wall. An industrial sink, pans hanging from an iron rack. Where was everybody?

The sound of a gun discharging echoed through the old walls, and she bit back a cry of fear. She heard a scream. What could she use besides her keys to protect herself? She chose a small cast-iron skillet from the rack and gulped.

There was a phone in the foyer on the butler's table—she'd call the police.

If Graham was behind the attempts on Shawn's life in the house, who had killed Charles?

Theadora?

Why?

It made no sense. Paislee wondered if Theadora felt betrayed, but Shawn seemed to think they'd concluded their business on good terms.

Paislee cautiously made her way out of the kitchen. Midge had showed her how to get into the dining room behind the tapestry, but the sound hadn't come from there. Or the drawing room. Paislee tiptoed to the hall and the foyer. The grand staircase was to her left. The butler's tall table was vacant. She reached for the hand-set of the old-fashioned phone.

The wire had been cut.

What was going on?

Voices shouted angrily. From the study.

She kept her shoulder to the wall and crept down the long, narrow hall.

A memory from the night of the quarterly party rose, of how Aila had watched Shannon, Gavin, and Graham with longing. Aila hadn't felt well but had rallied later when her mother wasn't the center of attention. She'd drunk tea. No wine. She'd touched her stomach. Paislee paused by the two-foot tall brass nymph to gather her courage as she stared at the partially closed study door.

"I wish you'd stayed home," Dan said from behind her.

Paislee's heart hammered, and she whirled, bringing the skillet up in self-defense. Dan dodged her swing and raised up his hunting rifle. He pointed it at her face.

She froze in icy cold fear.

"Drop the skillet."

She lowered it to the ground. "I really, really don't understand. Dan, the DI is on his way. I thought—"

"Shut up. Go tae the study with the others." His friendly voice had a faraway quality as if he was disconnected from reality.

She didn't want to. "I heard a gun go off."

"Move or you'll be next."

Paislee's toes curled in her wellies, and she slowly took a step forward. "Just run, Dan, and get away. You don't have tae do this."

Dan shoved her hard, and her shoulder rammed the study door that had been left ajar. She cried out in pain.

Jealous. He'd been jealous of Theodora and Shawn. She recalled the remark about a Mercedes. "They aren't having an affair, Dan."

He rammed the nose of the rifle into her side. "Shut. Up." He gripped her upper arm and tossed her onto the long couch between Malcolm and Gavin. Malcolm had been bashed in the face, his nose bloodied. He slouched against the end of the sofa. Gavin glared, a bruise at his temple. Had Dan physically overpowered them, one by one, then dragged them here? Why?

Shannon was on Gavin's other side, her mouth gagged with the navy-blue scarf Paislee had given her.

Shawn was prone on the floor before them, his profile reminiscent of Charles that day on the path. The final piece clicked like the completed corner on their Big Ben puzzle.

"You thought Charles was Shawn," she breathed out, her throat parched. "It was a mistake tae kill Charles."

"You got it." Shawn roused, and Dan kicked him in the side. "Dinnae move."

A bullet had lodged into the wooden floor of the study, but Paislee saw no injuries.

Shannon struggled from her seat on the couch toward her son, as if to protect him with her own body. Dan jabbed the gun at her chest so she was forced backward, her calves bumping Gavin's knees. The lady of the manor emanated fury.

Dan placed his finger on the trigger, the tip of the gun to Shawn's temple.

"Dan, don't!" Paislee yelled.

"I'm a hunter," Dan informed Shannon, "Your son is my prey. Sit or I will shoot him now."

Shannon sank down. To Shannon's right, Graham and Aila were back to back on the floor, tied together. Aila had something in red on her lap.

Tension was thick as fog in the study, and she watched Dan calculate his next move. "Dan, please. You have every reason tae think that something was going on. But it wasn't."

His brown hair fell over his forehead as he scowled at Paislee, then Shawn. His boot drew back for another kick. Shawn grunted in pain.

A low whistle sounded from behind a floor-to-ceiling tapestry of a stag and nymph. Midge!

"Did the DI talk tae you?" Paislee would keep Dan preoccupied so that the maid could act. "Is that when you found out?"

Midge peeked from behind the tapestry, her brown eyes wide as she half-entered the study. Something shiny glinted in her hands.

Dan centered the tip of the rifle at Shawn's forehead.

"The DI doesn't know." Paislee's breath's quickened.

"He knows." Dan's voice was cold. "Detective Inspector Zeffer toyed with me and Theadora last night. We showed him our rifles. Our permits. All but this one."

"She was paid tae be a surrogate, Dan. Tae help financially."

Dan flashed a look of fury at Paislee but kept his aim at Shawn. "Thea told me aboot her deal with Shawn." He kicked Shawn again. "Fifty thousand pounds. She saved the businesses. What aboot us?"

He flexed his finger near the trigger.

"Wait!"

"She was so proud, thinking she'd saved us." His jaw clenched as he glowered at Shawn. "I wanted tae save us. No babies, no bakery. I'm a failure, Paislee." A tear slid from his eye. "Not guid enough."

Hadn't Theadora felt the same? That she hadn't been good enough?

Midge flew at Dan with the two-foot brass nymph, knocking him over with the heavy statue. He screamed in pain and surprise, dropping the rifle.

Midge hurried backward, her hands to her mouth. Dan lunged for her. "No!" Paislee shouted.

Gavin, hands tied, jumped from the couch and kicked the rifle beneath the table. Malcolm growled like a wounded bear and tackled Dan before he reached the maid.

Paislee raced for Midge and grabbed her in a hug.

The study door burst open as the DI entered, followed by his constables. "What's going on?" the DI yelled.

Zeffer strode toward Paislee. Everyone tried to speak at once until Midge let out a piercing whistle, and they quieted. Malcolm had Dan's arms behind his back in a tight hold. The baker was going nowhere on his watch.

Paislee patted Midge's trembling shoulder.

"Dan Barr," the DI said. "You are under arrest for the murder of Charles Thomson. For the attempted shooting of Shawn Marcus."

Her landlord blinked to consciousness, and Shannon, the gag free, knelt at her son's side to help him sit up.

"I told you he knew, Paislee," Dan muttered darkly.

"You were nervous," the detective said. "When I asked tae speak tae your wife alone, you spluttered and claimed tae know aboot their affair. Your wife denied it. You had a shaky voice. Clammy palms. I realized you were hiding something. Turns oot your registered rifle, the one you didnae show me last night, is a match for the bullet we found in Charles."

"Not an affair!" Shawn piped up. Sweat beaded on his orangish forehead. "I paid her fifty thousand pounds tae be my surrogate."

Dan bowed his head, emitting a single sob. "We dinnae want your blood money." He raised his head and sneered. "I'm going tae jail for killing a man I thought was you—might as well get the right guy for the crime."

Zeffer nodded to his two officers. That was a confession.

"Shawn, where did ye get fifty thousand?" Shannon's expression was one of utter disappointment. "The estate needs every bloody pound right now."

"Mum, I know that. But you said it was important that I have a baby." He listed to the left to look up at his mother. "I sold me Rolex."

Shannon raised her gaze to the ceiling, her arms outstretched. She'd reached her limit.

"Paislee, your message said Shawn was racing here tae kill Gavin?" Zeffer prodded. "Because Gavin was trying tae kill him, and sleeping with Aila?"

Gavin turned on Shawn in genuine anger. "Me—kill you? And Aila? That's ludicrous! Your mother has always had my heart."

Aila sobbed loudly, and Paislee turned to where Graham and Aila were tied together. Graham wore a look of defiance. The red in Aila's lap was from ribbon tied around a stack of letters.

Shawn tugged at his mother's sleeve. "It was guid that I arrived when I did."

The DI crossed his arms. "How so, Mr. Marcus?"

Shawn rose unsteadily, balancing against the couch. "Dan had them all rounded up because he thought they were lying and hiding me. I knew Paislee would call you, Zeffer. I just needed tae bide me time before help arrived." He appeared confused. "Who was in me room with a pillow? Pushed me down the stairs?"

Because of *when* the incidents happened, Paislee knew it had to be someone within the house. Someone desperate. "Graham." She gestured to the lovers sitting together on the floor. "If you were dead, Shawn, and Graham married Aila, he would inherit the Leery fortune. Shannon has clearly stated she isn't the marrying kind so Graham would get no security there."

Shannon broke down crying, and Gavin gathered her close to offer comfort, his hand on her trembling back.

Paislee turned to Midge, who watched Shawn with love and concern. "I heard you whistling in the woods that day. Why were you following Aila and Graham? Did you know that they were an item?"

Midge drew in a shaky breath. "After the party, I found the letters between Miss Aila and Mr. Graham in her drawer, just like Mr. Shawn said." Her brown eyes widened and she quivered with fear. "I saw Mr. Graham run tae Miss Aila's room after Mr. Shawn was pushed down the stairs. She's having a baby."

"Shut up, you stupid cow!" Graham yelled.

"Graham Reid—you are despicable," Shannon said. She sneered at her former lover and her daughter, her expression sour. "I failed with both my children." Shannon blocked the view of Shawn with her palm.

"Mum!" Shawn sank to the couch, his demeanor subdued.

The DI had his team arrest Graham and Aila along with Dan. Paislee shakily stepped to the door to leave, her upper arm throbbing.

The detective was at her side in an instant. "You're rubbing your shoulder. Are you all right?"

"I'm fine."

"Of course you are. No blood this time, m'dear," he murmured. "You'll be the death of me, Ms. Shaw."

"I hope not," she quipped, warmed by his genuine concern. "You're getting better at this detecting thing all the time."

His seafoam eyes darkened. "Constable Payne, please escort the lady tae her vehicle. Meet me at the station."

Now? She was already running late! "I have tae get Brody tae school, and then I've a meeting with the headmaster. Happy to do my duty as a concerned citizen *afterward*."

Zeffer snorted and strode away to help his officers sort the occupants of the room with their crimes.

Paislee risked Zeffer's wrath and crossed the room to Shawn and Shannon on the sofa. Aila sobbed for her mother as she was handcuffed, but Shannon refused to go to her aid. A female officer shuffled Aila from the study, after Graham.

"Goodbye," Paislee said to Shannon.

"Bye. Thank you, Paislee." Shannon squared her shoulders and folded her hands before her. "The only way I'll leave this bloody estate is when I die. Gavin? If your offer of marriage is still guid, twenty years later . . . I accept."

Gavin clasped her hand and brought her knuckles to his mouth, kissing her skin tenderly. "You've made me a happy man."

Malcolm bowed his head and glanced away. Midge patted his arm.

"Congratulations," Paislee said, wishing them the best. One thing was for certain—Gavin already knew what kind of family he was taking on.

# Chapter 26

At eight forty-five that morning, a frantic Paislee parked in her driveway and raced into the house.

Brody and Grandpa waited at the kitchen table, ready to go just as she'd instructed.

"Hurry, now."

"Mum!" Brody scowled as he looked her over. "Why are ye in your pajamas?"

Grandpa smoothed his beard, his eyes speculating. "Ye might want tae change before your meeting with the headmaster. Everything all right, lass?"

"Aye. Give me five minutes. Let Wallace out back!" Paislee flew up the stairs, then changed from pj's to a sundress and cardigan, and sandals instead of Wellingtons. Her hair was a disaster so she swept it into a messy bun.

Paislee dropped Grandpa off at Cashmere Crush first, with a promise to be in touch as soon as she could. Would she have saved her lease only to lose it all to the Fishers' lawsuit?

Nervous, she and Brody arrived at Fordythe at half past nine. "I promise I'll explain everything tae Headmaster McCall," she said to her worried son. She would take full responsibility for being late—meaning, doing the detention time.

Paislee, defensive, had her excuses ready.

Mrs. Jimenez was at her desk and didn't smile at Paislee like she normally did. "You're meeting in the conference room. Go on in. They're already there."

"They?"

"The Fishers," Mrs. Jimenez whispered.

Dread weighted each step. She knew that Hamish would be disappointed in her for being late, and now she had to face Holly's family after a rough start to the day.

The glass door was closed, but she knocked once and opened it, going in with her chin raised high. She'd done her best by Holly that awful morning. The facts had to speak for themselves.

Hamish, in a dark brown suit, rose from his seat at the head of the oval glass table. A woman who had Holly's round face and gap in her teeth sat next to a man who exuded arrogance.

"Sairy tae be late. I'm Paislee Shaw."

"Are you all right?" Hamish asked with concern.

"Aye. Thanks." She sat opposite the Fishers and smiled.

Neither of them smiled back.

"I thought Arran Mulholland would be here?" Paislee asked.

"No need," Hamish said. "The Fishers have retracted their lawsuit against Fordythe and you." He opened a manila folder and removed three copies of the papers they'd all signed releasing the school from liability.

"Our solicitor said that dinnae mean much," Mrs. Fisher declared peevishly. "We *chose* tae not pursue it. Holly said ye were kind tae her."

Mr. Fisher's eyes remained hard.

"It's welcome news." Paislee rubbed her sore shoulder even as the weight of worry eased. She would keep her house and her business. She bowed her head in thanks, then lifted it again. "Is that all?"

"No," said Hamish. "Your chaperone rights have been returned." He glanced again at her hair and then her shoulder. "Where were you?"

She kept her expression neutral, feeling undervalued by someone she'd hoped would be a friend. "You can read all about it in tomorrow's paper."

He didn't press the issue with the Fishers watching. Counting her blessings, Paislee stood. "Have a good day. Your daughter is a sweet lass."

"We're moving tae Edinburgh." The woman darted a peek at her husband. "Tae start over."

Now that really was great news. "Well, thank God, I mean, good luck with that."

Paislee lifted her hand goodbye, her gaze lingering on Hamish's handsome face, before she left the room.

The morning paper featured Dan Barr caught in a lover's triangle. He'd confessed to shooting the wrong man in a fit of passion. A picture of Shawn had been paired with Theodora. *Poor Theadora.*

Paislee dropped Brody off at school. Hamish waved to her, and she waved back but didn't linger.

She parked behind her shop and unlocked the door to Cashmere Crush with an immense feeling of gratitude. She'd almost lost this place, and her home to boot. She wouldn't take anything for granted for quite some time.

Paislee displayed the cashmere vest she'd finally finished next to a matching cinnamon cap in her front window.

At ten on the nose, Shannon Leery sauntered in like Audrey Hepburn, wearing an ivory sun hat and suit, with the navy cashmere scarf Paislee had made stylishly draped over her throat.

"Morning, Lady Leery."

"Shannon, my dear. Soon tae be Shannon Thornton, after all this time."

"That's wonderful. Congratulations. How's Shawn?"

"He's resting at home. All of this"—she hesitated before settling on—"drama hasnae been guid for him. He's agreed tae take his health seriously. We speak tae the doctors tomorrow aboot dialysis."

Paislee nodded, not sure what to say.

"I've decided tae skip the memorial service for Charles, despite Father Dixon's disapproval. It seems hypocritical, considering he was blackmailing us all. Aila said he wanted a quarter million pounds tae keep their affair secret."

"Och. I'm so sorry." Paislee walked toward the back counter. "When did they decide tae"—she swallowed—"harm Shawn?"

"Graham's idea, according tae Aila, so that the two of them could one day rule Leery Estate. Rule." Shannon gave a delicate snort. "It's bloody hard work running the estate, and neither would last a day."

Paislee rounded the counter. "How is she?"

"Home. On bail." The lady's chin quivered, but then she raised it. "I do feel guilty aboot giving her up. I cannae let her sit in jail, especially with a babe on the way."

"And Graham?"

"Him I don't care aboot. But he's the father of my first grandchild." Shannon's skin had a green tint. "If he and Aila stay together, they'll have tae live in London, not the estate—I couldnae bear it." She sounded faintly horrified. "I feel like the star of me verra own TV drama."

"It's a lot tae carry."

"I cannae thank ye enough for helping me. Shawn was in too deep. You didnae have tae care." Shannon ran her hand over a skein of cashmere on a shelf by the register.

Paislee's smile was gentle. "That's not how we do things in Nairn."

"Don't I know it? I should've made Shawn stronger," Shannon lamented. "It's never too late, as Gavin keeps encouraging me. I'm considering a move tae Gavin's house. It's only twenty years old and has all of the amenities. There's a view of the Firth where we watch the dolphins."

"It sounds lovely."

"If you ever need anything, Paislee, call me. You've earned a friend in me."

Shannon left, and Paislee sank down on the stool, emotionally exhausted. She imagined Gran in heaven, rocking in her chair, and knitting. "I sure hope you get tae watch all this, Gran. Never a dull moment, considering it's such a quiet town."